THE THIRTY-FOOT ELVIS

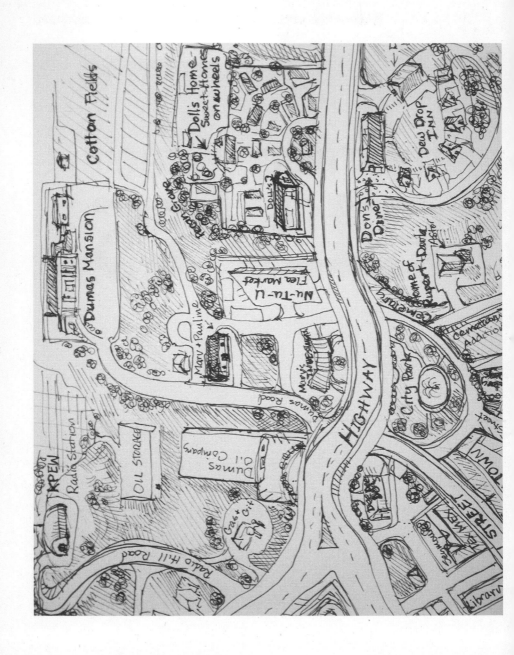

VOLUME TWO OF THE PEAVINE CHRONICLES SERIES

THE THIRTY-FOOT ELVIS

A NOVEL BY

JANE F. HANKINS

PARKHURST BROTHERS, INC., PUBLISHERS

Parkhurst Brothers, Inc., Publishers

Marion, Michigan

www.parkhurstbrothers.com

Parkhurst Brothers books are distributed to the trade through the Chicago Distribution Center, and may be ordered through Ingram Book Company, Baker & Taylor, Follett Library Resources and other book and e-book wholesalers. To order from Chicago Distribution Center, phone 1-800-621-2736 or send a fax to 800-621-8476. Copies of this and other Parkhurst Brothers, Inc., Publishers titles are available to organizations and corporations for purchase in quantity by contacting Special Sales Department at our home office location, listed on our web site. Manuscript submission guidelines for this publishing company are available at our web site.

Printed in the United States of America

First Edition, 2013

2013 2014 2015 2016   16 15 14 13 12 11 10 9 8 7 6 5 4 3 2 1

Library of Congress Cataloging-in-Publication Data
Hankins, Jane F., 1950-
  The thirty foot Elvis : a novel / Jane F. Hankins. -- First Edition.
    pages cm. -- (Peavine Chronicles series ; Volume 2)
  ISBN 978-1-62941-004-3 -- ISBN 978-1-62491-005-0
 1. Mobile home parks--Fiction. 2. City and town life--Arkansas--Fiction. 3. Arkansas--Fiction. I. Title.
  PS3608.A71485T45 2013
  813'.6--dc23   2013019778

This book is printed on archival-quality paper that meets requirements of the American National Standard for Information Sciences, Permanence of Paper, Printed Library Materials, ANSI Z39.48-1984.

Cover illustration and interior art by: Jane F. Hankins
Cover and page design: Charlie Ross
Acquired for Parkhurst Brothers Inc., Publishers by: Ted Parkhurst
Proofreaders: Bill and Barbara Paddack

112013
>CP

Dedicated to . . .

The loving memory of my mother:

Margaret Stuck Frier,
who peacefully "Crossed Over" from this world
twenty days after "Madge" was launched.

And to my daddy:

Sid Frier,
a master storyteller in his own right!
He left us far too soon in 1985 . . .
but I'm sure he's still sending me
jokes and inspiration from the Great Beyond.

ACKNOWLEDGEMENTS

First, I want to thank all the kind readers of *Madge's Mobile Home Park* who gave me such wonderful feedback and encouragement. Every book club meeting, fundraiser, reading, and signing party was a delight!

I especially want to thank Cousin Kitty and the Arkansas Chapter of the National Museum of Women in the Arts for their lovely "Welcome to Peavine" events! That is an organization near and dear to my heart. You fed us well, helped enormously with sales, and gave me a great opportunity to have a hilarious time performing readings from the book with my beloved loudmouth husband!

There is a *real* David the florist who gave me the name Violet X-pressions while I was writing *Madge* … (This led to my Peavine floral shop and Aunt Violet). He also shared a very funny story about the trials and tribulations of his experience dressing up as Morticia Addams (of the Addams Family) for a Halloween costume party.

More resource information about the Drag Queen experience was given to me by my faithful longtime hair stylist, Lindy. He also is helping my red hair to get a little more blonde every three weeks. Yes … Shirleen, Lucille, and Tammy have convinced me that blondes do have more fun!

Thanks again to my wonderfully kind and encouraging publisher, Ted Parkhurst. He rolled up his editing sleeves and did a great job helping me iron out my run-ons, adjectives, antecedents, and all the other boo boos that occurred as I went dashing through this wild year of writing. He had so much fun, I made up a Peavine persona for him (newspaper editor) … and I *promise* that I will change the *Peavine Times* to the new name he thought up – when I write more about him in Book Three.

"There's always a special somebody for everybody in this world. I'm sure of that!"

– Loretta Doll Dumas

"Baby, I've found out you're never too old for romance."

– Krystal Bridges

CHAPTER ONE

The Arrival of a Tall Dark Stranger

December 1, 1984

Home-Sweet-Homes-on-Wheels RV and Mobile Home Park

It was three o'clock on the coldest morning of the year so far. The only light burning in the lavender double-wide was the pink neon sign buzzing in the window by the door overlooking the newly expanded front deck.

Upon the occasion of her passing, the former owner, Doll Dumas, had bequeathed her luxury mobile home to Rhonelle DuBoise, Peavine's official psychic and a former exotic dancer from New Orleans. Accompanying Rhonelle's inheritance was the responsibility of managing the park – no problem for her since she had assumed that duty a year and a half ago, when Doll became too ill to do the job. Rhonelle enjoyed helping tenants, chatting with the maintenance guy, and joking with delivery personnel – all of which helped to ease her loneliness since her old friend Doll "moved on to the next life" on Christmas night the preceding year.

The interior of the luxury double-wide had undergone a drastic do-over since the previous year. A large part of the generous amount of money Doll included in Rhonelle's inheritance had been spent on an eclectic mix of redecorating projects.

Doll's rented hospital bed had been replaced by a queen-sized one with a red velvet coverlet and ornate brass headboard. Upon her lavish new Sealy Posturepedic mattress, Rhonelle tossed feverishly as she tried in vain to sleep. The stack of ten New Orleans jazz albums was half through playing on the hi-fi in the nearby living room.

Behind her eyelids, Rhonelle visualized the face of her Creole Granny, Laurite. Although she had long ago passed to the "Other Side," Laurite frequently contacted her psychic granddaughter. The sound of jazz music faded, and Granny Laurite's face grew larger, breaking into a grin so wide her gold tooth glinted in the dark. Granny Laurite chuckled and spoke to her granddaughter. *"He's a comin', Cherie! Doan worry, you find each other real soon!"*

Rhonelle smiled and with a sigh of contentment, pulled her red velvet coverlet up to her chin, and fell fast asleep.

Three and a half hours later, Miss Violet Posey was out walking her obese cocker spaniel, Hero, just as the sun began to lighten the horizon. She preferred walking him while it was still dark so he could do his business undetected.

Since Violet still occupied the apartment above her downtown Peavine florist shop, Violet X-pressions (now run by her nephew, David) – there was no place for Hero to "go" except in Herman Municipal Park just a block away. As he did every morning at this time, the old dog was dragging his mistress to the park at this moment. Violet was shivering against the bitter cold, even though she had her heaviest winter coat on over her nightgown and warm socks in her quilted slippers.

A stiff wind blasted from the north as she turned to walk the short stretch of sidewalk beside the highway toward the park. Violet cussed the wind like a sailor; one thing she hates is cold wind down her neck. Hero was the only soul ever to witness her profanity, a fault he graciously ignored as he paused to leave a marker for any prissy little poodle that would come by later.

"Can't you wait until we get out of this G.D. wind and into the blankety-blank park, you silly old mutt," Violet hissed through chattering teeth. She pulled the fur collar of her coat up to her nose and around her ears since her curler bonnet didn't offer much warmth. With her head down, she and pulled the dog toward the park.

Just as they approached the arched memorial entry to Herman

Park, Hero stopped in his tracks and emitted an ominous, low growl. Violet cussed louder with her face in her coat and yanked at Hero's leash in frustration, but he wouldn't move. He was staring up at something. The first rays of the rising sun blinded Violet as she squinted up over her fur collar at a huge formation in the middle of the park. So tall, it cast a shadow reaching clear across the highway, the newly constructed – monument? – gleamed between the blinding rays of morning sunlight.

"What the *hell?*" Violet stood there dumbfounded, trying to understand what she was seeing. It was an *enormous* statue of a man in a cape. That was unusual indeed. She knew Doll Dumas had built this park after her husband Herman Junior passed years ago. Could the new monument be a likeness of him, she wondered?

"Why the cape though? Is it some kind of tribute to Confederate soldiers?" Violet's heart leapt at the thought of *that* possibility. Then as the sun crept higher and the sky brightened, she was able to make out more details.

Violet's gasp of horror caught her dog's attention. Hero looked up at his mistress in alarm. "That is the biggest, most *vulgar* gawd damn thing I've ever seen!" Violet didn't care if anyone heard her this time.

The sun rose higher, reflecting off the shiny patina on the brightly painted fiberglass sculpture. A new day had dawned in Peavine and the appearance of the sleepy little town would forever be altered. Smack dab in the center of the city park, lovingly maintained by the Peavine Garden Club, stood a likeness of none other than the "king of all things tacky" as far as Violet was concerned.

The hips were captured masterfully in mid swivel. The raven-haired head was thrown back in song with a microphone in hand. His white bell-bottom jumpsuit and red-lined white cape sparkled in the sunlight.

In Peavine, the first day of December in 1984 will thereafter be remembered
as:

Day 1 of – The Thirty-Foot Elvis!

CHAPTER TWO

Bo and Lucille's Big News

At the much more sophisticated wake-up time of ten forty-five on that same morning, Rhonelle began to rouse from her dreams. The first thing she noticed was the sound of heavy traffic outside on the highway and car horns honking. Her eyes fluttered open at the commotion of people hooting, laughing and shouting not far from her bedroom window.

Sensing some momentous event, she slid out from under her warm covers and donned her robe in one gracefully fluid motion. Rhonelle never rushed herself, considering it unhealthy and self-defeating to do so. She did feel a growing excitement, however, and was just about to open her red drapes and look outside when she heard knocking at the front door.

She stepped into her satin mules, checked her hair, pinched her cheeks, applied a thick coat of glossy "Red Hot Momma" lipstick and sauntered to the door as the knocking grew louder and more insistent.

"Rhonelle you get yourself out here!" It was the unmistakable voice of her diminutive neighbor, Teenie Brice. "We know that even *you* couldn't be sleeping through this ruckus." By the time she got to the living room, Teenie's AKC toy poodle, Pitty Two, was also yapping at her.

Rhonelle opened the door and looked down at her small friend standing below her. Teenie always made Rhonelle feel positively statuesque. Teenie, wearing his red hat with the ear flaps and a plaid woolen jacket, held his tiny poodle so bundled up only her nose and eyes were exposed. Rhonelle was about to say something clever but stopped when she was overcome by a sensation of warmth and expectation. Her eyes traveled up over Teenie's red cap and out to the highway just beyond the mobile home park entry. Cars were lined up bumper to bumper. She brushed past Teenie who was gawking at her in her red satin robe.

"Rhonelle, don't you think it's a tad chilly for you to go out in that ... ah negligee?" His voice trailed off as she strode across the yard toward the highway. He hitched up Pitty Two and ran after her.

She didn't hear Teenie or anything else for that matter. She had to see what "*it*" was. Weaving through the crowd of onlookers and cars she walked faster until she rounded the curve and saw the shining figure of Elvis towering over everything around it. The crowd began to notice the tall dark-haired woman, with her red satin robe flapping in the wind. A hush spread amongst Rhonelle's fellow citizens as they elbowed one another and pointed in her direction.

Rhonelle stopped at the base of the sculpture and reached out to touch the base of it. Instantly she felt a stronger thrill. Warmth spread from her stomach and throughout her body so she did not notice the cold wind. There it was – the signature of the artist who had created this monumental statue. She traced the name with her finger tip: *Sergio Mandell.*

"Isn't this beyond your wildest dreams, Rhonelle?" Lucille Lepanto had grabbed Rhonelle from behind and crushed her in a firm hug.

"Momma must be dancin' in heaven over this!" Lucille hooted in delight and gave a lung-rattling laugh, as she released Rhonelle (who was feeling dizzy and disoriented at the moment). "This has got to be the biggest surprise little ole Peavine ever got! We even snuck it by *you* this time"

Rhonelle blinked at Lucille and gazed back up at the statue. "How ... did you do this? How did it get here without anybody knowing?"

She indicated the statue firmly bolted to the concrete pad Lucille had mysteriously ordered poured in the center of the park about ten days ago. All she would tell anybody was that it was going to be for a special gift to the town in memory of her mother, Doll Dumas. The Peavine Garden Club had assumed it was there in preparation for the City Christmas Tree Project that the holiday committee members were planning.

Rhonelle clutched at the neck of her robe as a shiver trickled down her spine. Her warm glow was fading and she was getting chilled. *How does one transport a thirty-foot tall sculpture of Elvis undetected, much less erect it overnight?*

Lucille guessed what Rhonelle was thinking. "Come on Bo," she called out to the stocky man sporting a mullet haircut and a sly grin. "We got some explaining to do, but we'd better get this woman inside before she freezes her tail off. What were you thinking, Rhonelle coming out in this cold wearing next to nothing?"

Bo Astor looked like he was about to make a comment on that, seeing as how Rhonelle had once upon a time made a good living by wearing "next to nothing," but thought better of it. He put his jacket around Rhonelle's shoulders and took her arm as he and Lucille steered her through the crowd, back to the lavender double-wide where Lucille's mother had lived all those years.

As she allowed herself to be led by Bo and Lucille across the highway, Rhonelle felt an excitement, a strong current of energy buzzing between the couple. As nearly breathless, they took turns describing how the statue was transported in sections loaded onto two eighteen-wheeler trucks, Rhonelle realized she'd never seen them happier. In only two hours, the team of six guys reassembled the statue in the middle of the night under the direction of the sculptor, Sergio Mandell.

Once again, Rhonelle felt a prickle of excitement from the pit of her stomach at the mention of that name.

After the threesome returned to the warmth of the double-wide, Lucille shut the door and started to literally dance with excitement. Bo Astor was grinning from ear to ear as he put his arm around Lucille.

"Lookie here, Rhonelle!" Lucille squealed in a voice an octave higher than usual, as she waggled her left hand so close to Rhonelle's face that Rhonelle had to take a step back in order to focus on the diamond engagement ring!

"Lucille and I are gettin' married," Bo announced, his chest expanded in self-satisfaction. "I went down on my knees last night and proposed at the foot of the Elvis statue. This time Lucille finally said "yes," so we picked out the ring first thing this morning just as soon as

Falkner Jewelry store opened!"

"We owe it all to you, Rhonelle," Lucille said as tears welled up in her eyes.

Rhonelle could only stare at the happy couple in confusion. *Ah Granny, what have you cooked up now? You were supposed to be helping* **me** *this time.*

CHAPTER THREE

Best Cure for the Post-Holiday Blues

After Rhonelle succeeded in shooing the happy couple out the door, she immediately brewed herself a pot of strong coffee with chicory and heated a pan of milk on the stove. No wonder she felt befuddled and irritated. To go wandering outside like that before she'd drunk a drop of coffee was ill advised. No civilized person can think clearly before their morning – or in this case nearly midday – coffee. She needed to settle her mind and get several important things figured out before she went another step into this day.

Rhonelle settled down in Doll's old overstuffed chair that her friend and decorator, Darla, had recovered in a red tapestry fabric decorated with silvery blue moons and stars. Curling up like a cat she pulled a purple chenille throw across her legs and cradled her mug in both hands. Savoring the first few sips of her café au lait, Rhonelle gazed around the living room, so different now from less than a year ago. She and her friends had extensively redecorated since Doll passed.

Rhonelle drifted back in memory to the previous January. It had been almost a year ago when she and Lucille had started the seemingly insurmountable task of clearing out Doll's things. They had to make room for Rhonelle to fix up the trailer to suit herself. It was a sad time, so soon after Doll's passing on Christmas night. They had begun on the day after New Year's, January the second, 1984. That was when Rhonelle first noticed something was going on between Bo and Lucille.

Ten Months Earlier, January 2, 1984

Rhonelle and Lucille had been working for the past four hours, sorting through Doll's keepsakes and collectibles to divide amongst her closest friends and neighbors. Lucille had just finished packing the last of the ceramic poodle collection in a box for Teenie and Mavis Brice when she burst into tears.

"I can't take this anymore," she wailed. "I know Momma's better off now, but I just keep thinking about all the years I missed being with her when I ran off with those dumb bikers. Poor Momma! She didn't know if I was alive or dead." She sobbed and wiped her nose on the sleeve of her sweatshirt. "I just wish there was something else I could have done to make up for all the pain I caused her. Gawd, I was such a *mean* little bitch when I was in my teens."

Rhonelle watched her friend patiently while this latest wave of grief and regret waxed and waned. Over the past 16 years since the return of Doll's prodigal daughter with her darling four-year-old Tammy in tow, Lucille had brought nothing but happiness to her mother. Rhonelle had also become quite fond of Lucille – actually considered her as a younger sister after a time.

She allowed Lucille to collect herself before she spoke. "You know you made your amends to your mother years ago. Your return and bringing Tammy into her life has been her greatest joy.

"Your problem is you are completely exhausted – mentally and physically. I think what you need is a break from all this."

Lucille nodded and stood up, tugging at her tight jeans and adjusting her hot pink sweatshirt. "Yeah, it's high time we headed over to Don's for some food. I'd better repair my face first." She wiped at the mascara running and smeared under her eyes. Snatching a tissue from a box on the nearby dressing table, Lucille glanced at her reflection in the mirror. "Good Lord, I look a wreck!" She trotted into the nearby bathroom and used a few of her mother's cosmetics still sitting out on the fake marble vanity. She smiled at the memory of her mother's daily ritual of "putting on her face" right up to the last. She wouldn't use Doll's deep plum lipstick though. She had some of her own signature "Pouty Pink" in her purse.

Thinking about her pink lipstick reminded her of her secret date with Lil Bo Astor on New Year's Eve, and the joke he made about her pouty pink lips. To her alarm, the memory actually made her blush. She glanced back at Rhonelle who was still sitting on the floor staring at her in that unfocused way of hers. Lucille wasn't quite ready to let Rhonelle know about Bo. He's at least ten years younger than her and never married.

"You ready to go?" Lucille hoped Rhonelle hadn't picked up on anything. "I need me some fresh air and something fattening," she said casually as she rummaged in her purse and pulled out the tube of lipstick, not daring to look Rhonelle in the eye." Having a close friend who also happens to be psychic could be a real pain in the butt sometimes.

"You need more than that," Rhonelle said as she got up off the floor in a single graceful movement.

"I need more than what?" Lucille wondered how much Rhonelle knew.

"You require more than a pie and coffee break," Rhonelle said with a shrug as she wrapped her red fleece poncho around her shoulders. "I suggest you take a *real* break after all you've been through with your mother these past few months. You're bound to have a letdown now that she's passed and you put in all that work on the big Memorial Bash for her."

"Just what did you have in mind then?" Lucille hooked her arm in Rhonelle's as they headed to the door and out onto the front deck.

Rhonelle smiled mysteriously and cocked her head to one side as if she were listening to something Lucille couldn't hear. "Well . . . now *that* would work nicely," Rhonelle said to thin air.

Lucille stopped in her tracks and turned Rhonelle to face her. "What idea is your Granny Laurite putting in your head now?" she demanded.

Rhonelle's eyes refocused on Lucille and she beamed that surprisingly beautiful smile of hers. "We think you need to get out of town for a few days, go somewhere fun and pay homage to your good memories of your mother."

Before Lucille could ask where the heck she supposed that place would be, the answer formed in her mind. "Graceland," she said in surprise. "Momma and I went there three years ago to celebrate Elvis' birthday!" Lucille laughed out loud at the thought. "We thought that was way more fun than memorializing his 'death day.'

"Dang, we got in the biggest giggle fit over his closet full of jump-suits arranged in order of size – expanding over the years. We had to skedaddle out of the room 'cause Momma was laughing so hard she got to coughing. Then when I told her to lean over to stop her cough-ing fit, she let loose a noisy fart and that got us laughing all that much harder! I'm surprised they didn't ban us for life. They are a pretty seri-ous bunch over there at Graceland."

Rhonelle noticed a flicker of sadness return to Lucille's face and added quickly, "You should take someone with you. How about Bo As-tor, since he's such an expert on all things Elvis these days?"

Lucille stopped and narrowed her eyes at Rhonelle who just smiled knowingly back at her. "Are you aware he's at least ten years younger than I am? What would people think if I was to go off like that with Lil Bo? After all, he has a reputation to protect being a Radio DJ."

"Since *when* did either of you get so prim and proper that you would care what anybody says?" Rhonelle smirked at the idea of wild-child Lucille caring about the Peavine gossip circuit.

"Besides, it's nobody's business where you go and who goes with you. You're both adults. So what if he's younger – he's just the tonic you need to help you get over your post-holiday blues."

"He's good medicine, that's for sure," Lucille said as her good spirits returned. She dug back into her purse and pulled out a bag of Tootsie Roll Pops. "Want one?" She held out the bag to Rhonelle who shook her head. "Bo gave me these yesterday to help me keep my New Year's resolution," she said as she popped one into the corner of her mouth. "Every time I want a cig, I suck on one of these instead … works so far."

Arm in arm the two women crossed the highway and went over to Don's Diner. As soon as Rhonelle touched the door with "Happy New Year" painted on it in pink tempera paint, she knew who she would encounter inside. This caused her to pause slightly and take a deep breath before pushing the door open.

CHAPTER FOUR

The Return of Mary Lynn

The clang of bells on the door caused some of the people inside the café to shift their glance to the entrance as Lucille and Rhonelle came inside. Don and Dorine were in the midst of a lively conversation with a middle-aged couple sitting at a booth near the window overlooking the highway.

The auburn-haired woman in the booth talking to Dorine had her back to the door, but Rhonelle knew that it was Mary Lynn, the "mysterious stranger" who had turned up in Peavine last week on the day of Doll Dumas' funeral . . . *Thanks to the machinations of Granny Laurite along with the spirits of Doll and that other man named Johnny.*

Rhonelle wondered how things had turned out after that night. All her Granny would tell her was, *Doll had "moved on" and had settled all her "Madge" issues.*

The first change that Rhonelle noticed in Mary Lynn's aura was the absence of the Spirit of Johnny, her long-lost fiancé. His presence had startled Rhonelle when she first met Mary Lynn at the Doll Dumas Memorial Bash a few nights ago. Her Granny Laurite had failed to mention that *another* ghost would be there when she told her all the other details about Mary Lynn.

The vision of Johnny – invisible to everyone but Rhonelle and standing right behind a very anxious Mary Lynn – resulted in a rather uncomfortable introduction. Rhonelle was so flustered by the sight of an unexpected apparition along with her Granny Laurite whispering instructions at her; she came across as seriously deranged! Fortunately, Rhonelle was able to effectively communicate her message from the spirits to Mary Lynn by the end of the evening without frightening her too badly.

The second thing Rhonelle noticed was a much lighter glow to Mary Lynn's aura, as if a heavy cloud had finally lifted. The man sitting with her must be her husband, Leroy. The apparent affection on his face as he watched his wife talking to Don and Dorine showed how much he loved her. Evidently Leroy also was aware of a change in Mary Lynn and delighted with the results.

I wonder if he knows what I know about Mary Lynn? Rhonelle had been the only living person who knew Mary Lynn's big secret. This sweet unassuming middle-aged woman was actually once the notorious *Madge DuClaire*. Even though Granny Laurite had filled her in on the whole history, Rhonelle still found it hard to believe that Mary Lynn had concocted a completely different personality called Madge in order to ensnare poor drunk Herman Junior into a fake marriage. The fact that seventeen-year-old Mary Lynn bamboozled so many people for more than three years portraying the most notorious gold digger in the history of Peavine made her performance worthy of an Oscar for best actress!

The most amazing realization was that if Mary Lynn/Madge had never tricked Herman Dumas Junior into marrying her and coming to Peavine, history would have been very different. Doll would never have been able to do all her good works over the years. Rhonelle's own life trajectory might very likely have been one of a tragic degeneration of an aging stripper. No telling what tragedies she had forestalled by coming to Peavine and helping to find Lucille … and Tammy. She couldn't bear to think of it!

"Let's sit over here where it's quieter," Lucille interrupted Rhonelle's reverie, steering her to a corner booth near the other end of the plate-glass window. Lucille plopped in the side facing the door so she could see everybody coming in to the Diner. Rhonelle slid in opposite – her back to the room and the booth with Mary Lynn and Leroy.

Rhonelle was gazing out the window at nothing in particular while Lucille waved at Dorine who was making her way slowly over to their booth. Dolly the poodle actually got to them first, wiggling and happy to see Lucille. The dog outfit for the day was a pink sequined sweater and tulle skirt. She stood on her hind legs waving her front paws (poodle for "pick me up and put me in your lap").

"Hey sweetie," Lucille cooed to the elderly canine, lifting Dolly to face level. "You've still got your party dress on. I guess you and Whutzit had a late night . . . yeck!" Dolly licked Lucille's nose before she could dodge.

"That does it for me." Lucille set Dolly back down in the floor. "Go get your Momma."

"Speaking of Whutzit," Lucille wiped the dog slobber off with a grimace. "Where is that ugly little mutt? Have Kristy and Misty left already?"

"They left yesterday after my birthday party, and don't let Dorine hear you call that poor creature an ugly mutt," Rhonelle added quietly. "He's simply a very unusual combination of canine genetic factors."

"Whatever," sighed Lucille, "at least he don't smell as bad as he looks. That reminds me; I'll bet Don has some of your cake left for us. That no-peek coconut cake only gets better with age."

"Just like I do," Rhonelle said with a smirk. She had never been sure of her exact birth date, so Doll had started the tradition of celebrating it on New Year's Day every year since Rhonelle had moved to Peavine. However, no one except Rhonelle knew her true age. This year marked a big one. She had just turned fifty, and that felt peculiar to her. She'd been too busy helping Doll, Lucille, and Tammy to notice her forties come and go. To turn the half century mark was something she could neither ignore nor accept as reality.

"And what would you like with your coffee, Rhonelle?" Dorine had been standing there timidly waiting for Rhonelle to stop staring out the window. Lucille had asked for coffee and some cake and was trying not to laugh as Dorine's eyes grew big as saucers. Dorine always assumed Rhonelle was communing with the dead whenever she appeared distracted. "I'll have a turkey sandwich and some of my birthday cake for dessert," Rhonelle requested with a smile. After a slight pause she added, "Add one more piece of cake. Shirleen will be joining us in a bit."

"Okay, coming right up." Dorine began to relax. "You want mayo and dill pickles on that sandwich, right?"

"Why, Dorine – you read my mind," Rhonelle said in mock astonishment.

"Lordeee, you gals love a good laugh at my expense. Come on Dolly, let's go tell Poppa what to fix." Dorine stuck her pencil behind her ear and shuffled over toward the kitchen, smiling the whole way with her loyal doggy at the heels of her fluffy pink house shoes.

"So Madam Psychic, how do you know Shirleen will be joining us?" Lucille leaned forward on her elbows.

"Because you are going over to Cottage #5 to get her for me," Rhonelle said as she twirled a strand of her salt-and-pepper hair around her finger. "I assume she hasn't left for Nashville yet, *and* she has everything she'll need."

Lucille pushed herself back from the table and gaped at Rhonelle. "You're finally gonna do it?"

"I'm going to let her do it." Rhonelle ruffled her bushy gray curls. "I'm tired of all this gray. I'm going for the full shebang – *complete makeover*."

Lucille clapped her hands with delight at the prospect of having Shirleen Naither do one of her famous "makeovers" on Rhonelle. She, Doll and Shirleen had been trying to talk her into it for the past ten years. "I'll go get her right now. It'll make her day!" She scooted out of the booth and turned to Rhonelle with new tears threatening to form. "Momma would be so happy for you." Then she walked quickly to the backdoor of the Diner and turned toward the Dew-Drop-Inn Cottages.

As Rhonelle watched Lucille leave she felt a familiar presence take her place in the booth seat recently vacated. The sounds of conversation and cutlery on plates muffled and faded. She turned to see the spirit of her Creole Granny Laurite sitting primly with her hands folded in her lap and a very self-satisfied expression on her face.

CHAPTER FIVE

Granny Laurite Has Her Say

*I*t *be about time you did some nice ting for yo self, Cherie."* Laurite smiled warmly at her granddaughter Rhonelle. *"You not get fixed up pretty since your dancing days. Doll would be glad you get rid all dat mess of gray hair!"*

Rhonelle rested her chin on her hand and sighed at the thought of her dearly departed friend. Doll certainly had a love for her bottle of Nice 'n Easy raven black hair dye. Except for one strand of frosted white in her later years, she kept her beehive black to the roots ... until most of it fell out. Shirleen found her some wigs to wear after that.

"I know you be sad and missin' her company. She was a fine lady. She do good for a lotta people," Granny added.

To her embarrassment and surprise, Rhonelle felt hot tears welling up. Unaccustomed to expressing or even awareness of her own emotions, she was suddenly very uncomfortable. On top of that she had to pretend no one was there since she was the only person who could see and hear her Granny. She had to "think" her conversations and try not to look insane. *Will I ever get to see Doll again . . . on this side, Granny?*

"Course you will, just not quite de same way I do it. She always be wid the ones she love." Laurite seemed truly sympathetic, and much gentler than she usually was with her granddaughter. *"Miz Doll was like a real momma to ya. She still be wit you when ya need her."*

Rhonelle cocked her head to one side and squinted through one eye at the apparition sitting across from her. Something about Laurite was definitely different. *Granny, you've changed. What's happened to you?*

To her amazement Laurite let loose a girlish giggle and pulled at the red kerchief on her head. *"Ooooh I doan know, but I tink it may have sumptin do with dat spirit, Johnny. He was some kinda special fella!"*

Rhonelle couldn't stop a smile at the thought of her granny being smitten in the Afterlife with some fine looking scoundrel. She knew he made for a handsome apparition, because she'd gotten a good look at him standing beside Mary Lynn at the Memorial Bash. *You say "was". . . where is Johnny now? I didn't see him with Mary Lynn today. Did he finally decide to "Move On," too?*

All Laurite would do was roll her eyes and look mysterious. The ambient noises in the restaurant grew louder as the ghost quickly faded to one tiny silver flash before she disappeared. *Well that's a new one . . . very dramatic, even for Granny!*

"Ahem. Excuse me Miss DuBoise." A timid voice beside Rhonelle made her jump. It was Mary Lynn Stanton. "I'd like to introduce you to my husband, Leroy. It's his first time in Peavine, and I wanted him to meet a . . . uhmm, real psychic." Mary Lynn stammered a little, not being sure whether it was okay to label Rhonelle as she had. She was still a little creeped out by the idea of someone who possessed telepathic abilities. At least she didn't call her a retired exotic dancer (to her face anyway . . . Uh oh, what if she just read my mind!).

Leroy stepped forward and shook Rhonelle's hand and smiled warmly.
"Glad to meet you, Miss DuBoise. Mary Lynn has told me how kind you and your friends were to her the other night, welcoming her to your big party like that. She says you taught her how to do the Mexican Hat Dance."

Rhonelle smiled and winked at Mary Lynn. "Yes, we had a lively time that night, didn't we. Your wife is quite a dancer. She even kept pace with Teenie Brice. That's no easy task!"

"He's the little man I just told you about who raises AKC toy poodles." Mary Lynn looked across the room to Don and Dorine's Wall of Fame. "There's a picture of him with his wife over there." She looked back at Rhonelle.

"Do you think Leroy and I could go over to their place this afternoon before we leave? I need to buy a couple of Mavis' Poodle Angels to take back to my friends at home."

"I'm sure they'd be delighted to have you come by." Rhonelle raised her eyebrows and pointed toward the framed photograph of Teenie and Mavis Brice.

"You'd better show Leroy that photo before he meets them, so he'll know what to expect."

Mary Lynn giggled at the thought. "I guess that's a good idea. ... Oh, excuse me!"

Dorine arrived with Rhonelle's lunch, lurching between Mary Lynn and Leroy to get to the table.

"Don't mind me. I can manage." She slid the sandwich and coffee deftly in front of Rhonelle, straightened up and put her arm around Mary Lynn's shoulder. "Don and I have been having a fine time hearing about the food Mary Lynn and Leroy ate while they were down in New Orleans. Don's been inspired to try new bread pudding recipes with real hard sauce."

Dorine leaned in and whispered, "He's even considering making oysters Rockefeller . . . but that sounds way too high falootin' for Peavine."

Rhonelle shrugged her shoulders. "I don't know Dorine. I'll bet you could find several customers that would love something like that for a change. I know I would." She took a bite of her turkey breast sandwich on white bread and thought about how much she'd rather be eating a fried oyster po' boy on a French baguette. "I know where Don can order top-notch seafood wholesale," she said after a sip of coffee.

"We'd better let Miss Dubois eat her lunch, Mary Lynn," Leroy said, taking his wife's arm. "Thanks again . . . for everything," he added, suddenly shy.

"Yes, thank you Rhonelle," Mary Lynn briefly touched Rhonelle's shoulder before she and Leroy turned to leave the Diner arm-in-arm. Rhonelle watched them walk to their car through the window. Mary Lynn put her arm around her husband and leaned her head on his shoulder. At that point Rhonelle looked away and focused on her half-eaten sandwich. Tears had blurred her vision.

What is wrong with me? I'm not usually this sentimental.

"It about time you soften up a bit, Chérie. Dat a good ting . . . shows

you really livin'." Granny Laurite had reappeared in the seat opposite Rhonelle. *"You been concerned wid the Other World too long now. You gotta live in dis one a little more fully now!"*

Rhonelle looked up at her Granny and dabbed at her eyes with the edge of her napkin. She knew Laurite was right . . . as usual.

Trouble is Granny, I don't even know what I want anymore . . . but I know there's something missing. I feel it more than ever now Doll has Crossed Over.

"When you know what dat is you want, I be ready to hep you." Granny faded except for her smile with a gold tooth twinkling. *"I know what you need, but you gotta figure it out!"* Granny's fading laughter was replaced by the excited squeals of Shirleen and Lucille as they clattered in through the Diner's back door, each carrying large pink bags of beauty products.

CHAPTER SIX

Rhonelle Gets a Makeover

Back at the lavender double-wide, Shirleen clapped her hands gleefully.
"I have been waiting *years* to get a hold of you!" She whipped the pink
polyester cape around Rhonelle's shoulders, secured it at her neck,
and lifted the copious mass of salt-and-pepper curls, holding it in both
hands like a sculptor examining a block of precious marble, envisioning a future masterpiece.

Shirleen and Lucille had gulped down their coconut cake,
wrapped up Rhonelle's piece to go and practically shoved her out of
the Diner and frog- marched her across the highway. Within minutes
they set up a makeshift hair salon in Doll's master bathroom with
Rhonelle sitting on a kitchen chair facing the wall-sized mirror over
the lavatory. Lucille arranged Shirleen's lotions, potions, scissors and
hair color implements like a surgical nurse preparing an operating
theater.

"I have the perfect shade of black hair color with me. I don't think
I'll need to do much more than trim a little on the ends and put on
some conditioner to hold down the frizz." Shirleen pulled at a tendril
and wrapped it around her finger.

"Good gawd, Rhonelle do you have *any idea* what a fantastic head
of hair you've got? Half of my clients would kill for curls like yours."
Shirleen fluffed the cloud of hair back down around Rhonelle's shoulders, pulled on a pair of plastic gloves and reached for two tubes of
color chemicals.

Lucille handed over the clear plastic bowl and something that
looked like a paint brush to Shirleen. "Shirley girly, I think we ought
to make her hair look like that disco singer, Donna Summer." She
studied Rhonelle's reflection in the mirror. "She's got about as much
hair, don't she?"

Shirleen carefully measured the hair color ingredients as she squeezed dark purple goo into the bowl. "Actually Rhonelle has more hair than Donna Summers. That's a wig she wears . . . or extensions at the very least.

"This will look fabulous and Rhonelle is gonna look ten years younger when I get her into the right makeup and a proper *bra*, for God's sake!"

"Excuse *me*, girls," Rhonelle lifted her hand out from under the pink cape. "I may be getting older, but I'm not deaf and I'm not senile yet, either. What's this about a new bra?"

"Good Lord, Rhonelle!" Far from eliciting an ounce of respect from Lucille, this just brought on one of her deep rattle laughing fits. "You've been flopping around braless long enough. You need to pull those tits back up into something with real support."

"I'm not braless," Rhonelle insisted. "I just prefer something thin and comfortable . . . well, sometimes I even leave that off, but nobody notices when I do."

"Oh yes they do!" Shirleen and Lucille shouted in unison.

After three hours of intensive hair coloring and styling, followed by a makeup consultation and application, Shirleen pulled out a lavender bag and handed it ceremoniously to Rhonelle.

"Here's a little late birthday present from both of us. We just wanted to find the right time to give it to you . . . in private."

After they'd rinsed and washed her hair, Lucille moved Rhonelle into the bedroom, where the bureau mirror was covered by a flowery, fringed shawl. They didn't want their "pet project" to see what they were doing to her until they had completed the whole new look. It was supposed to be more exciting this way, but the suspense was wearing on Rhonelle. However, she really did admire Shirleen's skills and knew that if anybody could improve her looks, Shirleen could.

"I have a pretty good idea what this is." Rhonelle cautiously accepted the bag emblazoned with the name of a famous lingerie shop. "How do you know it's the right size?"

"Because we're smart . . . and sneaky," Lucille proclaimed proudly. "Mavis told us your measurements from when she made that costume for you last time you went to Mardi Gras. She keeps all that information in a file."

"And I know all about bra sizing from when I used be a part of the Penny- Rich franchise." Shirleen quickly added, "Don't worry, this one won't make you look pointy, but it sure will give you a lift and make your tits perky. It's got real good push-ups in it. Give it a try before you make up your mind."

Rhonelle cautiously reached into the bag and slowly pulled out a red satin low-cut underwire bra. She held it up and considered the possibilities. She had to admit the combination of fashion and engineering comprised the most beautiful brassiere she'd ever seen (without tassels). "All right, scoot out of here and let me put it on so I can make my dramatic appearance . . . and *finally* see how I look after what all you've done to me."

The fact that a former stripper had shown the modesty to halfway disrobe in privacy was a huge joke to the girls. Shirleen and Lucille left the room laughing raucously and shut the door. Rhonelle found herself smiling over the irony of it, too.

Rhonelle squeaked the bathroom door open and found herself stunned at the woman looking back at her from the now-undraped mirror. She had not realized she could still feel so good about looking younger and – *what?* She . . . looked . . . *sexy!*

Thick black glossy curls fell below her shoulders. It was full – not bushy, styled just as she hoped. Shirleen also had masterfully covered the dark circles under her eyes and smoothed and brightened her olive complexion. She still had the eyeliner, yet applied mostly to her upper lids with a smoky eye shadow and plenty of mascara. Blush and deep red lipstick completed the transformation. Rhonelle *really* liked that lipstick; it made her lips look full and glossy.

She hadn't worn much makeup except black eyeliner pencil since her days in New Orleans. Over the years, she watched her hair turn salt and pepper with dismay, but didn't concern herself much about it. Mostly, she focused on her hands. Arthritis had made her knuckles go all knobby. She tried wearing turquoise and silver rings and bracelets, because she'd read somewhere that would help. Well, her hands were hardly noticeable now!

She tore off the flannel shirt and camisole she was wearing and put on the new bra. After a little scooping and pushing she got the look she was hoping for without terrible discomfort. "Not bad ... *not bad at all*," she said to her reflection, smiling seductively into the mirror.

Digging through one of the boxes of clothes that she had yet to unpack, Rhonelle found what she was looking for: her purple spandex top and matching skirt. Snatching her shawl off the mirror where Lucille had hung it, she wrapped it around her shoulders.

"Are you ready, girls?" Rhonelle called from inside the bedroom.

"More than ready," they shouted back with excited giggles.

Rhonelle flung the door open, sashayed in and dramatically tossed aside the shawl to reveal her new décolletage. Lucille and Shirleen hooted and shrieked with delight! "Where can I order some more of this lingerie?" she asked the girls as she beamed her lovely smile at them.

CHAPTER SEVEN

A Timely Call From Krystal Bridges

In the days following her big makeover, Rhonelle reveled in the reactions of her friends and other residents of Peavine to her new look. Most of them were at first astonished, and quickly complemented her on her appearance. Even Marv's not-too-subtle leering at her was pleasant (although his wife Pauline didn't care for that).

Don, Dorine, and the Brices were the first to see the "new Rhonelle" when Lucille and Shirleen dragged her over to the Diner for her first presentation. They cheered and applauded when Lucille got all their attention by a loud two-finger whistle when they walked in the door. Teenie was in shock for a few seconds, then got so excited he jumped up on his chair clapping enthusiastically before Mavis could stop him.

After a week of practice with her new makeup and acquiring the habit of wearing a bra every day, Rhonelle noticed some internal transformations as well. She liked feeling attractive again. Her mood evolved as she re-evaluated other things she had not allowed herself to feel for a long while.

When Lucille and Bo returned all aglow after their three-day clandestine trip to Graceland, Rhonelle was surprised by the sudden stab of jealousy she felt when she saw them grinning like fools, full of secret whispers and blushes.

She didn't want Bo for herself by any means. On the contrary, Rhonelle was delighted to see Lucille so happy. It made her realize how much *she* could use the attention of a man with the proper looks and skills for a few days and nights. Of course absolutely no one like that existed in Peavine. She had to get out of town for that form of recreation.

Sexual intrigue was an area of her life she had kept carefully crated and insulated since her move to Peavine so long ago. Except for a few brief encounters on yearly visits to her old friends in New Orleans, there were no men in her life, except for those special male friends of hers that were of a different persuasion.

That's why the almost supernaturally well-timed call from her old New Orleans friend Krystal Bridges made her whip around to see if Granny Laurite was standing beside her grinning with mischief. *Has it really been ten years since I last went to visit Krystal?* Rhonelle found that hard to believe. She'd been so involved with Doll Dumas and all her projects over the past several years there was precious little time for her to get out of town.

"Baby, you have *got* to come down for Mardi Gras this year," Krystal scolded in her high-pitched childlike voice. "I won't take any excuses this time. I need you to be my maid of honor!"

"Your maid of *what*," Rhonelle asked in disbelief.

"Yeah," Krystal giggled. "I know this comes as a shock to you, but Sammy and I are back together after all these years and I am not about to say 'no' to him this time!"

Rhonelle was completely taken by surprise by this news and couldn't think of anything to say. The long pause made Krystal ask, "You still there honey? You didn't faint or nothing did ya?"

"Champagne Crystal," as she was known professionally back in their dancing days, had carried on with Sammy the saxophone player from the club where she and Rhonelle were headliners. (Rhonelle, known as "Little Sheba" at that time, did a mighty racy version of the Arabian Dance of Seven Veils.)

Krystal would appear on stage perched in a giant plastic champagne glass, wearing gold balloons around her breasts and hips. She would climb down a short ladder accompanied by Sammy's sultry sax solo riff and proceed to pop her balloons one by one until she was down to her pasties and two balloons front and back on her g-string. After an incredible demonstration of tassel twirling, she would pop the last two "bubbles" and run off stage.

"I'm still here." Rhonelle answered calmly. "Don't you think I might be a little too long in the tooth to be 'maid' of anything?" She silently counted up how old Krystal was now, since she knew her to be at least four years her senior.

"Girl, we are both getting *up there!* I know I sound like a fool," Krystal added. "Baby, I've found out we're never too old for romance!

"How about I call you my 'best woman'? Would that suit you better?"

Rhonelle found herself grinning at the idea of it all. "That would suit me perfectly. What am I supposed to wear to this gig?"

Krystal gave the expected response, "Why honey, you just pick out the sexiest costume you can find and come strut your stuff. This is gonna be a *Mardi Gras* wedding so everybody will be playing dress-up, and of course Sammy is making sure we'll have the best jazz band in town!"

This was sounding better and better to Rhonelle. "I take it this won't be a church wedding,"

"Aw, hell no . . . we won't go that far honey. Sammy was able to reserve us a party room at the Royal So-Nasty (their nickname for the Royal Sonesta Hotel on the corner of Bourbon and Royal). Now that he's moved back to NOLA and taken over the family seafood business, Sammy's got some clout in this old town. He booked all this months ago."

"That sounds wonderful, Krystal." Rhonelle truly was delighted to hear from her old buddy. "I will be honored to be there for you. Can I bring a friend with me? There is a guy here that's been dying to go to a drag queen party. Not much of an opportunity for that kind of thing up here."

Krystal loved that. "Oooooh boy, he can be our flower girl!"

"That's even more appropriate since he's a floral designer." Violet Posey's nephew David had been badgering Rhonelle to let him take her to New Orleans ever since the Doll Dumas Memorial Bash. That's when he met the Gay Caballeros band members. Louise Dolesanger's grandson, the lead singer, told him about the Drag Queen Ball they were playing for during Mardi Gras this year.

"Who is going to be Sammy's best man?" Rhonelle knew she'd get the full story on Krystal's surprising decision to marry her old flame but was curious about her counterpoint in the wedding party.

"We aren't positive about that yet . . . still waiting to hear back from somebody, but I'll make sure he's a good match for you," Krystal said mischievously. "Don't worry honey – I know good looks and recreation are all you're asking for, right?"

Rhonelle knew exactly what Krystal meant. While that was an appealing thought, she wasn't sure she was still up for that kind of thing anymore. "Just make sure he has a good sense of humor and can dance . . . and the 'No Real Names Please' rule still applies just in case it goes anywhere," said Rhonelle, referring to a rule strictly adhered to on all of her extracurricular jaunts. She thought to add one other requirement, "not too young either, Krystal. Some maturity sounds good."

Krystal thought that was hilarious but agreed without debate. "We got you covered, baby. I got the perfect guy in mind and I'm not gonna say another thing!

"We'll put you down for two rooms here at the So-Nasty. Sammy was able to get a deal on a whole floor." Within an hour, Rhonelle had made her arrangements with David (who was beside himself with excitement) and talked to Marv and Pauline about taking care of the business at Home-Sweet-Homes-on-Wheels during her absence. Since the park had no vacancies, there would be no need for background checks on prospective tenants.

Teenie could be counted upon to cover any emergency that might arise. He was the expert when it came to thawing out frozen water pipes, a common hazard during the winter at a trailer park. He was the only person small and brave enough to crawl under structures with a blowtorch.

She called Lucille, who was pleased to hear that Rhonelle had finally allowed herself to have some fun.

"High time you took your own advice sweetie. I think you ought to do some shopping for an updated wardrobe to match your new look while you're down there . . . if you have enough time and energy left after all yore partyin' . . . and *other* activities," she added suggestively. Not even Lucille was privy to what Rhonelle did on her excursions, but she was a pretty inspired guesser.

"I might stay a couple of extra days to get some shopping done,"

Rhonelle said, ignoring that last comment and changing the subject. "If my driver doesn't mind, I could get a few things for the house while I'm at it. I think I'll ask David to take the delivery van, convince Miss Violet Posey it would be good PR."

Rhonelle had never before had this much money to spend on herself. Doll Dumas had made sure she had plenty of funds to fix up the double-wide as she wanted.

It was the first time in her life Rhonelle had anything resembling a real home that belonged to her. She anticipated redecorating as much as her trip.

"Don't get too carried away on furniture down there," Lucille warned. "Remember those French Quarter stores have their prices jacked up for tourists. Vaudine and Darla can probably find whatever you need for wholesale or less."

Look who's giving advice now. "Okay, sister," Rhonelle relented. "I can at least look around for some inspiration, but there are some things I'll want that can't be found anywhere else. Even Vaudine can't get them for me. Believe me Lucille; I know how to handle those antique dealers down there." Indeed she did!

After Rhonelle hung up the phone, she sat there stunned at the decisions she had just made without really thinking twice about the consequences. She realized she was at the cusp of a new stage of her life. Not at all sure what that was going to be, she supposed it was high time for some big changes.

Granny, what have I gone and done now?

"*You done good honey. Dis jus be de beginning,*" was all she heard.

. . . Meanwhile: From the "Other Side" in the Afterlife . . .

Laurite watched unseen as her granddaughter made plans for the trip to New Orleans. She cackled and rubbed her hands together as she rocked back and forth in a cane-backed rocking chair on the front porch of a pretty little Creole style cottage covered in bougainvillea vines. She viewed Rhonelle through a window-sized hole in a bank of clouds that faded into pinks and purples where they met the velvety darkness.

Since her experiences with Johnny and Doll in the "Moving Theater," Laurite decided to create her own personalized Afterlife environment. She found it very pleasant and peaceful and kept adding things as it occurred to her, such as a second rocking chair on the porch beside her.

The screen door of the cottage opened with a creak of springs and slammed shut behind a glowing white figure that moved forward and sat down in the second rocker. Laurite turned with the sound and smiled warmly as she watched the bright light resolve itself into the recognizable form of a tall man with wizened brown skin and shoulder-length snow white hair. He was plainly dressed in a red plaid shirt, jeans and soft deerskin boots. His face was a handsome mixture of Native American and Hispanic features that shone with wisdom and kindness.

He turned to Laurite and winked as he gave her a thumbs up.

CHAPTER EIGHT

The Lady With a Bird on Her Shoulder

The day after the call from Krystal Bridges was a Saturday, so Dorine's daughter, Darla, was helping out at Don's Diner as an extra waitress. Rhonelle's makeover and upcoming trip to New Orleans were already subjects of most of the conversations amongst her friends.

"It's about time that woman did something *close to normal* for a change," Dorine said to Darla as she opened the pie case. Evidently, Dorine considered being an attendant at a wild-costumed wedding ceremony uniting an aging exotic dancer to her old flame during Mardi Gras "normal" when compared to her *usual* activities – talking to dead people.

Darla couldn't conceal a smirk. She watched her mother search for a pencil before gently removing one from behind Dorine's ear and handing to her.
"I agree with you, Momma. It will be good for her to get away and have some fun. She certainly deserves it after all her hard work helping Doll the past several years." Darla poured two cups of coffee and placed them on a tray with two servings of coconut cream pie.

"By the way, Mom, Vaudine is on her way over with Leviticus. She just called to tell me. We're working on a plan to redo the décor at the double-wide and she needs to show me some pictures."

Dorine raised her eyebrows at the mention of Leviticus. "I'd better put them at that table over there. Where's Dolly?"

"She's over at the Brice's table," Darla indicated with a tip of her head. "I'll put her in the closet after I take them their order."

"Well . . . okay," Dorine sighed. "I hope Vaudine brings her own newspaper this time. Your daddy hasn't had a chance to read ours yet, and I don't want it ruined."

Darla delivered the pie and coffee to Teenie and Mavis Brice, made a brief explanation and enticed Dolly the poodle into the closet with a dog biscuit she had in her pocket and closed the door. Mavis quickly scooped up their gray poodle Pitty Tat (dressed in a white dress with red hearts), tucking her safely into the folds of her very ample lap. Teenie glanced warily toward the window.

Moments later the door to the Diner opened with the usual clang. In marched a woman with flaming red hair and a leopard print coat. Perched upon her right shoulder was a large, brightly plumed parrot. Vaudine Fortney of Forever Formica Used Furniture and Collectibles had arrived with her infamous bird, Leviticus (also known as "Mr. Nasty").

Darla waved at Vaudine and led her and Leviticus to their table. The bird hopped off Vaudine's shoulder and landed lightly on the back of one of the chairs to allow his mistress to remove her coat. Vaudine plopped her large black patent leather handbag onto the table and pulled out a newspaper and spread it out on the seat of the chair under Leviticus' perch. Darla went back to the kitchen.

The bird watched Vaudine settle into her chair then turned his gaze toward the Brices across the room. He cocked his head to one side and his pupils expanded and contracted in an alarming manner. Teenie was glaring defiantly back at him.

"He had better stay right where he is and leave these little old dogs alone," he said quietly to Mavis, wrinkling his nose in disgust as he noticed the newspaper on the seat of the chair

"If the Health Department were to see Mr. Nasty in here, Don and Dorine would be shut down quicker than a New York minute." Teenie hated to admit how greatly that bird unnerved him. The fact that Leviticus hated dogs increased his concern. Teenie glanced at his wife. Their poodle poked her nose up from under Mavis' large upper arm between sneaked licks from the pie plate in front of her.

"Keep Pitty Tat out of sight for Pete's sake!" Teenie was about to call even more attention to his dog by hopping out of his chair to drape his woolen neck scarf over her. Mavis merely waved him away and readjusted Pitty on her lap.

"Settle down, Teenie," she whispered, never missing a bite of pie. "The worst that bird could do is cuss at her. He's mature enough to know his manners. He don't even really need that newspaper." She looked up and thought a minute. "You know . . . I figure he's got to be around forty, forty-five years old by now. Don would know."

The kitchen door opened and Don burst out with a big grin on his face. He considered it a real occasion whenever Vaudine brought her bird to the Diner. He strode over to their table wiping his hands on his apron.

"Hey Vaudine . . . hello there Mr. Nasty, to what do I owe the honor of your company today?" Don bowed to the bird who had turned his attention from the Brices and studied his favorite chef with his right eye as the feathers on his head ruffled excitedly. Leviticus knew when he was appreciated, and Don was one of his biggest fans.

"Today is Levi's birthday so I brought him over for a treat. Fred's watching the store for us while we take a little break." Vaudine reached over and stroked her bird's head with her finger. "Leviticus, tell Mr. Don what you'd like to have," she said to him.

"Cookie please . . . yes cookie . . . hmmm," the bird mumbled.

Don loved the idea that the bird could order for himself. "What kind of cookie do you want sir? We've got chocolate chip, oatmeal raisin, and sugar cookies." He ticked them off as he held up three fingers. Leviticus cocked his head, scooted closer to Don, and looked up at him with his pupils rapidly expanding.

"Gimme a chocolate chip cookie and a cup of red fruit punch," Leviticus announced loudly in a perfect imitation of old Lester Astor (may he rest in peace). He punctuated it with a squawk and several head-bobs.

Don howled with laughter and slapped his knee. "Coming right up, sir," Don said as he bowed to Leviticus who bowed back – delighting Don even more.

"I swear Vaudine, that's the smartest most hilarious animal I've ever seen! It's almost like having a part of your old Dad with us again."

Vaudine gazed at her fine-feathered companion appreciatively – stroking his head again.
"That's probably why we get along so well, right fella?" She smiled up at Don. "Maybe that's why he likes you so much. Daddy always loved

to show out for you."

"Well, feeling was mutual," Don said bashfully. "Guess I'd better go tell Darla what he wants . . . and you too Vaudine. Will you have your usual?"

"He's been talking like Daddy all day." Vaudine squinted at Leviticus whose stare had returned to Teenie Brice. "Yeah Don, I'll have my pickles, potato chips and a diet cola as usual. Can Darla take a break for a few minutes so we can discuss Rhonelle's redecorating?"

"Sure, sure Vaudine." Don never understood why Vaudine never ordered desserts, but he didn't take it personally. "I'll have her bring over your order so y'all can visit." He turned back to Leviticus.

"As always, it's a pleasure having you here buddy. I feel like you brought old Lester along with you."

"Thank you," Leviticus said quietly as he watched Don return to the kitchen.

CHAPTER NINE

The Story of Vaudine Fortney and Mr. Nasty

Vaudine's mother, Eulelie Astor, had been a very religious, straight-laced woman, and her father, Lester Astor, was a real card – famous for playing practical jokes on the salesmen down at his dealership, Astor Pontiac and Buick.

The locals would come in to the dealership mostly to hear Lester's new jokes and stories. While there they'd take a look at his new cars. "Lester the Jester" is what they all called him.

Most of the wives would shake their heads over poor Eulelie Astor and say, "How on *earth* does she put up with that husband of hers?" For Eulelie's sixtieth birthday, Lester thought it would be a hoot to give his long-suffering wife a real talking parrot as a gift. He'd seen one at a pet store in Little Rock while he was up there on a car-buying trip. After a few cocktails over lunch with some old college buddies, he decided on a talking bird so he could teach it to say dirty words. The last thing Lester expected was Eulelie's absolute delight with that bird. She doted on it like a new grandbaby. Some saw this as another jab at her daughter, Vaudine, for never bearing her a grandchild. It didn't seem to count for much that her sons, Rodney and Bodine, had each dutifully produced a whole passel of rowdy grandsons.

Vaudine paid no mind when her mother hinted disappointedly about her lack of motherly instincts. Ever since eloping to marry Fred Fortney, a career military man, she stayed far enough away from Peavine to insulate her from parental pressure.

Meanwhile, Eulelie Astor worked with her parrot day and night, teaching it to talk. She repeatedly read aloud from the Bible her favorite Psalms and Proverbs to the stone-faced bird. One blessed day, he began to talk back to her!

Eulelie named him Leviticus, because that sounded so "Biblical." Eulelie had wanted to give all her children Bible names, but Lester wouldn't hear of it.

Leviticus the parrot proved to be a very talented mimic. Not only could he repeat what he heard, he could do an uncanny impersonation of whomever it was that said it. The Bible verses were in Mrs. Astor's soprano; the swear words and dirty jokes in Lester's baritone. Now *that* was an opportunity that ole Lester the Jester could not pass up.

Eulelie ignored the ribald selections of Leviticus' repertoire, the same way she'd ignore Lester's salty humor. She made an effort to concentrate on what she referred to as the *Lord's* words that the bird spoke to her.

Eulelie noticed that Leviticus would spontaneously quote Bible verses each time she rolled her eyes toward the Heavens to ask the Lord what she should do (which was at least once an hour). Living with Lester Astor would have been a difficult challenge for any woman.

First thing every morning, Eulelie would stumble out of bed to uncover Leviticus' cage. She waited patiently for his first words of the day. She referred to his utterances as one would consult their horoscope to discover what kind of a day to expect. Her entire mood depended on the first words mumbled by that bird at the crack of dawn. Some days Eulelie would come down to the kitchen neatly dressed and anticipating a happy day, cheerfully whistling "Onward Christian Soldiers." Those were the days when Leviticus had quoted something she found inspirational or uplifting. On other occasions she crept down the stairs in her nightgown, fixed her coffee in solemn silence, and scuttled back up to her bed, where she would stay under the covers until she heard the bird call out something more positive.

Leviticus was intelligent enough to figure out that some phrases had the effect of getting him his Polly-Wanta Treats much faster. He quickly learned to recite uplifting Bible quotes when he was hungry, saving Hell-fire and brimstone verses to use when Eulelie's cheerfulness bored him.

Eulelie's second son, the most righteous Pastor Bodine Astor, was mortified by the way his mother carried on about her talking bird. He tried to explain that it was downright *sacrilegious* for her to think a dumb animal could possibly be telling her what God wanted her to hear.

Bodine was probably just jealous because until Leviticus came along he had been his mother's pride and joy. She took pride in Rodney for prospering with his Astor Eternal Rest Funeral Home; but, in her eyes, watching her Bodine pastor his own church was pretty hard to beat.

Meanwhile, Lester Astor considered his wife's obsession with a talking bird hilarious. He added the Leviticus Forecast for the Day – with Eulelie's reaction to it – as a part of his daily comedy repertoire down at Astor's Buick and Pontiac.

Lester passed away a few years later, suffering a massive heart attack and keeling over right in the middle of one of his favorite traveling salesman jokes. At first, his buddies thought it was part of the act. It took a minute or two before they figured out he wasn't kidding. If Lester had to go that probably was the best way – doing what he loved. Even if his theatrical departure was a pretty big shock. After the death of her husband, Eulelie's behavior grew weirder by the day. She must have been a lot more attached to Lester than anybody realized.

Whenever Leviticus would start telling jokes or cussing (in Lester's voice of course), Eulelie decided that her dear departed Lester was contacting her from beyond the grave.

Finally, there came a day, after Pastor Astor started up his radio station KPEW, Mrs. Astor insisted that he put Leviticus on the air for his "Quote of the Day." The pastor felt so sorry for his mother that he gave in to her wishes, and granted Leviticus his radio debut real early one morning. Putting a talking parrot on a live radio turned out to be a *bad* idea! Leviticus had never cared much for Pastor Astor. When the pastor came striding into the control room and pointed his finger at Leviticus – the cue for the bird to start talking – the bird didn't like that one bit. Leviticus figured he'd show that pompous human who was boss.

The first "Quote of the Day" out of the bird's beak was the opening line of one of the *saltiest* of Lester Astor's traveling salesman jokes. That was followed by the bird squawking, "What the HELL do you think you're up to!?" when Pastor Astor frantically lunged for the microphone. A *terrible* commotion was heard by listeners when Leviticus flew up to the top of the pastor's head and sank his beak into the poor man's left ear lobe, nigh unto *piercing* it!

Immediately, Pastor Astor *himself*, cut loose with a whole string of the most blasphemous passel of cuss words ever heard over the airways! (Confirmed listeners were sure that discourse was due to the excruciating pain the pastor was feeling at the time.)

Eulelie fainted from the shock of it all and fell flat out on the floor, distraction enough to keep Leviticus from biting Pastor Astor's earlobe clear through. The parrot lit on the left shoulder of his unconscious mistress and inspected her shallow breathing with a downturned eye. Little Bo Astor who was running the control room, cued up a recording of "How Great Thou Art" while things could settle down long enough to call an ambulance for poor grandmother Eulelie. Leviticus insisted on riding with her.

Little Bo happened to have his tape recorder going the whole time during the first and final episode of Leviticus' Quote for the Day. He still plays the tape at parties around town when he deejays. It's a big hit with all the local folks. He replaced the profanity with *bleeps* so as not to be offensive, but that just makes it funnier. Little Bo seems to have a lot of his granddad Lester in him.

After the Leviticus' Quote of the Day fiasco, Eulelie Astor's health drifted downhill. She must have knocked herself in the head pretty hard when she passed out onto the floor at KPEW. The shock of hearing her saintly son cuss like a sailor couldn't have done her any good either.

Rodney and Bodine, very worried about the condition of their ailing mother, decided it was Vaudine's duty to move back to Peavine to look after her.

Fred Fortney, Vaudine's husband, had just retired as a major in the Army and was looking forward to moving to Hot Springs, where he planned to work part time at the Oaklawn racetrack. His plan was for him and Vaudine to travel around the country going to various horse racetracks throughout the rest of the year. Fred, a huge horseracing fan, had dreamed on his plan for a long time, and was not happy about moving in with his mother-in-law. Mrs. Astor didn't hide the fact that she had never forgiven Fred for convincing her darling daughter Vaudine to run off at the tender age of twenty-one to marry the likes of *him*, thus forsaking her family and friends in Peavine.

Fred and Vaudine worked out a compromise of sorts by purchasing a mobile home and settling in at Doll's park among her earliest tenants. Fred had always liked Doll, so that helped a lot. Vaudine told Fred he could drive up to Hot Springs as often as he wanted during racing season, and he did so at least once a week.

Fortunately (for Fred anyway), Eulelie Astor didn't linger too long. She went to join her late husband Lester only eight months after Fred and Vaudine had moved back to Peavine.

The one big hitch to all this was in her will. Mrs. Astor left Pastor Bodine all the money from the sale of Astor's Pontiac and Buick for his evangelical radio outreach. Rodney Astor got her house. Vaudine inherited Leviticus.

Bodine and Rodney would have gladly buried that bird alive and squawking with their mother; however, in the reading of the will, Eulelie had expressly stated that her beloved Leviticus was to go to Vaudine since *she* never did have any children.

Leviticus quickly bonded with Vaudine. Perhaps this was because she reminded him a little of Mrs. Astor, and he always preferred being around women more than men. Leviticus learned to happily perch up on Vaudine's left shoulder. She could smoke a cigarette, clean the trailer, and cook dinner – and Leviticus wouldn't budge (except to excuse himself to do his business in his cage). Fred taught him to say, "Pieces of Eight ... . . Pieces of Eight!" like the bird in Treasure Island.

Leviticus took to Fred right away, too. When the bird wasn't riding around on Vaudine's angora-clad shoulder, Leviticus would watch TV with Fred. Their favorite show was "Dragnet." Leviticus would sit on the back of Fred's **Barcalounger**, watching out of one eye and repeating some of the actor's lines. Fred also began to notice Leviticus mumbling some of Lester's dirty jokes and a few choice cuss words. That's how Fred and Vaudine got started calling Leviticus "Mr. Nasty."

Before long, even Leviticus started repeating "Mr. Nasty" without interruption until the name stuck. Doll Dumas decided the bird *had to be* smart enough to know what he was saying. She claimed his personality had changed for the better since he came to live with Vaudine and Fred. Doll officially nicknamed him Mr. Nasty, although he was sometimes referred to by his proper name, Leviticus. That depended on what kind of mood he was in at the time.

Life for the Fortneys had become pretty sweet. They were free of responsibilities with their home on wheels. Fred, Vaudine, and Mr. Nasty were able to travel to lots of racetracks, and still come back to Peavine to live and enjoy being with their friends.

While they were on the road, Vaudine didn't want to go to all the horse races with Fred, so she took up a new hobby. She would drop him off at the track and drive around looking for unusual finds at the local rummage sales, antique stores, and her favorite, estate auctions. Mr. Nasty stayed in the car or the trailer while his mistress shopped. Vaudine enjoyed these outing enormously. It wasn't long before she was hooked on those auctions as much as Fred was with the horses. While Fred would sit for hours analyzing the racing form, Vaudine would be there beside him with a city map and the local newspapers, checking out all the classified ads and auction notices.

At first this was merely an innocent pastime for Vaudine. She was always on the lookout for anything that had to do with poodles to bring back for Doll's collection. While she was at it, she started looking for objects with a parrot or bird theme. Pretty soon she had acquired poodle and parrot figurines, salt and peppers, vases, plates, dish sets, tablecloths, tea towels, painted furniture, paintings, postcards, note cards, even hats and sweaters.

After discovering the incredible bargains on furniture at these auctions, Vaudine started buying those great fixer-uppers she was sure somebody could use. Fred was pretty handy at refinishing, and Vaudine decided this would give him a kind of hobby to pursue when he wasn't playing the horses. It only took about a dozen horseracing/

shopping trips before the Fortneys' trailer and two portable outdoor storage units began to overflow with the items Vaudine had collected. Fred set himself up a little workshop area in a third portable building that Doll had moved over near their trailer. However, within a few months *that* got so cluttered up Fred could barely fit in there to work on all the honey-do projects Vaudine had so kindly found for him.

The straw that broke the camel's back was the day Fred came home from a lousy day at the races up in Hot Springs. He was tired and disgruntled because none of his horses had finished in the money. He walked into the doorway of the trailer with his head down in his racing form still trying to figure out what calculation he had gotten wrong about this or that horse when . . .

KALAAANNNGG! Fred knocked his head right into the swag lamp Vaudine had found and put up that afternoon so she and Doll Dumas could see how it looked before she bought it.

"What the HELL is that thing doing there!?" Fred shouted as he clutched his hand to his bleeding forehead. Doll and Vaudine were horrified at the sight of blood running down Fred's face. Mr. Nasty got terribly agitated and started squawking and flapping around the trailer. Fred pulled out his hanky to staunch the bleeding and sat down at the dinette table. When Vaudine ran over to tend to him, she tripped over a large box of porcelain figurines she had bought that afternoon (and hadn't had a chance to hide from Fred). As she grabbed the table to keep from falling, she knocked a whole set of Depression glass dishes set out on the table crashing onto Fred's lap!

Doll attempted to stay out of harm's way, but that wasn't easy with Mr. Nasty shouting, "Gawd dammitt ... gawd dammmiitt," while trying to get a claw-hold up on top of Doll's famously tall, black beehive hairdo.

Fred stood up, flinging broken dishes off his lap. His face looked as if he was about to explode. After a few choice epithets of his own, Fred announced that Vaudine had better get rid of all that "crap" she'd been wasting their money on, or he was leaving her for good! Then the old wounded soldier walked out, slammed the door ... and hobbled over to the Diner where he asked Don to drive him to the doctor.

Mr. Nasty disentangled himself from Doll's hair, and flew over to the Barcalounger. "Goodbye Fred," he said, followed by the same recitation of curses just delivered by the departing Fred. He topped that off with, "As ye sow shall ye reap," in a perfect imitation of Eulelie Astor.

Vaudine followed Fred to Don's Diner, her red eyes exaggerated by purple mascara running down her cheeks. Doll came along too, with her beehive tilting dangerously off-kilter. Mr. Nasty was attempting to hang onto Vaudine's pink sweater and his feathers were all ruffled. Dorine brought out the first-aid kit, where she had found a pint of iodine. After a generous application of iodine, Dorine was trying to stitch Fred's forehead back together with a row of Band-Aids across his noggin, and she was trying to do so with her eyes shut so she wouldn't faint from the sight of blood. Needless to say, she wasn't having much luck. Gratefully, Dorine let Vaudine take her place.

"Mind if I have a smoke, Fred?" Doll asked as she lit up a fresh cig. She sucked in a big drag and blew it out slowly to emphasize the drama – and to be sure she had everyone's attention.

"I have an idea that could be the best of all worlds for the both of you," she said with a smile as she rolled her eyes up at the ceiling. This hooked everybody's attention.

"I've been percolating on a scheme for the past month," Doll said nonchalantly as she tried to set her beehive straight.

"Vaudine, have you ever considered opening up your own shop to sell this stuff you've been buying for the past two years? You can't even begin to make use of it all, and wouldn't it be a thrill to make an income off a' doing something that you love to do?"

Fred looked up, "You mean make up some of the money she's wasted from being such a dang packrat!"

"Well, that's one way to put it," Doll interrupted before Vaudine could start to cry again.

"Dumas Oil Company has an abandoned building just down there across the highway. It hadn't been nothing but an eyesore since it closed down five years ago. I believe it would make a perfect place for you to start selling your wares.

"There's just enough time before the next Peavine Poodle Pageant and Style Show to get it ready for the tourists. You know you've already got enough poodle collectibles to fill most of the place up!" Vaudine began to warm to the idea. Fred, Doll, and Vaudine talked on about that shop while Don and Dorine served apple pie and ice cream. By then even Fred was getting a little excited about fixing up the old used furniture and reselling it at a good profit. Dorine thought it would be a great idea for Mavis Brice to put some of her dog outfits for sale in the shop. This was how Vaudine Fortney's Forever Formica Used Furniture and Collectibles was born right there in Don's Diner. They were ready to open for business by the week of the first Poodle Pageant.

Doll had saved Fred and Vaudine's marriage – and sanity. It was later that Mr. Nasty became a *hero* on the night of the Fifth Annual Poodle Pageant.

CHAPTER TEN

Leviticus Saves the Day

During the second night of the 1963 Poodle Pageant, Peavine was packed with pandering pet owners and their stylishly attired poodles. Just about everybody in town was at the VFW watching the talent finals and style show. Vaudine had been selling poodle collectibles like gang busters at the shop all day.

Two young guys from out of town had been hanging around Don's Diner and Vaudine's all day looking as if they were up to no good. Nobody thought too much about it with so many strangers in town. Most folks assumed they were with somebody in Peavine for the poodle competition.

That night Dorine was still cleaning up at Don's Diner to prepare for the next morning's rush. She had decided to stay home because their pup, Dolly, had the sniffles, and Dorine didn't want her to feel left out of things.

Walking back over to the cottage office after locking up, Dorine noticed a car with its headlights off pulling around to the back of Vaudine's. She didn't like the looks of that one bit so she slipped into the house and called the sheriff.

Marcella the receptionist was the only person at the station that night because the sheriff had his poodle, Fiona, in the finals of the talent contest. There wasn't any way to call him with his radio turned off, so Marcella said she'd run over to the VFW to fetch him herself.

Dorine was all in a dither because she knew how slow Marcella could move. She got out the binoculars that she kept by her picture window, turned out the living room lights and watched the store across the highway. Sure enough, she saw two men skulking around to the back of the building. Too frightened to go over there by herself, she tried to read the license plate on the car and prayed Marcella could pry the sheriff away from the finals in time.

After a few minutes the interlopers came running around the building back to the parking lot. They were stumbling and pushing each other out of the way as if they were scared witless. The strange thing was it looked like they were empty-handed.

The boys jumped into their car and backed up so fast, their drive wheels fell into the ditch beside the road. For a moment, their car wouldn't budge, which gave Dorine enough time to get their license plate number by the light of the streetlight, and she wrote it down. Just as they managed to get their car unstuck, here came Sheriff Tilley.

When he saw that car peal out of Vaudine's parking lot he tore out after them with a vengeance, sirens wailing and lights flashing. Furious about having to miss the most exciting part of the pageant, *and* his poodle Fiona's talent performance, he floored his cruiser in hot pursuit. Sadly, Fiona didn't do nearly so well on her dance number without her beloved owner there to egg her on.

Vaudine had been in such a big hurry to get the store closed down and get to the VFW for the big finals, she had not cleared out her cash drawer. There was too much money to stuff into her purse, and she was out of time to run by the bank. Under the circumstances, Vaudine decided to simply lock up the shop and drive on over to the pageant.

Neither did she have the time to take Mr. Nasty back home. She certainly couldn't take him with her to the pageant either. There was no telling what he might start shouting since he detested dogs almost as much as he hated Pastor Astor. He was better off staying in the dark shop until the pageant was over. Vaudine had been bringing Leviticus/ Mr. Nasty with her to work every day since she opened her store. He enjoyed all the attention from the customers, and kept a sharp eye out for shoplifters. He learned to say, "You break it, *you buy it!*" To drive the point home he would cock his head to one side and give the unlucky offender the "stink eye," as Teenie described it. Mr. Nasty turned out to be the most efficient security system Vaudine could have ever wanted. On that fateful night of the Poodle Pageant, Mr. Nasty was rudely awakened by the noise of shattering glass when the two boys broke in the back window of the shop with a brickbat. Immediately, the bird went into his loudest warning mode, starting off with a few of Fred's best cuss words followed by some favorite lines he'd learned from the Dragnet television show. It must have worked as a powerful deterrent because the two would-be robbers were too spooked to get anywhere near Vaudine's cash drawer. Fortunately for everybody, Mr. Nasty ended up not only saving all of Vaudine's money, but, as it turned out, he also saved those boys from a life of crime. The two potential criminals, John and Stanley, were only a couple of misguided teenagers who'd watched Marlon Brando movies a few too many times.

Vaudine decided she wouldn't press charges if they would agree to repair the window they broke, and come to Peavine once a week for the next six months to help Fred get caught up in his workshop. Fred whipped those boys into shape with his military discipline; and after many weekends spent working on "honey-do" projects, they ended up with polished resumes as furniture refinishers.

With Fred's wholehearted encouragement, John and Stanley enlisted in the Army when they turned eighteen. After serving four years they returned to El Dorado and opened their own business building furniture and repairing antiques. Even though Vaudine never had any kids of her own, she and Fred felt like they had a hand in raising two juvenile delinquents up into fine young men.

Later on when Stanley married and had a son, he asked Fred and Vaudine to be the boy's godparents. They were delighted to have that honor, and the two families kept up a close relationship. When their godson finished two years of technical college, he moved to Peavine. Fred recognized his talent as a mechanic and helped to set him up with a job down at Buddy Cheever's Tire and Auto Repair.

He was a sweet-natured, shy young man with red hair and an easy blush. His name was Cecil Swindle and he fell madly in love with Doll Dumas' lovely granddaughter, Tammy, the very first time he laid eyes on her.

CHAPTER ELEVEN

Going Back to the Big Easy

R honelle was already packed and sitting in a spot of sunshine on the front deck of the double-wide by ten-thirty on a Thursday morning in early February. She was waiting for David Posey to come pick her up so they could arrive in New Orleans in plenty of time to gussey up for Krystal and Sammy's rehearsal dinner that evening. She didn't mind getting up a little early if it meant a free dinner at Antoine's. Sammy's family had been the seafood wholesaler to the famous restaurant for years, thus the opportunity to reserve a party room during the Mardi Gras season.

It had been far too long since Rhonelle had indulged in any sort of a vacation, and she had to admit she felt as excited as a youngster about this trip. Not only would there be plenty of fabulous food and drinks, she looked forward to seeing her old friends . . . and possibly meeting someone new and *interesting*. That thought caused a shiver of excitement to run up her back. She had to smile at her own audacity.

In years past when Rhonelle would quietly return to New Orleans for an annual *rendezvous*, Krystal Bridges would set her up with a handsome stranger. It would always be during the Mardi Gras season so costumes cloaked reality and only imaginary personas were accepted. Rhonelle never knew the true identities of these men and didn't care to find out, or for them to ever find her again. This was the true "one-night stand" and it suited her just fine.

She always took sensible precautions, although having a hysterectomy in her thirties ruled out any fears of an unwanted pregnancy. Rhonelle relied upon her psychic abilities to steer clear of any man that might become a problem. Granny Laurite could always be counted upon to give her a warning if needed, yet always respected Rhonelle's privacy. Laurite was not one to judge other people's sexual mores as long as the liaison was all in good fun.

Now that ten years had passed since her last fling, Rhonelle didn't seem to have the will or energy to pull off another sexual masquerade. She admitted to herself that she definitely felt more attractive since her makeover, but for the most part, she was looking forward to buying a new wardrobe at Violet's Dress Shop in the French Quarter. The luxury of spending money on herself was new and exciting enough for her. She and her young friend David planned to go shopping for fancy dress-up gowns first thing tomorrow.

At the last minute, Rhonelle had decided to pack the beautiful red satin and black lace antebellum dress that Mavis had made for her Mardi Gras costume a dozen years ago. It still fit perfectly, and was very flattering with her olive skin. The effect of newly dyed hair curling down past her shoulders confirmed that the vintage gown was just the ticket to wear to the rehearsal dinner that night. She couldn't keep from smiling at the memory of the last time she had worn that dress as the mysterious lady in red!

I'm not up to that kind of shenanigans anymore . . . but I just wish . . . Oh well, I'm too old for all that now.

"Don't be so sure of dat, Chérie," Granny Laurite said as she appeared in the chair next to Rhonelle. *"Might be de one you lookin' for is right dere waitin' to find you!"*

Rhonelle decided to ignore that comment. This trip was under entirely different circumstances. *Hey Granny, want to go down with us as a chaperone for me and David? You can help us spot the speed traps on the way.* Granny Laurite swung her bare toes and looked sideways at her granddaughter with a mischievous expression on her face.

"I'll be glad to go back to de Big Easy along wid you. Dere a whole lotta tings I can hep you watch out for." One advantage of traveling with Granny Laurite was that she could warn of a hidden radar miles ahead. However, it was probably a good idea not to let David know they'd have a ghost riding along with them since that might make him a little jumpy. Driving his Aunt Violet's precious ten-year-old Lincoln Continental, he had orders to get it back to her without the least hint of a scratch.

Maneuvering that land yacht through the crowded narrow streets of the French Quarter would be nerve wracking enough without being distracted by the spectral presence of Granny Laurite giving directions from the back seat. Once they made it to the hotel located on the corner of Conti and Bourbon Streets, Rhonelle would insist he leave the car in the parking garage for the duration of their stay. They could walk everywhere they needed to go from there.

Just be sure you don't try any of your tricks on David. This is his first Mardi Gras and he's beside himself with excitement about being invited to that Drag Queen Ball. I want this to be a memorable experience for him. "I'm sure it will be!" Granny rolled her eyes. "You wanna have some fun, too. I see to dat."

Rhonelle was about to say something back to Laurite when her granny quickly disappeared with a tiny silver flash and was gone. "What are you looking for Rhonelle?" Teenie Brice stood on the steps of the front deck staring nervously at her, then whipped his head around to be sure no haunt lurked behind him. "*She* isn't here is she?" "If you're speaking of Granny, no. She's elsewhere at the moment. I was just wondering where David is." Rhonelle looked down to check her watch so Teenie couldn't see her stifle a laugh over his antics. "We ought to be leaving soon to beat the worst of the traffic. Come on up here and keep me company while I wait on him," she said, patting the chair Granny had vacated only seconds ago.

"Be glad to, Hon," he said as he trotted up the deck steps and took a seat. "It's turned out right pleasant this morning," he said, squinting up at the sun and swinging his feet in much the same fashion as Laurite. "But don't let this sunshine fool you," he waggled his finger at her. "I heard on the radio this morning we have a cold snap a coming . . . could even have an ice storm by the weekend if conditions are right."

"I'll have peace of mind knowing you and Marv will be here taking care of things for me while I'm gone." Rhonelle had witnessed Teenie fearlessly crawling under the double-wide armed with a lit blowtorch three years ago when the pipes had frozen. Marv could handle just about any other emergency. Now that Doll had passed, Rhonelle felt free to take a vacation for the first time in years.

Her dear friend's precarious health and need for Rhonelle's support running the Homes-Sweet-Homes on Wheels had kept her in town. For some reason that thought caused Rhonelle to suddenly feel sad and empty. Tears sprang to her eyes, and she fumbled in her purse for a tissue.

This did not go unnoticed by Teenie, who quickly handed her a cotton hanky from his jacket pocket. "Aw now, don't you worry about a thing, honey. We'll be just fine here." He peered up into her face with sympathetic understanding. "You *need* to get away and have a good time after all you done for Doll . . . and for all of us over these past few years."

Rhonelle dabbed at her eyes and looked at the mascara stains on the handkerchief in dismay. "I didn't think anyone carried these anymore. Sorry about the makeup."

"Don't you worry about that Hon, just keep it. Mavis has tons of these around." He patted Rhonelle gently on her shoulder. "We all have our own way of grieving."

Rhonelle realized that this big-hearted little man was the first person who had been able to console her, and she was very grateful. She arose, leaned over and gave him a long hug.

A crackle of gravel alerted her to the arrival of David in his Aunt Violet's Lincoln. He rolled down the window and slapped the side of the car.

"Woohoo y'all! Break it up or I'll start me some wild gossip!"

CHAPTER TWELVE

Dinner at Antoine's

Rhonelle and David drove through Tallulah and Vicksburg, expertly dodging the usual speed traps. They didn't encounter increased traffic until they reached the Interstate 10 causeway. Rhonelle opened the car window and inhaled the gulf air: a distinctive mixture of brackish water and petroleum refineries. "Ah . . . smells like bread and butter!" She sighed and leaned back, closing her eyes and savoring wind in her face.

David sniffed and wrinkled his nose. "Smells kind of polluted to me."

"Exactly," agreed Rhonelle. "Oil companies and fisheries are a big part of the economy in the area."

David drove on in silence. He was beginning to feel a little nervous about the whole Mardi Gras drag queen experience. What would his family think of him if they ever discovered he'd been gallivanting around dressed as a woman? This was just a silly thing he wanted to try, harmless as a Halloween party . . . right?

It was pretty obvious to his Aunt Violet that he was gay, and she didn't seem to have any problem with it. She considered it a side effect of being in the floral business. This new experience was taking things a bit farther out into the open though, and . . .

"You'll be *fine* David. Don't worry about anybody finding out anything from me." Rhonelle understood, even without her sixth sense, that he had concerns. "You have no idea the things I was up to when I used to come down here. It's one big, wild party and no tattling to worry about . . . unless you get arrested."

She laughed at his look of sudden concern. "That's not likely to happen to a nice guy like you! We will keep each other out of trouble."

David felt reassured at Rhonelle's words. He wasn't sure what

Rhonelle might get up to, but he was not going down there to get in over his head with one of those wild musicians or drag queens. The Gay Caballeros were pretty "out there." All he wanted was to play dress-up and party. He hoped he wasn't walking into an orgy or something.

"Relax; we're going to have a great time. Louise Dolesanger's grandson is a nice boy in a monogamous relationship. He won't steer you wrong.

"Wait till you get a load of my old buddy Krystal. She's quite a character. You'll love her shop off Jackson Square. It's called Krystal Gardens and has all kinds of cool New Age stuff mixed in with little fairies and pixies. You can get a thank you gift there to take back to your Aunt Violet. It was generous of her to loan us her *very comfortable* car."

Rhonelle glanced in the rear view mirror just in time to see her granny wave and wink out of sight. *I suppose she'll be back later.*

In the Afterlife at the Creole Cottage

Laurite took a seat and began rocking back and forth in an agitated fashion. She squeezed her eyes shut and repeated his name over and over hoping that would make him appear sooner. She would have to be patient. Grandfather White Cloud would arrive only when he was ready and not a moment sooner. As soon as she accepted the fact that Time on the Other Side was not linear, she calmed down and opened her eyes. The tall Native American man was sitting in the other rocker – also watching Rhonelle through the hole in the clouds.

"Is he gonna be there?" Laurite asked him hopefully.

"Your granddaughter is a beautiful woman, strong spirited, too," he nodded appreciatively and leaned back in the chair. He turned his gaze upon Laurite, which immediately had a warming effect upon her. "Yes, he is on his way to the city heading from the other direction. He prefers the longer way so he can cross the long bridge."

"Will he get to the dinner tonight as we planned?" Laurite's excitement was building now. "All de signs say she need to meet him on dis trip."

"It must not be too easy for them or it will not work," White Cloud chuckled. "My stubborn grandson's decision to attend at the last minute will cause a few … complications. They will turn out to work in our favor in the end."

"What do you mean there is only one room? We were told we would have *two* rooms reserved for us." Rhonelle was at the front desk checking them into the Royal Sonesta Hotel while David stood across the lobby sipping a cocktail and gawking at the crowd of people coming and going. It was already six-thirty after a harrowing entry to the city. David missed two turns, almost turned the wrong way down Royal and barely missed hitting some drunken revelers on his way through the French Quarter. She could have kissed the ground when they finally arrived safely.

The rehearsal dinner was at eight. Rhonelle was anxious to freshen up and change into her party clothes. She had a slight headache and was finding herself irritated by the noisy crowd of revelers in the lobby. "Check again won't you? I'm here for the Bridges-LeBeaux wedding party," she shouted over the jazz band starting to play nearby.

The large black woman running the check-in counter wearing a wig and false eyelashes didn't seem concerned about Rhonelle's distress. She looked again and discovered an envelope with "Ms. R. DuBoise" written on it.

"Oh yeah, this must be for you from Krystal. She came by with it this morning and I forgot all about it. Sorry baby, hope this explains the mix-up." The desk clerk looked across at David who appeared to be feeling pretty loose at this point.

"I don't think your young man will mind," she said raising an eyebrow and winking at Rhonelle. "It's a really nice room … actually a small suite."

Rhonelle sighed and let it go. It *was* Mardi Gras after all. She was lucky to have even one room. After registering and getting a couple of keys, she stepped aside and opened the envelope. Krystal had scrawled a cryptic message in her distinctive large handwriting.

Hey Baby!
Sorry about your room but I think you'll thank me! Wait till you meet the guy who got the other room!!! So glad you're here. Save your costume. Dinner tonight is real clothes.
See you there!
XXOO
Champagne Crystal

David's reaction to their room situation was relaxed. "Hey, it's just us girls!"

It was a nice suite, *very* nice – and at the end of the hall. Fortunately, there were two beds in one room and a fold out sofa bed in the other with two bathrooms. When she stepped inside, Rhonelle almost tripped over a large gift box with a fancy gold ribbon tied round it. The card had "To Our Little Sheba" written on it. She sat down on the sofa to open the card.

Here's your bridesmaid gift from Sammy and me. Wear it to dinner tonight! Add it to your seven veils.

"Ooooh, what's that?" David joined Rhonelle on the sofa after inspecting the larger bathroom. He picked up the envelope and read the inscription. "What's this mean, 'Little Sheba'? That's a funny nickname for somebody like you." He swigged down the rest of his cocktail and put the plastic cup on the coffee table. "Come on – open it!"

"I'm enjoying the wrapping for a moment. It's something Krystal wants me to wear tonight. By the way," she said as she put her hand on his arm, "You'll have to ditch the pirate outfit for tonight's dinner."

He was visibly disappointed. "*Dang* it, why's that?" It was a beautiful Captain Hook costume Mavis made for him when the Peavine Community Theater performed Peter Pan three years ago. It had been such fun – a very unusual production directed by Teenie Brice that included poodles as some of the lost boys.

"Krystal's future husband is from an old New Orleans Cajun family and his two brothers will be there. They want to be able to see our faces and know what kind of people are attending the dinner." When she saw David begin to look anxious about that, she added, "Don't worry honey, they're Cajuns. They might be racist but they are far from snooty. Their beloved eldest brother is marrying an old flame that happens to have been a striptease dancer in her prime so they're bound to be curious about her friends."

"What will I wear to this shindig?" David wrung his hands. "I have kind of a sport coat but I didn't bring a tie."

"We'll buy you one on the way to dinner." She turned her attention back to the box and opened it. "I want to see what Krystal has gotten for me. She has excellent taste in spite of herself."

Rhonelle pulled back the tissue paper to reveal a beautiful velvet shawl – black with bead-embroidered red and purple flowers and long-beaded fringe. When she held it at arm's length, both she and David gasped at the sight of it. "Krystal has outdone herself with this!"

"Put it on! I want to see how it looks on you." David jumped up and clapped his hands. "You look gorgeous in that! Can I borrow it tomorrow night?"

"You most certainly *cannot*," Rhonelle declared as she swished the glittering shawl around and across her shoulders. "We can find you something spectacular of your own on our shopping trip tomorrow morning." She smiled, "First we need to get you a proper coat and tie for tonight – my treat."

An hour later Rhonelle, in her purple spandex leotard and skirt topped by the lovely new shawl, steered David into the men's clothing store off the hotel lobby and bought him a dark purple velvet jacket. Then she left him looking at ties while she went next door to pick out some new earrings in the gift shop.

On her way she stopped by the lobby bar and ordered a cocktail to go. Rhonelle hadn't eaten much since she left Peavine that morning because she didn't want to spoil her appetite for the gourmet dinner awaiting them. She saw a lady sipping a pink drink with a lime in it. "I'll have one of those," Rhonelle told the bartender as she pointed to it.

When she returned to the men's clothing shop, David was looking spiffy in the purple jacket and a lavender tie he'd chosen to go with it. She was paying the bill for David's new clothes when she noticed a man watching her from a nearby rack of dress shirts. Tall and broad shouldered with gray hair pulled into a ponytail at the nape of his neck, there was a certain twinkle in his eye that she found very appealing. Rhonelle found herself powerless to keep from smiling back at him.

"Your son looks very nice in that," he said. "Where do they sell those velvet dinner jackets – in here?"

Rhonelle's smile quickly frosted over. "That's *not* my son!" She flipped the shawl over her shoulder and slid the credit card back into her beaded evening bag.

David stood at the door to the shop, waiting for her and holding her drink. "Come on, Gorgeous!" he shouted over the music in the lobby.

Rhonelle turned away from the man with the ponytail and sinuously walked over to David who offered his arm and handed her back her drink. She took a long swig and hooked arms. They left giggling and dancing across the lobby into the sights and sounds of Bourbon Street without a single glance back. The tall man in the ponytail watched them with a strange little quiver in his heart as he saw Rhonelle lean her head against David's shoulder.

"Wonder what those Cajun boys would say if I walked into Antoine's wearing this?" David had ducked into a souvenir shop on Bourbon Street and held up a tie that had caught his attention. An oversized penis was printed on it, eliciting a howl from Rhonelle over the idea of him wearing it home to Peavine.

"You wouldn't get past the city limits without Sheriff Tilley giving you a citation for indecency," Rhonelle said as she swatted it out of his hand. They had taken a detour on the way to dinner so David could get his first glimpse of Bourbon Street.

It was already a little after eight and she was getting lightheaded from hunger and the effects of that pretty little pink cocktail. "Let's get a move on *son*; we're going to be late for dinner." She told David what the man with the ponytail said to her and it became their latest private joke.

"Coming, Mother," he answered as he pranced back over and took her arm. "Careful you don't take a fall."

They arrived at Antoine's at eight forty-five. The maître de escorted them to the private dining room near the back of the famous old restaurant. They attempted some degree of dignity as they followed him through the crowded main dining room, but the thought of the scene that would have ensued had David actually worn the penis tie in *there* kept causing Rhonelle to giggle.

She almost tripped on the stairs to the party room. At that they both started laughing again. Krystal must have recognized Rhonelle's voice because she came running out to meet them, grabbing her old friend in a fierce, tight hug. Rhonelle winced slightly in pain as Krystal's large, pointy, overly firm breasts pressed against her. It was like leaning into two footballs.

"Oh here's my Little Sheba!" She leaned back and assessed Rhonelle. "Baby, you look fabulous! What have you done to yourself?" Before she could respond, Krystal shrieked and grabbed a handful of Rhonelle's luxurious black curls. "You finally did it! You got rid of all that nasty ole gray!" She dropped the hair and looked Rhonelle up and down. "Let me see you twirl around in that shawl. Oooh it's perfect on you!"

"I love it Krystal!" Rhonelle obliged her friend with a dramatic turn and flourish at the top of the stairs. "You always know exactly what I want better than I do."

"I know that's right, baby," Krystal said with a wink and an elbow to Rhonelle's side.

Meanwhile, David was standing on the stairs openly gawking at Krystal Bridges. She was a sight to behold with her pale blonde hair in a Farrah Fawcett hairdo, heavy makeup and short sequined cocktail dress. This get up might have worked on a younger woman, but looked rather bizarre on someone her age. She couldn't have been much more than five feet tall without the high spiked heels she was wearing. She was thin with skinny legs, and had enormous boobs for a woman her size . . . and they defied gravity in a most unnatural way.

"Shut your mouth David, you don't want to look country," Rhonelle chided.

"Krystal, this is my friend David Posey, and I believe he will do the honor of being your flower girl tomorrow night." Rhonelle giggled again and tottered precariously. David ran up the last step to grab her arm to steady her lest she fall. He had never witnessed this kind of behavior in Rhonelle before and was slightly unnerved by it. "Girl, I believe you need something to eat," Krystal looked over at David appreciatively. "You are a cutie . . . come on in y'all. They're about to bring the appetizers – oysters Rockefeller – your favorite!"

When they entered the dining room, Sammy jumped up to show Rhonelle and David to their seats. Around the table, guests were spooning and spearing at large platters of oysters and decoratively arranged vegetables. Rhonelle realized she was famished. Laid before her was a sumptuous classic French Quarter repast – the object of her dreams for several years. Rhonelle ordered a champagne cocktail from the waiter at her elbow. So engrossed in the process of wolfing down oysters and other delights, Rhonelle didn't really notice the person seated next to her . . . *until* Sammy introduced him.

"Rhonelle meet my childhood friend and soon to be best man, Sergio. I couldn't choose between my two brothers for that honor so me and Krystal coerced him into coming down for the wedding at the last minute."

Daintily wiping the butter that had dribbled down her chin, Rhonelle swallowed indelicately. Turning to offer her hand in her best lady like manner, Rhonelle froze in mid-gesture as she recognized him. There sat the man with the ponytail from the clothing store grinning back at her.

"Pleasure to meet you . . . properly this time," he said taking her hand gently and brushing his lips across it. His golden green eyes fixed on her face. Despite her attempt to appear aloof, Rhonelle felt a warm vibration course through her at his touch. She couldn't deny that he was extremely attractive, tastefully attired in a green velvet jacket similar to David's new one, paired with a gold tie over a crisp white dress shirt. A small gold hoop earring pierced his left ear.

Oh God. I'd better watch myself with this one! I'll do a quick read on him before I get myself in trouble. Where's Granny when I need her?

She disengaged her hand from his and took a long sip of water, using the pause to start a gentle psychic probe. He had a lovely aura but a small dark shadow was lurking somewhere near the edges. Just as she was about to focus in on it she felt something close off abruptly like a door slammed suddenly in her face.

He's blocking me!

Rhonelle was so startled she choked on her water, causing David to turn and thump her on the back. "You all right Rhonelle?" then he looked up and noticed Sergio. "Oh . . . and who might you be?"

Rhonelle recovered quickly and introduced him. "David, this is Sergio. He will be my counterpoint at tomorrow night's ceremony as best man. Sergio, this is David, my . . . *traveling companion.*" The two men reached across the table to shake hands. David was as smitten as she was.

As Sergio sat back down and picked up his napkin, a small flash of gold on his left hand caught her attention. He was wearing a wedding ring. Her initial dismay was replaced with relief. She could relax around this one. Married men were definitely out of bounds, like David and anyone else from Peavine, as a matter of fact. She decided to let down her guard on this Sergio guy and just enjoy his company. That was all she really wanted in the first place, to meet someone new and interesting.

Sergio fit the bill in both areas. Besides his charm and good looks (she'd already forgiven him for the remarks in the clothing store), she was almost positive that he was also a talented psychic. Since he was the first of her kind she had encountered besides Granny Laurite, Rhonelle was dying to know more about him. Despite her intense curiosity, Rhonelle certainly didn't want to invade his privacy. Flashing her best smile at Sergio, she lifted her champagne cocktail in a salute. "Cheers to the bride and groom."

He nodded and clinked his glass of Diet Coke against her champagne flute and took a sip while holding her in his green-eyed gaze. *Truce*.

Truce, she heard back in her head. The sensation of his voice in her mind was so startling, Rhonelle almost let the glass slip out of her grasp in surprise. Then she began to laugh out loud. David looked back at her and Sergio. "What? Did I miss something?"

"This is the man from the store I told you about," she said with a snicker. "He's the one who so tactlessly called you my son!"

"I was only having a little fun at your expense," Sergio explained in his deep voice and a twinkle in his eye. "This young man is way too fair skinned and blonde to be yours."

"You *are* a scoundrel!" Rhonelle bashed him with her beaded bag and laughed even harder. David was not sure if it was okay to laugh along with them, but he did not mistake the look of frankly carnal appreciation in Sergio's eyes as he watched Rhonelle throw her head back, tossing her glorious black curls and baring her long neck (and newly supported décolletage – courtesy of Shirleen Naither, bless her heart!).

One delicious course followed another along with plenty of wine.

Those LeBeaux brothers knew how to order up a fine meal – with plenty of fresh seafood, of course. After three hours of rich food, fine wine, and hilarious toasts (the brothers were good sports about Sammy marrying a woman with Krystal's background), the meal was topped off by flaming Bananas Foster and brandy-laced coffee.

A *very* relaxed and happy Rhonelle was accompanied back to the hotel by David on one arm and Sergio on the other. She had babbled on to Sergio and David about her dancing days with Krystal, hilarious stories about costume malfunctions and strip club pranks.

David was amazed to see Rhonelle talk like this. Normally she revealed very little about herself. He had been in conversation most of the evening with one of Sammy's brothers and had lost interest in Sergio pretty quickly. He'd also seen the wedding ring and was going to make sure Rhonelle didn't let this fella with his sexy ponytail and earring take advantage of his friend. She had had plenty to drink and he was feeling very protective of her.

"So, Sergio," David asked casually as they neared the door of the Royal Sonesta lobby. "Where is your wife? Didn't she want to come down here with you?"

Sergio glanced at Rhonelle before he answered.

"She is in Italy at the moment actually, taking some art courses over the next three months." His formerly jovial mood vanished, Sergio held the door for Rhonelle, who did a little pirouette as she danced through.

"Wow that sounds really cool! What kind of art does she do?" David couldn't help but be impressed. However, Sergio didn't elaborate further as they proceeded to the elevators. The loud clamor of music and people in the lobby covered the silence. Both men reached for the seventh-floor button once they were in the elevator.

Once again, Rhonelle was captivated by the beauty of Sergio's strong brown hands. She wondered if he also was an artist. That's when she realized that she still knew next to nothing about him because she'd spent the entire evening talking about herself. Two important facts she had *not* revealed were her age and that she now lived in Peavine, Arkansas. Her strong sense of privacy had held up through the fog of alcohol. Old rules die hard. He may know her first name but not where to find her.

When they got back to their suite, David turned to Sergio. "Well, we'd better turn in now. Rhonelle has had enough party for one night and tomorrow is a big day. If I want to get her up before noon, we'd better hit the sack." Then he unlocked their door and pulled her into the room as she smiled and blew a kiss at Sergio over her shoulder.

Sergio stood dumbfounded for a moment outside their door, laughed at his own foolishness and went down the hall to his own room shaking his head.

CHAPTER THIRTEEN

The Royal (Sonesta) Wedding

The next morning was chilly and overcast, not a good sign for a wedding ceremony in an outdoor courtyard. Rhonelle had slept like a log despite having to share her hotel room. David, always the perfect gentleman, had slept on the sofa bed in the sitting room, giving her the bedroom with two double beds. This suite must have cost Sammy a pretty penny, but certainly helped smooth over what could have been an awkward situation.

The suite was so comfortable Rhonelle didn't mind having to share. There were even French doors and a small balcony overlooking the courtyard. Rhonelle sat at a small table beside the window in silk pajamas with her new beaded shawl around her shoulders, sipping her cup of café au lait.

David had already been up for two hours. After a brisk walk over to Café Du Monde on Jackson Square, he brought Rhonelle beignets to go with the pot of coffee and hot milk he ordered from room service. How nice it was to be pampered and protected by a man again. It didn't matter that he was only twenty-eight and gay as the month of May; it was the thought that counted.

He was in the bathroom showering and shaving for the day while Rhonelle took her time with her coffee. She gingerly bit into a fresh beignet, savoring the sweetness. Powdered sugar littered the table and her knees but she didn't mind. Ah, how she had missed the cuisine of her youth! Maybe Don could learn how to make some of these; they were only a type of donut after all. She'd have to bring him back a box of the mix that's sold in the souvenir shop.

Speaking of shopping, she and David would have to start their outing pretty soon. Krystal had recruited him to help with the flowers and balloons for the wedding ceremony, which meant they needed to be back earlier than planned. The antique and furniture stores would have to wait until tomorrow.

Their first stop today would be the costume shop for Rhonelle's outfit. Then, it would be on to the Big Diva Couture Salon for David's dress, shoes and wig to wear to the Drag Queen Ball. He had scheduled an appointment with a makeup stylist specializing in drag do-overs two weeks ago. The stylist would meet them at the hotel around six to help him get his wig, fake nails, makeup and a few other tricks of the trade all done in time for the wedding. He planned to ride to the Ball in a limousine with the Gay Caballeros right after the wedding was over. It was all so exciting, no wonder he got up so early.

At close to ten already, Rhonelle decided to make this her breakfast and shoo David downstairs for the hotel's hearty brunch while she dressed for the day. The headache she awoke with had almost faded away now with her second cup of coffee. She had not had that much to drink in more years than she could count. Tonight she would have to be more careful; she wouldn't have David hanging around as her knight in shining armor.

"He a mighty tempting fella – dat Sergio" Granny Laurite materialized in the chair across from Rhonelle. *"Oooooh, nice room. Where dat sissy boy sleep?"*

It's a good thing I had my "sissy boy" with me at that dinner last night, Granny. You sure weren't around to help me. He slept on the sofa by the way.

Rhonelle glanced at the bathroom door, which was still shut. The shower was off and she could hear David singing "Copacabana" while he shaved.

Yeah, that Sergio is a real piece of work, very attractive but out of bounds. I don't fool around with married men.

Granny furrowed her brow. *"Cherie, he not married. Least he not married anymore. His wife done run off wid a younger man two year ago."*

Rhonelle narrowed her eyes. *How do you know all that . . . and why does he still wear his wedding ring since you know so much?*

"You have to ask him bout dat, but it not because he still in love if dat what you wonderin'. He be mighty bitter over it all." Granny Laurite looked sideways and rolled her eyes. *"Oh, I know I'm sayin' too much*

already."

Granny . . . did you know he's one of us?

Laurite smiled and nodded right before she faded and winked out in a tiny flash.

By seven that evening David and Rhonelle were dressed for their big night. Rhonelle had decided to replace the red dress with a harem girl costume and a sheer purple face veil that drew attention to her heavily-lined dark eyes.

David's stylist had pulled, shoved, padded, plucked and tucked him into his slinky gold-sequined evening gown and topped his creation off with a huge auburn wig. With high heels, David stood well over his normal six feet. Artful application of long red press-on fingernails and plenty of expertly applied makeup were the final touches. The stylist, who was a short, bald-headed man in leather biker clothes, stood back with his hands on his hips and cocked his head to one side as David stood anxiously before them.

"Done! You're gorgeous, kid." Then the biker-dude/stylist packed up his makeup case and held his hand out for the one hundred dollar fee, which David nervously handed over to him. "Thanks kid," he said. "Don't break your neck in those shoes." Then he was out the door.

David looked into the full-length mirror and back at Rhonelle. "I feel like Frankenstein."

Rhonelle studied him a moment. "You're very glamorous, but you also look like you could kick somebody's ass if you had to."

David considered this a moment. "I'll take that as a compliment."

"At least you don't look like you need to be wearing a few extra veils like I do." Rhonelle wasn't very confident about her bare midriff even though her stomach was still flat and firm thanks to her yoga and dance exercises. "I'll bring the velvet shawl with me to stay warm during the ceremony."

David practiced walking around the room in his new high heels while Rhonelle gathered up her beaded bag and tied the shawl around her waist. They had to get over to Krystal's room to help her with her very unconventional wedding gown. She looked down at the court-yard. It was lovely thanks to the two hundred gold helium balloons she and David had inflated and tied to the orange trees and the extra tiny white lights twinkling among the leaves.

"Let's hope the rain holds off until later." Rhonelle closed the drapes and picked up the sequined evening bag that David forgot he was using. "Come along Mademoiselle DaVita," she bowed and opened the door as he toddled out precariously. "Proceed to the bridal chamber!"

"Gawd this is weird," David said to the empty hallway as they ap-proached the suite where Krystal awaited her two handmaidens. "I've never seen a wedding like this one. This outdoes Teenie and Mavis' poodle weddings by a long shot."

"Nor will you ever witness another like this one," Rhonelle said. "This is definitely a once-in-a-lifetime event."

"That's for sure . . . ouch!" David winced and pulled at his under-garments. "I feel like I got my privates in a straitjacket." He gave his hips a wiggle and shook his leg. "There, that's better."

Rhonelle watched his little dance a moment with raised eyebrows. "You'll fit right in with those antics."

David was too busy adjusting his falsies to notice the expression on Rhonelle's face. "I hope so," he said as he tugged once more at his crotch. "Oh, excuse me . . . anyway, I've been meaning to ask you why Krystal and Sammy have waited so long to finally get married. She was going on about falling madly in love with him way back when she worked at that club with you."

Rhonelle halted a moment, her hand on one hip. "Yes, well *way back* then in the olden days . . .

The Long and Winding Road to the Altar for Sammy and Krystal
It was bad enough that Sammy dropped out of college to become a musician. Playing saxophone for a strip club was a disgrace to the

family, but they hoped he'd grow out of it. Had he married someone like Krystal, he would have been disowned. That's the last thing Krystal would have wanted, knowing how wealthy his family had become. They started out as simple Cajun fishermen, but ended up with one of the largest wholesale seafood companies in the parish – and were mighty proud of their new place in society.

While Krystal refused to marry him, she and Sammy were committed to each other, young as they were. When a job offer from a big Las Vegas casino turned Krystal's head, Sammy went with her. Soon, he was a Vegas musician. Krystal's novelty act with balloons was a big hit and she started making good money – more than Sammy.

When his father became too ill to continue running the business, the family pleaded with Sammy to come home and take over. Sammy refused to leave Krystal. He kept begging her to marry him, but she wouldn't do it. She didn't want to start off their life with scorn heaped upon her as a tarnished gold digger. Sammy decided Krystal didn't love him enough, so after a year he gave up and came home to New Orleans.

Krystal was devastated. Still, she knew she was right not to give in to Sammy. After saving every penny she earned over the next two years, one night she put a dollar in the mega jackpot after work when she was feeling really blue. She hit the jackpot! Even after taxes, Krystal was very well off.

She quit her job the next day and made plans to go back to the Big Easy as Sammy's equal. Her calls to him went unanswered. When she got back home she heard through the grapevine that he was living in Memphis at one of the company offices. Undeterred, she proceeded with her plan to start a business of her own. She bought a building off Jackson Square, used one space for a small shop, and rented out the rest.

Krystal wanted to try her hand at a dress shop, but knowing Krystal's questionable taste in clothing, her friend Rhonelle suggested a gift shop. By then Rhonelle had moved to Peavine and convinced Krystal to merchandise quartz crystals from Arkansas and those Swarovski crystal figurines and jewelry – combining two rising trends. (Thanks to Granny Laurite for the heads up on that one!) Using Krystal's name on the shop was also Rhonelle's idea. After a few years the French Quarter underwent a cleanup and makeover, so that tourists looking to spend money at Krystal Gardens were plentiful. Some customers delicately commented that Krystal Gardens was a nice counterpart to all the Voodoo shops.

Tragically, this was all lost on Sammy LeBeaux. One day Krystal picked up the *Times-Picayune* to read in the society page that Sammy had married a Memphis socialite.

Over the next ten years, Krystal had several loveless affairs and Sammy was miserable. Finally, Sammy divorced and moved back to New Orleans, appearing sheepishly at Krystal's door. They have been happily together ever since, and none of the LeBeaux brothers and sisters complained about that. The reason for their very unconventional wedding was to ensure Krystal's Social Security and inheritance rights should anything happen to Sammy. Plus, they both love a good party! "Baby, I've found out you're never too old for romance!" *How true that is, Krystal, well said indeed.*

A short pudgy man wearing a feathered mask, black and white harlequin costume approached Rhonelle and David from the other end of the hallway. Stopping to look David over appreciatively, he exclaimed, "Oooo la la!" before pivoting and walking on. "See there, Rhonelle," whispered David. "I told you that harem girl outfit looked sexy on you."

"I think he was commenting on *your* appearance 'DaVita' darling," Rhonelle whispered back.

This caused David to look back at the harlequin just in time to see him blow a kiss his way before stepping into the elevator. "Eeeuu!" David shuddered. "I think that was one of Sammy's brothers."

"You'd better get used to it honey," she said. Rhonelle thought his reaction was humorous. "The way you look tonight there'll be a lot more – and worse – where that came from." Right on cue the elevator opened to raucous hoots and loud wolf whistles. David turned around ready to shut up the rowdy rascals when he recognized the Gay Caballeros Band members coming toward them.

"Honey, you are superstar material for sure!" Gary (Louise Dole-sanger's grandson) was applauding appreciatively. "Turn around and let us get a good look at you. What do you think guys, should we get him up on stage with us tonight?" The other band members agreed David would be spectacular as their guest backup singer.

"You just said the magic words, 'up on stage.'" David struck a dramatic pose to the delight of all. Rhonelle was relieved to see his confidence return.

She handed David his evening bag containing the other room key and his lipstick. "You go on down to the courtyard with these guys and start handing out the beads to the guests. There are three boxes full over on the table by the guest book."

"What about Krystal's gown? You sure you don't need me to help get that together?" David fiddled with his sequined purse not sure what to do with it.

"Those red talons you're wearing would do more damage than help," Rhonelle said, pointing to his big hands adorned with long press-on nails.

"See what you mean ... Okay, we'll meet you down there." He happily teetered away, towering at least two inches over the tallest of the band members. Rhonelle's smile turned wistful as she watched him go. She wondered if this was how a mother felt watching her child go off for the first day of school. *Hmmm, on second thought – probably not.*

Rhonelle found Krystal purposefully trotting around her bridal suite clad in a lacey bra, panties and high heels. Her hair was still up in hot rollers. "Nice look for you Krystal. I hope that's not all you'll have on tonight."

"No baby I got something really special ... and don't worry, it's appropriate for the reception party." Krystal pulled out a slinky little chemise covered in silky gold fringe. "Isn't this the most darling flapper dress you ever saw?"

Rhonelle had to admit it was.

A large black woman in a purple choir robe stepped out of the bathroom, squealing when she saw Rhonelle. "Honey baby, when did you get here?" She enveloped Rhonelle in a soft comforting hug. Nobody could hug you better than Etta Mae Pearl. After the embrace she held Rhonelle at arm's length."Look at you all dressed up like Little Sheba again. *Soooo cute!*"

Etta Mae would officiate and sing at the wedding ceremony. She missed the rehearsal dinner because of a service at her church the night before, but since there really wasn't any rehearsal needed that was okay. Her day job, so to speak, was solo jazz singer with several local groups, including the one that Sammy played with down at the Palm Café in the French Market.

Rhonelle and Krystal had been friends with Etta Mae since they all worked down at the Exotic Dance Club on Bourbon Street, where she was costume mistress, not a dancer. Today, Etta Mae was here to help Krystal dress for the biggest runway of all. "Get them thangs outta your hair Krystal and let's get your wedding dress blowed up," Etta Mae chided as she pushed Krystal toward the bathroom. "It's almost seven-thirty and time's a wasting baby!"

At eight-fifteen the Dixieland band in the courtyard began to play a jazzed up version of "Here Comes the Bride." Etta Mae took her place at the end of a gold satin runner with Sammy Le Beaux on her right, dressed in a swashbuckling pirate costume. Next to Sammy stood his best man, Sergio, dressed as the Sheik of Araby.

First to come down the makeshift aisle was David, pretty adept at walking in his high-heeled shoes by now. He carried a basket of Mardi Gras beads, gaily tossing them to the costumed guests before coming to stand on Etta Mae's left. Next Rhonelle came down the aisle dancing and gyrating to the music until she stopped beside David. If the sight of Sergio's costume threw her for a loop, she hid it well.

When a trumpet blared out a fanfare, everyone stood and turned toward the courtyard entry, which was draped in garlands of tulle and white lights accented by three bouquets of gold balloons. There she was in all her glory – "Champagne Crystal redux!"

Krystal sidled into the archway sideways to accommodate her wide, floor-length wedding gown, its train and bodice *all made of gold balloons!* On top of her curly head was a glittering tiara with a rhinestone champagne glass in the center from which three tall feathers sprouted. The band syncopated the wedding march to Krystal's bumps and grinds as she danced down the aisle. Cheers and whistles from the thrilled crowd briefly drowned out the music.

When she stopped in front of Etta Mae, Krystal turned to curtsy to the applauding guests before taking her groom's arm. Subtly, Etta Mae took the microphone from her tall, skinny husband, Deacon Joe Riley, who was attired in a silk top hat and bright red tailcoat.

"Dearly beloved friends of Krystal and Sammy … y'all get quiet and set down so's we can finally get these two hitched!" Short and sweet, the service ended with the Lord's prayer and a soulful rendition of "Let Us All Come Together on Our Knees," sung by Etta Mae. The Dixieland band resumed the festive mood with "When the Saints Come Marching In." Then Etta Mae announced, "They's legal now!"

The "Second Line" parade back down the aisle and on to the reception was led by the bride and groom, Etta Mae, and the Dixie Land Band, followed by Rhonelle and Sergio, and David surrounded by the Gay Caballeros. Dancing along behind the bridal party were all the rowdy guests waving beads and helium-filled balloons over their heads.

All the way around the hotel lobby and into the party room Krystal systematically popped her balloon dress with her special sharp pin ring she used in her act years ago. By the time the last of the parade was assembled in the party room, cheering and whistling, Krystal was down to her last twenty balloons. Sammy did the honor of popping each one to a dramatic drum roll as the crowd counted down, "10, 9, 8 . . ." and so on until all the balloons were gone. Krystal, now clad in her little fringed golden chemise, broke into an impressive shimmy and shake to heightened applause. The band started some familiar dance tunes; champagne bottles popped and the party began.

Guests danced gaily and Rhonelle cut loose like she hadn't in years. Now entirely uninhibited, Sergio danced over-dramatically 'round her acting like Rudolph Valentino out of an old silent movie. Fascinated with Sergio's mystique and cracked up over his playful Rudolf moves, Rhonelle never even noticed when David left in the white stretch limousine to go to the Drag Queen Ball down at the end of Bourbon Street.

She noticed that Sergio stuck to soft drinks, unlike all the other guests who swilled down copious amounts of alcohol. Rhonelle was careful to limit herself to only a couple of glasses of champagne and ate a hearty sampling of the delicious buffet. The chocolate-covered strawberries and wedding cake were irresistible.

While she and Sergio sat to take a break from dancing, Rhonelle kept watching his beautiful, strong hands *without the wedding ring* as he picked up the strawberries and popped them in his mouth. She liked the way his lips were shaped, too. Abruptly she noticed Sergio was smiling at the fact that she was openly staring at his mouth.

Immediately, Rhonelle's guard sprang to full alert. She refocused her eyes and looked away quickly. They seemed to have agreed not to use their psychic gifts to invade each other's privacy, but the expression on her face must have been way too obvious.

"I don't suppose we could get some coffee around here at this hour," she said to break the spell.

"I always can find coffee," Sergio said, as he pulled her chair out for her. "Come Little Sheba; follow me to the hotel bar."

Once they left the crowded reception, a cool blast of air hit Rhonelle. She untied her shawl from her hips and pulled it around her shoulders for warmth. Sergio draped his arm and white robes around her, steering her toward the bar. She snuggled against him, allowing herself to be led.

Ah me, this situation could possibly turn into something after all. It's a pity he's such a handsome mess of a man . . . way too tempting . . . a heartbreak waiting to happen. But just being around someone like this is so nice after such a long dry spell.

"Careful Chérie, dis one needs someone strong. Don't forget you a strong woman."

Granny Laurite was sitting on a stool at the bar between two oblivious drunks, swinging her feet. With her gold tooth glinting in the dark, she grinned like the Cheshire Cat.

Rhonelle stopped so abruptly Sergio almost tripped over her. "Is anything wrong?" Noticing her expression, he followed her eyes to the hotel bar just as Granny Laurite vanished. Sergio cocked his head to one side and squinted at the exact spot where Laurite had been a second ago.

Rhonelle suspected that he may have felt or seen something. "Uh, no . . . I just thought it might be quieter over at that table in the corner there." She broke away from him, moving through the crowded room to slide onto a padded loveseat by a low table. Sergio smiled and followed.

After their coffee arrived, Rhonelle sipped and watched Sergio stir a packet of sugar with his left hand, which no longer sported a gold wedding band. Upon closer examination, she could see no trace of indentation or a tan line on his ring finger.

"So, Valentino . . . how long has it been since you split with your wife?" Rhonelle was going out on a limb here, but she had nothing to lose by asking.

"You *are* fascinated with my hands," he said nonchalantly, side-stepping her question. He looked into her eyes. "It's been long enough for me to know I want to stay single."

This could have been taken as a rude rebuff by anyone else, but Rhonelle was perceptive enough to see it as proof that he'd been badly hurt and was steering clear of any chance of involvement. All she said back was, "I've been single long enough to know I want to stay that way, too. In my case, I've always steered clear of long-term entanglements. Never married, never cared to."

The tension broken, they both relaxed and laughed. "What are your plans tomorrow afternoon," Sergio asked. "I was wondering if you would be interested in checking out some new art galleries." The surprised look on Rhonelle's face prompted him to add, "Yes, I am an artist, too ... full time for the past two years."

"I would enjoy that very much," Rhonelle beamed at him. *No wonder I'm drawn to his hands. They are an instrument of his creativity.* "I wanted to have a look around at the antique stores and galleries in the Quarter. It's been about ten years since I've been down here and I'm in the process of buying things for my new home."

"Interesting," was his only comment before changing the subject. "Will you be attending the send-off brunch in the morning?" Krystal and Sammy were leaving for a Caribbean cruise the next afternoon and had invited a few close friends and family to a brunch at Brennan's at eleven-thirty.

"I believe I might be able to get myself up and dressed in time." Rhonelle finished off her coffee. "I'm sure David will be up early." Sergio started to ask something but changed his mind. "We can have a look around the Quarter after brunch. One of the galleries I want to see is right down the street from Brennan's."

"It's a date," said Rhonelle smiling as she gathered up her shawl and beaded bag. "Shall we return to the party?"

Sergio reluctantly rose and took Rhonelle's hand as they left the cocktail lounge under the watchful eyes of Granny Laurite and Grandfather White Cloud.

Alas, the rest of the evening didn't go as Sergio was secretly hoping it would. They had only been back at the reception for about an hour when they were interrupted in the middle of a slow dance number in which Sergio was very much enjoying the undulations of Rhonelle's sinuous body against his.

Suddenly, there was David, disheveled and panicky, standing behind Rhonelle, tapping on her shoulder. "Excuse me . . . excuse me . . .

Sorry but this is an emergency. Rhonelle, I need you *right now*."

Disentangling herself from Sergio, Rhonelle turned to David intending a display of irritation at his intervention on her behalf. One look at the agitated expression on his face and his disheveled condition stopped her. He was obviously in a great deal of discomfort and she had a pretty good idea what was the cause.

"What's the matter, dear?" She tried not to look amused but wasn't very successful.

David pulled her away from Sergio and talking directly into her ear frantically explained his predicament. She nodded and patted him on the arm. "I gotta go now," she shouted over to Sergio who was standing in the middle of the dance floor looking deflated, his arms empty, and his mouth open. "I'll see you at the brunch!" She blew him a kiss and hurriedly left with David who was limping a little and holding his body at an odd angle as Rhonelle supported him.

"I am definitely *not* cut out for this drag queen business," David said as he ripped off his wig at the door of their room while Rhonelle fetched her key out of her beaded bag. He had mislaid his own evening bag. "Do you realize I've been trapped in this getup for over six hours now, and there is NO way I can even take a piss! I could do permanent damage to myself with these claws," he said as he frantically picked at the fake fingernails. "I don't know how you women stand all this."

He pushed by her into their suite and kicked off his shoes and danced around in a circle as he attempted to reach the zipper in the back of his gown. "Dammit, I am in *a real hurry* here!"

"Well hold on, Miss Thang, until we can get those claws off," Rhonelle said as she grabbed the bottle of nail glue solvent that was still out on the table and began to calmly dab at each fingernail while David jigged in place. "We have to remove these first, because you're on your *own* when it comes to relieving yourself."

CHAPTER FOURTEEN

Breakfast at Brennan's

Even with Rhonelle's assistance, it took David almost an hour to peel off all the accoutrements of his costume and remove his makeup. By the time Rhonelle was able to get to bed, it was close to two in the morning. Her last thoughts before drifting off to sleep were of Sergio and his despairing face when she left him on the dance floor. Better to leave them wanting more. That's my motto.

Her dreams were pleasant at first, Sergio's beautiful hands reaching out to pull her toward him. They were dancing again with the whole ballroom just to themselves, when he suddenly stopped and looked toward the windows. With a worried look on his face, he strode over to them and pulled back the curtains. Gray daylight spilled into the room. Taking the cue, the musicians stopped playing.

He looked back at Rhonelle, his face filled with regret. *"I'm so sorry,"* he said as he came back to her and brushed her mouth briefly with his lips. *"I'll have to go back now."* As she stood watching him, he dissolved into a pile of silvery glitter on the floor. She knelt down and tried in vain to sweep it up into her hands.

Before she opened her eyes, Rhonelle could hear a clicking sound against the window panes. She opened her eyes to take in her surroundings and slowly rose from her bed with the dream clearly etched in her mind. Pulling aside the curtain, she saw that rain and sleet were pecking against the glass and falling onto soggy wedding decorations in the courtyard below. Shivering, she retrieved her shawl from the other bed and draped it around her shoulders.

David was already up and dressed, watching TV silently in the sitting room. "I got us some coffee from the lobby," he said. He hopped up and handed Rhonelle a tall, lidded cup. "I hope I had them do it right for you."

"I'm sure it will be fine; thank you darling." She sat on the sofa and pulled a spare blanket over her feet. David had already folded up the hide-a-bed. "It's pretty cold this morning. Have you seen anything about the weather on the television?"

"There's rain mixed with sleet out there right now," David said as he turned up the volume on the TV and tried another station. "A man in the lobby heard that there was a chance of snow as far south as Jackson, Mississippi, by tomorrow, and record cold down here in New Orleans. Do you suppose we'll have bad weather at home?"

"Teenie told me he'd heard about a possible ice storm this week-end." Rhonelle recalled her dream and the strangely familiar sadness she had felt as she knelt to sweep up the silvery dust. "What time is it?"

David checked his watch. "It's about ten till eleven. What time is the send-off brunch? I'm starving."

Rhonelle threw back the blanket and quickly rose from the sofa. "Krystal said the reservation is for eleven thirty. You call down to the front desk and order a cab while I get dressed." Feeling a sense of urgency, she moved faster than her usual languid morning pace. Picking up her coffee, Rhonelle gulped it down as she returned to her bedroom. She had planned to wear one of her new dresses purchased the day before. The thin material wasn't warm enough for such a cold damp day, but the way she looked in it made up for a little discomfort. She would wear her coat and take the shawl.

"I never got to ask you if you had a good time at the reception last night." David was sheepish while he and Rhonelle waited in the lobby for their cab. "I'm afraid I broke up your little party with Sergio last night. I'm sorry if I cramped your style, but I was *this* close to having me a full-blown panic attack."

"Your timing was just right," Rhonelle reassured him. "If I had stayed on the dance floor much longer with that handsome rascal, I'm pretty sure I'd have ended up making a fool of myself before the night was over." She spied the cab and they stepped out into a cold, light rain. "Besides," she added right before she got into the cab, "we have plans for this afternoon. He wants to show me a few galleries after the brunch."

David raised his eyebrows but he kept his mouth shut until they were on their way to Brennan's. "So … the fact that he's a married man doesn't make any difference to you anymore?"

Rhonelle was amused at David's suddenly elevated moral standards. "Darling, if he were married, I certainly would not have any qualms about going to a few art galleries with him. However he is very *not* married at the moment." When she saw David's disbelief, she added, "He only wore his old ring to avoid entanglements. He knew Krystal would likely have set him up with someone … me as a matter of fact. He needn't have worried; our attitudes are very similar on that particular subject."

"I still think he's a jerk," David mumbled under his breath. Rhonelle decided to pretend she didn't hear that remark, but it did make her smile.

"This sure is yucky weather," he said to the cab driver to change the subject. "I didn't think it could get this cold down here."

"Sometimes it does." The driver looked at David and Rhonelle in his rearview mirror. "It's sure gonna put a damper on the festivities dis evening when the temp drops down to twenty-five like I hear it's supposed to. It's already down to thirty-six degrees right now."

Fortunately, David had bought an umbrella for them at the hotel, and he came around the side of the cab to hold it over Rhonelle after she paid the cab fare. Thinking nothing could feel colder than New Orleans at thirty-six degrees, they huddled against each other to stay warm and dry as they entered the restaurant.

It was warm, fragrant and crowded inside Brennan's. This being a Saturday during Mardi Gras season (a very unseasonably cold one) the place was packed with tourists. Krystal was standing and waving her napkin at them from her table. A quick scan of those seated at their table revealed three empty chairs, and no sign of Sergio. Rhonelle felt a pang of disappointment. *He's not going to be here after all.*

A waiter was instantly at Rhonelle's elbow. She ordered a Bloody Mary for herself and a Mimosa for David, who was too busy gawking at the surroundings to order. Rhonelle acted as if everything was just fine as she pulled her velvet shawl around her new black, red and purple flowered print dress. It was low cut and form fitting. "Wow, baby!"

Krystal exclaimed when Rhonelle shed her coat. "I can tell you've been to Violet's for a little shopping. You look spectacular ... doesn't she, Sammy."

Sammy nodded enthusiastically. "Sergio is gonna be real sorry he had to leave early." Sammy reached into his shirt pocket and drew out a small envelope. "He had to get back home and see about his studio. Once he found out about that big winter storm headed toward Arkansas and Tennessee, he had to leave early this morning." He handed the envelope to Rhonelle. "He left this for me to give to you, baby. I think you must have made quite an impression on my old buddy."

Rhonelle took the note and casually put it in her purse while smiling at her fellow brunch mates to hide her disappointment. She would read it later. She realized that she'd known Sergio had already left since awaking from that dream. *It's just as well he's gone before we could have gotten into something neither of us was ready for.*

David watched Rhonelle, relieved to see her apparent lack of concern. He, on the other hand *was* concerned – about the weather, not his friend. "How big a winter storm is this?" he asked Sammy. "I don't want to end up sliding off into a ditch in Aunt Violet's precious car!"

Rhonelle looked at him and put her hand on his shoulder. "We'll be fine if we leave by mid-afternoon. In the meantime, we can enjoy the best Eggs Benedict in the city." She raised her glass in the air. "Cheers everybody, and bon voyage to the bride and groom!"

CHAPTER FIFTEEN

Back to the New Normal

David and Rhonelle approached the outskirts of Peavine at ten-thirty that night, just as heavy snow replaced intermittent sleet. The winter weather had not slowed them down until they encountered occasional sleet in Vicksburg. After that – and out of excessive caution – David refused to drive over fifty miles an hour.

Along the way, Rhonelle had kept the focus on David and his impressions of New Orleans, now that he was grown. The only time he'd ever been there before was as a child of eight when his family spent the night there on the way to Biloxi, Mississippi.

His most vivid memory of that trip was an embarrassing stroll down Bourbon Street when he wandered off from his family, who later found him in a dubious gift shop, pouring over titty tassels and record albums with photos of nude women playing various string instruments. He was trying to figure out what kind of music they were playing when his mother grabbed him by the arm and yanked him out of there. His dad enjoyed telling the story at family gatherings for years.

On this trip David found himself shocked and bewildered by many new developments. "Did you know they have male strippers in those places ... and they get to spinning their *you-know-whats* instead of tassels?" David shook his head. "I had a good time getting up on the stage with the Gay Caballeros until things just got too kinky for me. No wonder I lost my purse. I couldn't get out of that club fast enough. I think I'll just stick to the Community Theater from now on. Wearing that drag queen stuff is downright painful." They decided he could donate the sequined gown to some deserving overly tall young lady needing a dress for the PHS Prom. Mavis could make it fit. As for the wig, his Aunt Violet would love it, especially if she believed David had bought it *for her*.

The talk of home, made Rhonelle eager to return to the sanctuary of Peavine and the extended family of friends waiting for her there. Even though Doll Dumas was gone, her gifts and memories were all around town. Best of all, Rhonelle now had a real home of her own and a business to run.

Sergio and the intense feelings he had aroused in her began to fade the farther they got away from New Orleans. She had not read his note yet, and didn't intend to look at it until she was good and ready. For now, Rhonelle had other concerns and responsibilities to occupy her mind. A rare winter storm was upon them and she had to be sure Teenie would not get too wild and crazy with his trusty pipe-thawing blowtorch.

The entire Home-Sweet-Homes-on-Wheels Park was covered in snow on top of a coating of ice. When David pulled up to the lavender double-wide, Rhonelle noticed that someone had turned on some lights for her. The double-wide looked cozy and inviting. She almost slipped and fell on the stairs to the front deck. Fortunately, David, following right behind her with her suitcase and shopping bags, was there to steady her.

As soon as he deposited her bags inside the front door, David gave her a quick hug and hurried back to the car. Blowing a kiss and waving as he slowly circled the drive and headed back out onto the highway. Rhonelle leaned against the door, grateful for the warmth and thoughtfulness of whomever had turned up the heat for her while she was gone. She closed her eyes and took a deep breath of the air in her new home. It even smelled new. When she switched on the kitchen lights, she had a big surprise.

There were new curtains in the windows and a matching set of dish towels and hot pads on the counter. The cabinets had been repainted a deep blue and had new drawer pulls and handles. Doll's old dishes were packed in a box on the floor and a whole new set with a more contemporary design had been stacked on the cabinet shelves.

An arrangement of fresh fruit in a blue glass bowl drew her attention to the counter, where Rhonelle found a loaf of Don's banana bread.

Darla and Vaudine had already started in on redecorating the double-wide. When Rhonelle walked into the living room she saw that more of Doll's furniture was gone, replaced by a new sofa uphol-stered in a deep red fabric. Rhonelle was thrilled with what they had done so far. Fabric samples lay across the sofa and on the coffee table. A set of drapes yet to be hung signaled more changes to come.

They sure did get busy over the past two days. A lot of changes in such a short time, my goodness!

Rhonelle turned on the hi-fi record player and loaded up five jazz albums. Mellow sounds filled the home while she took her bags into the bedroom and surveyed her bed. Not much had changed in there. *That's what all the other fabric samples must be about.*

Her old twin bed from her tiny trailer she'd lived in all the years since coming to Peavine was just as she had left it two days ago, but now it appeared small and cold. *Hmmm. Looks like I have made some changes in myself over the past two days. I'm going to have Darla order me a queen-size bed right away . . . and I want a fabulous headboard to go with it!*

Rhonelle giggled in sheer delight. She grabbed her purse and shuffled through the contents until she found the envelope containing the note from Sergio. She held it up with a mischievous smile, opened her lingerie drawer and tucked it under a stack of new lacey panties. *That will be the perfect place to keep Sergio for a while. I can wait and open this . . . on Valentine's Day!*

She sat up for two more hours examining the fabric samples. Turn-ing on the gas wall heater made to mimic a small fireplace, Rhonelle sat in her favorite chair drinking hot tea and reading from a racy novel Lucille had loaned her. Occasionally, she peeked outside to see if it was still snowing. From what she could tell by the outdoor light, it had not let up at all. At least three inches had piled up on the deck.

Rhonelle finally drifted off to sleep around one in the morning while watching the swirling snowflakes through her bedroom window, with the drapes left slightly open. *There's no place like home, there's no place like home ... thank you, Doll, wherever you are.*

CHAPTER SIXTEEN

Snow Day!

At four in the morning, the first ice-and-snow-laden tree branch fell on a major power line out by the entrance of the mobile home park. The loud buzz and explosion of the blown transformer awoke everyone nearby. Of course, the electricity went off immediately.

Rhonelle, startled awake by the loud noise, quickly assessed her situation. In the pitch dark room, she was able to feel her way to the bedside table drawer where the flashlight was kept. She was relieved the batteries were still good, so she was able to find her way around the room. Pulling one of Doll's old comforters out of the closet, Rhonelle spread it on her bed. Then she went into the living room to relight the fake fireplace and turn up the burners a little.

She peered outside and everything was dark except for an eerie glow coming from the snow-covered landscape. Snow was such a rare and beautiful event; she didn't mind the inconvenience of a power outage. Rhonelle quickly slipped back into bed and snuggled under the covers. Once again, she felt gratitude toward Doll, this time for installing new propane gas tanks for the double-wide and all the other permanent residents in the park. It didn't take her long to fall back to sleep.

The next morning was eighteen degrees and blindingly bright as the sun reflected off a six-inch accumulation of snow. Teenie was the first resident of the park to go outside and had measured the depth of the snowpack, declaring it a record amount for Peavine. Even though that declaration was doubtful, nobody argued with him. Teenie dutifully made the rounds with his trusty blowtorch, knocking on doors and waking his neighbors to be sure they were not suffering from hypothermia or frozen water pipes.

Mavis finally coaxed Teenie back inside after Louise Dolesanger called and complained about him banging on her door and peeking in her windows when she couldn't answer her door right away. Louise had been on the pot and was very annoyed by his intrusion on her privacy. She did appreciate his concern for her well-being (bless his heart), but she was just fine, thank you very much.

About eight o'clock, Marv came over to the Brices' to get Teenie so they could go over to the double-wide. Marv planned to turn on the gas fireplace, thinking Rhonelle was still out of town. They came clumping into the kitchen door stomping snow off their boots and laughing loudly over the fact Louise had been indisposed all the while Teenie was tapping at her windows.

Imagine their surprise when Marv was in the middle of a rather ribald remark about how he'd pass on Louise but wouldn't mind a chance to rescue Rhonelle, only to walk into the living room and find her glowering at them from her bedroom doorway.

There she stood, wrapped tightly in the comforter, her dark curls tangled into a black bushy halo around her pale face. Both men stopped in their tracks. Teenie actually let out a high pitched scream and Marv shouted, "Shit fire!"

"To what do I owe the honor of this early morning visit," Rhonelle asked pointedly as the two men almost fell on top of each other in fright. She had already forgiven them for the intrusion, but she did not feel very hospitable this early in the morning. "I will not require your services this morning seeing as how I've already taken care of the heat *and* my pipes in the wee hours! I *was* sleeping soundly until you two came thundering in here."

"Good God, Rhonelle, you about gave us both coronaries," Marv gasped, holding his hand to his chest. Teenie stood there wide-eyed, clutching his blowtorch, looking scared and letting Marv do the talking. "We thought you was still in New Orleans, so Teenie and I wanted to check that everything was okay."

"Hon," Teenie piped in. "We are so sorry. We just wanted to make sure you didn't come home to a cold house and . . . frozen pipes." His voice trailed off under Rhonelle's visage of cold disdain. "We better go now." He tipped his red cap, ear flaps trembling, and backed out of the room.

Rhonelle couldn't possibly stay angry at Marv and Teenie, knowing full well they only had her welfare in mind. Her face softened into a smile as she shooed them out of the living room and toward the back door. "Come back later after I've had a chance to make myself some coffee. And thanks guys; I know you meant well, but *knock* first next time."

As Teenie and Marv made their way sheepishly through the deep snow, Marv gave a low whistle and shook his head. "Man oh man, she liked to scare the peewaddling outta me! Looked like some kind of a witch or something." He glanced nervously back over his shoulder. "You reckon she's inherited some of that voodoo stuff from her granny?"

Teenie plowed alongside Marv trying to keep up. "Naw, she wouldn't hurt a hair on our heads. She just don't like two men crashing in on her first thing of a morning." He squinted at the glare of the sun on the sparkling snow. "Rhonelle definitely ain't a morning person."

Rhonelle watched her two friends cross the yard and head over toward the highway. She assumed they were continuing their assessment of the winter storm damage by checking on Don and Dorine over at the Diner. She had nothing but dearest affection for them in her heart.

She knew it would be impossible for her to go back to sleep now, and since she was now the official proprietress of the mobile home park, she should be able to lead her flock through this latest crisis. However, first things first . . . start some water to boil for coffee.

Rhonelle dashed into the bedroom, dressed in several layers of clothing, and quickly applied lipstick, including a dot on each cheek by the light of her flashlight. She attempted to tame her wild bushy hair by tying a silk scarf around her head. *No wonder Teenie and Marv were startled. I must've looked like a banshee standing there in the semidarkness.* Every time she thought of the look on their faces she had to laugh. She didn't want to frighten anybody else who might come by for her help.

Later as she contentedly sat by the fire sipping her café au lait and nibbling Don's delicious banana bread, she heard a timid tapping at the front door. Rhonelle looked out her window and saw a woman so heavily bundled up against the cold only her sunglasses and tip of her nose were visible. When Rhonelle opened the door, she realized it was Louise Dolesanger.

"Louise, come in and get warm," she said as she guided the plump woman inside and quickly shut the door. "Would you like some hot coffee and banana bread?"

"That sounds real nice, don't mind if I do." Louise's voice was muffled by the woolen scarf wound around her face and head.

"Let me help you with that," offered Rhonelle as she reached for the puffy down-filled coat and one of the two cardigans Louise wore underneath.

"Whew! Thanks dear." Louise plopped down heavily on the sofa. "I think I may have overdressed. I kind of worked up a sweat walking over here. This snow is really pretty, isn't it?"

"Yes it is." Rhonelle moved the large pile of Louise's outerwear over to another chair, out of their way. "I'm hoping the electricity will be back on before too long. I guess we'll have to wait for the roads to melt enough for the repair trucks to get through." She looked out at the bright sunshine and snow melt beginning to drip from the roof. "In the meantime, how would you like your coffee?"

"Black with a teaspoon of sugar would be nice, and I never can pass up Don's banana bread." Louise looked around the living room while Rhonelle was in the kitchen. "Looks like Vaudine and Darla have been busy while you were gone." That's when Louise noticed something was missing. "Where's your television going to be? Are you putting it in your bedroom?"

"Actually I hadn't even thought about it, since I never have owned one before." Rhonelle came back with a thick slice of banana bread and mug of coffee using new dishes from the cabinet. "I never got into the practice of watching TV and don't intend to start now … Too many other things I'd rather do with my time."

Louise was shocked to hear such a thing. She'd never known anybody to choose to go without a TV since the 1950s. "I don't know what I'd do without mine. I'm already in a tizzy over what to do with

my time now that the power is out. I can't watch my shows or practice on my organ without electricity. Even my little cooking range is
electric." She gazed out the window, a worried expression on her face.
"They better fix this by tomorrow so I can watch my soaps."

Rhonelle went over to a pile of boxes in the corner of the living
room and rummaged through one until she found what she was looking for, a portable tape player and radio. "I could loan you this for now.
There are batteries in the kitchen drawer."

Within minutes she had loaded the boom box with batteries and
tuned into KPEW radio. Bo Astor was on the air with an update on
power outages and how soon they were likely to get the downed lines
repaired. Not much was likely to happen until the next day. Since it
was Sunday, he returned to a pre-recorded service from his brother's
church. Because of the snow and power outages, today's service had
been canceled. Rhonelle turned the volume down but left it playing in
the background.

Louise settled back and sipped her coffee. "Well at least I don't
have to feel guilty about skipping church today."

"Amen to that," Rhonelle said, raising her coffee mug in a salute.
"You know David and had quite an adventure with your grandson
Gary and his band down in New Orleans this week."

"Oh I'm so glad you took David down there with you." This put
a smile on Louise's face. She was so proud of her grandson and his
musical career; his sexual preference made no difference to her. "It was
nice for him to be with Gary and all his little friends. They need to
have a chance to be with their own kind once in a while to relax and
just be themselves."

"Oh they did plenty of *that*," said Rhonelle, *a little too much for
David's sensibilities*, but she decided to keep that to herself. "We had a
wonderful time, but we're glad to be back home, even though we had
to return early because of the weather." She sat down and held her
hands up to the warmth of the gas flames in the cozy fireplace. "I have
my job managing the mobile home park now and a real home of my
own for the first time in my life."

"You're starting on a brand new chapter in your life," Louise said as she watched Rhonelle. "It's sort of like what Doll did for me, God bless her. I never would have gotten into show biz if it hadn't been for her finagling.

"Doll Dumas had a gift for setting the stage and getting it ready for someone to step up and start on their second act in life … third act in your case. I'd probably be drooling in some nursing home if not for what she did for me."

CHAPTER SEVENTEEN

Louise Dolesanger, Musical Entertainer at Seymour's Tex-Mex

Throughout most of her adult life Louise Dolesanger was the organist and musical director at the Fourth Baptist Church and Highway Prayer Club. She *never* missed playing for a single service during the thirty some-odd years that the church was open. Pastor Astor was no slouch when it came to holding services either. He normally had at least five or six events a week that required Louise's musical talents. In addition, there were the occasional weddings, funerals, and spontaneous revivals.

Louise was such a trouper she provided the music for both her daughter's weddings *and* even her husband's funeral! She claimed she was the only one she could trust to "do it right." Her friends all agreed with her there, but knew that had to have been hard on her. Nobody in Peavine had ever come close to playing the organ as well as Louise, but losing her husband seemed to take all the wind out of her sails. Once she realized she didn't have anybody to look after anymore, her life seemed to lose purpose. Despite the protestations of Pastor Astor and all the choir members, Louise resigned as church organist and musical director. She decided to offer her services as a full-time grandmother to help with her daughters' children. Both Katy and Lulu had moved to away to Texas with their husbands, and Louise hardly ever got to even see them.

She sold her house and bought a mobile home so she could move down there and be near each of them – in order to be at their beck and call should they need her. Sadly, Louise got neither a beck nor a call from her daughters. Both of the ungrateful daughters insisted they were doing just fine, thank you, and the church needed her talents much more than they needed her to babysit. Her grandkids were all in their teens by then, anyhow.

Soon after that, the Fourth Baptist Church and Highway Prayer Club Church burned down, the organ with it, and Pastor Astor went all weird trying to build a fireproof bunker. So poor Louise decided to move her trailer into Doll's park, and waited. For what, she didn't know.

Before long, Louise got into the habit of staying home all day to watch her favorite soap operas on TV. Doll first realized there was a problem when in most all of her conversations with Louise, she would talk on and on about the characters from "As the World Turns" and "Days of Our Lives" as if they were *all real people*. Doll decided it was time to perform an intervention on poor Louise just as soon as she could come up with some way to get the poor woman back in touch with the real world.

One Saturday evening, Doll was at Seymour's Tex-Mex in downtown Peavine picking at a plate of hot tamales that according to Dorine were probably straight from the can. She noticed the crowd was pretty sparse for a weekend. Seymour's food was not particularly bad . . . it just was not especially *good*.

Seymour's wife, Lolita, was the head cook. The only thing remotely Mexican about her was her name. She had a tendency to rely upon prepackaged ingredients like canned chili and cream of chicken soup, Rotel tomatoes, and large quantities of processed cheese. She had no idea that such a thing as fresh cilantro existed. Only recently, had she started to use the occasional daub of gelatinous canned guacamole.

What the place needed was something new and catchy to bring in customers, something that would distract them from the unexciting entrees. A year earlier they had added some decorations to the rather drab décor. The new wall mural painted by Claudine Laudenberry, the art teacher at Peavine High, was not quite enough to spice up the atmosphere. Doll found that viewing snoozing seniors in sombreros sitting up with their backs up to an adobe wall only reminded her that she probably would have to sleep upright that night if she was to avoid a bad case of heartburn.

As usual, Doll had a sudden inspiration so perfect that it made the hair on her arms stand up. She could help Seymour and her friend Louise at the same time! This caused Doll to stand up and holler at Seymour to come over to the table *right then!* Scared half to death, Seymour thought she'd found something really horrible in her food, and came running over to see what it was.

Doll sat Seymour down and told him about a Mexican restaurant that she and Herman Jr. used to love to frequent up in Little Rock, called Island X. They had "Edie at the Organ" for their entertainment. Edie was a sweet, smiling lady who had recently retired from a state government job and was pursuing a career she really enjoyed by playing music most evenings for Island X diners. Having taught herself to play by ear, Edie was so accomplished she could play just about any tune the customers requested. If you could hum it for her, Edie would play it.

"Now who do we know that lives right here in Peavine and has that same kind of talent?" Doll asked Seymour (who was so relieved that the food was okay, he couldn't think of an answer).

"Uuuh . . . I dunno, I guess I don't know many musicians."

"Oh yes you do . . . our very own Louise Dolesanger," Doll answered for him triumphantly.

"We could get Louise in here to play at your restaurant a few nights a week – just during the dinner hour, not too late or anything. I could help you out on getting an organ … and maybe have a stage built.

"Oh boy! You'll have so many customers in here on a Saturday night … you may even have to hire another waitress! This will be just what Louise needs right now, a new stage to perform on during this new 'stage' of her life!" Doll would get real excited when she discovered a way to help someone, and to come up with an idea that solved two problems at once was double the pleasure! What she had to do now was to convince everybody involved that this was as great an idea as she *knew* it was.

All Louise played music on since the church burned down (organ and all) was a small electric practice organ she had at home. Since acquiring her soap-opera addiction, she had refused to even play on that because she didn't see any point in practicing if she never played much for anybody else these days.

Being the only Jew in Peavine, Seymour Hidelman never set foot in the Fourth Baptist Church, but he knew about Louise's musical expertise. He had heard her play the piano accompaniment for the annual Peavine Poodle Pageants for years, so he knew she had a full repertoire of secular tunes.

He recalled overhearing the Brices at supper just the other day talking about how concerned they were because Louise had become very listless and disinterested. Teenie said that she was so absorbed in her favorite television shows, that they couldn't get her to commit to the upcoming pageant. She had told them to just use a record player and leave her alone.

"So you see, Seymour," Doll told him. "You'd be doing us all a big favor if you'd let me buy you an organ setup like I saw in that Little Rock place. I know Louise would perk up and her music would bring you a crowd of customers. That would be a favor to you!"

Seymour couldn't see a thing wrong with that deal so he and Doll got busy the following Monday.

Mavis and Teenie Brice were included in Doll's scheme. Mavis created a darling Mexican-style blouse and skirt to fit Louise's ample figure. To top it all off, Teenie ordered an authentic Mexican sombrero to complete her outfit.

Doll figured that they would need the blessing of Pastor Astor for the whole project in order to convince Louise that it wouldn't be a sin for her to play music at an eating establishment. (They did not dare mention Seymour's application for a liquor license or plans for a dance floor to the pastor at this time.)

It took about three weeks for Doll and Seymour to get the organ, speakers, and side-man rhythm machine ordered and set up it up on the newly constructed four-foot-high stage. Lolita decorated the walls and stage with bright crepe paper streamers and tissue paper flowers. Doll and the Brices managed to pry Louise loose from the television and convince her to go out to supper on a Thursday evening. They told her it was Pitty and Rufus' wedding anniversary and insisted that they needed her to help them celebrate. Poodles were welcome in all eating establishments in Peavine, providing they were appropriately dressed. One exception was Doll's doggy Rufus. The rules were bent for him, but he was required to wear a bow tie.

When Doll, the Brices, the poodles, and Louise entered Seymour's Tex-Mex, all of Louise's friends – gathered at the restaurant beforehand – stood around a mysterious lump covered by a large tarp on the stage.

Pastor Astor stepped forward and, in his best preaching voice, announced: "Sister Louise, the LORD has told me that you have been hiding the light of your musical talent under the bushel of your bereavement and addiction to those cursed daytime TV programs! And Sister, GOD has said that if YOU, Louise, can overcome your weaknesses and start blessing us all with your music again. . . . HE will give ME the courage to begin again and rebuild HIS Church . . . Say Hallelujah!"

"Hallelujah!" the crowd of friends shouted.

On cue, Seymour and Lolita whipped off the tarp to reveal a shiny new electric organ – bigger and better than anything Louise had ever seen, much less played.

Louise almost fainted when Doll explained that Seymour wanted to make her the main attraction at the Tex-Mex. Louise insisted that she was too old and too out of practice to consider doing such a thing. She couldn't use the excuse that it was a sin because Pastor Astor already said it was okay . . . and he was the town specialist on sin.

Everybody cajoled and pleaded with Louise to get up there and give it a try. Even the poodles whined at her. It is believed that the deciding factor was the costume that Mavis had put together for Louise. When Mavis pulled the blouse and skirt out of the big red box that was sitting on the table next to the organ . . . Louise's jaw dropped. She clasped her hands to her ample bosom.

"No one's sewed such a pretty thing for me since my momma did when I was a little girl," she said, her voice quivering with tears.

Doll and Mavis gently escorted Louise into the ladies' lounge and helped her change into the beautifully embroidered white blouse and red skirt with bric-a-brac trim. When Doll placed the authentic Mexican sombrero on Louise's head and made her take a look at herself in the full-length mirror, an amazing thing occurred. That costume completely transformed their old friend Louise. Right then and there, she took on the persona of Louisa the Mexican Entertainer! Costumes often can trigger unusual behavior in people.

Louise strutted out of the ladies lounge to cheers. She climbed up the steps to the stage waving and blowing kisses to her audience. Then she sat down to that quadruple keyboard, flipped on the drum machine, and started playing "Lady of Spain" like she'd never missed a day of practice!

She played nonstop for two hours before they could convince her to take a break and eat a quick supper. While she ate, Seymour switched on some recorded music so it wouldn't get too quiet. When she returned to the stage, the customers cheered and shouted out requests. If you could hum it, Louise could play it. Everybody almost forgot to eat because they were having so much fun watching Louisa and singing along with familiar tunes.

This was the beginning of Louise's entertainment career, or second life, as she likes to call it. When Louise became *Louisa,* she let her light shine. The only thing shoved under the bushel was Louise's strict Baptist upbringing. Seymour was awarded a beer and wine license. When he cleared out a few tables to make room for a dance floor, Louisa never even batted an eyelash.

CHAPTER EIGHTEEN

Candlelight Dinner at Don's

The telephone rang as Rhonelle and Louise sat by the fireplace reminiscing about Doll. It was Dorine calling from the Diner to let Rhonelle know Don was cooking up a pot of vegetable beef soup and grilled cheese sandwiches for lunch. Dorine said to tell everybody at Homes-Sweet-Homes-on-Wheels that they were welcome to come on over free of charge.

"Don can't get the oven lit but the gas stovetop and grill work just fine." Dorine sounded pretty cheerful about their predicament. "This is kinda like camping! Oh and if anybody has some extra flashlights or batteries they can spare, we sure would appreciate it if they bring them along so Don can have enough light to cook supper. He wants to fix up a big dinner tonight for y'all."

"I have plenty of candles," Rhonelle said. "We could have a candlelight dinner for . . . what, about twenty?"

"I figure at least that many." Dorine had another idea. "Say, you know there are gas space heaters in the Dew Drop Inn cottages and they're all vacant right now. Ask around and see if any of your tenants need a warm place to stay tonight. We won't charge 'em of course. I heard it's supposed to drop down to about fifteen degrees tonight and that's too cold for an unheated trailer."

Rhonelle agreed to call on everybody by lunch time to see who would need lodging for the night. She invited Louise to stay there with her. They could camp in the living room by the fireplace where it was the warmest. She would also have Teenie warn everybody to leave their faucets dripping to prevent frozen pipes.

During a very convivial lunch hour at Don's Diner, plans were made for park residents without heat to find a warm place for the night. Even though the sun was shining at the moment, the temperature was predicted to drop below thirty degrees that night. Snow that melted during the day would refreeze at night, leaving roads slick as ever.

Don brought a battery-powered transistor radio over to the Diner so they could hear Bo Astor's music and constant weather updates. Who knew when power might be restored to different areas around Peavine!

Lucille Lepanto would miss the candlelight dinner because she was out at KPEW helping Bo keep the station on the air. She called Rhonelle from Radio Hill after lunch and told her Bo had picked her up in his four-wheel drive vehicle. She had packed herself an overnight bag. They planned to pull an all-nighter to keep the generator fueled up and running.

Lucille couldn't quite get through that announcement to her friend without letting loose a few giggles. "I'm sure we'll be able to keep each other warm!"

"I have no doubt you will," Rhonelle said, smiling to herself. "You two are the last ones I'd need to worry about. I've gotten all my tenants settled in a warm place for the night, thanks to Don and Dorine. You and Bo will be missing a nice hearty meal at Don's."

"Actually we're gonna have plenty to eat thanks to Ozelle's grandchildren out there at the Brisket Basket," Lucille told her. "They fired up the smoker and grill this morning and brought us a Sunday dinner barbecue feast a little while ago. Said it was a thank you to Bo for keeping everybody's spirits up. Their daddy, Doc Ozzie, has a Jeep in case of an emergency house call. He brought the food out to us. Wasn't that thoughtful of him?"

"Sounds just like something his father, Ozelle, would do." Rhonelle was pretty sure it was Mr. Washington who came up with that idea. "Well, take care of yourself and Mr. Bodine Junior tonight. I've got to go dig up enough candles to provide light for our dinner."

"Okay, go burn down the Diner," Lucille retorted. "You and I've got to get together after the snow melts so you can tell me about New Orleans. I'll bet that wedding was something else!"

Rhonelle had anticipated Lucille's curiosity and decided she would only divulge wedding details and highlights of David's drag queen escapade. She was not ready to discuss Sergio yet. *Better warn David to keep his mouth shut about him, too, if that was possible.*

"Sure, till then, and remember like you always tell me; if you can't be good, be careful. Bye, Lucille."

Rhonelle hung up the phone to the sound of Lucille's undiminished lung-rattling laughter.

Since Louise had gone over to the Diner to visit with the Brices and Dorine until dinnertime, Rhonelle decided to take a short nap on the sofa. She had dragged her twin-bed mattress into the living room and made it up for Louise, who would be staying with her for the night. She spent most of the morning making rounds of the mobile home park with Teenie and Marv, confirming everybody had what they needed and a warm place to stay. This was her first test as the official new proprietor of the park. Rhonelle felt she had handled it pretty well.

Fortunately, most of the temporary RV tenants had left before the weather turned bad, so there was a place for everyone to stay warm and plenty of hot food. Most of Peavine was without power except for two blocks downtown that had buried lines (thanks to the wisdom of the city council) and hardly ever lost their electricity. That was a good thing because it meant the grocery and drugstore could stay open and Violet X-pressions wouldn't lose any of its inventory. The elementary school also had power and could set up a shelter for those who needed it. Most were able to work out something with friends, families or neighbors.

Out at the Dumas Mansion Rest and Retirement Home, a generator kept electricity on for the elderly clients. Christabelle Tingleberry and her dog, Cutie Boy, got a ride out there the day before. She wanted to help out with cooking as well as patient care. Nobody could brighten up a cold dreary day better than Christabelle. Now that she didn't have Doll to care for, she needed to find ways to be useful. She was there purely as a volunteer. Doll had left her enough money to retire on. Fortunately, Christabelle's windfall was carefully managed by Marv's investment company, so she avoided any temptation to enter any more Publisher Clearing House sweepstakes.

Rhonelle thought of all this as she drifted off to sleep, envisioning the entire town enveloped in the warm rosy glow of communal caring and commitment. *Why would I ever want to live anywhere but Peavine? I wouldn't leave this place for anyone . . . not even someone as handsome and intriguing and sexy as Sergio.*

That the very idea of leaving Peavine to be with Sergio should occur to her startled her slightly. Too sleepy to consider what that meant, Rhonelle drifted into a dream. *First she saw Granny smiling fondly at her from the front porch of a small Creole cottage. This was replaced by Sergio leaning in to kiss her . . . only to dissolve quickly into sparkling dust. The last thing she remembered was a new face, a wise and loving man with brown creases, strong Native American and Hispanic features, framed by a cloud of shoulder-length, snowy white hair.*

When she awoke, she noticed a change in the light coming through the picture window. The sky had darkened and clouded over. Thick snow was falling again. She wrapped her blanket around her and got up to watch it falling. It was a beautiful event, even though it caused so much inconvenience. She knew this miracle of nature would last only a short time. All too soon people would slip back into their routines. She could think about her odd dream later. There was too much to do in *this* world for the time being.

CHAPTER NINETEEN

How to Restore a 1964 T-Bird

The snowstorm of 1984 went down in the Peavine record books. Because of unusually frigid temperatures, much of the record six-inch snowpack took five days to melt completely. Home-Sweet-Homes-on-Wheels Park was without power for four days. Don and Dorine got their power back on after two days and helped Rhonelle handle her "snow refugees" by providing a warm place to gather and take a hot shower. By the end of the five-day event, all of Peavine was back online and returning to their homes.

Fortunately, there was little permanent damage, and tempers held until the end of the week. Minor inconveniences can become mighty irritating over time. Louise's snoring and early hours grated on Rhonelle. Much to her relief, Don and Dorine invited Louise to come stay in their extra bedroom after the second night. This allowed Rhonelle some peace and quiet to get the sleep she needed to handle the daily maze of maintenance issues. It also gave Don and Dorine a reasonable excuse to tell their son, daughter-in-law, and three noisy grandchildren they would have to stay with Rupert and Darla at the Astor Eternal Rest Funeral Home until power was restored.

Sleeping at a funeral home sounds pretty creepy, but the mortuary was on the same power grid as downtown and still had power. With all the plush carpeting, heavy draperies, and soft chairs and sofas in the grieving salons, it probably was one of the most comfortable places in town. Fortunately, there were no newly departed occupants in the morgue or otherwise. This fact did not keep Dora Lee from tormenting her two younger brothers with manufactured bumps in the night and other ghostly noises for the two nights they spent there.

The following week, their winter wonderland was only a memory and by Valentine's Day the weather turned warm as spring. Rhonelle opened her lingerie drawer that morning and spied the envelope con-

taining Sergio's note peeking out from under a pair of red satin panties. She picked it up and looked at his handwriting where he'd written
her name. She was holding it up to the window light when the front
doorbell rang. Startled, she dropped the envelope and guiltily covered
it with three new bras before slamming the drawer shut.

*Saved by the bell! Better go see who this is, and I'll take it as a sign I'm
not ready to look at this yet. Sergio, you can just stay right where you are
. . . for now.*

She had to smile at the thought of keeping him imprisoned under
a pile of her new beautiful brassieres. It was such a perfect place to
hide him. Standing at her front door was Tammy Lepanto, beloved
granddaughter of Doll Dumas, accompanied by her latest and most
serious boyfriend, so far, Cecil Swindle. Cecil's clean auto repair uniform fit tightly over his husky physique and his carrot-colored hair was
slicked back with gel.

"Hey, Auntie Rhonelle," Tammy gushed as she hugged her beloved
friend and dance mentor. "Happy Valentine's Day! Me and Cecil
wanted to bring you this candy and talk to you about a . . . proposi-
tion. Isn't that right sweetie?" She handed Rhonelle a large red satin
heart-shaped box of chocolates and pulled her beau forward. Cecil had
been hanging back, shuffling his feet and blushing.

"Er uhm, a proposal," he stammered. "I mean a suggestion." Since
nothing seemed to sound right, he blushed even more. Rhonelle's eyebrows rose higher with each word until Cecil gave up and let Tammy
do the talking.

"It's real exciting!" Tammy bounced up and down in her red high
heels she wore to complement her acid-wash jeans and red blouse.
With her blond hair pouffed up into "mall bangs" and those two-inch
heels, she towered a good three inches over Cecil. It was obvious he
didn't mind the difference in height one bit. He still looked as if he
couldn't believe his luck to have landed a girl as sweet and beautiful as
Tammy.

"Come right on in. I'd love to hear all about your *proposal*,"
Rhonelle said as she smiled at Cecil and led them into the living
room. "Have a seat and help me eat this candy."

She was so proud of how the redecorating was going. Darla and Vaudine had found some lovely material for new slipcovers for Doll's big old easy chair and Mavis had sewed it up in no time. It was red with pale blue stars and moons scattered across it; the chair was now perfect for her psychic reading sessions. A floor lamp with a fringed shade stood beside it.

"Ooooh, it looks soooo pretty in here now!" Tammy was impressed at the transformation. It didn't bother Tammy to see her grandmother's space redecorated, perhaps because now she had so many of Doll's favorite things moved over to her own house on Pecan Street, behind the mobile home park. "Darla and Vaudine sure have been busy. I like all this red."

Tammy sat on the sofa gazing around the room and thoughtfully chewing on Rhonelle's chocolates until Cecil quietly cleared his throat. "Oh yeah," she giggled. "Aunt Rhonelle. It's about your car."

Rhonelle wrinkled her brow in confusion. "What are you talking about? I haven't had a car for ten years . . . unless you're talking about that old piece of junk out back that I don't know how to get rid of."

"That's where you're mistaken Miss DuBoise," Cecil interjected. "I don't mean no disrespect, but that's a 1964 T-Bird, a rare classic automobile. It's the only year they made 'em with the 'Jet Bird' design. I've been looking for one like that I could afford for years." He glanced over at Tammy to be sure he hadn't over spoken.

" I uh, hope you don't mind ma'am, but me and Tammy went and took a look at it after she happened to mention you still had that car you come up to Peavine in. Good thing you've kept that canvas tarp covering it all this time."

"He got all excited when I told him about your old car out back," Tammy giggled and hugged Cecil's shoulders. "Cecil's a car repair genius! Aren't you honey."

At this point even Cecil's *ears* were blushing. He grinned and went on to explain their plans for the 1964 T-Bird. "I been fixin' up old cars since I was big enough to hold a wrench. With my daddy it was furniture restoration, but I've always had a thing about cars. In the past few years I've really gotten into refurbishing antique cars so they're just like new."

"Antique? It's not *that* old!" Rhonelle was defensive of the age of her automobile (and herself by reference).

"No ma'am, but any car that's around twenty years old is considered a ... classic!" Cecil reassured her.

He was smarter than he looked, Rhonelle decided.

"So you think you can make it run again, perhaps be safe enough to travel on the highway?" This was giving her some options, but she wondered how expensive it would be to take on a project like this. "How much would this cost me?"

"Oh, it won't cost you anything!" Both Tammy and Cecil spoke at the same time. Rhonelle waited patiently for the explanation.

Cecil started. "My daddy and Mr. Fortney my godfather are putting up the money for parts and such. Mr. Cheever at the auto repair shop where I work is helping out, too."

"Here's the best part, Aunt Rhonelle." Tammy looked with the utmost pride upon her dearest Cecil. "Go on and tell her honey."

"I plan to enter your T-Bird in a regional auto show for antique ... and classic cars. If I win the top prize, and I feel like that's a good possibility, I'll be able to set up my own car *bidness!*"

"And you would have a shiny new car to drive again," Tammy added. "I don't know how you can stand not having a car."

"For one thing I don't have to keep getting a driver's license." Rhonelle shrugged. *Or reveal my true age.*

She noticed Tammy and Cecil were literally on the edge of the sofa cushions waiting for her answer. "However, this sounds like such a good deal for me, I'm sure it's worth the driving test." *Which is something I definitely don't intend to take again.*

"You mean you'll let us fix it up for you?" Tammy was thrilled.

"I will gladly let you do whatever you want with it," Rhonelle beamed at the happy couple. "You can't make it any worse off than it is now."

Tammy certainly is invested in this project . . . ah, proposal. That's what all this really is about. Cecil wants his own business so he can propose to her and she knows his pride demands it. How sweet!

"Thanks, Miss DuBoise," Cecil stood and shook her hand on their deal. "I'll be over tomorrow to have it hauled over to the repair shop. "This means a lot to me." After gushing numerous expressions of gratitude, Tammy and Cecil left the trailer. Rhonelle watched the happy couple walk across the yard, hugging and kissing before they got into Tammy's car. *They're probably going over to Don's Diner for the Sweetheart Luncheon special.* Don had one every year at Valentine's, but Rhonelle had never gone to it. She'd never had a date with anyone in Peavine. *No Valentine sweetheart for me in this town and no way that's going to change.*

"*Dat* **could** *change you know, Chérie. All you gotta do is ask, and I hep you all I can.*" Granny Laurite had materialized and was standing right beside her.

I know that, Granny. I just hope it's not too late for me by now. I've been thinking about how nice it could be to have a true soul mate . . . but I'm just not quite ready for any commitment yet.

"*I know, baby. Don't you worry. It not gonna be too late for you.*"

Thanks Granny. I love you.

"*I love you too, Chérie.*"

As Granny Laurite's presence faded away, Rhonelle felt a little less lonely than before. She thought of the hidden letter from Sergio and warmth spread throughout her chest. *It's not the right time yet, but pretty soon perhaps. I'll know when it is . . . and so will he.*

Another pleasant thought came to mind. *I'm going to have a new car!*

CHAPTER TWENTY

Peavine Poodle Pageant Time Again

The brief winter quickly gave way to an early spring. In Peavine, springtime meant one thing: Poodle Pageant time once again! Teenie and Mavis made this year's theme a special tribute to the pageant's beloved co-founder, Doll Dumas.

Teenie, who did all the grooming for his own little doggy, had figured out a way to let the fur on top of her head grow long enough to dye black and tease up into a poodle version of Doll's famous beehive. It took months to grow out enough hair to achieve the desired look, so he sent out early notices of this year's show theme in January to give other participants time to attempt the same look. The rest of Pitty Two's costume, designed by Mavis, was to be kept secret until the night of the pageant.

Planning for the first annual Doll Dumas Memorial Poodle Pageant was well under way when Marv and Pauline came up with a suggestion. Since a larger-than-usual crowd was expected this year, he thought Rhonelle ought to consider expanding the mobile home park. More visitors were sure to arrive in their RVs. Most out-of-town dog owners, who previously had to park their campers in parking lots of area motels, would be much happier staying at Home-Sweet-Homes.

Marv's investment firm handled the trust fund Doll left behind to take care of the park's needs. He and Pauline now lived in a very nice new home they built on a property adjacent to the mobile home park, just a stone's throw away from Tammy's neat little house. She'd lived with her momma there until three years ago when Lucille decided her daughter was grown enough to take care of the house on her own. Lucille had built a log cabin out by Too-Tite Tavern when she bought the business, and had planned on moving out there eventually. Lucille knew that Marv and Pauline watched over Tammy as if she were their own child.

This still left a large open field behind the mobile home park right up to Vaudine Fortney's Forever Formica parking lot. The three-person committee of Marv, Teenie, and Rhonelle decided that was a perfect place for an expansion. Construction was started in early March and the addition was ready for temporary campers by mid-April in plenty of time for the pageant days during the first week of May. Fred Fortney and Cecil Swindle constructed a handsome wooden privacy fence to separate the permanent residents' area from the temporary campsite. Three new bath houses were built to allow tent campers for the first time. The permanent residents voted to name the new area "Poodle Trot Camp Ground."

All of Doll's friends and family were extremely pleased with the renovation and expansion of the park, and felt like it was an admirable addition to the northern entrance of the town of Peavine. Rhonelle surveyed her new domain with pride each day, and swore she could feel Doll's approval from the Great Beyond. Unfortunately, not everyone in Peavine was as pleased about this new development as these dear folks.

Vestaline Dalton, wife of the mayor and longtime president of the local Garden Club, had her own band of loyal followers, none of whom were fans of Doll Dumas in the first place. Having to look upon a bigger and more vulgar version of Madge's Mobile Home Park (as they still called it) was near to unbearable every time they were forced to drive by.

David's Aunt Violet Posey was one of Vestaline's best friends as well as a frequent customer at Vaudine's. She openly gave the park a sneer of frank disapproval whenever she passed by. Marv and Teenie were putting up the new sign at the camper entrance one sunny day when they witnessed her drive by slowly and glare malevolently out her car window. Teenie later swore he saw Aunt Violet mouthing unheard words as she passed.

Teenie stared in disbelief. "I believe that old lady is saying some cusswords at us." He put his hands defiantly on his hips and shouted at the retreating Lincoln Continental, "Same back at you, you uptight old dingbat!"

"Man, that was harsh," Marv smirked at Teenie. "Hope she didn't hear you say that. No telling what she might tattle about you when she gets back to the mayor's wife."

"Well, I just don't give a *poot* what those snobby old ladies say about us." Teenie bent back down and fluffed the brand new arrangement of iridescent pink and orange plastic flowers he had stuck into the large pot beside the new sign. "We've caved into enough of their demands already. We got rid of those white tires, didn't we?" Tammy had lovingly relocated thirty-seven whitewashed half tires that formerly lined the mobile home park entrance in her grandmother's days. Tammy had relocated the tires to her own front yard and driveway. Rhonelle had replaced the tires with twelve bright pink flamingo yard ornaments and dared anyone to complain about them.

"Vestaline is just pissed off because she couldn't boss her husband into finding any municipal regulations to stop this expansion," Marv said with a shrug. "Nothing they can do about it now. I made damn sure we were legal ahead of time."

Teenie chewed his lip and wrinkled his brow. "I sure hope they don't make trouble when this place fills up next week. Rhonelle told me all the spaces were booked up three weeks ago."

"Teenie, you got enough things to tend to with running the pageant. You don't need to worry over those biddies. Leave 'em to me and Rhonelle. Most of them are scared of her anyway." Marv put his arm around Teenie. "Come on little buddy, let's get us some lunch over at Don's."

One big consolation Teenie had almost forgotten about was the fact that this was an election year and after two decades of running uncontested, Mayor Herbert Dalton was about to meet his match. An exciting new up-and-comer in politics, Billy "Buckshot" Bradley, had filed a month ago and was about to give old Mayor Dalton a run for his money!

Buckshot, as he was known around the county, was an avid sportsman and clever politician. He'd started out as an attorney for the oil company, but switched to politics when he ran for state representative the year after he married Ginny Leah, known as "Sugar" because of her weakness for desserts. Both Buckshot and Sugar had children from previous marriages, her two girls and his three boys. They became known as the Bradley Bunch, and there wasn't a handsomer family to be found in Peavine.

Buckshot had a head of thick gleaming white hair and a magnificent smile. Nobody could work a room or county fair like Buckshot. Whenever he listened to you, it was as if you were the most important person in the room by implementing his constant eye contact, firm handshake and the occasional consoling hug. Buckshot also had a phenomenal memory for names and faces. He claimed it was a secret method taught to him by none other than the Honorable Dale Bumpers.

Despite never passing up a dessert or sweet, Sugar was delicately thin and petite with pale blonde hair. She dressed with impeccable style, and was extremely ladylike. She was always outgoing and friendly to everyone she met. Sugar and Teenie became mutual admirers when she adopted one of the Brice's AKC toy poodles as a Christmas surprise for her daughters six years ago. The puppy was white as snow and they named her Princess.

"I never have gotten into politics much," Teenie said out of the blue to Marv as they waited to cross the highway. "I believe I'm gonna do all I can to help Sugar get her husband to beat old man Dalton this year."

"That's very civic minded of you," Marv agreed. "I think a new mayor is exactly what this town needs. I plan to make a sizable donation to his campaign myself."

That year the annual Peavine Poodle Pageant/Doll Dumas Memorial version was the best attended, most highly publicized event ever held in Peavine. The Poodle Trot Camp Ground was full to the brim with happy campers and poodles. Teenie insisted on adding a fenced-in dog play area so the poodles could get acquainted before the competition. A couple of the purebreds got a little *too* friendly and left town carrying the seeds of a new dynasty.

The "Best Poodle Beehive Contest" was a hilarious hit. Pitty Two won the best beehive, of course, thanks to her hair being the tallest and stiffest in the show. She also proceeded to win first place in the talent competition with her uncanny impersonation of Doll Dumas.

Mavis had complimented Teenie's carefully coiffed dyed black bee-hive doggy hairdo with a small pair of cat eye glasses, and a dog outfit with purple slacks with pink ruffles and a tiny flower print halter top. Teenie slipped Pitty Two a white rawhide stick to chew on. When the dog walked onto the stage on her hind legs, it appeared she had a cig in the corner of her mouth while prancing about the stage as Louise played "You Ain't Nothing but a Hound Dog." It brought the house down!

The title of "Most Beautiful Poodle" went to Sugar's dog, Princess, for the third year in a row. Her beehive was dyed pink with glitter sprinkles, and she wore one of Mavis' famous pink Cinderella-at-the-Ball gowns. All the judges were impartial officials from the AKC Toy Poodle Association so there would be no charges of bias, even though they all were huge fans of Teenie and Mavis and looked forward to this event each year.

It was a wonderfully profitable week for the community. Even the weather cooperated with cooling breezes and sunny skies. All the area motels were at full capacity, including the Dew Drop Inn cottages. Rhonelle knew the mobile home park had never run at a profit in all the years she had been living there. She had never been so proud of her management skills until now. It was if she had built something bigger and more meaningful than at any other time in her life.

She had a brief image of Sergio the day after the pageant. His face was spattered with paint and he had a look of total concentration. He was building something very large and felt good about stretching his boundaries. He turned and winked at her. "*Soon, baby . . . just not yet.*"

Abruptly, the vision winked out like a television set being turned off.

CHAPTER TWENTY-ONE

The Long Hot Summer

The second week of May brought an abrupt end to springtime in Peavine and an early arrival of summer. Rhonelle didn't mind hot weather, claimed it kept her muscles loose and limber. She had been walking much more than usual since becoming manager and noticed an improvement in her stamina. She always kept up her daily yoga stretches and still taught the jazz class at Tammy and Amber's School of Tap, Cheer and Baton.

Rhonelle was so busy tending to her tenants, checking campers in, and doing the occasional psychic reading here and there – she barely gave Sergio a thought during the day. However, almost every night he entered her dreams in a very pleasant way.

Sometimes it was merely a glimpse of his face or watching him concentrate on some project; although she couldn't quite grasp what it was exactly he was working on. Each time she got close to figuring it out he would take her into his arms, and once again they were dancing in costumes at Krystal and Sammy's wedding reception. Some nights they had long intimate conversations, details of which faded like mist in the morning sun. Then there were other nights when these encounters were as hot and steamy as the weather. Those visions weren't so easily forgotten.

Almost all of the dreams were satisfying and pleasant and she often awoke with a smile on her face. She was positive that she and Sergio were communicating in their own way – telepathically. This was all the involvement she could tolerate for the time being. The envelope containing the note from Sergio was still unopened, hidden at the bottom of her lingerie drawer and practically forgotten. She often talked to her Granny Laurite about her strange feelings concerning this new man in her life. (She definitely felt like they had some sort of a relationship.) She could not quite bring herself to ask Granny to tell her what she knew about Sergio. The time for that would come soon enough. For now, she'd rather not know too much.

The new larger front deck that Cecil Swindle had built on the lavender double-wide became the favorite place for friends to gather on long summer evenings for a cold beer or glass of sweet tea. Most days Rhonelle would sit there with her cup of coffee as she gazed off into distant realms of the spirit world. At least that's what most people assumed. If they knew what earthy visions she actually mused upon, they would most probably be shocked – except for Lucille.

On some occasions, her friends and tenants brought over food. On those days, Fred Fortney would fire up Doll's old charcoal grill for a good, old-fashioned cookout. This was usually on Sunday evenings so Don and Dorine could enjoy having someone else do the cooking on their one day off. Of course, Don always brought a scrumptious dessert.

Darla had finally convinced her parents that they needed to hire a permanent waitress at Don's Diner. During the Poodle Pageant, they had been so busy that it took two girls as well as Darla, who usually came in on Saturdays to help when she could. Tammy had suggested two of her twirl and dance students to work at the Diner during that busy week. One of the girls, Lorna Mae Monett, was graduating this year and was looking for employment. They hired her to stay on. Lorna Mae was a shy, slightly mousey young woman, yet very efficient and a big help to Dorine. It had been a puzzle to Dorine as to why Lorena Mae would have ever enrolled in majorette training in the first place, until she met her pushy mother. Fortunately, Lorna Mae was now eighteen and moved out right after graduation. Tammy found her an old trailer to rent at Home-Sweet-Homes so all she had to do was walk across the highway to work at the Diner.

Cecil and Tammy were practically joined at the hip these days.

Tammy helped him on the many evenings Cecil worked after hours to restore Rhonelle's 1964 T-Bird. Tammy's principle jobs were to hold the flashlight for Cecil and entertain him with amusing stories of the goings on at her Summer Cheer and Baton Camp.

He could not have been happier. Both his relationship with his beloved Tammy and the T-Bird project were progressing nicely. The Regional Classic Car Competition was coming up Labor Day weekend in Branson, Missouri. Rhonelle planned to ride along with Tammy and Cecil in the car transport van as their chaperone, a purely symbolic gesture to please Marv and Teenie, who were overly protective of their darling Tammy.

Ever since Marv first laid eyes on little four-year-old Tammy when he and Pauline found the long lost Lucille Lepanto in a Texas roadhouse, he loved that child as if she were his own. Teenie also was fiercely loyal to Tammy. Both he and Mavis doted upon her like loving grandparents. Doll Dumas' whole circle of friends had quickly surrounded Lucille and her precious daughter Tammy as a diverse and supportive extended family. Little Tammy's childhood names of "Teenie Pop" and "Unkie Marv" had stuck through to adulthood as her favorite endearments for the two men.

Cecil had a lot to live up to in the eyes of Teenie and Marv, especially Marv because of a long simmering feud with Cecil's godfather, Fred Fortney. The fact that Fred could regularly go to racetracks around the country as if he were visiting harmless amusement parks drove Marv crazy. Marv was well aware of his own weaknesses in that area. He was a recovering gambling addict who had sworn never to go near a racetrack ever again (so help him God!).

So far, things had stayed fairly cordial between the two men for the sake of keeping peace in this tightly knit community. Rhonelle wondered how well things would go when Marv realized just how serious the relationship had become between Tammy and Cecil. Fortunately, both Fred and Marv were more focused on the almost magical transformation of the 1964 T-Bird. Cecil had completed the exterior paint job, polished up all the chrome and replaced the stained and worn out convertible top. There was nothing like a shiny bright new toy to make a man happy.

Even Rhonelle, who had managed quite well without a car for the past ten years, was getting excited about driving her own beautifully refurbished vehicle. She was most curious about the rebuilding of the motor, because she wanted assurances that the car would be safe for traveling. She was looking forward to the possibility that she could go on a private road trip again if she so pleased. The time was drawing nigh when she would want to do just that ... when she found out *where* she was supposed to find her mysterious Sergio.

One hot June afternoon, Rhonelle was sitting on her deck sipping iced coffee and musing upon all of the recent makeovers in her life: Doll's lavender double-wide (still lacking a new bedroom suite), the new deck, the campground annex, her old car, and her own new look. She was just thinking about needing another touch-up on her hair dye job when Lucille pulled up in her cherry red Mustang convertible. Sitting in the front seat beside her was her old cohort, Shirleen Naither.

"Hey Rhonelle, look what the cat just drug into town," Lucille shouted. Raucous laughter followed and out hopped Shirleen waving her magical pink "bag of beauty" in her hand. "Shirl Girl is here to help her niece get set up with her new salon – Snazzy Styles."

"I thought you might need a little expert re-do by now," Shirleen blithely stated as she climbed up onto the deck and took a look around. "Oooooh this is a nice improvement! Have you had time to do some redecorating inside too? Lucy girl says you've been mighty busy of late." All the time Shirleen was talking her eyes were assessing the condition of Rhonelle's hair from roots to ends.

Rhonelle was beginning to feel a little self-conscious. She had carelessly pinned her hair up off her neck while she did a bit of yard work earlier. "You caught me at a rather style impaired moment," she said as she tried to push a few errant curls back away from her face. Humidity had doubled the already thick volume of her copious head of hair. At least the graying roots hadn't grown out terribly much since her last touch-up . . . or were they glaringly obvious?

"Would you girls like something cold to drink?" Rhonelle turned and opened the door.

"Good gawd, yes," Lucille gasped, fanning herself. "It must be one hundred degrees. I don't know how you can stand to sit out here in this heat." She and Shirleen brushed past Rhonelle in their rush to get into the air conditioning. Lucille immediately went into the living room and switched the window AC unit from low to high. Rhonelle was so used to this behavior she only shrugged and went to the kitchen to fetch a couple of cold Diet Cokes from the fridge. She would turn it back down after they left.

Rhonelle returned and sat in her big red chair with the stars and moons. She wrapped her flowered shawl around her shoulders to protect her from the chill of the AC. "Your timing couldn't have been better. I'm about out of the hair color you left me, and I really hate fooling with all that mess."

"It's certainly worth the trouble." Shirleen grinned at Rhonelle. "You look really good. I swear you've got a new glow to ya."

"I've noticed the same thing, Shirl Girl." Lucille peered at Rhonelle. "If I didn't know better, I'd say she's got her a secret fella stashed around here somewhere." Lucille cut loose with her rattley laughter. "I don't think you could sneak anything past me though. This may be a double-wide but there ain't that many hiding places around here."

Rhonelle sat quietly smiling while the two women guffawed and slapped their thighs at her expense. *Lucille is more intuitive than she realizes.*

"What have you and Bo have been up to on those trips you've been taking to Memphis lately?" Rhonelle asked Lucille, diverting the conversation from the idea she could possibly have a hidden lover. "I know you're up to something, but I have declined to pry out of courtesy for your privacy."

This caught Lucille off guard. Rhonelle noticed a slight blush and hesitation before Lucille answered. "Well . . . I just might be up to something *more* than what you're thinking." She cleared her throat and sat up straight, adding casually, "Bo and I had some business dealings to see about."

"Yeah," Shirleen sneered. "I'm *sure* you did." Then she elbowed

Lucille before taking a sip of her Coke.

"I'll have you know Bo and I have gone in fifty-fifty on a new sound system and live broadcast van for KPEW," Lucille announced proudly. "He's gonna use it to cover events around town for 'remotes' like . . . uhm . . . store openings, big sales, and special events. It'll really add to coverage of the Peavine High School football games."

Rhonelle knew there was something Lucille was purposely leaving out, but Shirleen beat her to the punch. "That's great for Bo and the radio station, but what's in it for you?"

"That's the exciting part!" Lucille leaned forward and giggled. "The sound system is mostly for me. As of August first, the Too-Tite Tavern will have *live* music on Saturday nights and an Open Mike night once a month that we will eventually broadcast late at night on KPEW. Won't that be a hoot?" She glanced from Shirleen to Rhonelle.

Rhonelle immediately saw two problems with this idea. "What do you think Bo's brother and father are going to say about using the radio station to promote a drinking establishment? After all, they're both Baptist preachers."

Lucille's shoulders slumped a little and she bit her lip. "We thought about all that, believe you me, but Bo is pretty sure he can work around them."

"I'd like to see how he'll do that," Shirleen snorted.

Lucille looked at Rhonelle sheepishly. "For one thing, I done bought out his brother, Joe Don Astor. I'm half owner of KPEW now."

Both Rhonelle and Shirleen were dumbfounded.

"It's okay," Lucille rushed to reassure them. "Momma left me plenty of money to invest and of course I talked with Marv about all of it before I did anything. We plan to ease into the Too-Tite shows. We probably won't start that up until after Christmas sometime. I'll have the musical acts on for a few months and only advertise at first."

"That sounds pretty secular for a gospel station Lucy." Shirleen was familiar with the original format for the station and knew Pastor Astor would have a conniption over all this.

"That's the thing," Lucille insisted. "KPEW is a whole lot more than a gospel station now. That's what makes it such a goldmine. It's the *only* radio station in Peavine, and we have a lot to offer besides religion, which is still broadcast live from Reverend Joe Don's real church every Sunday. All day Sunday is still gospel music and Bible stuff."

Rhonelle was amazed that she hadn't picked up on any of this before now. She was well aware that Bo and Lucille had been spending plenty of time together romantically. The business side of their relationship came as a big surprise.

"I guess my psychic abilities have slipped," Rhonelle sighed dramatically. "You have become quite adept at hiding things from me."

"Oh, I've got an even bigger secret you don't know about." Lucille rolled her eyes up to stare at the ceiling with a mischievous smile. "And don't you dare try to get it out of me or you will spoil a big surprise."

"Lucy, don't tell me you've let yourself get knocked up!" Shirleen grabbed Lucille by the arms and jerked her around to face her.

"Gawd no," Lucille shouted, shocked that her friend would jump to that conclusion. "I'm not that stupid! I'm a whole lot older now and hopefully a tad wiser." She straightened up and smiled at Rhonelle. "I just happened to have a real nice Christmas present in the works. Bo and I are going to great lengths to keep it under wraps, so no psychic snooping okay?"

"You have my word," Rhonelle crossed her heart and held up her hand. "Now, if you have finished your soda, Shirleen how about getting to work on this." She unpinned her hair and shook out a full halo of bushy black curls (with one inch of graying roots).

Lucille and Shirleen chattered on about the new hair salon preparations and the future of KPEW while they worked on Rhonelle's hair. Meanwhile, Rhonelle silently watched the two of them – especially Lucille. *I can't believe I haven't picked up on any of this*.

The thought of a Christmas surprise was exciting. Rhonelle certainly did intend to honor her promise not to pry. For some odd reason she couldn't shake the feeling that whatever they were planning would have a profound effect upon the whole town, especially on her.

There was a sound like static in her mind and Sergio's face flashed into view before quickly disappearing with a tiny silver spark. *Granny has been up to something!*

July was hotter than usual. Shirleen had tutored her niece well and Snazzy Styles Salon was a big hit with the younger set. The Blue Hair Brigadiers still went to Dee Dee's Do's. The new salon was in the downtown area close enough for Rhonelle to walk over for her monthly color touchup. Trudging back home in the sweltering heat reminded her of the benefits of having her own car again.

The T-Bird was practically finished now. She had been invited for a test drive with Cecil that weekend, and hoped she could remember how to drive. Except for a few times when Doll Dumas had lent her a big old Pontiac, Rhonelle had hardly driven for ten years. She knew in her gut she would be traveling in the near future to some place out of town . . . no idea where yet, but she wanted it to be in her own vehicle.

She needn't have worried about her driving skills, and the car ran even better than she remembered. The newly repaired air-conditioning had made the whole experience of tooling down the highway on a hot summer night refreshing as well as exhilarating. Best of all, she felt sexy driving that car.

Ah Cecil, what a godsend you are!

Despite her gratitude and sincere hopes that he would win the prize money for the fantastic restoration of her T-Bird, Rhonelle had to renege on her offer to play chaperone when Tammy and Cecil went to Branson for the Labor Day Classic Car Rally.

The Poodle Trot Campground had been booked up for weeks, so she would have to stay home to manage the crowd. Tammy's dance academy partner, Amber, was thrilled to go in Rhonelle's place and assure things were pure and proper between the young couple.

Poodle Trot Campground stayed busy all summer as word got out after the Poodle Pageant that it was a very pleasant place to stay – especially if you had pets. Because the campground was busy, so was Rhonelle. The steady stream of extra money the campground generated had padded her redecorating fund.

She had done little to her bedroom except to add some fancy red drapes with a lacy sheer panel, all designed and hand made by Darla. Now Rhonelle had money and a great opportunity to find the perfect bedroom suite.

Vaudine Fortney had cajoled Rhonelle to leave the mobile home park in the capable hands of Teenie Brice for two days in midweek so they could attend a stupendous estate sale in Vicksburg, Mississippi. After plenty of coaxing and reassurance from her friends, Rhonelle decided to take a break and go along with Vaudine and Darla on their hunt for antique treasures among the trash.

They were headed to a very large, old estate with plenty of furniture for sale – a veritable goldmine in Vaudine's eyes! She was fortunate enough to have received an invitation to the "dealers only" preview, one of the perks she had earned after years of collecting merchandise from estate sales.

Rhonelle decided it would be a nice break for her – something entirely new and different. She'd not taken a day off since returning from New Orleans and facing the ice and snow storm. The possibilities of numerous psychic vibrations she might encounter also intrigued her. There was no telling how many spirits and past lives she might pick up on in that old southern mansion. Just handling the antiques could give her a buzz.

Fred and Cecil had hooked up Vaudine's brand new horse trailer to Darla's used hearse from the Astor Eternal Rest Funeral Home, so they had plenty of room to bring back their finds. Cecil had tuned up and repainted the hearse a pretty blue color and replaced the funeral home logo with Darla's Denim and Lace on the side. Dorine declared it still looked like a hearse, no matter how hard you tried to tart it up.

The threesome set off for Vicksburg the day before the big sale, checking into a motel near the Mississippi River bridge. The plan was for Darla and Vaudine to get up at the crack of dawn so they could get a good place in line before the sale started. Rhonelle would sleep in and join them later using the special entry ticket that Vaudine had left for her. All three women were piled into a room with two double beds and a rollaway. Darla offered to sleep on the rollaway since she was the youngest.

Rhonelle tossed and turned most of the night, only falling into a deep sleep after Darla and Vaudine left *not so quietly* at five in the morning.

She dreamt she was wearing the red and black satin dress Mavis had made for her. Sergio was there, too, dressed in an antique suit of clothes that went naturally with his ponytail. They were walking through a large house from room to room, commenting upon scenes displayed in each room as if it were a museum.

When they came to one bedroom, she was immediately struck by the beauty of the bed with an ornate brass headboard and red velvet coverlet. It was exactly what she had been looking for all this time. They both agreed they had found something valuable that they'd thought was gone forever.

What!?

Rhonelle's eyes flew open as she sat up in bed, wide awake. Looking at the bedside clock, she was shocked to see it was already almost ten o'clock. After gulping down a vile cup of hotel room coffee, she hurriedly dressed and applied red lipstick, smearing a little on her cheeks to brighten her pallor. She nibbled some peanut butter crackers Vaudine had stashed in the room, grateful that Mr. Nasty wasn't along for this trip.

In the middle of recalling her dream she was startled by the phone ringing. It was Darla.

"Rhonelle, are you ready yet?" Darla usually tended to speak in a slow detached manner, but this time there was breathless excitement in her voice. "I think we've found something you might like. I'll be by in ten minutes to pick you up at the front lobby door."

A half hour later Darla and Rhonelle had made their way back to the estate sale. Maneuvering and parking a hearse with a horse trailer attached takes a while. Vaudine was practically doing a jig on the front porch while she waited for them. As soon as they stepped onto the portico, Darla and Vaudine got on either side of Rhonelle and expertly serpentined their way through the mob of antique dealers rummaging through tables of fine china, crystal, and porcelain figurines. They squeezed through the kitchen and up the back stairway to the bedrooms.

Walking down the hall they passed two bedrooms filled with vintage clothing and linens. When they entered the third bedroom Rhonelle stopped suddenly and her jaw dropped. There was the exact same bed she had seen in her dream. She walked over to it as if she were in a trance. *Superimposed over the scene in front of her was another vision. She saw herself with Sergio under that red velvet cover in the midst of a joyfully passionate act of completion!* Her face reddened and she went weak in the knees.

"I told you she would like it," Darla said to Vaudine.

CHAPTER TWENTY-TWO

Falling Into Fall Again

Needless to say, Rhonelle could hardly wait to get the new bed back to her lavender double-wide. It was a challenge to fit into Vaudine's horse trailer, along with the other fabulous finds the three-some had bought. Rhonelle was very grateful now for that pesky snow-storm. Without it, she might have stayed in New Orleans and wasted her money on the wrong furniture.

"You would have spent twice as much down there," Vaudine reminded her smugly. "You'd never have found that oriental rug to go in your bedroom either if it hadn't been for Darla here."

"I know that," Rhonelle conceded happily. "I never would have guessed that going to a sale like that would be so rewarding. (*Nor did I ever think it would be so exciting either.*) Here I am going home with the bedroom of my dreams (*literally*)!"

Darla drove along absently, smiling as she visualized exactly how she would rearrange Rhonelle's bedroom. "All you need now is a mirror on the ceiling," she added, out of the blue.

Vaudine hooted over that idea as she assumed Darla was making a joke in her own droll manner. Rhonelle secretly thought that would be a nice addition but wasn't sure it would be possible to install a mirror on the ceiling of a trailer, even one as large and luxurious as the lavender double-wide. Then she surprised herself with her next thought. *What would people think of me if I were to do such a thing?*

Darla shot a sly glance at Rhonelle, who quickly retorted, "That kind of a mirror might show me more than I would want to see. Some things are best left to the imagination. Besides, word would get around town pretty quickly that I was running a bordello."

Vaudine had a good laugh over that. "Yeah honey, those snooty Garden Club ladies would have a heyday over that tidbit of information." She poked Rhonelle with her elbow. "Darla, I think that big brass bed is a little risqué for Homes-Sweet-Homes, but I sure do like that oriental rug you found. That is classy! This is the most fun I've *ever* had at one of these sales. We'll have to do it again sometime."

"I doubt I could afford another shopping spree like this one," Rhonelle sighed as she mentally calculated the balance in her bank account. "I think from now on, I'd better let you and Darla shop for me."

"What else do you think you'll need?" Darla asked, not taking her eyes off the road.

Rhonelle had not really thought about that, but she suddenly pictured something in her head. "I need something for the living room. Like an easy chair with an ottoman, preferably in leather . . . kind of modern sixties style."

Darla's eyebrows shot up as she glanced across Vaudine at Rhonelle. "We should look for a Herman Miller chair. They're pretty expensive, but we might be able to find a used one that needs repair at one of these sales."

Vaudine was always on the lookout for usable broken furniture. "If anybody can find you one of those Herman what's-his-name chairs, I can, and Fred will fix it!"

The three women rode along comfortably in the plush front seat of the blue hearse, the back packed to the gills with collectibles and antiques. The trip to Vicksburg had turned out to be a rewarding experience for them all.

Labor Day came and went in a haze of humid heat and a crowded campground. Cecil, Tammy and Amber rode home with the T-Bird in tow and a second-place trophy from the competition. The prize money was less than Cecil had hoped for, but in Branson he met an affluent antique car collector willing to hire Cecil to restore several of his latest acquisitions. He was going to have them shipped to Peavine the very next week, along with several thousand dollars down payment toward Cecil's expenses.

Tammy planned to let him unload the cars at her house to park in her backyard while Cecil rebuilt them – one at a time – in the workshop Fred had found for him. Things had not worked out exactly as Cecil and Tammy had hoped, but a better-than-expected outcome overcame their disappointment.

This collaboration with a wealthy car collector eventually would earn Cecil a good deal more money than he'd have won for first prize. It just wouldn't all come at once. Cecil was willing to be patient. Rhonelle wasn't sure Tammy could wait too much longer, though. She could almost hear the wedding bells ringing in her ears. To protect her daughter from a fate much like hers, Lucille had started Tammy on birth control pills while she was still in high school under the pretense it would help keep her periods regular. Rhonelle knew that Lucille was doing all she could to prevent her sweet beautiful daughter from getting herself into trouble. She agreed with Lucille that Tammy was naïve and overly affectionate, which might lead some horny young football player to believe he could "get to third base and slide into home."

Rhonelle was convinced that Tammy had way more gumption than her mother gave her credit for. She also had learned self-defense from her "Unkie Marv" and knew when and how to use her skills. All that dance, cheer and twirl training had given her a surprisingly strong grip. Rhonelle's only concern about Tammy was her tendency to be a little spacey. She hoped she'd remember to take those pills on a regular basis when the time came that she really needed them.

Tammy had never tried to hide anything from Rhonelle. She was as easy to read as an open book. After the trip to Branson, Rhonelle didn't need Amber to tell her that Tammy spent most of each night in Cecil's motel room. They are, after all grownups now . . . but that didn't keep Rhonelle from worrying. She hoped Tammy hadn't – in her excitement – been careless about taking her pills. Her one consolation was that Cecil seemed extremely conscientious. *He'll take good care of her.*

Lucille and Bo made two more mysterious trips to Memphis and constantly looked like they were up to something. They had not announced their business merger to anyone besides Shirleen and Rhonelle. Lucille had asked them not to talk about it until Bo had figured out how to break the news to his dad, Pastor Lyle Bodine Astor.

Fortunately, an unexpected event soon solved their dilemma.

"God works in mysterious ways." Lucille proclaimed as Rhonelle opened the door to find her standing there one fine morning in late September. Lucille raised her hands to the heavens and said, "Can I hear a Hallelujah please."

Rhonelle blinked at the sun in her eyes and leaned on the door frame. "Hallelujah and get inside. I haven't had my coffee yet." She was still in the process of brewing a pot and heating her pan of milk. "Whatever it is, you'll have to wait a minute."

Lucille plopped down on the sofa and sprawled her legs up across the armrest so she could admire her new pair of red and gold cowgirl boots – which oddly enough reminded her of Rhonelle's fancy new bed.

"Why don't you use Mom's microwave to heat up your milk? It sure would be faster."

"I don't believe in those contraptions – radiation is bad for my health." Rhonelle had tried the microwave once but the milk got too hot and formed a skin on it. She enjoyed the ritual of stirring the pan of milk while her coffee brewed. It allowed time to think about her dreams, another more recent pleasant ritual.

After her café au lait was perfectly prepared, Rhonelle sauntered into the living room and nestled into her favorite chair. "Okay, tell me what momentous event has transpired that caused *you* of all people to come knocking on my door so early on a Saturday morning." (Ten o'clock was considered early for Rhonelle).

"The Lord has taken care of the Pastor Astor problem!" Lucille put her feet back down on the floor and faced Rhonelle.

"He's not passed away has he?" Rhonelle assumed Granny would have already informed her of that event.

"Oh, Hell no," Lucille giggled. "This is way better.

"Yesterday morning Reverend Brother Joe Don got a frantic call from ole lady Dalton, that snooty wife of the mayor that lives next door to Pastor Astor. She told Joe Don he'd better get over there to see about his daddy before somebody called the sheriff for indecent exposure!"

"The sheriff was indecent?" Rhonelle couldn't help teasing her friend.

"No, but the pastor was," Lucille slapped her knee. "If you call standing on top a ladder in your front lawn in nothing but yer drawers and a pair of black socks while preaching about the end of the world indecent, I guess he fit the bill."

"Oh my," Rhonelle's eyebrows shot up and she couldn't keep from smiling. "How on earth did they get him to come down off the ladder?"

"Joe Don made an emergency call to Doc Ozzie before he left his house, and they arrived at the pastor's place about the same time." Lucille felt a little guilty about enjoying this story so much, but that didn't stop her. "Poor Vestaline Dalton was wringing her hands and crying while her esteemed mayoral spouse kept trying to get the pastor to let him put a blanket around him. It was quite a scene. Several of the neighbors had come out in their yards to see what in the world was going on by the time Joe Don and the doctor arrived."

Rhonelle couldn't help but feel sorry for the old pastor. "What a shame they all had to see him like that. What did he do when he saw Joe Don?"

"Not much really," Louise shrugged. "He didn't seem to recognize his own son. It was the sudden appearance of Doc Ozzie, pulling up the driveway and hopping out of his SUV that got his attention. Once he saw that black-skinned face, he shouted out –'look, a heathen Hottentot has come to me for salvation!'"

Rhonelle couldn't stop herself from a quick snort of laughter. "Oh good Lord, I hope the good doctor didn't take offense."

"Naw, he took it all in stride," Louise waved her hand. "It cracked him up, too, as a matter of fact. He and Joe Don convinced the pastor to go back into the house and maybe they could have themselves a little impromptu baptism."

CHAPTER TWENTY-THREE

Saving Pastor Astor

Within twenty-four hours all of Peavine was abuzz over the embarrassing spectacle of Pastor Astor's early morning sermon on the ladder in his skivvies. Once Joe Don got his daddy down off the ladder and wrapped in the mayor's blanket, the old man was quite docile as they led him back into his house.

Doc Ozzie listened patiently to the pastor's religious rambling while he gently took the old man's vitals. He was pretty sure a raging urinary infection was the cause of the sudden confusion and aberrant behavior. Joe Don bundled him up and whisked him off to the hospital in El Dorado. They kept the pastor there for a week of tests and plenty of antibiotics.

By the time Pastor Astor was ready to be released from the hospital, he was less dazed and confused, and fortunately for his pride, totally unaware of the spectacle he'd caused with his now famous "Sermon on the Ladder." It was obvious to his two sons that their daddy could no longer live on his own. His mental and physical health had been declining ever since the KPEW scandal with the IRS. The death of his quiet little wife, Velma Jean, five years ago had been a serious blow to his well-being and a grave concern to Joe Don and Bo.

Joe Don's wife immediately made it crystal clear she most certainly would *not* allow his father to move in with them, nor have their young family move over to the pastor's house. She knew she would end up taking care of her father-in-law in addition to the three rambunctious young boys, two hunting dogs and her own aging parents, already in her charge. Bo wasn't an option either. So at that time they had hired a housekeeper to come in six days a week and hoped for the best.

Now the day they long dreaded had arrived. Decisions could no longer be delayed. An Astor family meeting was convened, with Doc Ozzie to discuss care options for their once proud and fiery patriarch.

Pastor Astor's sister, Vaudine Fortney, and sons Bo and Joe Don were gathered in a patient conference room. They had just left the pastor's bedside. Seeing him tucked into the hospital bed, gazing sadly out the window at nothing in particular was hard to bear. He seemed to have shrunk three sizes that week.

To everyone's surprise and delight, Peavine's own cheerful angel of mercy, Christabelle Tingleberry, intervened as soon as she'd heard about Pastor Astor's prognosis. She spun into action after Lucille told Rhonelle about the early morning spectacle of the pastor's melt-down. Rhonelle decided Christabelle would be the one to call on for help.

Christabelle required a "cause" to keep life interesting now that she no longer was the caregiver for Doll Dumas. She didn't really need a salaried job since she had been blessed with the "sweepstakes sur-prise money" Doll bequeathed to her.

At this time in Christabelle's life, she was aware of a new calling even better suited to her cheerful disposition. During the ice and snow-storm the previous winter, she had stayed out at the Mansion Rest and Retirement Home to volunteer her nursing care. During that time, she discovered a glaring need that she was confident she could fill.

Many of the residents at the Mansion Rest Home had been sitting around in their rooms watching TV most of the time except during meals. That week when the electricity and cable went out, the resi-dents were in dire distress from boredom. The generator was only used for the most basic needs and even if they could have turned on their televisions there wasn't any cable. Christabelle made sure there was a battery operated radio available on each floor so everybody had access to KPEW. (Thank God for Little Bo and Lucille for keeping the station on the air!) Christabelle had the care aides dig out all of the board games, dominoes, and decks of cards from the storage closet. She arranged chairs and tables around a roaring fire in the beautiful fireplace in the main common area.

She organized tournaments amongst the residents. Christabelle even talked Rose Posey into playing the piano in the drawing room for an old-fashioned sing- along. She dearly wished Louise Dolesanger could have been there as Rose's playing had gotten pretty rusty. The old folks were joyously singing off key. Most were hard of hearing so the quality of the accompaniment didn't matter all that much.

By the end of the five-day snowstorm, a new sense of community had been forged among the residents. Many claimed that storm was the most fun they'd had in years. However, after months of weekly visits as a volunteer answering the phone and serving meals, Christabelle noticed the residents were slipping back into their old routine – sitting isolated in their rooms watching TV. Nobody on staff had the will or time to keep things organized so that there was always something fun and interesting for the residents to do together.

That's when Christabelle decided to offer her services as full-time activity director at the Mansion Rest and Retirement Home. At age sixty-five, she was qualified to be a resident of one of the retirement living apartments. All she asked for was a rent-free apartment in exchange for her services as a full-time activity director.

She and her little dog Cutie Boy could be on site every day to bring their own special brand of enthusiastic cheer, and she would have the security of a place to stay should she need nursing care in the future. The arrangement also allowed her to fulfill a long-held but never expressed dream. Now that she could afford it, she wanted to travel. At the top of her wish list was a trip to the Hawaiian Islands. She had secretly been collecting brochures at a travel agency during her shopping trips to Pine Bluff.

Christabelle mulled over all these momentous decisions on the day Rhonelle and Lucille called to ask her advice about what to do with Pastor Astor. Within just a few days, Christabelle had negotiated an agreement with the Mansion Rest and Retirement Home. She talked things over with Bo and Lucille and consulted with Doc Ozzie about the pastor's medical needs. Christabelle had carefully maintained her Registered Nurse accreditation and had twenty-three years experience of geriatric care on her resume, making her advice invaluable.

Christabelle Tingleberry entered the Astor family care meeting that day armed with a sense of purpose and *mission*. Her cheerful attitude quickly dispelled the guilt and unease that accompanies the difficult decision adult children must face when the time comes to put a parent into a nursing home.

First thing, she passed a Tupperware container of fresh-baked chocolate chip cookies around to the family. With their permission, she took over the job of convincing Pastor Astor that the Mansion Rest and Retirement Home was the best option for his care. Christabelle promised that by the time she was through talking to him, he'd feel like it was *his* idea in the first place!

Christabelle breezed into the pastor's hospital room with a cheerful hello and aroma of fresh-baked cookies. She pulled up a chair and took the old man's large speckled hand in her warm, pudgy little fingers. "Pastor Astor," she said, gazing earnestly into his pale, sunken face. "I have been praying hard for many days now asking for God to show me a sign." This seemed to get through to him. His watery blue eyes turned to focus on her face. "Yes, Pastor, it's me, Sister Christabelle Tingleberry. I've come to tell you God has answered my prayers and shown me the path I need to follow now after the years I cared for our dearly departed friend, Doll Dumas. God bless her eternal rest in Heaven."

The pastor's lips stirred and he whispered, "God bless her rest in Heaven. Amen."

"Amen," Christabelle repeated as she squeezed his hand and proceeded. "Now I want you to know that God has a new mission for me and this is the exciting part, Pastor . . . He has a new mission especially for you!"

The pastor's eyebrows raised but he didn't say anything.

"Pastor, you have got to get up out of this bed tomorrow so you can come with me to a flock that needs a shepherd. *You* are the one that God has chosen to be His shepherd. We got us some missionary work to do out there at the Mansion Rest and Retirement Home. Just think of all those souls you could save before they leave this life! Say Hallelujah!"

"Hallelujah," the pastor repeated weakly with a look of wonder on his face.

"Yes sir," Christabelle said with more determination in her voice.

"Our mission is to get you moved out there and set up shop for Jesus! Those poor elderly folks can have a better quality of life and receive the comfort of the Lord – with your help."

"I feel so weak," the pastor said as he looked wistfully into Christabelle's face. "I don't know how I can go on."

His words just about broke Christabelle's heart. Still, she had expected him to respond in this vein initially. At least she knew he was paying attention. That was a good start.

"Lyle Bodine don't you worry one bit about that." Christabelle released his hand and patted his thin arm consolingly. "I'll be there to take care of you and help nurse you back to health. Remember, the Lord will always give you the strength you need to do what he asks of you. God *loves* you and He won't be asking any more of you than you can bear."

The pastor's eyes flooded with tears. He clasped Christabelle's hand with more strength. "God still loves me?" He looked down sheepishly. "I thought I was being punished . . . for my sinful pride."

"Of *course* God loves you," Christabelle reassured him. "Maybe He has given you this weakness so you can witness what it feels like to need His strength to carry on . . . just like the Apostle Paul bein' struck blind afore he could really see what Jesus was all about."

There was nothing like hearing the Gospel to engage the pastor. He nodded his head. "I've been blind, but now I can see," he muttered.

Christabelle kept on preaching to the preacher. "God loves those old and lonely people out at the Mansion . . . even those that have gotten so ornery. That's why we got to go out there to *save* them!" She reached over for the box of cookies and handed it to him. "Here, have a little something sweet. It'll make you feel better. Your dear neighbor, Vestaline Dalton, made a batch of her special chocolate chip cookies for me to bring over to you. She knows how much you love 'em."

Pastor Astor sat up a little straighter in his bed and slowly reached for a fresh cookie, still soft from being baked that morning in Christabelle's own oven. She didn't mind a *little white lie* if it would reassure the pastor that his neighbor had not written him off as a total basket-case after seeing him in his underwear. Knowing the fickle nature of Vestaline Dalton as Christabelle did, however, the woman probably had stricken his name from her sacred list of "acceptable" people who would enhance her social standing.

"What about my house?" the pastor asked suddenly with the cookie halfway to his mouth.

Christabelle had already figured that out, too. "You don't need to worry one tiny bit about that either." She folded her hands in her lap and smiled a bit smugly as she thought of how well she had worked out this part of the dilemma. "Your little sister Vaudine will take very good care of your lovely home. She and Fred are willing to stay there as long as you need them to." The Fortneys had run out of storage in their trailer and sheds, and were delighted by the idea of moving into the spacious three bedroom home – even if it meant putting up with the Daltons next door.

"Here honey, have some milk to help wash that down." Christabelle was relieved to see a little color return to the pastor's cheeks as he swallowed his cookie and eagerly reached for another. Pastor Astor paused after finishing his second cookie and formed a question in his mind. "Do you know what a CIA is?"

Christabelle had to admit she had no idea where he was coming from now. She was aware that his CAT scan had shown some stroke damage and expected him to get some of his words confused. "Well . . . I'm not real sure I do know what a CIA is unless you're talking about a government agency."

Pastor Astor looked nervously at the hospital room door and said quietly "Doctor Ozzie and the new . . . the neurologist told me I am having CIA's. Are there feds watching me?"

Christabelle couldn't help letting loose her high-pitched, tinkling laughter.

"Oh my goodness no, dear. They were talking about something called TIA's. You aren't in trouble with the law you're just having some little tiny strokes now and then, that's all."

The pastor visibly relaxed and took a great sigh of relief. "Thank you, Sister, for relieving me of a terrible burden." His soft voice filled with gratitude as he gazed steadily up into Christabelle's astonished face. True humility coming from Pastor Astor was a rare and precious thing.

"Pastor," Christabelle said as she handed him another cookie. "I think we've had us one of God's own miracles today!"

Fifteen minutes later a nurse poked her head into the conference room and told Doc Ozzie and the Astor family they needed to get on down to the pastor's room. Rushing down the hall, they were greeted by the unexpected sound of "Amazing Grace" being belted out with gusto in Pastor Astor's deep baritone and Christabelle's high pitched soprano. Bo and Joe Don peered into the room over two giggling nurses. There stood the pastor with Christabelle's support, singing every word and note of the lovely old hymn with intense feeling. After the last verse, the pastor sat back down on his bed and motioned for them to come in.

"I have something to tell you all," he said in an unfamiliarly gentle tone of voice. "I will be moving out to the Mansion Retirement and Rest Home, there to live from this day forward. Sister Christabelle and I have the Lord's own missionary work to do out there." He slowly swung each leg back up onto his bed and lay back on his pillow, smiling contentedly with his eyes closed. "Now if you'll excuse me, I need my rest so I'll be ready for tomorrow's journey."

Once again, Christabelle had done her job with loving care and good humor. The results most certainly could be called miraculous!

CHAPTER TWENTY-FOUR

One Thing Leads to Another

October saw several moves and relocations in Peavine. Vaudine and Fred Fortney moved into the Astor house while Bo and Joe Don got their daddy out of the hospital and settled in the Mansion Rest and Retirement Home. Vaudine immediately began the humongous chore of sorting through the family heirlooms to see what she could include in one massive estate sale, come November. Cecil Swindle, bless his heart, was helping to haul and move the Fortneys' possessions. As a way of thanking their godson, they offered their trailer as his new home, replacing the small one-room apartment attached to the garage where he worked.

One week after Pastor Astor's arrival at the nursing-care facility out at the Old Dumas Mansion, Christabelle Tingleberry packed Cutie Boy, three suitcases full of green and red outfits, and a few cherished belongings into her old station wagon, and moved into a Mansion retirement apartment. Since the new apartment was furnished, she left all her furniture in her trailer for Louise Dolesanger's use when she moved out of her trailer and into Christabelle's newly vacated one.

Not having to move furniture made things easier for Louise. All she had to ask Cecil Swindle and Tammy to move out of her tiny mobile home were her clothes, music books, a reliable old clock radio, and the small electric organ on which she worked up new musical arrangements. Christabelle had left her favorite cast-iron frying pan and a small extra set of dishes for Louise in her spotlessly clean kitchen. Since Louise hardly ever cooked for herself, she left her seven-piece set of 1972 avocado green aluminum cookware for the next tenant.

The next tenant for Louise's vacant trailer was the object of discussion one warm October morning as Rhonelle sat on her front deck with Teenie, Marv, and Louise sipping coffee and solving the problems of the world.

"Tammy thinks we should let that mousey little waitress Lorena Mae Monett move out of her old drafty trailer into Louise's," Marv drawled with a pinched look on his face. "I don't know why that girl insists on dressing the way she does. Don't use a bit of makeup and never wears nothing but frumpy brown pant suits. At least the pink uniforms at the Diner give her a bit of color. I understand Tammy and Pauline have decided to make 'Little Miz Wallflower' their latest makeover project. They've been trying to lure her into Snazzy Styles for over a month."

"You know what Lorena Mae told me the other day?" Teenie sat up with indignation. "When I asked her if she might be getting herself an AKC toy poodle any time soon? I was going to give her some of my expert guidance just to be neighborly. She said she wouldn't be getting no poodle 'cause she's *allergic*."

Louise cut in on Lorena's behalf. "Well we can't blame her for her health conditions. She certainly is neat and clean, and I'm certain she would take good care of my trailer and my things. She doesn't have any furniture or household items of her own – just a small TV – being so young and first starting out on her own and all. I hear from Tammy that all the poor girl has to sleep on is an air mattress! She must have been in a mighty big hurry to get away from her overbearing mother."

Teenie wasn't ready to let go of what he considered Lorena Mae's unfair prejudice against AKC toy poodles. "Then that girl had the *nerve* to tell me she was considering buying herself a *Chihuahua* puppy as soon as she'd saved up the money! I was just too shocked to say a word."

Rhonelle placed a consoling hand on Teenie's boney shoulder. "A Chihuahua is a nice clean little breed, actually therapeutic for asthma sufferers. Another point to remember is all the poodle outfits would fit her puppy. You could give her some clothes for it and branch out Mavis' dog clothing designs."

"I'd never considered that." Teenie mused upon the possibilities. "I wonder how photogenic a Chihuahua is."

Interrupting Teenie's thoughts, a white Cadillac convertible with a "Buckshot Bradley for Mayor" poster taped to the side pulled up to the lavender double-wide. The Bradleys' nineteen-year-old son Tad was driving, his blond hair gleamed in the sunlight as he flashed his winning smile at the group gathered on the deck. "Good morning, folks," he shouted cheerfully as he got out of the car. "How is everybody doing today?" The tall, handsome young man strode up and hopped up onto the deck. He politely shook hands with each person present.

"Mr. Brice, Mom wanted me to offer you a ride over to the fundraiser luncheon so you could help her greet the guests, if you don't mind coming a little early."

Teenie was flush with pleasure. He had been a strong and vocal supporter of Buckshot Bradley, mostly because of his admiration and devotion to Bradley's wife, Sugar. Teenie stood up to his full four-foot-eleven height, smoothed out his dressy brown trousers and adjusted his bowtie. "Yes son, I'd be delighted to help out with the hosting duties." He couldn't suppress an excited giggle. "I love riding in the campaign car!" He turned back to Louise as he was about to walk away. "I say we get that girl moved into your old place as soon as possible. Maybe we can get her straightened out. Least we can do is see to it that her new doggy is well dressed."

Rhonelle watched Teenie gleefully climb into the convertible while Tad held the door for him. She could barely see his head as they drove off. Teenie waved enthusiastically at everyone they passed.

"Well *that's* settled then," Louise stated abruptly. "Now, I want us to talk about Thanksgiving." Louise's sudden change of topic took Marv by surprise, but Rhonelle had been expecting the subject of their first Thanksgiving without Doll to come up. Rhonelle could sense another underlying anxiety was troubling Louise besides the fact she was missing her dear old friend. She suspected it had much more to do with Louise's daughters, Katy and Lulu, who normally ignored their mother, being embarrassed by her career as a musical entertainer. They only invited Louise to visit twice a year – for Thanksgiving and Easter.

She would take a bus down to Longview, Texas, for a few days, staying at Katy's for Thanksgiving and Lulu's for Easter. Both girls had married young men who worked for Dumas Oil Company and were

moved to the branch office in Texas not long after they married –
within two years of each other. Lulu's husband was an engineer who
worked at the refinery. He made twice the salary of Katy's husband,
which made for some friction between in-laws. If it weren't for her
grandchildren, Louise would gladly stay in Peavine with her friends.

Her younger daughter, Lulu, had shown some unaccustomed
daughterly concern when she took the trouble to drive up for a short
visit right in the middle of Poodle Pageant week. She couldn't have
chosen a worse time for a surprise visit to her mother since that's the
busiest week of the year for Louise. In addition to playing the piano
for rehearsals and talent competitions at the Poodle Pageant, she was
entertaining later than usual at Seymour's Tex-Mex every night for
the pageant week for larger-than-usual crowds. All of her musical duties left Louise with hardly a moment to spend with Lulu.

To make matters worse, there wasn't a single motel room or Dew
Drop Inn cottage available for her because of the huge crowds. Lulu,
who wasn't about to camp out in the new campground surrounded
by dogs, ended up squeezing into Louise's tiny trailer, sleeping on the
recliner. She only stayed one night, so fortunately she only had twenty-four hours to follow her mother around, wringing her hands with a
constant frown on her face

Before returning to Texas, Lulu dropped by the lavender double-
wide to be sure to inform Rhonelle about her deep concerns over her
mother's health and welfare. "I just don't see how she can keep up this
lifestyle much longer," she told Rhonelle, skulking furtively in the
front door while glancing back over her shoulder. (As if Louise had
the time to watch what her daughter was up to!) "I think Katy and
I are going to have to look into some kind of an arrangement where
Momma will be more comfortable." Lulu sniffed and glanced disap-
provingly around Rhonelle's newly decorated living room. "Having
her live this far away from us is really hard on me and my sister."

The hell it is, Rhonelle thought to herself. She smiled pleasantly yet
did not offer to let Lulu come in and have a seat. She didn't want to get
into this kind of a discussion with her. "I think your mother is doing
beautifully. She is involved and active, always a good thing for us as

we get older. You needn't worry about a thing; she has plenty of friends here to watch out for her."

Lulu stared hard at Rhonelle and hesitated before she spoke. "Did her friend Doll Dumas leave her any money?"

Ah, now I see why the sudden concern. Rhonelle shrugged and smiled. "I have no idea. I make it a practice not to pry into my friends' financial matters."

She began to lead Lulu back out the door. "Now if you'll excuse me I have several new guests to check into the campground. Have a safe trip home." Lulu blushed and frowned, leaving without so much as a thank you or goodbye. Recalling that unpleasant scene, Rhonelle looked over and grinned at Louise. "So just what do you have in mind for Thanksgiving? I take it you want to break with your tradition of turkey in Texas."

"I sure as heck do!" Louise slapped the arm of her chair in anger. "It's bad enough my daughters are conniving to get me into assisted living in Longview." Louise's eyes began to tear up as she quickly drew a tissue from her sweater sleeve and wiped at her nose. "To make matters worse, Katy won't allow her own *son* to come home just because he wants to bring his boyfriend, Jay, with him. That just breaks my heart!"

Marv's eyebrows shot up and he gave a low whistle. "That's really harsh Louise. We all know your grandson, Gary, has been the light of your life."

He leaned forward with his elbows on his knees and glanced at Rhonelle before speaking to Louise. "Give your boy a call and tell him he's welcome to come up here and bring Jay and the whole band with him if he wants to." Then an idea occurred to him. *Why don't I go have a word with Don and Dorine? Maybe we could use the Diner for a great big dinner for everybody that needs a place to come to.*

Rhonelle thought that was a splendid idea, since she wasn't sure how to prepare a turkey dinner. Doll had hosted Thanksgiving for all the tenants in the trailer park for many years, and Rhonelle assumed that responsibility came with her inheritance of the lavender double-wide. The last two years had been potluck and Christabelle did the organizing. Lucille bought a huge fryer last year and learned to deep-fry a whole turkey in the backyard. She did two small ones and they were delicious. One of the birds exploded, but that was her first try before reading the instructions.

"That sounds fantastic to me, Marv, just as long as we can still have Lucille's fried turkey again," Rhonelle said enthusiastically.

Louise began to feel better sitting there between her two caring friends. She was so grateful for their acceptance of her grandson. She couldn't find the words, so she sat there blinking away tears, grinning at Marv and Rhonelle.

Marv looked down at his watch. "It's lunch time already. How 'bout we mosey on over to the Diner and talk this over with Don and Dorine. I'll call Pauline to come join us."

The threesome strolled along the driveway with Louise in the middle. She hooked her arms around Marv and Rhonelle and gave them both a squeeze. "You all are my real family now."

Louise remembered something important she'd meant to tell Rhonelle. "Honey, I want you to have my old TV. . . . No, I insist. You might need it for news, and I can use Christabelle's old one, now." They crossed the road and entered Don's Diner filled with the familiar sounds of clinking cutlery, friendly conversation, and the aromas of chicken and dumplings, fresh turnip greens, and best of all, hot apple pie.

CHAPTER TWENTY-FIVE

Pink Birthday Cake and Elvis

Before Thanksgiving, the calendar held a few other important events for the citizens of Peavine. First of all, the honorable Mayor Herbert Dalton had – for the first time in twenty years – an opponent who could be considered a serious challenge. "Buckshot" Bradley was really giving old man Dalton a run for his money. Younger, more energetic, and certainly easier on the eyes than Mayor Dalton (who had recently celebrated his seventy-third birthday), Buckshot brought the house down with his smart answers and folksy humor at the debate held four weeks before Election Day. The courthouse was packed to the gills with a boisterous audience, thanks to the excellent promotion of the members of the Ladies League of Political Activities (LLOPA for brevity).

Mrs. Vestaline Dalton took all this personally. She considered it an outrage for anyone to be so brazen as to contest her husband's divine right to lead the town of Peavine. After all the fine steward-ship and sacrifice he had selflessly given for twenty years, she couldn't comprehend the motives of such ungrateful citizens. Truthfully, what Vestaline couldn't face was what in the world she would do without the entire package of honor, prestige, and privileges that she felt were owed to *her* as the wife of the mayor.

Vestaline Dalton was founder and longtime reigning president of the Peavine Garden Club, as well as treasurer of LLOPA. She con-tinually sought reassurance of loyalty from her fellow club members and even went so far as to draw up a re-elect Mayor Dalton pledge for them all to sign until Maude Simmons reminded her that was illegal and smelt of fascism. Maude, a liberal Democrat, was the new LLOPA president and secretly delighted to be supporting Buckshot Bradley.

The most ardent and vocal Buckshot Bradley supporter was none other than Teenie Brice. He had become a trusted confidant of Sugar Bradley and an honorary "uncle" for all five of the Bradley children. He wore his "Buckshot is the Best" campaign buttons every day and printed up "Bradley for Mayor" T-shirts for every tenant in the Home-Sweet-Homes-On-Wheels Park. His poodle, Pitty Too, wore her tiny shirt, but Mavis' XXL version didn't quite fit. Rhonelle wore her extra-large Bradley shirt as a nightshirt and a couple of times while she did her yard work. Blatant campaigning just wasn't her style.

Rhonelle didn't need to be a psychic to have a pretty good idea as to who would win this race. Dalton's days were over and a new era for Peavine was about to begin with Buckshot Bradley. She could have recommended that statement as a campaign slogan for Teenie, but thought better of it. If word got around that she was making psychic predictions about politics, she'd *never* have a moment's peace.

Rhonelle's mind was in enough turmoil as it was. She was having vivid dreams about Sergio more frequently, and hardly any visits from Granny Laurite. For some reason she was having trouble getting in touch with her Granny, now that she wanted her help with Sergio. Rhonelle finally admitted to herself that she yearned to see him again (awake, not asleep). The problem was, she had no idea how to get in touch with him. He was still blocking her attempts to contact him telepathically. She feared she might be losing her psychic ability or that somehow losing contact with Granny Laurite had weakened her powers. It was all very troubling to her.

Rhonelle was experiencing a crisis of confidence for the first time in many years. She considered calling Krystal to get the information she needed about Sergio, yet that seemed humiliating to her. Intimidated by his note, which still laid unread and hidden in her underwear drawer, she feared opening it would only bring a definite rejection. Yet when she and Sergio came together in her dreams, everything was wonderful. The conundrum was enough to make her doubt her sanity.

Fortunately, during the daytime hours Rhonelle felt competent and in control. She was preoccupied with the everyday business of running the trailer and camper parks and didn't have time to stew over otherworldly concerns. To her surprise, she had never felt so alive and connected to the world of the living as she had in the past nine months. Perhaps that was why Granny Laurite wasn't coming to her lately. Maybe she wanted to give her granddaughter some room to flourish in her own life, instead of dwelling on those who had passed to another plane of existence.

Of all those who were no longer in this world, Rhonelle missed Doll Dumas the most. Hardly a day went by when she didn't think of her friend and wish she could sit and visit with her as they did so often while Doll was alive. She found herself talking to Doll anyway, as if she was listening from the Other Side. Rhonelle wasn't sure she could get through since Granny had told her Doll chose to *Move On*. Rhonelle wasn't familiar with the rules about that area of communication since all of her contact had been with those spirits still in the In Between. She certainly didn't want to disturb Doll's peace, yet there was no one she would rather talk to at this time.

Around midnight on October 24, which was Doll's birthday, Rhonelle lay on her red velvet bed, staring at the ceiling desperately missing her dear friend. She had just put the last of the pink birthday cake in the refrigerator and been so exhausted she had not even bothered to start her bedtime jazz on the record player.

She had hosted Doll's first posthumous birthday party in the lavender double-wide that evening. She'd scheduled it after the Diner closed so Don and Dorine could come. Marv, Pauline, Lucille, Tammy, Louise, Christabelle, and Vaudine Fortney (with Mr. Nasty on her shoulder) had attended. They sat around eating pink cake and vanilla ice cream, retelling their favorite memories of Doll. Ozelle and Sally Washington weren't able to come to the party, but sent over a beautiful arrangement of pink roses that morning.

Herman Junior had started the tradition, presenting his beloved wife Doll a dozen pink roses first thing in the morning on her birthday every year of their marriage. After Herman's death, Ozelle and Sally had continued the tradition, honoring every single one of Doll's birthdays with a dozen pink roses. That afternoon, Tammy and Lucille tearfully placed this year's bouquet on Doll's grave, next to that of her beloved Herman Junior.

Teenie and Mavis were late for the party. Teenie's campaign strategy meeting at Bradley Headquarters had run long. Most of the party talk was upbeat. They all agreed Doll would have been delighted with this year's Poodle Pageant, Buckshot's run for mayor and the extension of the camper park.

There were a few tears (mostly from Dorine), but the overall mood never became maudlin. Rhonelle hadn't shed a tear herself, but remained calm and cool as she listened to her friends share their experiences. Perhaps the effort to restrain her emotions explained why she felt worn out by the time her guests had left. Tears were flowing freely now as she pictured Doll's kind face, not as it was when she lay frail and dying but as Rhonelle saw Doll the stormy night Rhonelle first showed up at her door. Despite her obvious shock at the sight of Rhonelle, her dark eyes exaggerated by running mascara and her wild black hair billowing in the wind, Doll had invited her in and listened to the outrageous things Granny Laurite had told her to say.

I will always be grateful that you took me in that night dear friend. I miss you so much right now. If only I could tell you about this strange man who has come into my life. . . . I think I've fallen in love with him, but I am so scared I will lose him and I can't even really find him. I'm so confused, don't know what to do.

Very softly, Rhonelle heard music coming from the living room. She realized it was not her New Orleans jazz but Elvis singing "Are You Lonesome Tonight." A pink glow glimmered under the living room door. That pink glow seemed to fill her chest with warmth and serenity. She rose from her bed and opened the door with joyful certainty.

Doll, you're here!

The living room filled with a rosy pink glow and the faintest whiff of a Pall Mall cigarette. As Rhonelle stood stock still, the light coalesced into a figure sitting in the newly upholstered, overstuffed chair. As the luminous figure dimmed, there sat Doll Dumas, smiling at

Rhonelle. Doll exhaled a plume of cigarette smoke that formed into a perfect halo over her tall beehive hairdo.

"*Of course I'm here, Hon.*" Doll laughed at the astounded look on Rhonelle's face. "*I've been here all evening. When I feel that much love from my friends and family, I cain't help but show up! And you know my weakness for Don's pink birthday cakes!*"

Rhonelle gleefully jumped onto the red sofa and pulled a purple chenille throw over her bare knees. *I wasn't sure you could be reached by any of us since Granny told me you'd Moved On. The last thing I wanted was to disturb your peace . . . that, and I couldn't bear the thought of calling out to you and not getting an answer.*

"*Aw bless your heart, honey! I've heard every word you've uttered to me since I crossed. You of all people should have known that even if we Move On, a part of us is always with those we love. You can talk to me all you want. I'm always gonna be here to listen and help any way I can.*"

Rhonelle started to blubber and cry harder than she ever had since Doll's passing. Once somewhat composed, Rhonelle had to laugh at her own ignorance and profound sense of relief. Of *course* Doll would always be a part of her. How could she not know that?

So I assume you know about Sergio then? Rhonelle wiped her tears and gazed hungrily at her friend's kind face smiling back at her with one perfectly drawn eyebrow cocked high above the sparkling cat eye glasses.

"*Oh yeah, your Granny Laurite has let me know all about that feller. He's a pretty sexy guy, I must say!*" Doll blew another stream of smoke from the side of her mouth. The smoke formed the shape of a heart before dissolving and reforming into something resembling a face.

Rhonelle couldn't take her eyes off the various shapes Doll's cigarette smoke kept forming. It reminded her of the caterpillar from *Alice in Wonderland.* She had to shake her head and blink a few times to keep herself from falling into a trancelike state.

So you've been talking with Granny? Why has she been so distant from me lately? I hardly ever get a visit and she rarely answers my summons anymore.

Another possibility occurred to Rhonelle and just as she was about to ask, Doll spoke, *"No, you're Granny hasn't Moved On yet. She's still In Between waiting for* **you** *like she promised."* At the look of confusion on Rhonelle's face, Doll continued. *"First of all* **that's** *not happening any time soon, you've still got a long life ahead of you right here.*

"Laurite is changing. I saw the beginning of a kind of softening after she got to know Johnny. You remember him don't you?"

Rhonelle nodded. *He's Mary Lynn's fiancé that got killed on what was to be their wedding night. I suppose you became acquainted with him while you were In Between. I got a glimpse of him at your Memorial Bash standing next to Mary Lynn . . . but I thought he'd Moved On by now.*

Doll shrugged and looked around the room. *"Actually he decided to come back. I think some call it reincarnation."* She turned back to Rhonelle. *"That happens a lot more than you'd expect. Sometimes people decide to return for another chance to find their true soul mate, a kind of do-over. Pretty chancy decision to make, but Johnny always seemed a bit rash to me."*

Is Johnny Mary Lynn's true Soul Mate? Rhonelle was suddenly intensely interested in this do-over thing.

Doll stamped her cigarette butt in a small ashtray that appeared on the arm of the overstuffed chair. *"No Hon, her husband Leroy is the one for Mary Lynn. Johnny never even intended to marry Mary Lynn. His plan was to leave her in Memphis at the Peabody and let his friend there get her a job and do something about that baby.*

"He had a change of heart though on the way to pick her up that night, and decided to go through with it anyway even though he knew he was making a mistake. When he took his eyes off the road to look down at that silver cigarette lighter he never saw the truck that hit him."

Then . . . why did he come back?

Doll leaned forward and winked at Rhonelle. *"I'm sure we'll know something about that later when the time is right, but right now I'm here to talk about you, not Mary Lynn."* She rubbed the arms of what had once been her favorite chair.

"I love what you've done with the place. This new upholstery suits you to a T." Doll looked askance at the oversized "Bradley for Mayor" T-shirt and calf-high tube socks Rhonelle was wearing. *"I can't say the*

same about your choice of bedtime attire."

Rhonelle blushed and pulled the chenille throw a little higher. *I wasn't expecting company tonight.*

Doll raised her eyebrows and chuckled. *"That's not what I've been told. I hear you've had quite an interesting dream life lately."*

Rhonelle wondered just how much Doll did know. *But that's only dreams. The problem is I'm ready for more than that. I want a real relationship with him. Good lord, I can't believe I just said that. I've never wanted any kind of real relationship with a man before now.*

"Well you've got one with this guy honey!" Doll slapped her knee and began to cackle. *"It's just a pretty darn unconventional romance . . . and I'd expect no less from a gal like you.*

"Things are going to work out, you just wait and see." Doll reassured her. *"Your Granny and her new cohort on the Other Side are doing all they can on their end to see that you and Sergio get together pretty soon. The rest is up you and Sergio."*

This caused a jolt of excitement in Rhonelle's stomach. *How soon will I see him? Wait a minute; you said Granny has a new friend. Does he have long white hair and sort of look like an Indian?*

"Oh you've met White Cloud already?" Doll was impressed.

No I haven't met him; I just got a glimpse of his face once in a dream. I kind of wondered if he was . . . God or something. Rhonelle felt embarrassed to admit that last part.

"Well he does look a lot like those old paintings you always see. Ah, we all have such limited ideas till we learn better." Doll smiled kindly. *"White Cloud is a very wise old soul. I'm sure you'll get to know him before too long.*

"In the meantime Hon, you'd better go get you a pretty new nightgown . . . just in case. Sergio is coming to find you and you'd better be ready for him when he does."

Doll stood up and looked over to the bare spot where her old recliner used to sit beside the fake fireplace. Rhonelle had given it to Christabelle and was still looking for something more modern to replace it. Darla was on a mission to find a Herman Miller chair and ottoman. *"Darla will have your new chair next week. Yep I think that's gonna be just right in that corner,"* Doll said nonchalantly. *"I think it will be the perfect place for Mr. Sergio to park his butt."*

Rhonelle was accustomed to spirits talking about the future in this way. She slowly rose from the sofa, the chenille throw falling to the floor. Sensing Doll was about to leave, Rhonelle needed to ask one more question. *What should I do about that letter . . . from Sergio? For some reason I'm afraid to open it – afraid I will be hurt when I finally read it.*

"Rhonelle, honey it's about time you took a chance on opening up your heart. You got to stop being so afraid of losing someone you love. All you gotta do is love. Nobody is ever really lost. You ought to know that by now. You'll read that letter when the time is right."

Doll's face filled with light. The pink glow spread throughout the room and filled Rhonelle with warmth and an incredible sense of peace. As Doll began to disappear, Rhonelle heard her impart one last piece of advice.

"I think a red satin negligee would suit you real good!"

Rhonelle stood in the now darkened living room for a moment before she shambled back to her room and snuggled under the red velvet coverlet between her new satin sheets. *Thank you Doll, I love you . . . and I will be making a shopping trip to a Barbara Graves Intimate Fashions up in Little Rock real soon. I promise you that!*

CHAPTER TWENTY-SIX

The Gift

In the days following Doll's late night visit, several friends dropped by the double-wide to tell Rhonelle about dreams in which they were *positive* Doll had come back to tell them something important. First, there was Tammy, who glowingly recalled how pleased her Granny Doll was with her boyfriend Cecil. "It was the most wonderful dream, Aunt Rhonelle. I felt like Granny was really here. She told me Cecil was a truly good man and a good man is hard to find. She said to hang on to this one!" Tammy was beside herself with happiness. "It's like she gave us her blessing so we can like, go ahead and get . . . on with our plans."

Rhonelle wasn't fooled by Tammy's attempt at covering up the fact that she and Cecil were ready for marriage. Rhonelle expected an announcement sooner rather than later. Car restorations were going very well for Cecil. He had finished work on two of the five antique cars that the wealthy classic car collector had sent him. Now that he had found a large building to rent with the help of Fred Fortney, he was mostly working full time on these projects. It wouldn't be long before the restorations would pay a living wage.

Two days later, Lucille also mentioned having a very realistic dream about her mother talking to her. When Rhonelle asked what Doll had to say, Lucille merely winked and replied with a sly expression on her face, "She wholeheartedly approves of what ah . . . Bo and I have been up to – and let's just leave it at that."

On Wednesday, Rhonelle was about to take a couple of days off and drive her newly refurbished T-Bird up to Little Rock for some lingerie shopping when she got a call from her friend, Krystal, in New Orleans. Krystal was coming up to Arkansas that very weekend to buy some new inventory for her shop, Krystal Gardens, and wanted to stop by Peavine on her way to Hot Springs.

"Of course you can stay with me. I've been dying to hear about your honeymoon cruise," Rhonelle lied politely.

Then Krystal said something that stopped Rhonelle cold (or hot).

"I have to deliver a special gift to you from a very handsome guy you met back at my wedding. You remember Sergio don't you?" It was all Krystal could do to keep her giggles at bay.

Rhonelle could barely hide her excitement as her heart began to pound. "Yeah, I remember him, quite sexy for his age wasn't he. What kind of gift are you talking about?"

"Well Lil Sheba, it was the strangest thing," Krystal said. "I got a call from the La Chanteuse . . . you know, that special little boutique we love to go to?"

"Yes, what did *they* want?" Rhonelle didn't try to disguise her curiosity this time.

"Lorelei, you know her, the gal that owns the shop, called to tell me some man named Sergio had called her and ordered a special item. He told her to call and tell me that I was supposed to deliver it to a friend of mine called Little Sheba. Well she knew he must have been talking about you since we both have shopped there for years . . ."

"What is it?" Rhonelle interrupted Krystal's drawn out explanation. "What did he buy, for God's sake?"

"That's what's so *mysterious* about all this, it's gift wrapped and Lorelei said she had to promise not to tell me what was in this big ole box. Baby, it looks beautiful! She had her girls do a wonderful job of wrapping it with gold paper and a gorgeous satin ribbon. That Sergio may be a rascal, but I'll bet he has real good taste, being an artist and all."

Rhonelle began to suspect what this gift could be. "Is it very heavy – the box I mean?"

"Not too much, but it makes a thumping noise when I shake it," Krystal added with a giggle. "What's been going on between you and Sergio? I knew you two hit it off pretty good the night of my wedding. Too bad y'all had to cut things short 'cause of the bad weather."

Rhonelle avoided an answer by asking Krystal a question. "How much do you know about Sergio? I don't know where he lives or his last name. I haven't heard from him since the wedding." This was not entirely true if you count the dreams and the unopened note, but Rhonelle felt mostly honest in saying this.

"I'm surprised to hear that. Sammy told me he hadn't seen Sergio so smitten with anyone as he was with you!"

Rhonelle felt herself relax as pure joy swelled up in her chest, but she still kept her voice cool and slightly detached. "How long has Sammy known Sergio?"

"Oh baby, they go way back. They were like blood brothers when they was just boys running amok in the bayou. They kind of lost touch with each other when Sammy went to college and Sergio joined the Army for a while. It wasn't until the last few years – right before Sergio's grandfather passed away – that he came back here and he and Sammy got to be close again. Especially after he got rid of that bitchy wife of his. She hurt him pretty bad. Cleaned him out financially to boot."

Rhonelle wasn't interested in the ex-wife. She had suddenly remembered the gentle face of the wise old man with the long white hair she had seen in one of her dreams. "Krystal, was Sergio's grandfather Native American . . . you know, an Indian chief or something?"

"Girl, I keep forgetting about your psychic powers! As a matter of fact, he was an Indian, maybe with a little Spanish blood in there, too. Sergio used to call him an Indian name. Now what was that?"

"Could it have been White Cloud?" Rhonelle held her breath as she waited for Krystal to respond.

"Yes! That was it. He called him Grandfather White Cloud. I don't know why you ask me anything. You seem to have him pretty well figured out. Sounds like you are a lot more interested in him then you're letting on." Krystal sounded a bit suspicious of her friend.

"It's pretty complicated and I'm still trying to sort out my feelings," Rhonelle confessed. "I definitely am interested in what's in that gift box. How soon can you get up here?"

"I'll leave first thing Friday morning. I gotta get back home for Halloween next week. There's going to be a fantastic celebration in the quarter this year. You know how we love to play dress up down here!"

First thing in the morning for Krystal meant leaving town by eleven-thirty, so Rhonelle prepared for her friend to arrive in Peavine about time for an early supper . . . *after* she had opened that gift box to see what was inside.

At seven-thirty on Friday evening, Krystal appeared at the door of the lavender double-wide. It was her very first visit to the town of Peavine. She was two hours late because she had made a couple of wrong turns along the way. The large gift box wrapped in gold paper with a red satin ribbon and red silk rose was in her arms.

"Let me in, pour me a stiff drink, and let's get down to business baby," Krystal squealed as she kissed Rhonelle on the cheek and breezed past her, trailing a scented cloud of her favorite blend of Hove perfume. "Hey, this isn't bad at all. It's just like a real house in here," she called over her shoulder as she wandered into the living room.

Rhonelle glanced up and down the driveway before closing the door to be sure none of her neighbors had witnessed the arrival of her flamboyant old friend bearing such an ostentatiously wrapped present. There would be way too much explaining to do if Teenie or Tammy had seen this. To her relief no one was out because it was dinner time. Rhonelle poured Krystal bourbon on the rocks, decided on a double for herself and carried the drinks into the living room. The gift box was laid on the sofa. Krystal had found the bathroom.

Rhonelle heard water running as Krystal hollered out to her. "You got this bedroom tarted up like a bordello, honey! You sure there isn't something you're not telling me?" Rhonelle almost choked on her first sip of bourbon as she sat waiting for Krystal while staring at the box, which seemed to glow in the lamplight. When Krystal came back into the living room she trotted over to the sofa, grabbed up the drink, and took a long swig. "Ah, that's better. Well come on, baby, let's have a look." She nodded her head toward the gold box.

Rhonelle was resigned to having to share this with Krystal, along with some of her secrets concerning Sergio. She slowly rose from her chair, picked up the box, shook it a little, and sat back down with it across her lap. She knew exactly what was in it but that didn't diminish her excitement one bit. One more sip of bourbon and she was ready to open it.

"Oh my God, that is so *you*," Krystal exclaimed when Rhonelle pulled back the tissue paper in the box and held up the shimmering red satin negligee. The red satin slippers trimmed in red marabou were a nice addition. "I'll bet he even got the size right, didn't he . . . of course, Lorelei would have known that."

Krystal threw back the last of her drink and held out her glass for a refill.

"Baby, I think you got a whole lot of explaining to do."

After a couple more bourbons and a whopper of a ghost story, Rhonelle decided she'd better call David the florist to drive them over to Seymour's Tex-Mex for margaritas and a late dinner. By then it was nine o'clock and Don's kitchen would have closed for the evening. Rhonelle wasn't quite ready to introduce Krystal to Don and Dorine anyway. That could wait until breakfast, if she and Krystal got up in time. She remembered Louise Dolesanger was playing late at Seymour's since it was Friday night. *Krystal would enjoy some festive musical entertainment.*

Actually, Krystal enjoyed Louisa's antics on the organ a bit too much. Fortified with two margaritas and a bowl of cheese dip, Krystal decided to display some of her favorite bump-and-grind moves on the dance floor with David as her partner. Poor thing, he didn't know what to do or where to look. Rhonelle came to his rescue when she intervened to announce that their hot tamale dinners had arrived.

Krystal thought that was hilarious. "I'll show you some hot tamales!" she shouted as she danced her famous shimmy shake all the way back to their table.

The crowd that had watched her dance with David whistled and applauded their appreciation. Louise got a kick out of Krystal's uninhibited enjoyment of her latest dance tune arrangements. Rhonelle was speculating how best to fend off the inevitable questions that would arise concerning her friend. Folks in Peavine don't see many people like Krystal around town. Rhonelle decided Lucille would love to have witnessed that performance.

After dinner, David drove them out to the Too-Tite Tavern so Krystal could meet Lucille, have a nightcap, and watch open-mike night. Of course, Krystal wasn't content to just watch. Before she knew it, Rhonelle had been coerced into being a backup singer along with Lucille and David, while Krystal performed a full-throated rendition of "You Picked a Fine Time to Leave Me Lucille".

Lucille absolutely loved it! She wouldn't let David, Rhonelle, and Krystal leave the Tavern until after closing time – one o'clock in the morning.

Needless to say, Rhonelle and Krystal slept in the next day. Brunch was a strong pot of coffee and donuts. Teenie had brought by half a dozen glazed donuts bright and early and politely left them at her doorstep. He was in the habit of going on a run to the Donut Palace every Saturday morning and bringing donuts by to Rhonelle and Louise Dolesanger. He had bought extras that morning for Buckshot Bradley's campaign headquarters for the volunteer workers at the phone bank.

After tapping softly at the door and attempting to peer in through the window, Teenie gave up hope of meeting the colorful character whose antics had the Peavine gossip mill running overtime. He knew better than to wake Rhonelle before she was ready to get up. Maybe they would be over at Don's for lunch and he could introduce himself to this Krystal person. He sure hoped so.

Krystal had to get on her way to Hot Springs. She wasn't able to stay for lunch, much to the disappointment of Teenie, Marv, and Don, each of whom looked up expectantly every time the bells jangled on the Diner door throughout lunch hour. Rhonelle wasn't sure how much Krystal remembered of the details of her story about her strange psychic romance with Sergio. She wisely omitted that it was being nudged along by the efforts of three spirits from the Other Side. It must have sounded too weird even for someone as open minded as Krystal. When she left the lavender double-wide, Krystal wished Rhonelle good luck with "that guy," and didn't ask any more questions.

Rhonelle waved goodbye to her friend, watching her car pull onto the highway with a sense of relief tinged with a bit of sadness. Despite all of the drama and disruption that accompanied Krystal, she was like a sister to Rhonelle – kind of a loud, attention-seeking sister—but like family nonetheless.

Now that she was alone, she could once more take out her beautiful new gown and robe to get a better look at them. She took a long hot shower and put on makeup before trying on the whole set, including the slippers. Everything fit perfectly, of course. Rhonelle was so pleased; a squeal of delight escaped her lips when she looked at her reflection. She could not have done a better job of picking it out for herself.

Thank you, Doll, for making sure I have the proper attire!

She saw a quick flash of Sergio's face with a devilishly self-satisfied expression on it, followed by the faint echo of Doll's laughter.

CHAPTER TWENTY-SEVEN

An Unconventional Thanksgiving

Halloween that year was upstaged by the upcoming mayoral election. Teenie was so involved in the campaign, he didn't have time for the usual rounds with Pitty Too in her latest costume or the annual Halloween get together he and Mavis always hosted for friends, neighbors, and costumed AKC toy poodles. Mavis Brice was never one to complain, especially about her beloved Teenie, but Rhonelle could tell she was feeling left out. There was a noticeable droop in Mavis' face and shoulders as she lumbered up the steps to the deck of the double-wide. There, Mavis joined Rhonelle and Louise who were enjoying a sunny, day-after-Halloween afternoon.

Mavis' poodle, Pitty Too, followed at her heels, looking nervously up at her mistress. The dog's little tail that poked out of the back of her orange tutu was uncharacteristically tucked between her legs.

"Mind if we come up and set a spell," Mavis asked in her hoarse, whispery voice.

"It would be our pleasure." Rhonelle maneuvered one of the extra sturdy Adirondack chairs around for Mavis to sit in, and put a cushion down beside it for the dog.

"How's the world treating you, Mavis?" Louise was trying to sound cheerful, but also noticed a change in Mavis' usual easy going demeanor as she slowly lowered herself into the chair that creaked ominously upon receipt of her full weight.

Mavis' sighed loudly and gazed off toward the highway. Pitty ignored the cushion and hopped up onto Mavis' lap, snuggling into the copious folds of her orange and black printed caftan. During the long pause before Mavis said anything, Louise and Rhonelle looked at each other – eyebrows raised – and waited patiently.

Finally, Mavis realized she was expected to respond when Pitty pawed at her and gave a little whine. Mavis looked down and stroked the pup's curly top knot. After another deep sigh, she spoke. "Teenie's just not been himself lately." A handkerchief appeared from a hiding place up her sleeve and she wiped at the corner of each eye. "This'd be the first time he's ever missed out on our Halloween festivities. Politics has taken him over." She looked up at Rhonelle with fear in her eyes. "You don't suppose he's possessed or something, do you?"

Louise had to bite her lip to keep from laughing at the notion. She figured Mavis had been watching too many old Halloween thrillers lately. "Oh honey, he's not anymore possessed with politics than many another man I've seen," she reassured her. "My husband got so carried away one year with running for justice of the peace, I swore I'd leave him if he ever tried that again."

Rhonelle patted Mavis on her arm. "Don't worry about Teenie. He will be back to the poodle business as usual soon as the election is over. There's only five more days left to go."

Mavis slowly shook her head. "I don't think he'll *ever* be the same after being in such tall cotton." She glanced up at Rhonelle with a look of shame. "Don't get me wrong. I'm real proud he has done such a good job of organizing Buckshot's campaign. It's just . . . I don't fit in with that world. He's done forgot all about Pitty and me." A shuddering sob escaped her.

Rhonelle rose from her chair and squatted down in front of Mavis so she could look directly into her face. "Mavis Brice, how many times has Teenie proclaimed you are the love of his life?" When all Mavis could respond with was a sniff into her handkerchief, Rhonelle gently took hold of her large forearms. "You two are *soul mates*, and don't you forget it. Teenie is having the time of his life right now, and doing a fine thing for this community."

Louise chimed in with her opinion. "Lord knows we needed to get shed of old Mayor Dalton and elect somebody new with fresh ideas. I'd never have believed we could do that until Teenie convinced me Buckshot would be a great mayor."

Rhonelle could see that Mavis was feeling a little less forlorn. "Just bear with Teenie a little while longer. It would devastate him to think he'd hurt your feelings. I don't know what he'd do without your love and support, Mavis."

This brought a tiny little smile to Mavis' face. "Thanks girls. I just needed to vent a little." (If this was venting, it had to be the mildest form Rhonelle had ever witnessed.)

Mavis brightened up and her eyes regained their twinkle. "My man may be small but he sure is mighty, ain't he?"

Rhonelle stood up and put her hands on her hips. "That is for sure!" she said emphatically, before sitting back down in her chair. "Now back to the business at hand.

"Louise and I were just discussing Thanksgiving. We're going to have a big gathering over at Don's Diner this year. Louise and I were doing a head count on who all will be there." She picked up a small notebook and pencil from the table beside her chair. "Anybody you can think of we should include that we might have missed?"

Louise was relieved to change the subject and see her friend Mavis' mood return to normal. She started by explaining in a roundabout way the catalyst for the idea of an unconventional Thanksgiving dinner at the Diner. "My grandson Gary is coming with his little friend, Jay. I wonder if David might like to come too since he had such a good time with those boys when he went down to New Orleans."

Mavis pondered a moment. "What about that new waitress at the Diner? She might be glad to be excused from spending the day with her family. She could tell them that she had to work."

"Why that's a great idea, Mavis," Louise agreed enthusiastically. "Her mother is always so hard on her – going on about how she dresses too plain and won't wear a bit of makeup. The poor girl confided to me the other day that her daddy usually gets snookered in front of the football games on the TV every Thanksgiving. My goodness what a shame that must be," Louise tut-tutted.

"Well I'm all for comfort, and Lord knows I never did use make-up," Mavis added. "But if you ask me, Lorena Mae puts a might too much effort into trying to look plain. She could pass for one of them Mennonite girls."

Rhonelle knew Lorena's choices had nothing to do with religion but everything to do with making her mother crazy. "I'll bet you'd see quite a makeover if Lorena ever decided to catch the eye of a boy she fancies."

Mavis started to laugh quietly. "I know who'd be happy to help out with that. Tammy is trying to figure a way to get Shirleen to pounce on her the way she did you, Rhonelle."

"I've never regretted that intervention," Rhonelle admitted as she ran her fingers through her black hair. *I'm more grateful than they can imagine.*

"By the way, we'll have to be sure Shirleen joins us this year, too."

With Mavis restored to good humor, the three women sat on the deck making their plans until the sun set and it was time to go in for supper.

As Rhonelle had predicted, Buckshot Bradley won the mayoral race handily. Old man Dalton seemed to shrink three sizes while Teenie felt six feet tall. He stayed up late monitoring the vote count at City Hall before going to the post-election victory party at the VFW Hut. Bo Astor was on the air at KPEW until all the votes were counted. His new live broadcast van provided on-the-spot reporting. Teenie dancing on the table at the victory party was the highlight of the evening. That probably wouldn't have occurred had Mavis been there.

Mavis had considered going to the party but fell asleep before all the votes were counted. Teenie woke her up with a joyful late night phone call to give her the results. Telling him to go on without her, Mavis went back to sleep, grateful in the knowledge that soon she'd have her old familiar Teenie back (now that all this political nonsense was over).

Teenie got a ride home with Tad Bradley at one in the morning. He'd had three wine spritzers and was feeling pretty tipsy. The next day he strutted around town with a huge grin on his face while removing political signs and cleaning up campaign headquarters. It wasn't until the next day he began to feel the letdown, realizing all the excitement was over. Mavis was aware of the downturn in his mood and hoped part of it was due to fatigue. After two weeks passed by and her little man still appeared listless, it began to concern her.

On a Saturday morning, she and Teenie were sitting in their front yard eating donuts and watching Pitty Too have a romp with Sugar Bradley's pup, Princess, (who was spending the weekend while the Bradleys went on a trip) when they spied Tammy leaving the Fortneys' trailer after giving a long kiss goodbye to Cecil. He was the sole occupant of that trailer since Vaudine and Fred had moved over to Pastor Astor's house.

Teenie sat bolt upright in his chair. "Well, I'll be . . . I don't think I saw Tammy going in there. She must have come over pretty early this morning for me to have missed her." He stood up and waved at her and shouted, "Good morning, Tammy honey!"

Tammy swirled around quickly and her pretty face turned a deep shade of pink when she saw the Brices watching from across the street. "Oh! Hi Teenie Pop – Auntie Mavis . . . uh, sorry I can't visit. I have tap class this morning." She turned and walked very quickly up the road toward her house. "Well that's odd." Teenie sat back down as he watched his beloved Tammy hot foot it off in the opposite direction. "What do you suppose she was doing over there so early of a morning?"

Mavis watched Teenie and waited apprehensively as the reality of the "Tammy and Cecil situation" began to sink in.

"Oh my God!" Teenie had put two and two together. "You don't suppose our little Tammy could have been . . ." He looked over at Mavis helplessly.

Mavis simply nodded her head and said, "Uh hmm."

Teenie didn't know whether to be outraged, shocked or sad so he settled for all three. "You mean our little Tammy . . ." he sputtered.

"Ain't no innocent little girl anymore," Mavis finished for him.

Privately, Mavis was not at all surprised. She and Rhonelle had discussed Tammy and Cecil's burgeoning romance on several occasions lately. She hated for Teenie to feel the sense of betrayal he must be experiencing, but that was a whole lot better than moping around the way he had been lately. Her mighty little man was beginning to come back to himself at last.

Over the days leading up to Thanksgiving, Mavis was able to soothe Teenie's ruffled feathers a bit by reminding him that they needed as much tranquility as possible for the upcoming gathering of friends, family and neighbors. She advised him not to tell Marv what they had witnessed. There was enough bad blood between Marv and Fred Fortney over the gambling thing as it was. For Marv to find out his precious Tammy had been carrying on in a carnal fashion with Fred's godson had the potential to destroy the fragile truce the two men adopted for the sake of the young couple.

The unconventional Thanksgiving dinner at Don's turned out to be a large gathering. A lot of guests wanted to come and experience a new and fun holiday experiment to neutralize the occasional corrosive tensions that sometimes mar family holiday dinners.

It proved a welcome opportunity for several families to start a new tradition. Even the Bradley family accepted Teenie's invitation to join them. Rhonelle and Darla put a great deal of thought into seating arrangements, setting out a place card for each guest. They intentionally placed certain groups together or at separate tables to keep the dinner conversations lively and congenial.

Shirleen and her husband came in from Nashville. The Party Girls, Kristy and Misty, and their husbands arrived early from Benton to help with the cooking. They occupied three of the Dew Drop Inn Cottages. Louise Dolesanger's grandson Gary and his "little friend" Jay drove up late on Tuesday so they could help with setup. They also reserved a cottage.

Rupert and Darla were able to come because Reverend Joe Don Astor and his family were going to visit his wife's people in Mississippi. This granted Bo Astor and the Fortneys the freedom to come join in. They were planning to do so, anyway.

Pastor Astor had his dinner at the Mansion Rest Home, where he was granted the honor of leading the blessing. Christabelle decided to stay there too since she had so many activities planned for the residents and their families. She was planning to come by that night for leftovers, always her favorite part of Thanksgiving.

At the last minute, Lorena Mae Monett decided she would attend, bringing an extra large frozen pizza as her contribution to the potluck. (All the kids loved that!) She caused quite a stir when she showed up. Ditching her usual drab brown wardrobe, she wore a nice little hand-me-down blue mini dress given to her by Tammy. A touch of pink lip-gloss brightened up her complexion, and she actually went so far as to apply some rose blusher to her cheeks.

Shirleen had heard about Lorena Mae from Lucille and watched her from across the room after Tammy pointed her out. Shirleen saw a world of possibilities in that face, sort of like a clean canvas presented to an artist. With a few blonde highlights and a new hairstyle, she knew she could transform Lorena's dull brown pageboy into something much more becoming. Shirleen knew she would have to approach Lorena Mae carefully though, so as not to scare her off. Shirleen wasn't known for subtly when it came to giving beauty tips.

Teenie had commiserated with Don, Dorine, and Mavis ahead of time on the menu and potluck assignments so there was a wide variety and nobody had to prepare more than one item. This was a real break for Don. His sole duty on this day was to stay out of the kitchen and play the host. He stood at the door and proudly welcomed each guest, directing them to the buffet tables.

Dorine held court while sitting at her favorite booth by the window, her feet propped up on a chair. She was wearing her fancy gold house shoes with the curled up toes and bright orange socks. Dorine's poodle Dolly was in her lap wearing a pilgrim outfit. Mavis sat across from them holding Pitty Too in a darling little turkey costume. Whutzit, Kristy's weird little mixed breed mutt, cowered under the table shivering with excitement.

David brought flower arrangements for each table to complement the orange and yellow tablecloths Darla had found to use instead of Don and Dorine's usual paper ones. Dorine's granddaughter, Dora Lee, helped place paper napkins with brightly colored turkeys on them and set each table with steel flatware. There would be no plastic forks today. Vaudine's collection of ceramic turkey salt and pepper sets completed the festive decorations.

Turkey roasting duties were shared by Kristy and Misty in Don's kitchen. Lucille set up her big deep fryer in the courtyard. Unfortunately, the Party Girls slept too late and managed to overcook the twenty-five pound turkey they put on to roast at three in the morning. Lucille's two juicy deep-fried ones more than made up for their *faux pas*.

To complete the varieties of protein, Buckshot Bradley brought a platter of his famous smoked venison and Marv and Pauline baked a whole Petit Jean ham. Don had insisted on baking pies, but did so the day before. The cleanup crew consisted of all the able-bodied young men: Cecil, the Bradley boys, and Kristy and Misty's spouses. They knew they would get to watch the football games as a reward over in Don and Dorine's den.

Louise and Bo were in charge of musical entertainment. Bo had a playlist prerecorded for the radio suitable for background during the dinner. Gary moved his grandmother's small practice organ over and Louise played some favorite tunes before dinner, while guests were arriving and laying out their food on the buffet. Intoxicating aromas had the guests ravenous by the time the dinner was announced at one-thirty. The men were slobbering hungry.

Right before the stampede to the dinner buffet, Louise began to play "We Gather Together" on her organ. All the guests took a cue from Don and Dorine's family, joining hands and forming a convoluted circle around the dining room. Everyone was included.

Dorine had to holler at Kristy to come on out of the kitchen and quit trying to fool with her dried-out turkey. "Give up on it Hon, we can grind the meat and make soup out of the carcass later this evening!"

Kristy burst out of the kitchen wiping her hands on her apron, her hair standing on end and took her place between her husband and Misty. Misty gave her a wink and whispered, "That's okay. They're already so full of your cheese dip, they'll never miss it."

With everybody in place, Louise jumped up from the organ and happily joined the circle between her beloved grandson, Gary, and his beloved Jay. Dora Lee had requested the honor of saying the blessing, so after she proudly chanted, "God is great, God is good and we thank Him for our food." Everybody shouted "Amen!" Then dinner was officially served.

Seymour and Lolita won the prize for the most unconventional Thanksgiving offering – their famous hot tamales! A wide variety of salads, including tomato aspic (largely untouched), green bean casseroles, corn soufflés, four kinds of stuffing (Rhonelle had made her granny's old recipe for oyster dressing), twice-baked potatoes, sweet potato casserole, and all the meats were laid out on three long tables buffet style. Everybody helped themselves and went back for seconds. The desserts were arranged up on the counter and in the pie case.

Right before dessert, Lucille took Dorine aside and told her she had a very special announcement to make.

"Don't let it go on too long, honey," Dorine advised. "You know everybody's been eyeing Don's pies, and those men will want to get to the den in time to watch their games."

"It won't take more than a few minutes," Lucille said, grinning ear to ear. "I'll give everybody a chance to get their coffee … and then I promise we will cause some excitement." She nodded at Bo, who turned off the background music. Taking this as her cue, Louise got up from her table and trotted excitedly over to the organ. That caught the attention of half the diners. As they wondered what was about to happen, Lucille stood at the table where she had been sitting with Bo, Tammy, Cecil, Buckshot and Sugar Bradley, and the Brices.

Lucille tapped the side of her water glass loudly with a fork and waited for the room to get quiet. "Excuse me y'all. I got me a big announcement to make."

Rhonelle knew what was coming and carefully watched the faces of friends scattered around the room. Cecil pulled at his collar and straightened his tie, blushing deep red all the way to up to his ears. Tammy was happily radiant.

Lucille, delighted to break the news, felt her eyes begin to fill with tears as she announced, "We are gonna have us a wedding. . . . My Tammy and her fella Cecil have decided to get hitched!"

Louise started playing "Here Comes the Bride" as everybody

cheered the happy young couple. Lucille made them stand up. Tammy waved exuberantly, flashing her tiny diamond engagement ring. Cecil was much shyer. It was all he could do to acknowledge the cheers with his head held high and a couple of nods and waves. Rhonelle knew he was merely trying to hide his emotions. He was deeply in love with Tammy and still amazed by the fact she loved him back with so much ferocity. He also was a little intimidated by so much attention paid to something as personal as his relationship with Tammy.

Teenie was overcome with relief and began to cry as he hugged first Mavis then Tammy around their waists. Tammy and her mother hugged and cried. Buckshot reached over to congratulate Cecil with a firm handshake. Teenie hugged Sugar then Mavis then Tammy again.

Marv and Pauline were at the table with Rhonelle. Pauline was thrilled with the news, yet glanced nervously over at Marv who was applauding politely. His face wore a pained smile. Rhonelle noticed a small twitch in his cheek as he clenched his teeth and stared icily at Cecil. Marv displayed all the protective instincts of a doting father. In his eyes, *nobody* was good enough for his little girl, especially someone connected so closely with Fred Fortney.

Pauline was already heading over to Tammy and Cecil to give her congratulations. Rhonelle, Lucille, Mavis and Pauline were well aware for months that Tammy and Cecil had marriage on their minds. The sooner it came about the better in their point of view. Marv gulped the dregs of his wine, and in that moment resigned himself to make the best of the situation . . . for Tammy's sake.

Rhonelle quickly refilled his glass and pulled him toward her so he could hear her over the noise in the room. "I think a toast to the happy couple is in order, don't you? I'll let you do the honors." She smiled at him as if to say *I know what you're going through*. Marv looked at Rhonelle and grinned back. He clanked his spoon against his glass, Pauline jerked her head around at the sound. The look on her face was an urgent mute plea for him to *please be nice*.

"I have a toast to make," he said loudly, raising his glass. "Here's to the most beautiful girl in the world – uh, next to my Pauline, of course – and the luckiest guy I know . . . Tammy and Cecil!"

CHAPTER TWENTY-EIGHT

So Now What?

Back to the First Day of the Thirty-Foot Elvis
December 1: In the Lavender Double-Wide

Rhonelle sat staring out the picture window. The line of cars proceeded slowly along the highway barely visible beyond the pecan trees. The crowd drawn to gawk at the gleaming statue of Elvis had grown even larger.

Her half-finished mug of café au lait had turned cold. An hour had gone by since Lucille and Bo left her with the news of their engagement, and there she sat ruminating over all that had happened in the past eleven months. Rhonelle was still absolutely dumbfounded by the discovery she had made that morning.

His name was on the sculpture: Sergio Mandell!
I know that has to be him. All this time he's been secretly working with Lucille and Bo. Did they tell him about me? I've got to hand it to Lucille; she's finally learned how to keep things from me. I'm sure she doesn't have a clue that her secret artist also happens to be my secret . . . well, whatever he is.

Granny you have outdone yourself with this maneuver . . . and I know you must have been conspiring with Sergio's grandfather!

Rhonelle first heard the familiar cackle . . . before a tiny silver spark grew into a bright glowing light. The light dimmed and formed itself into the apparition of her Granny Laurite sitting on the Herman Miller chair, her bare feet propped up on the ottoman.

"*I tink your man gonna like dis chair. I tole you he a comin', Cherie . . . jus as soon as you really ready for him,*" Laurite said as she wiggled her toes and looked appreciatively at Rhonelle's new décor. When she took a good look at Rhonelle in her red satin negligee, her eyebrows shot up and she let out a low whistle.

"He really gonna like dat red gown you got on." She was grinning so big her gold tooth shone brightly.

He **ought** *to like it since he's the one that bought it for me, but I suppose you already knew that.* Rhonelle couldn't keep from laughing at the whole situation. She was absolutely giddy at the moment and very glad to have her Granny Laurite back with her after such a long absence.

Something suddenly occurred to her – Sergio could very well be right there in Peavine. *Granny, is he here in Peavine? I wonder if he knows I live here.*

"He knows it now!" Granny was delighted. *"I tink after dat big drama you put on out by de statue – he got him a big surprise, too!"*

So he **is** *here in Peavine. So now what?* Despite her happiness, Rhonelle was at a loss as to what to do next. She had never felt this way about a man before.

"You can start by reading that note he left you in New Orleans." To Rhonelle's surprise, Doll Dumas was standing right beside her. *"I believe now would be the right time, don't you think Laurite?"*

Granny Laurite nodded and grinned in agreement.

Rhonelle slowly rose from her chair, feeling as if she was floating into her bedroom. All the fears she had invested around the simple act of opening that envelope to read Sergio's letter slid aside as easily as the chenille throw fell from her lap onto the floor.

To her surprise, the note was no longer buried under her lace panties but laying right on top of her new bras. The white envelope gleamed in the low light of the bedroom when she opened the lingerie drawer. As if in another of her dreams, she picked up the envelope and tore it open. At that moment, Rhonelle felt the last of her resistance melt away.

Earlier That Day ...

Sergio Mandell was sleeping heavily and late in Dew Drop Inn

Cottage #3, exhausted from the all the work and planning over the past week and a half. Engineering and overseeing the disassembly of the thirty-foot statue of Elvis, securing and loading the sections, then driving from Memphis was enough stress. But the fact that his crew had barely enough time to reassemble and erect the statue *in the dead of night* made it truly a gargantuan task.

The crew of seven, three of them sculpture students from the Memphis College of Arts, was staying in a small motel north of town. The lady who hired him for this gig insisted that he stay in this cottage, the better to witness the reaction of the townspeople when they awoke to find his fiberglass masterpiece smack in the middle of their municipal park. She assured him it would be the biggest Christmas surprise this town ever had.

When Lucille first appeared at his studio back in January, with her outrageous idea, Sergio thought she must be crazy. However, after doing some research and receiving a hefty down payment, Sergio was convinced he could pull it off. He had enlarged his studio space and hired an assistant. This all transpired a couple of weeks before he went to New Orleans for his friend Sammy's wedding. Little had he known how that trip would change his life, the fateful evening he first met Rhonelle.

Lucky for him, Sergio had been forced to leave New Orleans before falling so far under Rhonelle's spell he'd never be able to get back to the huge project ahead of him. Also, he sensed that neither of them was ready for a commitment. He had his guard up after his nasty divorce. And Rhonelle seemed to hide a definite fear of loss beneath her cool attitude.

Now that he had finally completed the installation of the greatest sculpture project of his career, Sergio could relax. Perhaps he would allow himself to find her and experience more of their relationship than just those dreams. Unless she had decided to block his psychic messages, it shouldn't take very long for them to get together again.

Still in bed, Sergio stretched luxuriously with his eyes closed, smiling at her image in his mind. He wondered what she must have thought when she opened that nightgown. He had slipped up and allowed himself a telepathic peek at her for only an instant when she tried it on for the first time. It took a considerable amount of will-power for him to wait all this time and not mention to Sammy's wife Krystal how interested he was in Rhonelle. He didn't even want to ask where she lived.

"Wake up, Little Eagle. You will miss a wonderful thing if you sleep any longer."

That was the pet name that only one person had called him ever since he was a boy. Sergio opened his eyes and was greeted by the sight of Grandfather White Cloud sitting in the easy chair across the room. His heart filled with the warmth of unconditional love that he always experienced in the presence of his grandfather. The spirit's face was crinkled in that mischievous smile that always meant something exciting was about to happen. Before Sergio could rise from his bed, the apparition quickly dissolved.

He became aware of the sounds of cars honking and voices coming from outside. Glancing at the clock on the bedside table, he noted it was almost eleven o'clock. Excitement clutched at Sergio's stomach as he realized his sculpture must be drawing a crowd. What artist could resist the urge to see the reaction to his biggest masterpiece! Dressing hurriedly and shivering a bit from the cold, Sergio left the cottage, walking to the highway and toward the city park.

He was astonished at the commotion: cars were lined up bumper to bumper. On both sides of the highway, pedestrian crowds of men, women, and children headed toward the park where he'd installed the Thirty-Foot Elvis only a few hours earlier. Sergio's heart began to pound as he walked faster, weaving in and out of the crowd toward the park. He was eager to see how his masterpiece looked in the daylight.

When he arrived at the park, it was thick with gawkers. Sergio positioned himself beside a large oak tree so he could watch without drawing attention to himself. Then he noticed a change in the volume of nearby conversations. He heard a woman in front of him murmur to the man next to her, "Here she comes now. Can't wait to see what she does when she sees *this*."

"Do ya suppose *she* knew about it ahead of time? Wowie kazowie, look at what she's got on!" The man next to him was craning his head around for a better look. Sergio followed the man's gaze to get a better view. A hush fell over the crowd as it parted to reveal a tall woman with thick black hair wearing nothing but a red satin and lace night-gown and robe that billowed and whipped about her in the cold wind.

It's her! Rhonelle has been here all this time? Sergio was dumbfound-ed. His knees almost buckled as he watched her go up to the base of the statue and run her hand across the inscription of his signature. He felt his entire body react to her touching his name. She looked up and turned her head in his direction. Not knowing what else to do, he ducked behind the oak tree. There, Sergio attempted to calm his rac-ing heart and regain his breath. Then he started to laugh out loud at himself for acting like a shy teenager. *Grandfather, you trickster! How on earth and heaven have you pulled this off?*

Nearby, a small boy looked up curiously at this strange man whose gray hair was pulled back in a ponytail laughing so hard tears were streaming down his cheeks.

"You're not from around here are you mister," the boy said as he squinted up at Sergio.

"No son, just passing through. But I might stay a little while after all." Sergio peeked back around the tree and watched Rhonelle as she was approached by none other than that Lucille woman who had hired him to do this job. The DJ guy that had accompanied her was put-ting his jacket around Rhonelle and the two of them were leading her away. Following them unseen from a distance, Sergio watched the threesome cross the highway and enter a lavender double-wide trailer.

He looked to his right and there was Don's Diner. Realizing he was extremely hungry and in need of a strong cup of coffee, Sergio entered the crowded restaurant, taking a booth near the back with a clear view of the trailer park across the highway. He had a strong premonition that he could find the information he needed from the frazzle-haired old waitress wearily shuffling toward him in fuzzy pink house shoes.

CHAPTER TWENTY-NINE

The Long-Unread Letter

Rhonelle sat on the edge of her bed holding the letter in her hands. She was excited yet calm at the same time, with no sense of dread about the contents. She felt a small click in her heart as the lock that had held her deeply felt emotions hidden away for so long finally came undone. The warmth of love that came pouring forth grew stronger as she unfolded Sergio's letter and began to read.

My Dear Little Sheba,

I'm sorry I had to leave New Orleans so abruptly and get back to my studio, but I know it is probably the best thing for me to do at this point in my life. I might have frightened you away had I stayed. You and I know very little and yet everything about each other. For the time being there will be no last names and no addresses. Isn't that how you prefer it?

Neither of us is ready for a relationship right now. There are too many other things in the way. I do not even expect you to read this letter until you are completely ready for us to move onto another level.

Now that you ARE reading it — I will sense it and I'll know the time is right and you are finally ready for me to find you. Something tells me I probably will be closer than you think!

Until then I will have to be satisfied to see you only in my dreams.

Your Sheik of Araby (Sergio Mandell)

CHAPTER THIRTY

Hot Chocolate Celebration

Rhonelle sat staring at Sergio's letter after reading it three times in a row. She was delighted to be reassured of his feelings toward her, but also very impressed with his substantial psychic ability and intuition. His energy felt closer and more dynamic to her now than when they were together in New Orleans. Everything finally began to fall perfectly into place.

Oh boy, I have definitely met my match. Sergio is a more talented psychic than I realized. And what an artist! I still can't figure out how he was able to pull off that Thirty-Foot Elvis . . . overnight!

I'm sure I'll get to hear all about that very soon.

Rhonelle stood up and reached for the phone just as it began to ring. Lucille was on the line.

"Hey girl, I've got somebody I want you to meet," Lucille said, with a load of smug self-satisfaction.

Rhonelle couldn't resist showing off a little. "It wouldn't be the artist Sergio Mandell himself by any chance?"

"Yes it is!" Lucille was only slightly surprised. "Just wait till you get a look at him, though. If ever I saw a guy that's your type of fella, it's this Sergio."

"Let me guess," Rhonelle said. She could see Sergio so clearly in her mind, he might as well have been standing in right in front of her. "He's not too tall, plenty of muscles, handsome face, about my age, and wears his long gray hair pulled back in a ponytail. All in all it's a very sexy combination."

There was a long pause before Lucille said anything. "Rhonelle, dang it . . . can't I keep *anything* a secret from you?! Well I'm not even gonna ask how you know all that, but you're right as usual." Lucille gave a wicked snicker. "I think you'd better show up tonight at Don's Diner anyway. They don't grow guys like him here in Peavine."

Lucille was making calls to about fifty of her and Bo's nearest and dearest, inviting them to gather at Don's Diner that night for hot chocolate and cookies at eight. She figured it was time that she and Bo announced their engagement.

That afternoon, Lucille and Bo had hired a dozen men to hang red Christmas lights in Herman Park to decorate the area surrounding the Thirty-Foot Elvis. A lighting ceremony was scheduled for that evening at seven-thirty. Bo was going to have the live broadcast van there to carry coverage on KPEW and play Christmas music.

"Won't that be a gorgeous sight?" Lucille was so pleased with herself. "We've ordered four thousand strings of red twinkle lights. This will be the biggest, best Christmas display Peavine has ever seen! You were surprised a little bit weren't you?"

Rhonelle pulled aside her red drapes and gazed out her window. "Lucille, you pulled off a big one. I was more than a little bit surprised! Astonished is a more apt description."

"Oh goodie!" Lucille was dancing with excitement. "So we'll see you at the park at seven and then we can all walk down to Don's for hot chocolate. I've invited Sergio Mandell to join us. He was going to go back to Memphis today but changed his mind and is staying an extra night. I put him up at one of the Dew Drop cottages last night. He's so cool, Rhonelle. You have *got* to meet him."

"I'm sure I will enjoy that. See you at the park at seven." Rhonelle looked around in dismay at the clutter in her bedroom. "I've got to go now dear. My house is a mess and I haven't even gotten dressed yet. Bye, Lucille."

This ought to be an interesting evening.

The lighting ceremony had been announced throughout the day on KPEW so a large crowd was gathered by six-thirty that evening – only minutes after the last string of lights were hung. Lucille had bought a small generator to power the display. Bo had the KPEW van parked nearby blasting a live feed from the station, drowning out the generator's loud hum.

Rhonelle had spent the afternoon cleaning up her trailer and made a last-minute run to the Piggly Wiggly for extra provisions. She didn't want to eat lunch over at Don's and take the chance of running into Sergio before she was ready. She took a nap, then a long bubble bath before carefully selecting her attire. Then came the artistry of her makeup. Sergio was on her turf now and she wanted to exercise a little bit of control over the situation. (She was positive she would lose whatever tiny amount of control she believed she had over him the moment she set eyes on him.)

Don's Diner had been slammed with customers all day because of the huge number of people coming to see the Elvis statue. Since it was a Saturday, Darla was there but she and Lorena couldn't handle the crowds. Tammy and Amber had to come over to help out. Dorine was so worn out by eleven o'clock it was all she could do to just sit behind the counter managing the cash register. By noon she reckoned they had made as much money as they normally brought in over a week's time.

First thing Don did after he spied the giant Elvis on his daily trip to the grocer was to turn back for home and call Bo Astor. He knew Bo had to have been in on this somehow. Bo fessed up and in his excitement told Don about his proposal of marriage to Lucille at the base of the statue. He and Lucille were on their way out the door that very moment to go to the jewelry store, after waking up old Mr. Falkner to open early before Lucille could change her mind.

Don hooted and slapped his knee so loud, he woke up Dorine. Of course, she had to know what the heck was going on. When Don told her, she's the one that insisted on the cocoa and cookie party so they could have a proper announcement to all their friends. Don loved that idea. Before he let Bo get off the phone he asked him for "Elvis food" suggestions.

Fortunately, Don had stocked up on plenty of peanut butter, bananas, and white bread when he got to the grocery store. A peck of last-of-the-season green tomatoes he'd picked from his garden before the cold weather made a big mess of fried green tomatoes to go with grilled peanut butter and banana sandwiches. Don filled in the menu with a huge pot of chili (always popular on a cold day) and plenty of coconut cream pie.

The hungry crowds had started pouring into Don's Diner at breakfast and continued nonstop until four-thirty, when the Diner closed early because they ran out of food. Don was plum tuckered by then, even with his son Donnie there to help with the cooking.

Tammy and Amber stayed after closing to bake cookies for the party. They also made sure plenty of hot chocolate mix was on hand.

Tammy was thrilled about her mother's engagement. Lucille had called her early that morning to share the good news – not only of her and Bo's engagement, but also about the huge Elvis statue in honor of Granny Doll. She had wanted to let Tammy in on the Thirty-Foot Elvis Christmas surprise sooner, but knew her daughter was the worst when it came to keeping a secret.

Luckily, Tammy and Cecil were at Tammy's house this Saturday morning, far away from Teenie's vigilant watch, and carefully avoiding Marv and Pauline.

"Oh Cecil," she sobbed prettily, tears spilling down her beautiful cheeks. "This will be my Momma's very first wedding, too. I want to do all I can to make it special for her. I just wish my Granny Doll could be here to see this. It would have made her so proud."

"Aw honey, please don't cry." Cecil, a huge lump in his throat, took her into his arms and patted her back helplessly. Her tears always completely undid him. "I'm sure your Granny is watching down from heaven, and is so happy for you and your momma she's probably dancing a jig up there right now."

That brought a smile to Tammy's face. She chuckled at the thought of Granny Doll dancing a jig. "Oh sweetie, you always know how to make me feel better," she said as she wiped her face on the sleeve of Cecil's plaid shirt she was wearing instead of pajamas. "I love you sooooo much!" She hugged him tightly, then playfully dove back under the covers. "It's still early," she giggled. "We don't have to get up yet. That big ole Elvis will just have to wait on us a little bit longer."

Once again, Cecil wondered what he had done to deserve such happiness. Whatever it was … All he could think was *Thank you Lord, thank you Jesus for making me the luckiest man on earth!*

Rhonelle had everything ready by six o'clock that evening. She had the trailer tidied up, with clean satin sheets on her bed and plenty of scented candles placed strategically around the bedroom and bath. She'd opened a good bottle of red wine and set out two goblets beside it. She had arranged a small platter of cheeses, olives and sliced smoked sausage, and placed it in the fridge. Her hair and makeup were the best she could manage without Shirleen. The red lipstick matched her low-cut red sweater worn over a long black skirt and boots. She topped that off with the velvet-beaded shawl from New Orleans artfully flung around her shoulders.

She decided to leave off her silver and turquoise jewelry at the last minute and simply wore a delicate gold and emerald ring that had once belonged to her Granny Laurite. The beadwork on the shawl provided just the right amount of sparkle. It was still too early to go over to the park for the lighting ceremony so Rhonelle put on some slow jazz albums and poured herself a glass of the red wine. She sank back into the cushions of her special chair after a sip of wine and tried to relax. She closed her eyes and took a deep breath.

"*Cherie, I tink you more than ready for dis fella,*" cackled Laurite who was sitting on the sofa swinging her bare feet, smiling fondly at her granddaughter. "*He finally be good and ready to find you, too, after all dis time.*"

Opening her eyes, Rhonelle could not remember a time when she was more delighted to see her Granny sitting there talking to her.

I don't know how you managed to get him here, but I will always be grateful to you. I never should have doubted you'd bring Sergio to me. But ... will everything be all right? I'm not making a fool of myself getting involved with someone at my age am I?

Laurite threw her head back and guffawed at the age reference. *Why dis be just de right time for a good man to come along! I was older than you when I marry husband number three. You and Sergio gotta whole lot of catchin' up to do.*

"Doan you worry, Cherie, everything is gonna work out jus fine. You'll see!" Laurite smiled kindly at Rhonelle as she faded away to a silver spark with a pop. Then she was gone, but Rhonelle was left with a feeling of being loved, guided, and cared for.

Thank you Granny . . . for looking out for me.

Rhonelle knew Laurite wasn't the only one "up there" watching over her. She had plenty of help from White Cloud, Doll Dumas, and the One Granny called "The Boss."

There was a timid knock at her door. Teenie and Mavis had arrived to escort Rhonelle to the lighting ceremony. She rose from her chair relaxed and ready for a very interesting evening. A tall dark stranger had come to town and neither she nor Peavine would ever be the same again.

CHAPTER THIRTY-ONE

A Sweet Reunion

On the "Other Side" at Granny Laurite's Creole Cottage

Laurite sat on the porch of her cottage in her rocking chair. She eagerly watched the scene forming below her through the hole in the bank of pink and purple clouds. A large crowd had gathered in Herman Park for the Thirty-Foot Elvis lighting ceremony. The screen door of the cottage opened with a creak of rusty springs behind her. A glowing figure emerged and transformed into the familiar apparition of White Cloud. He stood at the edge of the porch with his arms folded, admiring the fine statue "Little Eagle" had made.

"You must be very proud of your grandson," said Doll Dumas, popping out from behind one of the purple clouds to the side of the cottage. "I'm just thrilled to have something as grand as that big Elvis in little ole Peavine!" She peered over her cat eye glasses down through the clouds. "He's really captured that famous hip swivel. It looks just like that rascal."

White Cloud turned to Doll Dumas, extending his hand to help her up the porch steps. "I am indeed proud," White Cloud said with a warm smile. "You are certainly worthy of such an honor. You have many people thankful for your love and friendship."

At the touch of his hand and kind words, the pink glow surrounding Doll brightened and she literally floated over to her chair beside Laurite, who extended a hand to bring Doll down into the seat. "Come watch dis, White Cloud. I tink I see dem comin'." Laurite's attention was focused on Rhonelle, Teenie, and Mavis as they entered the park. "Ah, she look so beautiful!"

"Look over there," Doll pointed excitedly at Sergio, who had just arrived from the opposite direction, accompanied by Lucille. Sergio was looking up at the statue judging whether the spotlight was properly focused, when he suddenly froze and turned his gaze directly toward Rhonelle. She had spotted him at exactly the same moment.

"Success at last," White Cloud shouted with joy. Crystal goblets of golden bubbly champagne appeared in the hand of each spirit.

"It has taken them almost two and a half lifetimes to be reunited, but now they will finally be together again. The rest is up to them.

"Blessings upon you, dear children," White Cloud said as he held out his glass for a toast. "Cheers!"

"Cheers!" Laurite and Doll joined in. As they clinked their glasses together in a beautiful sound; a shower of golden sparks sailed out over the porch, through the hole in the clouds covering the scene below.

At the very moment Rhonelle and Sergio saw each other across the park, she could have sworn she heard something. It was a bright ringing and she felt surrounded by the spirits of her Granny and Doll and someone else.

"Rhonelle, honey, are you all right?" Teenie asked as he looked up at her with concern. Without realizing it, Rhonelle had halted suddenly when she saw Sergio and almost stumbled as she went wobbly in the knees.

"It's probably them high-heel boots. I don't know how you walk around in those things." Mavis shook her head as she plodded along behind them in her rubber galoshes. "I don't know how anybody can walk in heels either. They's just nothing but torture . . . at least that's what I heard a man say," David Posey said as he emerged from the crowd and grabbed Rhonelle by the arm.

"Good evening Mr. and Mrs. Brice. Isn't this exciting?" he looked in the direction Rhonelle was staring. Mavis and Teenie did, too, after noticing the dazed expression on Rhonelle's face.

When David realized who it was that was next to Lucille Lepanto, walking toward them through the crowd, his jaw dropped. "Oh . . . my . . . gawd. What is *that* man doing here?"

Teenie stood on tiptoes to get a better view. "My goodness, what in the world is Lucille doing with that guy? He looks like an old hippie!"

David looked nervously at Rhonelle. "Did you know he'd be here?"

Mavis squinted at Sergio and back at Rhonelle who was standing still with a silly grin on her face – a very un-Rhonelle thing to do. "Well, who is this feller? Seems to me you know who it 'tis."

Rhonelle blinked and resumed a more familiar expression, although she still couldn't stop smiling. "That happens to be Sergio Mandell – the artist who created this magnificent statue." By this time Lucille and Sergio had made their way across the park to Rhonelle and her three confused friends.

"Hey Rhonelle, here he is!" Lucille presented Sergio to Rhonelle. Obviously excited, Louise was a little winded from the brisk walk. "Y'all this is the soon-to-be *very* famous sculptor, Sergio Mandell. Sergio, I want you to meet Teenie and Mavis Brice, David Posey, and my dear friend, Rhonelle DuBoise." Sergio nodded briefly at David, shook hands with Teenie and Mavis, but all the while had eyes only for Rhonelle, who let out an uncharacteristically girlish giggle.

He took Rhonelle's hand and said, "We've met. It is *very* nice to see you again, Little Sheba." Then to everyone's amazement, Sergio took Rhonelle in his arms and gave her a long kiss on the mouth.

Ah, nice to see you too, my love. And I don't care who is watching.

Lucille couldn't think of a thing to say for a few seconds, and burst out laughing. "Well I'm so glad I could help you two reconnect."

Sergio and Rhonelle broke apart as if nothing unusual had occurred. David and Teenie looked affronted. Mavis was surprised but delighted.

"Ladies and Gentlemen and everybody else – git ready because it's almost time for the countdown to the biggest light show this park has ever seen." Bo Astor was on the PA system installed in the KPEW live truck. In honor of the occasion, Bo was in his full-on Elvis impersonator wig and costume. He looked like a short plump twin of the Thirty-Foot Elvis.

"If the lovely Lucille Lepanto would care to join me at the base of the statue . . . with Mr. Sergio Mandell, we'll get this place lit so bright it'll be seen all the way from outer space!"

The crowd began to cheer at the thought of something so grand happening to little old Peavine. Tammy and Cecil were already up by the statue with Bo. Tammy was squealing and hopping up and down with excitement.

"I guess that's our cue," Lucille said as she tapped Sergio's arm, glancing apologetically at Rhonelle.

Rhonelle turned a reluctant Sergio toward the Thirty-Foot Elvis and gave him a little shove in that direction. "You two go on. Your public awaits. We'll join you at Don's Diner afterward."

Giving Rhonelle's hand a gentle squeeze before he turned, Sergio offered his arm to Lucille and they began weaving their way through the crowd toward the Elvis. After they'd gone about five yards, Lucille looked back over her shoulder at Rhonelle and mouthed, "He is gorgeous!" Rhonelle knew Lucille was dying of curiosity, but she was determined to return the focus to the announcement of Lucille and Bo's betrothal (and off whatever is going on between her and Sergio). Before David could get a chance to ask her anything, Rhonelle suggested they find a good spot over on the side of the park at the sidewalk that led toward Don's Diner. They found a park bench on which Mavis could sit and Teenie could stand to view over the heads of the crowd.

David gave Rhonelle a meaningful look and said, "I need to talk to you later Miss Thang! . . . Goodbye, Mr. and Mrs. Brice, I'd better go find Aunt Violet. She's been *fit to be tied* ever since she first discovered Elvis early this morning."

"Maybe she'll like it better when she sees all these pretty lights," Teenie said as he smiled and waved goodbye. "That boy is a *saint* to be so nice to his aunt the way she bosses him around," Teenie whispered to Rhonelle and Mavis. "She is one *mean* old lady."

"Okay everybody is now in place." Bo was back on the PA. Sergio and Lucille were standing beside the foot of the Elvis statue. **"This here is Mr. Sergio Mandell who created this magnificent work of art and was able to get it put up in a matter of hours while you all was snug in your beds. Let's give him a big hand."**

The crowd cheered and whistled.

"Now Lucille, since this was your idea as a way to honor the memory of your sweet momma who everybody in Peavine knew and loved ..."

More cheers and applause erupted.

"Come on over here and turn on the light switch. Everybody help me do the countdown . . . ten, nine, eight . . ."

When the whole park full of people got to "zero," Lucille threw the switch and four thousand strands of red lights – strung from tree limbs, streetlight poles, park entrance arches, even power lines – lit up. They cast a fiery glow like nothing ever seen in humble Herman Park. A communal gasp of awe and admiration arose from the crowd, followed by a moment of stunned silence, then the crowd cheered more robustly than before.

Before the applause died out, Bo Astor brought up the volume on a tape of Christmas song selections. The crowd began to walk off in various directions to admire their transformed municipal park. Groups broke out into spontaneous choruses happily singing along with "Jingle Bell Rock" and "Santa Claus Is Coming to Town."

Out on the edge of the admiring multitude, David stood with his Aunt Violet. Her old cocker spaniel, Hero, sat patiently, his leash slack as he watched the crowd for poodles. Hero had a great deal of disdain for dogs wearing silly little "human skins." Violet Posey had a great deal of disdain for just about everybody and everything in the park that night. When all the red lights came on, David looked hopefully at his aunt. "How about that Aunt Vi, don't those lights look pretty?"

There was a pause as Violet stared at her beloved Herman Park, favored location for the Garden Club's yearly Christmas Glory decorative project, now invaded by an enormous, tacky, fiberglass statue and hundreds of thousands of red lights. "It looks like one big gawd dammed *whorehouse* to me! Come on Hero, let's go home." Violet Posey mustered as much dignity as possible and dragged her old dog off with her.

Bo turned over broadcast duties to his young part-time announcer so he and Lucille could sneak out the back way and get over to the after-party at Don's Diner. After removing his sunglasses and wig, Bo was happy to remain in his sequined jumpsuit. After all, it was Elvis who had brought them together and witnessed his heartfelt proposal in the wee hours of that morning. Bo recalled kneeling at the foot of the statue to "make an honest woman" of Lucille and the tears in her eyes as she finally said "yes."

It hadn't been the first time Bo had asked Lucille to marry him. He'd been trying to get a commitment out of that woman for the past five months. He figured he'd been lucky at last because of perfect timing. Completion of the Elvis project they'd planned in secret since January added to Tammy's recent engagement just wore his woman down. For sure, Lucille could no longer use the excuse that she had to wait until her daughter was settled.

"Hmmm," Bo mused to himself as he waved at Tammy and Cecil to indicate they were headed for Don's. "There's my future step-daughter. That's kinda weird considering I'm only about ten years older than she is. ... Cool!" As Bo and Lucille distanced themselves from the crowd, they struck up a little conversation. "I just realized what a long day this has been Babe," Bo said, huffing a little because they were walking so fast.

"I know," Lucille shook her head and grinned. "So much has happened . . . I can't believe it's still the same day."

She slowed down and came to a halt right just before they reached the Diner parking lot. "It just hit me that I am worn out. This has all been so exciting, I didn't realize I was so tired."

Bo put his arm around her and hugged her shoulders, covering them under his red satin-lined cape. "Babe, I'm plum tuckered, too, but this has got to be the *best day of my life*."

Lucille gave him a kiss for that. "Mine too, honey ... one long wonderful day with more to come! I sure am glad I dragged you off with me to Graceland that day. I never would've thought to do such a thing if Rhonelle hadn't dared me to."

Lucille's jaw dropped and she stared ahead to the Diner. "Oh . . . my . . . *gawd*."

"What is it?" Bo asked, his wrinkled brow following her gaze. "Something wrong, Babe?"

Lucille started to laugh. "No, nothing's wrong, hon. It's just too weird how this has all worked out." Bo was still confused. Lucille turned to face him. "It turns out our friend Rhonelle has got something going on with Sergio Mandell. I don't know what exactly, but I'm gonna find out."

Bo shivered a little. "That woman is spooky sometimes. She's been looking pretty hot lately, though." He grinned at Lucille. "Not as hot as you do, Babe. C'mon, let's go on in. I'm freezing out here."

Inside Don's Diner, Dorine peered out of the window, watching for the guests to arrive.

"Looks like our hostess is a-waiting," Lucille said. A cardboard sign on the door read, "closed for private party" in hastily scrawled red magic marker. Dorine gestured for Lucille and Bo to use the back door.

"Hey Momma," yelled Tammy from across the parking lot. "We got Sergio with us. Dorine said to come in the back door, 'cause of all those people at the lighting ceremony would try to come in and order something to eat."

Cecil and Sergio – on either side of Tammy – sheepishly glanced over their shoulders at the family groups not far behind, folks returning to their cars parked along the highway. Marv and Pauline had arrived at the same time as Tammy, Cecil, and Sergio. "Hey Unkie Marv and Auntie Pauline," Tammy shouted, waving. "Come here and meet this famous artist who did our big Elvis!"

Sergio couldn't help from raising his eyebrows when he got a good look at Pauline. She was wearing a white fox fur jacket and white fur hat over her tousled blond hair. Large rhinestone snowflake earrings glittered at her ears. Her tight red slacks and white leather boots looks so urbane; he hadn't expected anybody as flamboyant as Pauline in a place like Peavine. Cecil noticed the look of surprise on Sergio's face. "They're not her real aunt and uncle," he explained quietly. "She calls most all her Granny Doll's friends that. Although if you ask me, Mr. Marv acts like he's her dad."

Sergio studied the uneasy look on Cecil's face as Tammy happily hugged Marv and Pauline before introducing them to Sergio. Pauline offered her red-gloved hand to Sergio, "Charmed, I'm sure," she purred as she looked him over. "Mr. Mandell, that sculpture is simply the most glorious thing ever to come to Peavine. I just can't imagine how you did it!"

Marv came forward and put one arm around Pauline's shoulder and shook Sergio's hand. "You creative types always amaze me. I'd sure like to hear how you and Lucille done cooked this whole thing up."

"We can do that later Unkie Marv," Tammy insisted excitedly. "We got more good news to share when we all get our hot cocoa."

"Really," Marv shot a suspicious glance at Cecil.

Pauline pulled Marv along toward the back of the Diner. "Come on sweetie, it's getting late. We don't want to hold anything up, do we now?"

Sergio excused himself and went back to his cottage to let the rest of the guests arrive. He needed a few minutes to himself to clear his cluttered mind. He wanted to take a moment to think back on his meeting with Rhonelle ... and that wonderful, blissful kiss!

Rhonelle, Teenie, and Mavis arrived at the Diner parking lot just as Vaudine and Fred Fortney pulled in. "Hey Rhonelle, I got something to tell you!" Vaudine shouted as she emerged from her car. "This is too strange even for Mr. Nasty."

"That's hard to believe," muttered Teenie, no fan of the Fortneys' talking bird.

Vaudine approached Rhonelle, her eyes as big as saucers behind black rimmed cat eye glasses. "Three weeks ago, I was looking through my wholesale collectible catalogs to get my orders in before the holiday, and Mr. Nasty was settin' on my shoulder like he always does 'cause he likes to look at the pictures." Vaudine – a bit breathless at this point – kept talking as they walked slowly toward the back of the Diner. "When I got to the page with Elvis memorabilia, he started doing that thing he does when he's excited. You know how he looks with one eye and the pupil gets all big and little at the same time."

"Yes we know *that* look all too well, don't we Pitty Too," Teenie inserted, hugging his well-bundled poodle close to his chest.

"Well ... anyways," Vaudine continued while Fred tried to distance himself from the conversation by whistling tunelessly under his breath and walking faster. "All of a sudden Mr. Nasty started saying 'Elvis . . . buy Elvis,' over and over." Vaudine continued, ignoring Fred. "He sounded so insistent I figured why not, so I ordered me a ton of Elvis stuff 'cause Doll loved him so much . . . and *now* look what we got standing in the middle of our city park."

Rhonelle did find this interesting. "I'll bet you've already sold a lot of things just today. Good thing that you listened to him." She looked up just as Sergio was coming their way from his cottage. "This day certainly has been *full* of surprises."

Wandering away from the Fortneys, Rhonelle took Sergio's arm and led him to the Diner's back door. The Fortneys and the Brices followed along slowly to allow for Mavis.

"What do you suppose is up with Rhonelle and that sculpture fella," Teenie whispered to Mavis.

"I dunno and tain't none of our beeswax honey," Mavis said. "Best we stay out of it."

It took a good thirty minutes for all of Bo and Lucille's friends to gather. In the meantime, moments after Bo and Lucille had arrived, Barry Zellhorn, the Peavine High football coach, burst into the Diner. One of his players, Harold "Ox" Osbey, followed, carrying a cumbersome video camera on his shoulder. "Hey Bo," Barry shouted from the door. "Mind if I interview you and Lucille about that big statue?" Without waiting for an answer, Coach Zellhorn motioned for Ox to hook up the microphone to his camera. "This won't take long. I already got some video with Mr. Mandell earlier this afternoon out by the statue while the fellas was putting up all those lights." Coach Zellhorn switched on the camera lights and made sure all the settings were correct, oblivious to the puzzled expression on Lucille's face, *and* Dorine angrily shuffling toward them from the kitchen.

"Okay Ox," Barry stood in front of the camera beside the corner booth where Lucille and Bo were cuddled up by the window, sipping hot chocolates. "Nope, nope that won't work. Too much reflection off that glass. Here we go Miz Lucille." Barry pulled Lucille up by the elbow while Bo looked on helplessly. "Come over and stand right here by me. That's right. Okay Ox . . . on three." He held up three fingers and counted down two, then one silently and addressed the camera. Right behind Ox stood Dorine glowering, her arms folded across her bosom.

"I'm at Peavine's popular local eatery, Don's Diner, just up the highway from the Thirty-Foot Elvis, and I'm talking with Lucille Lepanto, owner of the Too-Tite Tavern. Lucille is the one who came up with the idea of making this thirty-foot tall statue and surprising everybody in town with it this morning. What made you want to tackle such a huge fantastic project as this, Miss Lepanto?"

Lucille had quickly warmed up to the camera and Coach Zellhorn the moment he mentioned her Tavern. Dorine's hostility had also melted away at the reference to their Diner. Lucille patted self-consciously at her tightly sprayed hair. Instantly, her natural showmanship clicked in. "Well, I did this all as a tribute to my momma, Doll Dumas . . . who passed away almost a year ago. She loved the people in this town and they loved her back. I wanted to do something real special as a memorial to her – and give a big Christmas present to the citizens of Peavine."

Wiping away a tear from the corner of her eye, Lucille straightened up and threw back her shoulders. An inch more of her bountiful cleavage appeared above her V-neck pink sweater decorated with snowflake sparkles.

"I made a pilgrimage to Graceland back in January. See, Momma was about the biggest fan of Elvis I ever knew. Me and my friend Bo Astor of KPEW radio . . . uh, well, we saw these great looking life-sized Elvis statues on display at a place nearby . . . and I thought, what if we could get one of them for the mobile home park across the street there . . . where Momma used to live?

"Then I thought wouldn't it be *great* if we could get a really *big* one done and put it in Herman Park, which was built in honor of my momma's second husband, Herman Junior, after he died. Anyway, Bo and I talked to Sergio – the artist – and he said he could do it! The surprise part was Bo's idea."

Bo half stood out of his chair and waved at the camera. Coach Zellhorn took the mike and Ox turned the camera back to him. "Well folks, now you've heard how this little town of Peavine, Arkansas, has now become the home to a new, soon to be famous landmark, the Thirty-Foot Elvis . . . and cut!"

Ox shut off the lights and stopped the camera. Coach shook hands with Bo and Lucille. "Thanks y'all. I'm going to get this edited tonight and take copies of the tape up to the all three Little Rock TV stations first thing tomorrow morning. You'll be famous Lucille, so get ready."

Darla had quietly walked up with a plate of fresh-baked cookies. "Why thanks, don't mind if I do," said Barry as he and Ox each took a handful of cookies and hustled out the door.

Bo shook his head and grinned as he watched his buddy leave.

"Ever since Coach got that video equipment last year for the athletic department, he's been obsessed with movie making. Originally, that camera was for game films, but he uses it for other things during the off-season. He even had his football team help him go film a piece on a Civil War reenactment over the summer so he could use it in the American history class he teaches. I guess that still falls under the educational use category."

Tammy and Cecil came in the door right after the amateur film crew had left. "Momma!" Tammy rushed over and sat across from Bo and Lucille. "I just saw Coach Zellhorn, and he says you're gonna be on TV!"

"We'll see about that, honey," Lucille smiled and patted her daughter's hands. "Coach is a mighty big talker . . . but then he's a mighty persistent fella. He just might BS his way into a career as a TV news reporter."

"Oh I think he's aiming higher than that, Babe," interrupted Bo. "He told me this morning that he'd like to produce a full-length, documentary-style movie about our Thirty-Foot Elvis . . . that is if you and Tammy don't mind."

"I think that would be *fabulous*, don't you Momma?" Tammy's eyes took on a blurry faraway look over the dream of such fame and glory coming to Peavine. Then with an abrupt change in her stream of consciousness, Tammy brought her focus back to Lucille and Bo. "When do you want me to make the announcement?" she whispered conspiratorially.

"I think as soon as everybody gets here and takes a seat, you can stand up and do it," Lucille told her. "The sooner we get this show on the road the better, Hon. Bo and I haven't had but a couple hours of sleep in the past twenty-four and it's gettin' late. Good thing I've got Bud to help Joe run the bar at Too-Tite. I plan to hit the sack early tonight." Under the table, Bo gave Lucille's thigh an affectionate squeeze.

Tammy excused herself and went back to the kitchen to help Darla and Amber with the cookies and cocoa. Cecil decided to join them since he felt like three was a crowd at that table.

Within five minutes, everybody had arrived. Rhonelle had used the few precious moments while she accompanied Sergio to the back door of the Diner to make some discreet plans concerning later that night. She insisted on waiting to enter the Diner at the same time as the Fortneys and the Brices. She was relieved to hear David had gone home with his Aunt Violet and wouldn't be there to stare suspiciously at her and Sergio during the party.

When Tammy made the announcement that her momma was engaged to Bo Astor, the whole room cheered. Even Bo's brother, Jo Don the preacher, gave them his blessing. They decided there was no hurry to tell their daddy, Pastor Astor, about this any time soon. Christabelle Tingleberry was there, having taken the evening off. She agreed that it would be wise to wait until right before the wedding to break the news to Pastor Astor.

Toasts were raised to Lucille and Bo, the Thirty-Foot Elvis, Sergio Mandell, and once again, Tammy and Cecil – and last of all – their dearly departed friend, Doll Dumas. Then the happy group left the Diner, warm and full of hot chocolate and cookies.

Darla, Tammy, and Cecil stayed to help Dorine and Don clean up and close down for the night. Then each went their separate ways, home to warm beds. However, several of the partygoers had plans of their own for the rest of this special evening. Day one of the Thirty-Foot Elvis was *not over yet.*

Bo gave Lucille a ride to her log cabin behind the Too-Tite Tavern. He walked her to the door, glanced over his shoulder, and followed a giggling Lucille inside. They locked the door, turned out the lights and built a roaring fire in the fireplace. Bo made a mental note to see if he could find a place to buy Lucille a bearskin rug. He bet that Sergio would know where he could get one.

Tammy and Cecil took another stroll around the park to enjoy the splendor of the red lights and the huge shiny statue smack in the middle of it. "Isn't this romantic?" sighed Tammy as she clung tighter to Cecil and rested her head on his shoulder. "I'm so happy for Momma. It's about *time* she found somebody to marry. I'm just happy for everybody in the world tonight."

Cecil stopped and looked into her beautiful sweet face. "Me too, Tammy, 'cause as long as you love me, nothing too bad to bear can ever happen to me." He gave her a long kiss and held her for a while. They broke apart and started to laugh as they walked faster and faster back to the highway and ran all the rest of the way to Tammy's house. Cecil was hoping to God that "Unkie" Marv and Pauline had already gone to bed and wouldn't notice them taking a shortcut along their backyard fence.

He needn't have worried. Pauline returned from the party in an amorous mood, after all the talk of weddings ... and looking at that sexy sculptor. Marv wasn't interested in anything but Pauline and what was going on in their plush, well-draped bedroom.

Rhonelle let her hand brush lightly against Sergio's back when she walked by him on her way out of the Diner. He clearly heard *"midnight"* in his mind. Looking into her eyes, he nodded. Sergio gave Rhonelle a meaningful look as she left the party, accompanied by the short little man with the enormous wife.

Sergio excused himself a few minutes later and strolled over to the park once more to admire his masterpiece. He had spent the better part of a year working on and living with his gigantic creation. To his surprise, he realized he would miss the big fella. "I'll have to come visit you," he said aloud as he stood at the base of the statue.

Now he had an even better reason to come visit waiting for him right across the highway, two blocks down from where he stood at that moment. He still wondered at how well planned this whole drama had been from the beginning. He was so cautious and determined to finish this biggest-ever project, he had postponed his search for Rhonelle. What a pleasant discovery that his thirty-foot Elvis had always been the key to finding her.

How elegant, how clever and how *obvious* it now was that all of these events reflected the touch of his Grandfather White Cloud! The Sergio of two years ago would have been stubborn and sullen at being manipulated so. But he had grown in the past year – seemed to have discovered who he really was – and found something that had been long lost. He was only grateful, more so than he could ever remember.

Wiping away the tears that ran freely down his face, he turned and began to walk briskly back toward his Dew Drop Inn cottage. He had another hour and a half to wait. That's nothing compared to what he believed had been more than one lifetime of waiting to reunite with his woman.

At ten minutes to midnight, Sergio could wait no longer. Silent as a ghost, he let himself out of the gate to the Dew Drop court-yard, crossed the deserted highway and walked up the gravel driveway of the Home-Sweet-Homes-on-Wheels Park. The only trailer with lights on was the large lavender double-wide that he knew belonged to Rhonelle.

He kept to the shadows and went to the back door as she suggest-ed, before tapping lightly. He saw her outline as she walked by the curtained kitchen window.

When she opened the door, he saw that she was once again wear-ing the red satin negligee he had sent her. Her hair was a dark cloud of tangled curls … and she had on her reddest, glossiest lipstick. (*Thanks, Shirleen!*) The effect upon Sergio was devastatingly sexy. He followed her inside, too awed to say a word as Rhonelle smiled and locked the door behind him.

"*I believe our work here is done for a while.*" White Cloud sighed with a deep sense of satisfaction. He and Granny Laurite sat on the folding chairs in the backyard, a perfect vantage point to watch all the secret romantic comings and goings on this cold winter's night.

"*Yep,*" agreed Laurite with a chuckle. "*I tink dey all managing real well witout our help now. We need ta give dem a little privacy."*

"Yes, they certainly do deserve that." White Cloud stood and offered his hand to Laurite, who smiled coquettishly at him as she took hold of it.

"Love each other well this time my children," he said quietly as he held his other hand up in a blessing toward the lavender double-wide.

Both the spirits began to glow brightly and condensed into a ball of golden light. As they rose up into the sky, a shower of tiny golden stars fell upon Rhonelle and Sergio, who were deliriously happy to be together at last in the ornate brass bed with the red velvet coverlet.

CHAPTER THIRTY-TWO

Teenie's Bright Idea

Day two of the Thirty-Foot Elvis dawned clear, bright, and not quite as frosty as the previous morning. The sun had risen by the time Violet Posey went outside with her dog Hero for their usual walk to Herman Park. Still wearing her nightgown under her overcoat and curler bonnet on her head, Violet wearily dragged Hero along toward the center of the park, although he attempted several times to pause to relieve himself along the way.

Violet had tossed and turned all night as her dreams became a frightening series of nightmares. She dreamt of being chased all over town by that dreadful statue that had come to life as a Godzilla-like monster intent upon the destruction of Peavine. She awoke later than usual with a headache and a new sense of purpose.

By the time she and Hero arrived at the center of Herman Park, poor Hero's bladder was about to burst. It was there Violet stopped, smack dab at the base of the Thirty-Foot Elvis. She pointed to it and said, "Okay Hero, knock yourself out."

She smiled with smug satisfaction as Hero left a nice big puddle. Looking up with defiance into the face of her fiberglass nemesis, she said quietly, "Take *that* you son of a bitch!" She made a face and stuck out her tongue before happily marching back to her apartment above Violet Expressions Floral Shop.

About the time Violet was taking her small revenge on the Thirty-Foot Elvis, residents of the trailer park were stirring awake. Teenie sat straight up in bed so suddenly, he startled Mavis, who had been still snoring softly. "Good Lord, Teenie! What's the matter ... you got a charley horse in your leg?" Mavis asked with a voice filled with concern.

"No, hon," Teenie announced with a voice full of determination. "I ain't got no charley horse, but I do have the most wonderful best idea ever!"

Mavis struggled up into a sitting position eager to hear Teenie's latest bright idea. "I'm all ears. Tell me what you're a thinking." Teenie snuggled up next to Mavis' warm soft bulk and looked sweetly up into her face. "Weeeelll . . . we got us *two* weddings coming up now don't we?"

"Yes we do, bless 'em." Mavis smiled fondly at her diminutive spouse.

"I got this great idea about how we could do this thing better than the traditional kind of a wedding," Teenie continued despite the wary look evolving on Mavis' face. "Why do there have to be two weddings? Why not just have one?"

Now Mavis was really confused. "Of course there'll be two weddings honey . . . unless you're thinking somebody ought to elope like we did."

"Oh, no, no, *no* . . ." Teenie protested. "I wouldn't *dare* suggest that. You know I've regretted denying you the chance for a real church wedding all these years. I just hope you have forgiven me." Mavis curled her flabby arm around Teenie and practically buried him in her deep soft valley of cleavage. "Lord hon, I was so happy you'd marry me it didn't matter where we did it!"

Teenie always quite enjoyed this particular area of Mavis' anatomy so it was a moment or two before he came up for air, his toupee pushed dangerously far back on his forehead. "The feeling's mutual, Sweet Dumpling," he said weakly, a crooked smile on his face.

"So why are you talking about only having one wedding then?" Mavis loved it when Teenie called her "Sweet Dumpling," a private pet name he'd come up with for her early in their courtship.

"Well . . ." He paused as he pulled on the blanket to primly cover his knees. "What I want to do is have a *mother-daughter* wedding for Lucille and Tammy!" He held his hands out as if framing a scene in a movie. "I can picture it now. It'd be the first wedding of its kind in Peavine . . . or anywhere else as far as I know . . . and *I* would be their wedding planner!"

Mavis paused a long time so she could think of the kindest way to respond to this outrageous notion without hurting Teenie's feelings. She was pretty sure nobody else would think this was a great idea – especially Tammy and Lucille. It sounded more akin to killing two birds with one stone than the proper way to joyfully celebrate two marriages.

Teenie beamed at her. "I told you it was a great idea, I'll have to call Lucille and Tammy right away and tell them about it." He bounced out of bed, slipped into his striped flannel bathrobe and automatically straightened his toupee. He glanced at the clock on his way to the bathroom. "It's only seven-fifteen; you suppose they're up yet?"

"No hon. I doubt they'd be up this early on a Sunday." Mavis blew out a breath between pursed lips. Maybe she had time to head this off after all.

"That's right," Teenie gasped. "There's been so much excitement around here I done forgot what day it is." He let loose a high-pitched giggle. "I'll talk to the Reverend Joe Don about this right after services today."

"Oh well," thought Mavis. "I'd best leave this up to the Lord." She pulled the curtain open on the window beside their bed and looked out at the sunrise. With most all the leaves off the trees, she could see clear across the park to the lavender double-wide. She recalled the surprising interactions between Rhonelle and that stranger . . . Sergio what's his name. "Hmm, I wonder what really has been going on with those two?" She blushed at the thought and quickly closed the curtain.

Over in the lavender double-wide that morning things were just fine as far as Rhonelle and Sergio were concerned. Sergio was the first to wake up at ten-thirty. They had been carousing and talking until three-thirty when they realized they were starving hungry. They enjoyed a very late snack, devouring the cheese plate and bread, washed down with that bottle of red wine, another example of excellent planning by Rhonelle.

Making love in person had required plenty more energy and endurance but it was *way more satisfying* than dreams. Sergio propped himself up so he could watch Rhonelle sleep. Her hair was a tangled mass all around her face and covered most of her pillow. The red lipstick had worn off and she had a little smile on her face. He thought she was more beautiful than ever. She gave a little snort and rolled over, still sleeping soundly.

Sergio carefully got out of bed, wincing as he stretched a kink in his back. This little reminder that he no longer was the young stud he used to be only made him smile. He'd done all right last night, even though he had gotten a little rusty in the romance department over the past few years. He and Rhonelle were the perfect age for each other. All those impossible notions and expectations he once had about sex had flown out the window.

Last night they were able to laugh and just enjoy whatever happened ... and not mind anything that didn't. Both were comfortable with who they were and the fact they were both inhabiting bodies that happened to be fifty-something years old. Sergio reluctantly left Rhonelle asleep and searched for his clothes. They were piled on the living room floor next to the sofa where Rhonelle's red negligee was carelessly flung over the cushion. Seeing this caused Sergio to recall some pretty arousing memories. He almost went back to the bedroom right then, but decided he'd better go to the kitchen instead to make some coffee. He needed to clear his head and figure out how to get back to Dew Drop Inn cottage #3 unseen. And he needed a ride back to Memphis.

He would bring Rhonelle her coffee in bed and they'd figure out something. He really wanted her to come with him and stay in Memphis for a couple of days. He'd show her his studio and take her around town. She was embarrassed to confess to him last night that she'd never been to Memphis in her life. He'd love to be the one to show her around.

Rhonelle heard clinking noises in the kitchen and smelled coffee brewing. She opened her eyes, stretching luxuriously before rising sinuously from the well-rumpled bed and heading to the bathroom. Shivering, she grabbed her velvet shawl and wrapped it around her shoulders. Rhonelle had no idea where her red satin gown had ended up. Seeing her reflection in the bathroom mirror, she burst out laughing at the way her hair stuck out in all directions. She had a huge lovenest tangle on the back of her head. Washing her face, Rhonelle applied a fresh coat of lipstick and tried to drag a brush through her hair.

Sergio heard her stirring and called from the kitchen, "I've made us some coffee. How do you like yours?"

"Au lait, please." She stuck her head out of the bathroom door so he could hear her. "There should be plenty of milk in . . ."

"Found it . . . and the pan you use," he interrupted, followed by the clanging of pot lids sliding off and hitting the floor. "Whoopsee . . . sorry about the noise. Stay put and I'll bring it to you. I found your favorite mug, too."

Ah, what a luxury! Rhonelle put a dab of the leave-in conditioner and frizz tamer Shirleen had left with her and worked it through her hair. That got her curls a little better under control. Hopping back into bed and propping up the pillows behind her, she made sure to drape her shawl with just enough shoulder bared and smoothed out the red velvet coverlet across her legs.

When Sergio came into the bedroom with her coffee a few minutes later he almost tripped over her slippers that were still on the floor. He was too busy staring at the beautiful scene of Rhonelle seductively propped up in bed, clad only in a strategically arranged velvet shawl. Needless to say, the café au lait had to be reheated by the time she was able to get around to drinking it.

Forty-nine minutes later they were sipping their second cups of coffee in the living room, warmed by the gas logs. Rhonelle was curled up in her special chair, wearing her red gown and robe. Sergio was enjoying the comfort of the Eames chair and ottoman Darla had found for her.

"You look good in that chair." Rhonelle tilted her head and smiled at him through the steam rising from her coffee mug.

"Not as good as you looked in that bed," Sergio sighed contentedly.

"I bought that chair *and* the bed with you in mind," Rhonelle confessed. "I knew one day you'd end up in both of them."

"Yeah," Sergio grinned back at her. "Just like I knew I'd get to see you wearing that red night gown, too, Little Sheba. Isn't it fun being psychic friends."

"Indeed it is my love," Rhonelle said laughing. Then in a more serious tone, "it is helpful when we can't be together . . . not quite so lonely."

Sergio stared at her a moment before saying anything. "Would you be interested in giving me a ride back to Memphis today? I happen to know you have a pretty sexy vintage car that is begging for a road trip. You could stay with me a couple more nights; I could show you the real Memphis."

"I'd love to," Rhonelle answered without a moment's hesitation. "Now we have resolved that . . . how on earth am I going to get you out of here without anybody seeing you?"

"I have that figured out already," Sergio said. "If you'll just hand me the phone, I'll call Lucille and tell her that she and Bo won't have to take me back home. I can say I came over to your place this morning to see that fancy T-Bird and you agreed to give me a ride home since you'd never been to . . . ah, Graceland!"

"Excellent idea," Rhonelle giggled. "You do all the talking to Lucille so she can't ask me any questions. I'll call Tammy and see if she and Cecil can keep an eye on things for me while I'm gone."

A little while later Rhonelle made Sergio ride with his head out of sight as she drove him in her T-Bird over to his Dew Drop Inn cottage. Leaving him to pack and turn in his key, she instructed him to meet her after twenty minutes in the Diner parking lot. Don and Dorine were in church, so Sergio left the key under the flower pot Lucille had pointed out. She had the bill covered. It was much ado over nothing since nobody was around to witness their exit.

Tammy had finished the big breakfast she prepared for Cecil when Rhonelle called. They had slept in and planned to skip church. "We'd be glad to help you out, Aunt Rhonelle, so you can take a little trip . . . right, Cecil?" He almost choked on his waffle when Tammy as much as admitted he was there with her. "Y'all have fun. Graceland is just great!"

God bless Tammy . . . so open and accepting with no questions asked. I hope those two have set a date for their wedding, and it better be soon.

Rhonelle and Sergio lit out for Memphis in the shiny good-as-new T-Bird at high noon. That was just about the time Coach Barry Zellhorn was driving through Pine Bluff on his way to Little Rock. The tapes he'd made about the Thirty-Foot Elvis were safely stored in a briefcase on the passenger seat of his red pickup truck. Those three little video tapes could turn out to be life changing – not only for him but also for his fellow residents of Peavine.

CHAPTER THIRTY-THREE

The Marching Elvises

Coach Barry Zellhorn tried his best to get somebody to come to the door of the first two TV stations he called on in Little Rock. This being a Sunday there were no regular business hours or receptionist around to let him in. He got lucky at the third TV station when he caught up with the weekend anchor in the parking lot as he was coming in to work.

Coach had worn his best suit so he would look professional. He did not want to be mistaken for those downtown vagrants he'd heard about. Projecting all the confidence he could muster (of which he had a considerable supply), he approached the anchor and introduced himself.

"Sir, my name is Barry Zellhorn. I'm a documentary film producer from south Arkansas. How'd you do," he said, shaking hands as the confused newsman tried to remember who Barry might be. "Nice to meet you," the anchor replied earnestly.

"I have here a tape with a riveting personal interest story about a very exciting new landmark newly arrived in our state." Barry patted the briefcase he was holding. "I am willing to give your station an *exclusive* news breaking story on the fantastic Thirty-Foot Elvis statue that appeared *mysteriously . . . overnight* in the sleepy little town of Peavine just yesterday morning!"

The anchor studied Barry a moment then decided he liked the sound of a Thirty-Foot Elvis. "That's pretty crazy, just the kind of story to pick up a Sunday night broadcast. This has been a pretty dull news day anyway. Sure, I'll take a look at it and if the quality is okay, we'll try to use it. Thanks pal." The man flashed a smile full of unnaturally perfect teeth. Barry tried to keep his hands from shaking with excitement as he opened his briefcase with the three large video tape cassettes inside. "Here you are sir, and I'll include two extra copies for you to send to your affiliate stations — especially one in Memphis since the artist resides there." The anchor man was impressed with Barry's professional thoroughness. It never occurred to him the other two tapes were intended for rival local stations.

Before closing the briefcase, Barry handed the anchor one of the new business cards he'd been waiting for an opportunity to use:

Barry Zellhorn
Documentary & Commercial
Film Producer and Screen Talent

Barry's home phone number on the card would lead a caller to his answering machine, already set to sound like it was an actual office phone. He sure didn't want anybody calling the high school looking for Barry Zellhorn, the movie producer. He had handwritten Bo Astor's phone number at KPEW on the back as an alternate phone contact.

"This right here is the phone number of the owner of the local radio station in case you all might be interested in coming down for a live shot of the Christmas parade. It ought to be a humdinger of a photo op."

The news anchor put the card in his pocket and shook Barry's hand. "I'll pass on the information, thank you. If this gets on today it will be during the ten o'clock." With that, he unlocked the back door of the building and disappeared into the TV station carrying Coach Barry Zellhorn's dreams of fame and glory with him.

"Whew," Barry exhaled with relief as he strode down the street to his truck. "I've done all I can for now." Suddenly realizing he was mighty hungry, Barry glanced at his watch. It was already two-thirty. "I think I'll go reward myself with dinner at Franke's Cafeteria. I've got a real hankering for some roast beef and that eggplant casserole. Wish Don would try making that sometime."

After a delicious meal, Barry found a pay phone and called Bo Astor about the TV station possibly using his story on the ten o'clock news and to be watching for it. Bo was tickled to death to hear about

Barry's good luck and promised he would set up his VCR and tape it for him, just in case he couldn't get back in time.

The weekend news anchor and staff got a kick out of Barry's homespun video of the Thirty-Foot Elvis and all the hoo-rah it had caused. They made it the top story on the ten o'clock news that night. Come Monday morning, the news director liked it so much he sent copies to TV stations in Jonesboro and Memphis. He assigned a camera crew to go down to Peavine and cover the Christmas Parade on Thursday.

Meanwhile, imagine their surprise when Sergio and Rhonelle turned on the TV Monday evening while they were happily ensconced in a luxury room at the Peabody hotel and saw a story about the sudden and mysterious appearance of a Thirty-Foot Elvis statue in Peavine. Sergio and Rhonelle had decided to stay in the grand old hotel for a couple of nights before Rhonelle's return home. Having waited so long to be reunited, they were loath to go their separate ways again so soon. They decided to make an occasion of Rhonelle's first trip to Memphis. Sergio would have lingered in Peavine a few more days, but for his class "Modern Sculpture in Epic Scale" at the Memphis College of Art.

Sergio's 424-square-foot apartment behind his warehouse studio was not very comfortable for two people. In spite of that, Rhonelle was fascinated by his studio and his many projects in various stages of development. They were only checking the weather forecast that night when the story about the Thirty-Foot Elvis came on. The part with Sergio's interview was just starting. Sergio veritably sprang out of bed when his name appeared in big letters at the bottom of the screen:

"Memphis sculptor Sergio Mandell pulls a big one on small Arkansas town."

Sergio exclaimed that the camera made him look much too old, but agreed his Elvis looked grand.

Rhonelle couldn't hide her amusement at his reaction to the interview.

"You look very dashing, darling. Good thing you were wearing the gold earring. It's a very sexy look for you." She hid her head and giggled into the fancy blanket as he leaped back onto the bed, pulling up the covers. "My, my, I never thought I would be carrying on with such a famous artist!"

"Hey," he said as he came up from under the covers. "I *am* famous now aren't I?" His look of astonishment changed to glee and he reached for the bedside phone to dial room service. "I think we deserve a little celebration here … Hello, Room Service, I'd like to order a bottle of champagne and … fresh strawberries if you have any," he said, adding Rhonelle's request. Fruit would go nicely with the chocolates they'd bought earlier from the confectioner in the lobby.

Events in Peavine began to snowball over the next three days. Early on Tuesday morning, Bo Astor got a call from a Memphis radio DJ who interviewed him live on his morning show. Even though he was completely star struck, Bo held his own with the popular top 40 morning man. The subject of Elvis impersonators came up and before Bo knew it, the leader of The Marching Elvises had called into the Memphis radio station and challenged all his members to show up and march in the Peavine Christmas Parade … if that would be okay with Bo Astor, of course. That was more than okay as far as Bo was concerned. Best of all, he was asked to be the grand marshal and lead the cadre of Marching Elvises!

Both Rhonelle and Sergio awoke early the next morning with the same premonition; she needed to call Lucille Lepanto right away. Sure enough, Lucille was excited about all the news coverage. Bo wanted to be sure Sergio came back to Peavine, as the guest of honor for the parade, since he was sure there would be "tons of TV cameras" in town for the event.

Any excuse to spend more time with Rhonelle was fine with

Sergio. He planned to follow her in his pickup truck so he could bring six smaller-sized versions of the thirty-foot Elvis back to Peavine. Rhonelle was sure Vaudine would be able to sell them from the parking lot in front of her store. He had the half-dozen, five-foot-tall yard art statues packed in his truck, along with a half-gross of end-table-sized figurines he sold at shops near Graceland.

What a sight they made tooling down the highway, Rhonelle in her classic turquoise T-Bird followed right behind by Sergio in his red pickup full of Elvises. They got plenty of double takes and horn honks along the way. When they stopped for lunch at a Wendy's on the way, a large crowd of curious onlookers surrounded the pickup. The manager was so intrigued by their story of the Thirty-Foot Elvis (and grateful for the increase in business) that he gave Sergio and Rhonelle free lunch and made plans to go to Peavine himself.

Rhonelle and Sergio arrived in Peavine well after dark. Lucille and Bo were at the Diner waiting for them, along with everybody else from the trailer park. Vaudine was beside herself with joy when she saw the Elvises in the back of Sergio's truck. She figured she would sell out of them before Christmas.

Dorine laid plates piled high with steaming hot chicken and dumplings in front of Sergio and Rhonelle then laid her hand on Sergio's shoulder. "Shall I have Darla get your cottage ready for you, Mr. Mandell? I assume you'll be staying for the big parade."

Sergio paused with a fork full of a hot dumpling halfway to his mouth and glanced over at Rhonelle who smiled back at him. She calmly looked up at Dorine and said, "That won't be necessary, Dorine. Sergio and I have already made arrangements."

Dorine blushed when she realized what Rhonelle really meant, but didn't comment. Nobody said anything because at that moment Barry Zellhorn came bursting in through the door, followed by the bright lights of a video camera wielded by Oz Osbey and a microphone aimed at Sergio who was happily tucking into his plate of chicken and dumplings. Between bites, he was grinning foolishly at Rhonelle. From then on there was an understanding among Rhonelle's friends that Sergio was her man. They were together now; no questions asked. After all, they were hardly a couple of kids any more. Lucille's jaw dropped. She couldn't have been happier for her friend. Obviously, Sergio was a perfect match for Rhonelle. Lucille had the satisfaction of realizing she and Bo had been the ones to bring them together. (It was some time later that Lucille found out about New Orleans, but she still insisted that the order for the Thirty-Foot Elvis made everything possible.)

The night of the Peavine Christmas Parade was one for the history books. All three of the Little Rock TV stations and a camera crew from a Memphis station were there. The KPEW live broadcast van band played secular Christmas holiday tunes as they followed behind the Marching Elvises, whose elaborate routines complemented their flashy red and white jumpsuits, black wigs and dark glasses. Bo Astor, dressed in full Elvis regalia, waved happily from Lucille's cherry red Mustang convertible leading the parade up Main Street and around Herman Park where the Thirty-Foot Elvis – garishly lit by multitudes of red lights – loomed over the festivities. The Elvises were followed by a raucous troop of heavy-set Shriners in fezzes from the Little Rock Chapter. They were astride mini-motorbikes, weaving in figure eights and punctuating their routine with alarmingly loud backfires.

The Peavine High School marching band rounded the corner blaring out a medley of popular Christmas carols. They paused to allow head majorette Patti Jean Boling to showcase her incredible high-tossed flaming batons twirling exhibition. Nobody since Tammy had been able to pull off such a feat.

Following the marching band was the large group of PHS cheer and pompom girls – all trained at the Tammy and Amber Academy.

Next came an unusual assortment of proudly decorated annual holiday favorites. The Littlest Angels on the Church of the Vine float were adorable as usual. Seymore's Tex-Mex presented Louise Dolesanger perched atop a large piñata constructed of bright tissue paper stuffed in a large chicken wire sculpture that faintly resembled a donkey.

This formidable project was a remodel of a giant Peavine HS Boll Weevil from the latest homecoming parade constructed by Miss Laughtenberry's high school art class. Louise's small electric organ and speaker were installed inside the piñata, which allowed her to play "Feliz Navidad" merrily along the parade route. Santa at the North Pole was none other than Don Dinkins of Don's Diner featured on the float decorated with Luke's Barber Shop pole (on loan) and copious amounts of cotton bolls to resemble a snow scene. Teenie Brice was also aboard as Santa's helper.

Teenie played his role clad in a darling elf costume designed by Mavis – complete with large pointy ears attached to the sides of his cap. He gleefully threw candy to parade route crowds. Pitty Too, in her holiday tutu, yapped and ran around his feet occasionally biting at Teenie's curly-toed elf booties. Mavis was so proud.

A surprising new addition this year was Tad Bradley slowly driving his dad's white convertible with a lovely young woman singing "White Christmas" accompanied by the karaoke machine from the Too-Tite Tavern. Hardly anyone recognized the once mousey young Lorna Mae Monett soulfully crooning from the backseat. Tammy and Lucille had finally convinced Lorna to color her hair and wear some makeup. Pauline had loaned her white fox fur hat and jacket to complete Lorna's glamorous new look.

Two of Cecil Swindle's newly refurbished classic cars with the local beauty queens on board followed the singing Lorna Mae. Miss Peavine of 1984, Jean Ann Westbrook, dressed in a formal gown and blond mink stole, waved exuberantly from a 1966 electric blue Corvette. The 1984 Little Miss Peavine was the youngest of the Bradley girls, six-year-old Betsy Lee. She proudly held her Poodle Pageant queen doggie, "Princess" as she waved from a hot pink 1962 Cadillac.

At the end of the parade cheers rose as Peavine's beloved Black Santa, Ozelle Washington, turned the corner in a spectacular red sleigh pulled by Doc Ozzie's SUV. This was Ozelle's first return appearance in the annual parade since suffering a stroke two years ago. His rich laughter could be heard over the crowd as his six great grandchildren tossed small stuffed animals to the gang of youngsters mobbing the sleigh.

When the film from this event hit TV screens across Arkansas and Tennessee, Elvis fans took notice. Within days more and more curious onlookers found their way to Peavine. Vaudine sold out of Sergio's statues within two weeks.

Sergio returned to Memphis and taught his last few classes for the semester. Then he brought another load of Elvises to Peavine. After ten days away, he gratefully fell back into the arms of Rhonelle, who was eagerly awaiting his return to the lavender double-wide.

CHAPTER THIRTY-FOUR

A Very Elvis Christmas

After some discussion, Rhonelle and Sergio decided to spend the Christmas holiday together in Peavine. They would go to New Orleans for New Year's, visiting Sergio's great aunt and spending time with Krystal and Sammy. Rhonelle felt this first Christmas since Doll's passing was too important for her to be away.

Ozelle and Sally Washington had begun the tradition of inviting Doll to join them for Christmas Eve dinner while they were still living with her at the Dumas Mansion. Their dinner party had expanded over the years to include Doll's friends from the trailer park, Don and Dorine, and Lucille, who this year brought Bo Astor. Tammy brought Cecil, and now Rhonelle had Sergio with her.

The gathering was held at Ozelle's large home out at Washington Acres. Ozelle and Sally's children and grandchildren grilled and cooked. Their great-grandchildren sang a traditional Christmas blessing before taking their places at the decorated tables. For dessert, Sally still made her mother's famous peach cobbler. Food was plentiful and delicious. Dinner was at seven, conveniently between afternoon and midnight Christmas Eve services.

Many happy memories of Doll were shared around the three large tables set up in the Washingtons' grand dining room and parlor. After dinner, Louise Dolesanger sat down at the piano and the whole group sang along to a mixture of traditional and black gospel Christmas carols. All the kids sang "Santa Claus Is Coming to Town" at the end of the party as the guests began to leave.

Rhonelle walked out into the cold starry night clutching Sergio's arm for warmth. Looking up at one particularly bright twinkling star she thought of her Granny Laurite. She had not seen nor spoken with the spirit of her grandmother in a long while, but she was keenly aware of her love surrounding her.

Thank you, Granny, for whatever it is you've done. I have never had such a happy Christmas as this.

Sergio looked into Rhonelle's radiantly happy face and kissed her gently. "This is the best Christmas I can remember, too."

They still had not settled exactly on where they would spend most of their time together, Peavine or Memphis. There would be time to figure all that out. Sergio, who had been making good money off all the Elvis sculptures, decided to give notice to the university that he wouldn't be teaching next semester. He wanted to work full time as an artist now. Both he and Rhonelle could see success was in his future.

They hosted a Christmas brunch the next morning at the lavender double-wide for Tammy, Cecil, Lucille, and the Brices. Bo would have joined them but had to go out to the Mansion Rest and Retirement Home to be with his father and all the Astor family. Marv and Pauline were off to the Caribbean for the holidays like they'd done for years. They always celebrated Christmas on the beach with Little Larry's good-natured brother, Big Al, and his wife Tina, who used to work with Marv and Pauline during their notorious days in Miami, Florida.

Perhaps it was best that Marv wasn't present at this brunch when Tammy made her announcement. She and Cecil had decided they were going to be married on Valentine's Day . . . or rather on February the sixteenth since that would make it a Saturday wedding.

"Me and Cecil just *love* Valentine's Day! Don't we sweetie?" Tammy bounced in her chair while Cecil began to turn a bright pink at his ears as he nodded shyly.

"As a matter of fact, last Valentine's Day was when Cecil started to come up with his new business idea 'cause he thought he needed to start making enough money for us to get hitched." Cecil was even more flustered now and his pink ears had turned bright red to match the splotches on his cheeks. "Well . . . heh, heh, Tammy honey, that's not exactly what I meant."

"Well, anyway," Tammy blurted out happily, flinging her arm around Cecil, who looked like he was being choked. "The last thing we need to worry about is *money* after how Granny Doll fixed things up for me, but I guess Cecil making all those thousands off that rich car collector makes him feel better about it all."

She shook her head at her beloved beet-faced Cecil and held him at arm's length. "That's just the way you men are . . . so silly about those things!" Then she gave him a big kiss before dissolving in giggles while the rest of the party stared open-mouthed at the happy couple. A small "ahem" broke the silence after Tammy's fit of giggles subsided. "W . . . e . . . l . . . l . . ." Teenie started with a concerned look on his face. "Don't you think that's a mite hasty? I mean if we're gonna have us a big church wedding, especially the mother-daughter one I have already planned out, we'll need more time than that. I think you should wait till June."

Before Tammy could burst in with a flustered response, Lucille cut in.

"First of all, even though we love you dearly Teenie, there ain't gonna be no mother-daughter wedding and that's that." She turned to Tammy sitting beside her on the red sofa with Cecil on the other end, peering hopefully at his future mother-in-law.

"Honey, if you want a Valentine wedding that's exactly what you'll do. It will be the *pinkest*, most romantic heart-filled wedding that The Church of the Vine will allow. I want to be able to sit there and enjoy watching my little girl walk down the aisle and cry like every other mother of the bride!"

"Oh Momma, I love you." Tammy hugged Lucille tightly around her neck as Cecil beamed at them both looking visibly relieved. Teenie looked crestfallen. He would need some time to recover from the loss of his wedding planner role. However, he loved his two surrogate daughters enough to put their happiness before his own. Mavis patted her little man consolingly.

"I've already come up with five wedding gown designs for you to choose from honey," she said in a firm voice to Tammy. "Any one of them would look lovely with some red and pink hearts on them."

"Ooooh, really Aunt Mavis, you could put hearts on my gown? That would be fabulous!" Tammy bounced and clapped her hands, then looked worried. "Is there enough time for you to do all that and get my dress done?"

"Sure honey," Mavis reassured her with a wave of her hand. "Come on over tomorrow and pick out the one you want. Me and the sewing ladies will get started on it this week. You know I got me some help now."

Teenie was beginning to cheer up with the discussion of a wedding gown. Suddenly he broke in, "Tammy honey, you be thinking about what you want to do for the reception and I can get it all organized for you. I'm an experienced party planner now that I done all those political fundraisers for Buckshot. Sugar Bradley wants me to help her with the inauguration celebration plans, too." Teenie added that last bit of information with undisguised pride.

"Oh Teenie that would be so great if you could be Tammy's official wedding planner," Lucille said. "The Party Girls Catering Company will need plenty of supervision. … I just hope you'll have enough time with the *other* job we got in mind for you."

Teenie looked quizzically at Lucille as she gently elbowed Tammy who was sitting there staring blankly still seeing visions of her wedding gown adorned with pink and red satin Valentine hearts. Lucille tried again to get her daughter's attention. "Tammy honey, you need to tell Teenie Pop what we discussed." Tammy still didn't have a clue so Lucille continued for her. "Teenie, Tammy and I want you to walk her down the aisle so you can be the one to 'give her away,' just like you was her real daddy."

At first Teenie sat there stunned and (for once) speechless. When Lucille's request finally sunk in, he burst into tears and ran over to hug Lucille and Tammy. "That is just the sweetest thing anyone ever asked of me," he sobbed between hugs. "You know I'd be honored."

After many pats and kisses from the mother-daughter brides, Teenie sat back down next to Mavis, who handed him a small lace-trimmed linen hankie with a holly sprig embroidered on it. After being so well soothed, Teenie sat bolt upright with another urgent concern.

"What about Marv?" he asked Lucille. "Won't he want that honor since he and Pauline went down to Texas to find you two."

Rhonelle had been watching this little drama quietly. She was pretty sure why the wedding date had so suddenly been moved up. Now she spoke up for the first time. "Actually *I was the one* who told Marv where to find Lucille." (*With a lot of help from Granny Laurite.*) "Might I make a suggestion?" Rhonelle waited until all eyes were upon her before she spoke again. "I think Marv should be the one to walk *Lucille* down the aisle when she and Bo tie the knot."

Lucille let out a whoop and gravelly laughter. "Rhonelle, I think that's a great idea! Only thing is Bo and I won't be getting married in a church, but I reckon we'll figure out a way for him to hand me over to my groom."

Teenie looked relieved and curious. "Well, Lucille honey, where and *when* are you going to have your wedding?"

Bo looked at Lucille and grinned. "Well *that*, my friends, is a secret for now. Isn't it, Babe?"

"Yep," Lucille added. "Bo and I are hooked on surprises after what we pulled off with Sergio and that big Elvis." She looked over at the Brices. "Let's make sure our Tammy gets the wedding of her dreams before we go to planning all my stuff. Although I got a pretty good idea what I want Mavis to whup up for *my* wedding dress. I done already bought the fancy boots to wear with it!"

"My goodness Lucille," Teenie blinked at Lucille's brash idea. "You sound very non-traditional."

"That's one of the thangs I love about my woman," Bo Astor proclaimed with overly dramatic vehemence, dropping to his knees in front of Lucille, who responded by bopping him on the head with one of the decorative pillows on the sofa.

"Enough of all this mushy stuff y'all," Lucille cackled. "Let's open our presents!"

The traditional "doing the tree" proceeded Doll Dumas style. First, the album "Elvis Sings the Songs of Christmas" was started on the hi-fi. Then Tammy handed out gifts. Sergio abruptly stood up and excused himself.

"If you'll pardon me, I gotta go talk to Santa for a minute. Go ahead and start without me." (*I'll be right back darling. I think you and your friends need some privacy for a bit.*)

This last bit was said directly to Rhonelle's mind. She nodded and smiled at him, grateful for his sensitivity. "Okay, but don't take too long," she said out loud. After about forty-five minutes Sergio came back in the back door with a smug look on his face and his hands behind his back. Rhonelle sensed the door to his mind was shut tight. *Okay my love. I'll play along with the surprise. You're as bad as Lucille and Bo!*

This caused Sergio to guffaw suddenly while the rest of the people in the room looked curiously at this man who was still mostly a stranger to them. As soon as he composed himself again, Sergio pulled out a large bouquet of red roses from behind his back. "Roses for my lady; expertly chosen and arranged by our friend David, I might add." This caused a communal "Aawww ... how sweet" from the room.

When Rhonelle rose gracefully to accept the flowers and give Sergio a swift kiss on the lips, she found a red string tied around the tissue paper wrapped stems. The string went across the floor of the kitchen and under the back door. She held the string up and showed it to her friends. "Get your coats on. Looks like my dear Sergio has arranged for a follow-the-string game."

Murmuring excitedly, everybody bundled up and followed Rhonelle and Sergio out the back door, around the new carport that housed the refurbished T-Bird and Sergio's red pickup truck behind it. The string went all the way around the back of Louise Dolesanger's trailer and back to the front of the lavender double-wide.

Rhonelle stopped in her tracks and gasped. There stood a six-foot-tall, life-sized version of the Thirty-Foot Elvis right next to the corner of the front deck.

"Oh darling, this is perfect!" She really meant it. She had no idea how he had hidden this from her. She loved it and the whole surprise with the string made it even better. Everybody cheered when they saw it.

Bo came up and slapped Sergio on the back and shook his hand, "Man, you are just too cool for words."

Rhonelle gave Sergio a much longer kiss this time with Lucille hooting her encouragement. When they broke apart, Sergio said,

"There's one more little thing you haven't noticed yet." Rhonelle's eyes went from Sergio's smiling face and back to the statue. A small box was tied to one of Elvis' hands. She reached up and gingerly untied it and held it in her hands. She looked uncertainly up at Sergio. *Should I open this now, or later when we're alone?*

That's up to you my love. I have no problem sharing this moment with your friends. Sergio was speaking directly and only to Rhonelle and she felt all barriers to his mind fall away.

She wanted to open it *now*. There was a breathless moment of silence as her friends crowded closer to have a look at what could be inside the small gold cardboard box after she untied the red satin ribbon that secured it.

When she first took a peek at the contents, she snapped it back shut. Staring in astonishment at Sergio, she asked, "Where did you find this?"

She saw his face with another face superimposed over another one similar and familiar, but not the Sergio of today. They were alone in a strange room with music playing. Just as quickly as the vision had appeared, it vanished.

"Well, come on sister," Lucille brought Rhonelle back to the here and now. "Let us see what's inside the box," she said with a tinge of impatience. "It's getting cold out here."

Sergio opened the box for her and took out a delicate antique ring, a deep red ruby surrounded by small diamonds set in gold. He gently took Rhonelle's left hand and slipped it easily onto her finger. It fit perfectly over her swollen knuckle and once again she marveled at the beauty of Sergio's strong hands and his total acceptance of her own fingers, marred by the early damage of arthritis.

"I bought this little trinket in an antique store in New Orleans after we met there for Krystal's wedding. I've been saving it for the right occasion," Sergio said so all could hear.

"Oh my gawd," Lucille said with her hands on her hips. "Now we got us *two* psychics in Peavine. Lord help us if Bo's daddy ever hears about *this*!"

CHAPTER THIRTY-FIVE

More Elvis Than Ever

While Rhonelle was away with Sergio for a few days during the New Year's holiday, the Brices were in charge of Home-Sweet-Homes-on-Wheels. Teenie and Mavis planned to spend the days enjoying the comforts of the lavender double-wide. They packed up Pitty Too and Mavis' sewing bag and trudged over to mind the park office right after Rhonelle and Sergio left for New Orleans.

The red pickup truck wasn't out of the county before the Brices stood at the door of the lavender double-wide. "Now let's see," Teenie started patting at each of the pockets in his plaid wool jacket. "Where did I put that key?"

"It's under the flower pot by the door," Mavis whispered in case some thief might be listening.

"Oh, so it is," Teenie giggled. "How could I have forgotten that? Just too much wedding and inaugural planning on my mind I suppose," With an air of nonchalance he bent over and found the key under the pot of plastic red geraniums by the door. Teenie had brought it over to go with the red and white Elvis statue now standing guard in the front yard.

"After you, m'lady." Teenie held the door open while Mavis squeezed by him.

Mavis switched on the lamps in the living room and laid out her sewing things on the sofa. When Teenie came in with Pitty Too, her doggie bed and favorite toys, he found Mavis standing in there, dabbing furiously at tears running down her plump cheeks. I still can't get used to all these changes Rhonelle's made to the place," Mavis said, her small voice hoarse. "It's like Doll never was here . . . even her favorite settin' chair is all different." She looked mournfully at the overstuffed chair Darla had covered with moons and stars fabric. "Aw, honey, don't you cry," Teenie wrapped his little arms around

Mavis' waist as far as he could reach. "Doll wanted it this way. That was her gift to Rhonelle. And it's the first time that gal has had a real home of her own."

He led Mavis gently to the overstuffed chair. "Why don't you just set yourself down right here. See, it still feels the same," he added cheerfully. "Now you just relax and I'll go into the bathroom and get you a cool washrag for your face."

Mavis smiled up at him. "Thank you, Hon. That would feel good. My face feels all flushed." She settled back into the soft chair cushions and closed her eyes. The chair was just as comfortable as always and the new fabric had an almost velvety texture. She had helped make the slipcovers and had enjoyed the feel of it. She could hear Tee-nie humming a little tune as he went over to the bedroom door and opened it. She heard the light snap on. Teenie abruptly stopped hum-ming and let out a long low whistle.

"Oh good Lord in heaven," Teenie whispered in an awestruck tone. "I'd heard about this from Darla and Vaudine . . . but Oh – I can't believe she done all *this*!"

Mavis' eyes flew open and she called out to Teenie. "Hon, what is it? Did you break something?"

Then she heard a rather wicked little giggle as Teenie went into the bathroom and started running the faucet. "No dear," he shouted over the running water. "There ain't nothing wrong – exactly. You stay put. I'll be right there."

Returning to the living room carrying a wet red washcloth, Teenie was unable to hide a mischievous grin. "Here you go. You better cool yourself off before I show you what else our friend Rhonelle has been redecorating."

Mavis got up and went over to peer into the master bedroom. She hadn't set foot in there since Doll had passed last year. When she saw the red velvet bed with the fancy red and gold headboard, she let out a gasp. Teenie grabbed her by the elbow and dragged her closer to the ornate bed and pointed up at the ceiling. "Take a look at that."

A large rectangle of mirrored tiles surrounded by small glowing lights covered the ceiling over the bed – Rhonelle's private Christmas gift to Sergio.

"Hand me that cold washrag," Mavis held her hand out at Teenie. "My face is sure burning now!" Both Mavis and Teenie giggled simultaneously. By the time they sat back down in the living room, they were laughing so hard they were in tears.

Mavis sighed. "We always knew Rhonelle was a very private person."

Teenie squealed with new laughter. "Yes and now we know *why*. She is certainly a woman full of surprises. All these years and I never thought she'd have any kind of a *private* life."

"And why shouldn't she have a private life?" Mavis asked Teenie. "You think she's too old for … all that?" She waved toward the scandalous bedroom.

"She seems to have made a good choice with that Sergio fella," Teenie admitted. "They seem like such a good match . . . I wonder where he's been all her life?"

Mavis stared out the window in deep thought before she said quietly, "I think maybe he's been looking for *her* all his life."
Teenie shivered slightly. "Ooooh, you're getting kind of spooky on me." Mavis' face crinkled up into a smile again. "Why Teenie, I thought I was being romantic."

They spent the rest of the afternoon working on their projects before deciding to walk over to Don's Diner for an early supper. Teenie couldn't resist telling Dorine all about that "wild bedroom" Rhonelle had over at the double-wide.

Dorine sat down at their table and leaned in to hear about the mirror over the bed. "Oh Lordeee," she snickered and clapped a hand over her mouth when Teenie told her. "Of course I knew all about that bed and the other décor from Darla and Vaudine. They said Rhonelle liked to have swooned first time she saw the bed when they went to Vicksburg. But a mirror with lights – our Rhonelle has really been busy!"

"That's one way to put it," Mavis whispered. They all burst into laughter. After dinner Teenie and Mavis walked slowly back to the small Airstream trailer that had been their home these many years.

Teenie looked longingly across the park at the lavender double-wide, its Christmas lights along the roofline and around the deck still twinkling brightly. He could see the life-sized Elvis lit brightly with a new spotlight. It looked like a fancy resort to him.

He stopped and turned to Mavis before they went up the steps to their tiny built-on porch. "Hon, how long has it been since we took us a vacation anywhere?"

Mavis thought for a moment. "Well . . . I guess the last time was when we went up to Little Rock for the last dog show, but that was years ago."

"No, I mean a *real* vacation," insisted Teenie. "We always took our Airstream with us instead of staying in a motel."

"Oh," Mavis agreed. "I see what you mean, but that's because of the pups." She patted Pitty Too, who was sound asleep in the crook of her arm.

"Well," Teenie said, "wouldn't it be nice if we was to stay some place really nice for a few days . . . for a little vacation of sorts?"

Mavis sighed as she heaved herself up the front steps and unlocked the door. "I don't see how we could afford to go do something like that. Besides, you know how I feel about getting all dressed up. "

Teenie scampered in and around Mavis so he could look up into her face. "W . . . e . . . l . . . l . . ." I think I may have a good alternative." He had a very sly look on his face as he stood there making his eyebrows jig up and down as he jerked his head back toward Rhonelle's trailer."

Mavis looked across the way and back at Teenie as her mouth made the shape of a tiny o. "Do you think we could? I mean, would she mind?"

"Rhonelle told me we was to make ourselves right at home, soooo . . . I don't see anything wrong with us staying there while she's gone. That's a much better way to look out for her place . . . right?" Teenie fluttered his eyelids at Mavis and gave a perfectly innocent smile at her.

After packing their toothbrushes, PJs, and poodle, they snuck back over to Rhonelle's, giggling in the dark like a couple of kids. They had the most pleasant luxurious vacation of their lifetimes and all they had to do was go across the park to the lavender double-wide.

By the time Rhonelle and Sergio returned with another load of Elvises they had picked up on a side trip through Memphis, it was almost ten o'clock on a cold rainy night. They were pleasantly surprised to find the double-wide warmly lit and the Brices waiting up for them with a crock-pot of vegetable soup and a plate of pimento cheese finger sandwiches. The place was neat as a pin, cleaner than when Rhonelle and Sergio left it. A fire was lit in the gas log fireplace and Mavis was cleaning up the tea cups they'd just emptied.

"Thank you, Teenie and Mavis, for taking such good care of the place," Rhonelle said as she shook raindrops off her coat. "The soup was so thoughtful. You shouldn't have gone to so much trouble."

"I'm glad she did," shouted Sergio from the kitchen. "I'm starving. This looks great!"

"Well we better get on out of your way now," Teenie said as he and Mavis gathered their things and put on their coats. "It's way past our bedtime." Before he could stop himself, a shrill nervous giggle escaped his lips.

"Goodnight y'all," Mavis said. "Real glad you're back home safely." She hustled Teenie out the door after he picked up the poodle.

"Do you think she knows?" Teenie looked back nervously over his shoulder after they walked across the yard.

"Probably," was all Mavis said, but she had no regrets.

By the time Elvis' birthday rolled around on January 8, a huge amount of publicity had circulated about the statue in the park. Besides generous news coverage on TV, radio, and in the newspapers, Bo Astor had convinced the Peavine Chamber of Commerce to buy time for a TV commercial that he and Barry Zellhorn had produced using footage from the video Coach Zellhorn was compiling for his official

Thirty-Foot Elvis documentary. They could only afford to buy time on three TV stations; one each in Little Rock, Jonesboro, and Monroe, Louisiana, but that was enough to draw plenty of Elvis devotees, some of whom were already planning a stopover in Peavine on their pilgrimage to Graceland.

Bo and Lucille chipped in on a radio ad they made together and sent to as many stations as they could afford in the area. Bo had requested and been approved by the FCC to change the call letters for KPEW radio station to KEPW – now the only Elvis Presley-inspired radio station west of the Mississippi!

The Peavine school board had a large stash of funding remaining from a posthumous donation by the Doll Dumas estate. In a unanimous vote, they changed the name of the football team mascot from "Fighting Boll Weevils" (a name that had always been an embarrassment) to the Peavine "Hound Dawgs." The band got all new uniforms with a design very similar to the ones worn by the Marching Elvises in the Christmas Parade. Bo Astor came up with that idea.

With so much preoccupation over the new era heralded by the Thirty-Foot Elvis, the January fourth inauguration celebration for the first new mayor of Peavine in more than twenty years was in danger of going unnoticed. Teenie Brice recruited Bo Astor and Lucille to advise him on how to spice up the party and generate more interest.

Bo was more than happy to DJ an old-fashioned sock hop dance at the VFW. Lucille brought over the new karaoke machine and video screen that Bo had given her for Christmas. With plenty of free promotion on KEPW, a huge, multi-generational crowd of townspeople turned out.

The highlight of the evening was a nearly perfect rendition of "Heartbreak Hotel" by newly sworn-in Mayor Buckshot Bradley on the karaoke. Sugar Bradley was so proud of Teenie's party planning that she pulled him out on the dance floor to publicly congratulate him. The First Lady of Peavine said that he had put on the best inaugural ball in municipal history.

Teenie seemed to grow a foot taller as he stood in the spotlight, showered by applause. Mavis was so proud of him. She had taken a special effort to dress nicely for the occasion. Still, she was delighted to know she would be able to wear socks and sneakers to such a fancy event. She made a new caftan out of some fabric she mail-ordered: pink poodles and Eiffel towers printed all over it.

Mavis was determined to overcome her usual shyness during the inauguration. She told herself this was Teenie's night, that Teenie needed her as a part of his new stature in the world of high society and politics. Mavis was delighted to see her little man happy again. His disappointment over the rejection of his plans for a mother-daughter wedding was a thing of the past now, to her great relief. Teenie had also been too preoccupied to notice Tammy's slight pallor some recent mornings, and that her perfect figure was getting slightly fuller.

After the big party, the citizens of Peavine had to brace themselves for a wave of tourism the likes of which they'd never experienced. Don and Dorine hired three more waitresses. Lorna Mae trained them up in the way they should serve.

By the way, plain little Lorna Mae showed up to work two days before the Christmas Parade almost unrecognizable to Don and Dorine. She had decided on her makeover and it was a jaw-dropping transformation.

Tammy and Shirleen had always wanted her to bleach her hair blonde and maybe give her a perm. However, Lorna Mae had a mind of her own. She figured, since everyone else in Peavine seemed to be Elvis crazy, she would go for an Ann-Margret "Viva Las Vegas" look. Shirleen's niece dyed Lorna's drab brown hair a deep rich red and styled it with big rollers. When she added heavy eyeliner and coral lipstick, Lorna Mae looked like a million bucks.

Lorna started to wear more of Tammy's hand-me-downs and started leaving several of the top buttons of her waitress uniform strategically undone. Tad Bradley literally tripped over his own feet when he came into the Diner and saw her for the first time. Her new look certainly caused an increase in the number of young men eating Don's grilled peanut butter and banana sandwiches and plate lunches.

When it came time to train up the three new waitresses at the Diner, it became apparent that Lorna had acquired a new air of authority. She made certain helpful suggestions to Don and Dorine on handling the expected increase in customers over the next few days. Lorna had done some research since the first flood of people showed up December first. When they thought about it now, Don and Dorine honestly couldn't remember how they had gotten along before they hired Lorna.

A new bill board was erected north of town that said:

Welcome to Peavine,
Home of the Thirty-Foot Elvis!

It all but blocked out the traditional sign that for years had welcomed everybody to "Peavine – The Little Town That Grows on You." Local businesses thought they were more than ready for the first "Big Elvis Day," but the tidal wave of tourists that descended on Peavine that week was far beyond anyone's expectations. A steady stream of backed-up traffic along the highway was made worse by all the illegally parked vehicles along the side of the road. Sheriff Tilley and Deputy Joe Bob Roberts had their hands full writing tickets and directing traffic.

Vaudine Fortney's Forever Formica was swamped with customers wanting to buy miniature replicas of the Thirty-Foot Elvis. Within two days, she sold out of all the various-sized Elvises that Sergio had brought from Memphis. The shop was so crowded with customers at one point, Mr. Nasty had a mild nervous breakdown. He cut loose with so many expletives Vaudine had to cover his cage. Fred had to take the poor frazzled bird home for the day.

Elvis devotees packed Don's Diner and Seymour's Tex-Mex day and night. Louise taught herself some new Elvis tunes to play at Seymour's and ended up playing "Happy Birthday" to Elvis more often than she'd have liked while the tourists sang along. Ozelle's Brisket

Basket was selling barbecue in record-breaking amounts. Both of Ozelle's places were run ragged, the original restaurant south of town as well as from their catering truck set up near Herman Park.

Keeping the masses fed was one thing, finding a place for them to stay was a whole other matter. Despite winter weather, the Poodle Trot Camp was full to the brim with tents and campers. They built several bonfires to keep things toasty. Sheriff Tilley had to call on the volunteer fireman to check and be sure the park trees' low-hanging limbs didn't catch on fire.

Rhonelle was especially grateful to have Sergio around in case anything got out of hand with the people she had to turn away because they ran out of room. This crowd made the Annual Poodle Pageant regulars seem like a Sunday school outing by comparison.

Needless to say, most of Peavine was relieved to have that week over with. The restaurants and merchants saw huge profits but were beginning to doubt if all the turmoil that accompanied their new tourist attraction was worth spoiling the former peacefulness of their quiet little town. Only two people seem unfazed and openly delighted with it all: Bo Astor and Lucille Lepanto. Bo was having the time of his life with his radio station. Lucille designated once-a-month "Elvis Impersonator Nights." The live Open Mike Night broadcasts on KEPW every Saturday night were wildly popular. Whenever questioned about the date of her upcoming wedding, Lucille would claim she and Bo were just too busy . . . and besides, there was Tammy's wedding to finish planning.

Meanwhile, Vestaline and former Mayor Herbert Dalton were laying low, patiently waiting for the tide of public opinion to veer back onto a track of decency and modesty. Violet Posey was getting her revenge on a daily basis with her dog, Hero, delivering his little "gift" at the base of Thirty-Foot Elvis during their predawn constitutionals.

Even the loyal residents of the Home-Sweet-Homes-on-Wheels were beginning to wonder if perhaps all this attention might be a bit too much of a good thing. They had all been holed up in their trailers most of that week as if they were under siege.

A cold snap with a dusting of snow and sleet hit Peavine the next to the last week in January. Everybody took it as a good excuse to take some time off and rest.

As soon as the roads cleared, Sergio reluctantly left for Memphis so he could replenish his supply of Elvis statuary. Even his studio and roadside store near Graceland run by his two employees was picked clean. He promised to be back in time for Valentine's Day. This would be the longest time he and Rhonelle had spent apart since their reunion on December the first.

Rhonelle busied herself with wedding plans for Tammy. Mavis was finishing up work on the wedding gown and bridesmaid dress (thank goodness there was only one). The Party Girls came down a week before the wedding to finalize arrangements on the wedding reception with Teenie. Shirleen arrived the week before the wedding to coordinate hairstyling and makeup.

Fred and Vaudine decided to have the rehearsal dinner at Seymour's Tex-Mex and free up Don's Diner for the bridal reception food preparation. David was in charge of flowers. He ordered double the usual amount of pink and red roses for Valentine's Day. Violet Posey found plenty to complain about during their busiest day of the year.

Marv and Pauline insisted on paying for the flowers and all the expenses of a week-long honeymoon in Destin, Florida. They had wanted to give the young couple a trip to Hawaii, but Tammy had never flown before and the thought of such a long flight made her turn green. The beach on the Gulf sounded just right to her. The Thirty-Foot Elvis stood silently by as his importance faded in the light of Peavine's most-beloved daughter readying herself for the rite of matrimony.

CHAPTER THIRTY-SIX

The Wedding of Tammy Lepanto and Cecil Swindle

From the Amanda Hollingsworth Social Whirligig Column in the *Peavine Times:*

On Saturday evening of February sixteenth at seven o'clock, marriage vows were solemnly exchanged by Tammy Sue Lepanto and Cecil Alan Swindle during a lovely ceremony at The Church of the Vine officiated by Reverend Joe Don Astor.

The bride was presented in marriage by her surrogate father and close friend of the family, Teenie Brice (affectionately called "Teenie Pop" by the bride), and her mother, Ms. Lucille Lepanto. All of the guests were sure that the bride's late grandmother, Doll (Mrs. Herman Jr.) Dumas must have been smiling down from Heaven at this beautiful sight!

The bride's wedding gown was a custom-made confection of French tulle, lace, seed pearls, and small appliqué hearts of pink and red satin lovingly designed and constructed by Mavis (Mrs. Teenie) Brice. The bride's floor-length Spanish lace veil was an heirloom of the Dumas family, purchased in New Orleans by the late Adelaide (Mrs. Herman Sr.) Dumas, and was topped by a rhinestone tiara studded with red hearts and pink rosebuds. The bridal bouquet was a dozen red roses with miniature pink orchids and white tuber rose sprays.

The one bridesmaid, Amber Lea Hanley, wore a red satin floor-length gown with a ruffled neckline and hem. It contrasted in a most unusual yet pleasant way with Miss Amber's well-known head of curly orange hair, styled expertly in a daring up-do studded with sprigs of baby's breath. Miss Amber carried a bouquet of pink roses and baby's breath.

The groom's father, Albert Gene Swindle of El Dorado served as his son's best man. He and the groom wore all-white tuxedos with red cummerbunds and pink bow ties. Each sported a boutonniere of a single red rose.

The mother of the bride, Ms. Lucille Lepanto, wore a floor-length, two-piece gown of rather luminous pink polyester silk with an overlay of pink lace strewn with seed pearls. Her gown was also designed and made for the occasion by Mrs. Brice. Ms. Lepanto wore a wrist corsage of pink rosebuds and was accompanied by her fiancé, Mr. Bodine Astor the second.

Louise (Mrs. Charles) Dolesanger played the organ for the ceremony and provided the musical entertainment at the reception afterward.

A lavish reception followed the ceremony in the church's new activity hall. The basketball court was completely transformed into a romantic Valentine Garden by the floral artistry of Violet Expressions and head floral designer David Posey. Ivy and rose buntings wrapped in white lights hung from the walls and around three white gazebos built to frame the refreshment tables. Red and pink Valentine hearts of various sizes decorated the walls and were scattered upon the candle-lit tables.

Talented pastry maker, Mrs. Kim Lei Nan, who moved to Peavine from Korea and recently became the owner of the Donut Palace, outdid herself with a spectacular five-layer white wedding cake. Each layer was decorated with pink icing roses and marzipan red hearts. Don Dinkins made chocolate pies instead of the traditional groom's cake.

Other scrumptious snacks were provided by the Party Girl Catering Company, including their famous cheese dip at special request by the bride. Pink sherbet and ginger ale punch was served from two crystal bowls at the canapé table. Misty and Kristy (co-owners of Party Girls Catering and longtime friends of the bride) helped serve punch by pouring at both ends.

For those with a heartier appetite, Ozelle Washington's famous barbecue brisket was served on Sally Washington's delicious yeast rolls with slaw and baked beans served in dainty pink containers.

A grand time was had by all. At the end of the evening the newly married couple left in a perfectly restored vintage 1960 white Cadillac convertible as the guests blew bubbles (instead of throwing rice) from small pink ribbon-wrapped vials handed out to guests by Tammy's Tappers.

After a week-long honeymoon trip to Destin, Florida, Mr. and Mrs. Cecil A. Swindle will make their home here in Peavine at the house given to the bride by her late grandmother.

The newspaper was spread out across the red velvet coverlet as Sergio read the society article aloud to Rhonelle, who lay back on the pillows sipping her coffee. It was the Sunday after the wedding and they were enjoying a late morning.

"Oh, you were *right*," Sergio started to laugh when he got to the part about the Party Girls serving punch. "She actually does use the words 'pouring at both ends!'"

Rhonelle laughed so hard her eyes were watering. "That's why Kristy and Misty insisted on setting up punch bowls at each end of the table. They knew Amanda would write it up like that. Those girls are still full of it ... can't seem to help themselves."

"That's why I love this town and all of your interesting friends," Sergio smiled as he reached up and kissed Rhonelle.

"Do you really?" she asked, wondering if he was serious. "Do you like it here *that* much?"

"Of course, I do," he patted her on the thigh as he got up out of bed and took her empty coffee mug. "Peavine is a part of you now, so, of course, I love it, too."

As he headed toward the bedroom door with his back to her he added nonchalantly, "Yes, I *would* enjoy living here. I'm still working on the logistics of making that possible."

Rhonelle was left staring at the doorway with her mouth open and was about to speak but realized it wasn't necessary. Instead, she smiled and snuggled back into her pillows with a contented sigh. *Telepathy is so ... convenient.*

It is indeed, agreed Sergio.

CHAPTER THIRTY-SEVEN

Beware the Ides of March

Life in Peavine seemed almost back to normal during the last two weeks in February. The newlyweds returned from their honeymoon on the beach in Destin. Tammy was deeply tanned, glowing with health and happiness. Cecil was sunburned, but a great deal relaxed. They set up housekeeping at Tammy's, where Cecil needed a while to get used to the idea that he was now perfectly entitled to come and go at all hours without having to sneak by Marv and Pauline.

The weather was warming into another early spring. With the return of fine weather came an ever-increasing tide of tourists and Elvis-gawkers. Barry Zellhorn went by the statue at least once a day to take a few frames of video for the time-lapse montage that he wanted to use in his documentary about the Thirty-Foot Elvis.

If he encountered a crowd at the park, Barry called Bo Astor or one of his football players to come help him interview unusual strangers and the occasional Peaviner for reactions. Whenever one or more impressive Elvis impersonators showed up, Bo would drop whatever he was doing and come extend a hearty welcome. More often than not, he'd put them on his new mid-morning radio show, "Elvis Talk."

Business at the new KEPW radio and Lucille's Too-Tite Tavern was better than ever. Bo spent most nights out at Lucille's log cabin, but they hadn't yet gotten around to setting a wedding date. Whenever anybody had the nerve to ask about that, Lucille said it was too soon after Tammy's big day. "We'll get around to it sooner or later. Let it be a surprise."

However, beneath all this geniality, an undercurrent of discontent was brewing in Peavine. Old Mayor Herbert Dalton finally roused himself out of his post-election defeat doldrums when he caught sight of the new welcome sign north of town.

His wife Vestaline drove him out there expressly to make him look at the huge, gaudy billboard.

Welcome to Peavine
Home of the Thirty-Foot Elvis

It dwarfed and mostly obscured Herbert's familiar, small hand-painted: "**Welcome to Peavine: the Little Town That Grows on You**" sign that had been a landmark for the past twenty years. The sight of this travesty caused something to pop in the old gent's head. Determined to get revenge on these usurpers, he blamed this new "age of vulgarity" in Peavine directly upon the new mayor, Buckshot Bradley, and vowed from that day forward he'd make that man's life a living hell! (It seemed inconsequential to old man Dalton that the Thirty-Foot Elvis appeared during *his own term*, even though near to the end.)

Violet Posey was all too happy to help Vestaline and Herbert Dalton recruit other disgruntled citizens to their anti-Elvis cause. Some way or another they would get rid of that obscene gyrating rock-and-roll singer's statue. Having the former mayor as their spokesman gave them just the gravitas they needed.

Vestaline's vehement presentation at the March meeting of the Ladies League of Political Activities resulted in half of the members signing her petition declaring the Thirty-Foot Elvis a menace to the morals, health, and safety of the citizens of Peavine. Violet Posey had no problem collecting more signatures at the March meeting of the Peavine Garden Club, whose members were still stinging from the insult of having their annual Christmas Glory in the Park project so rudely snatched away from them.

Violet's older sister, Rose Posey, circulated the petition out at the Mansion Rest and Retirement Home and signed up plenty of the Blue Hair Brigadiers. Unfortunately, Rose talked to old Pastor Astor, who until then had been blissfully ignorant of the whole "Elvis thing." When he heard about Bo changing his beloved KPEW radio call let-

236 | JANE F. HANKINS

ters to KEPW, all his dormant hell-fire and brimstone oratory burst back into full flame. Pastor Astor felt his strength and vigor return as he led impromptu prayer meetings at the Mansion chapel. He used these opportunities to sermonize about the "dangers of worshiping false idols." Early onset dementia caused some remnants of his long-forgotten Shakespearian inventory to combine colorfully with his church rhetoric. He ended each sermon with a full-throated "beware the Ides of March!" He was very proud of himself for remembering what month it was.

While Christabelle Tingleberry was pleased to see Lyle Bodine Astor's cognitive and physical condition improve, she was quite concerned about the direction it was taking. Rose Posey had largely usurped Christabelle's position as activity director of events out at the Mansion. Rose was the one that went to the pastor's room to "remind" him it was time for a prayer meeting and cheerfully wheel him down to the Mansion Chapel. He could have made it there just fine using his walker, but Rose took advantage of the spectacle of Pastor Astor being ceremoniously wheeled through the halls as a way to gather worshipers along the route.

The Blue Hair Brigade ladies gathered as moths to a flame. They were longtime fans of the pastor and great admirers of his old-time preaching style. Christabelle hoped to gently steer the residents toward more positive activities like a friendly hymn singing or thinking up charity projects for the less fortunate. From the sounds of shouted cheers and "Amen to that" coming from the once quiet "meditation chapel," Christabelle surmised the only things that crowd of elderly ladies lacked were pitchforks and torches.

The day arrived when the pastor and his followers insisted on a field trip. Rose Posey with some help from her sister Violet cornered Albert, the Mansion bus driver, and booked a date and time for him to drive a whole busload of the clients over to Herman Park.

Their intention was to hold a prayer and protest rally at the base of the Thirty-Foot Elvis. Violet had coordinated the excursion with Vestaline Dalton and her band of followers from the LLOPA and the Garden Club. Poor Christabelle was powerless to stop them. She followed the bus in her 1969 Buick with her first-aid kit and blood pressure cuff on board – just in case an elderly protester was overcome in zealotry. She watched from the safety of the Buick, so as not to be mistaken for a member of the "anti-Elvis" movement.

Albert parked the bus as close to the statue as possible and helped escort his passengers between azalea bushes and other obstacles. For many, it was their first time to actually look up at the enormous "graven image." The Blue Hairs couldn't help being in awe of it. They had to agree it was an impressive structural and artistic achievement, far surpassing anything else in Peavine. When Pastor Astor was dutifully wheeled up to the base by a very nervous Albert, all the old pastor could do for several minutes was stare up at the gleaming statue, his mouth agape.

"Jumping *Jehoshaphat*," Pastor Astor mumbled repeatedly. "I had no idea he was this *big*." An appreciative smile slowly formed on his uplifted face. "Looks like my boy outdone himself on this one," he muttered to Albert, who had been watching the pastor with concern over his first reaction to the object upon which he had heaped such severe condemnation.

Christabelle's reluctance to be suspected of participating in the Blue Hair protest was trumped by her nurse's instincts. Worry over the pastor's possible adverse reaction to the Thirty-Foot Elvis provoked her to leap out of the Buick and jog bouncily across the lawn of Herman Park. More anti-Elvis groups were arriving and joining the Mansion residents carrying signs. In the vanguard of this group were Garden Club ladies and LLOPA members, marshaled by Vestaline Dalton with former Mayor Herbert Dalton in tow.

Christabelle saw real trouble ahead if the Daltons should involve themselves in the anti-Elvis movement. Slowing her pace to a brisk walk in order to catch her breath and push windblown hair off her face, Christabelle squinted at the poster board signs she saw being passed out to the protesters by Violet Posey. Christabelle thought *surely* she was misreading the crude printing on the bright orange and green signs. Heavy footfalls, accompanied by huffing and puffing behind Christabelle proved to be Barry Zellhorn with another one of his deep-bench-football-players-turned-cameraman.

"C'mon over this way Al," huffed Coach Zellhorn. "The light will be better if we can shoot from this direction. Oh, 'scuse me Nurse Tingleberry."

The young man carrying the camera stopped, laughed, and pointed at protesting ladies proudly carrying their signs as they lined up around the statue's base. "Coach, look at those signs!" Al said in disbelief.

"Do they really say what I think they do?" Christabelle shaded her eyes from the sun and suddenly clapped her hand to her mouth.

"Ha! I believe they do Miss Tingleberry," Coach said gleefully. "Oh this is rich . . . too good to be believed. We got us a real gem here today. I'll make movie history." He and his camera-toting student ran forward to film the gathering.

Christabelle started to laugh so hard she had to stop walking and simply enjoy the spectacle. She had *not* misread the garish signs with the bold black letters printed on them:

Peavine Opposes Obscenity (POO)

Nearby, Christabelle heard snorts of laughter. David Posey, Violet's nephew, was observing his aunt as he lounged on a bench under a nearby tree. Standing next to him was Theodore Patterson, editor of the *Peavine Times*.

"This ought to make for an unusual headline," Theodore noted dryly as he snapped several pictures with his telephoto-lens-equipped camera before turning calmly toward his office.

David stood up politely. "Care to have a seat and join me, Miss Tingleberry?"

"Why thank you, David," Christabelle said as she sat primly down next to him on the bench. "The view from here ought to be perfect." Seeing the POO signs had diluted most of Christabelle's anxiety. She knew she could step in and rescue the pastor from here, if needed. For now, she would allow things to unfold of their own accord, and enjoy the show while sitting in the company of this nice young man.

The POO protesters formed a circle around the Thirty-Foot Elvis. Holding signs aloft, they waited for former Mayor Dalton to take his place beside Pastor Astor, who sat patiently in his wheel chair smiling congenially. He was enjoying being out on such a fine day, even if the wind was beginning to pick up a little. Rose Posey had thoughtfully brought along a lap blanket for his comfort. Pastor Astor closed his eyes and basked in the warm sunshine and humid, almost summery, weather.

Mayor Dalton held up a battery-powered bullhorn and addressed the crowd. "Good afternoon ladies and gentlemen, may I have your attention please." Christabelle noted that the crowd was composed almost entirely of ladies. The only gentlemen present were the former mayor and Pastor Astor. Andrew the driver had gone back to wait in the bus.

"Fellow conscientious citizens of Peavine," continued Herbert in sonorous tones. "We are here today to reclaim the dignity of our town from the *ghastly* effects of this obscene form of idolatry, of all things tacky and immodest, erected here . . . nay I say *imposed* upon us here in the center of our town. *Without the slightest* bit of consideration for the wishes of us God-fearing, decent citizens." He paused to allow the crowd to agree with his expression of indignation.

"Not a single person in this town was asked for permission or consent before raising this atrocity . . . this *stain* upon our lovely little park. Just look at the turmoil this statue has caused: increased traffic dangers, drifters, and gawkers. Just about every kind of misfit and miscreant has been drawn to this . . . this . . . *unholy* piece of . . ." Herbert Dalton stammered . . . at a loss to come up with the most despicable word he could think of to describe the Thirty-Foot Elvis.

Violet Posey said, "shit" – under her breath, of course.

Vestaline grabbed the bullhorn from her husband and filled in that most dastardly of all words to describe the thirty-foot sculpture.

"***Modern Art!***" she shouted out over the crowd, in what she felt was the most scathing condemnation of all. She handed the bullhorn back, a smug look on her face. The gaggle of ladies hooted and booed at the Elvis (not Vestaline).

"Yes," Herbert Dalton continued after a loud feedback screech from the bullhorn caused everyone nearby to try to cover their ears. "Yes . . . who in their right mind would want such a garish piece of modern art in their city park? What kind of people do *they* think *we* are . . . some kind of hippies – or *liberals?*"

"NO!" shouted the crowd of ladies, almost in unison.

"I should think not . . . no indeed!" Herbert was good and warmed up now. "We are not going to let them force us to put up with this obscenity are we?"

"NO!" was the resounding response.

"Well here is what we are going to do about it." On cue Vestaline handed her husband a large thick tablet of white paper, which he held up over his head.

"What I have here is a petition I've had legally drawn up because I know how these things work, mind you. I wasn't mayor of Peavine for two decades for nothing!"

(He got lots of applause on that line.)

"Anyway, what I have here is our not-so-secret weapon. This here is a petition to have this statue declared a public nuisance and a danger to our community. So I say to you Mr. Mayor … I say:

"Tear . . . Down . . . this Elvis, Mr. Buckshot Bradley!"

The ladies cheered and waved their signs in frenzied excitement. Amid the clamor Pastor Astor slowly rose from his wheelchair. The lap blanket fell to the ground. Herbert Dalton was startled as the pastor reached for the bullhorn and held onto the former mayor's arm to steady himself. Pastor Astor took a deep breath and spoke firmly.

"Let us pray."

Silence settled over the crowd. Meanwhile, back on the bench under the tree Christabelle and David looked at each other in surprise.

"Dear Lord in Heaven, look down upon us miserable sinners here below. Show us the way to rid ourselves from all this evil that has come upon us in the form of this graven image of sin and idolatry." Pastor Astor paused to allow shouts of "Yes, Lord!" and "Amen!" to arise spontaneously from the crowd.

"We need all the power that You can give us, Lord." Pastor Astor was building to a crescendo. "We need ALL the powers of Heaven and Earth to take this Elvis down and wash away our many, *many* sins, Lord. Let me hear an Amen!"

"Amen!" shouted the shrill voices of the ardent POO protesters.

A strange thing occurred at that moment. At the very same time the pastor raised his face and extended his free hand to the heavens, a cloud moved overhead, dimming the sunlight dramatically. The wind blew across the park, ruffling the dresses and hair of the ladies, knocking their hats askew. Some of the signs blew out of their hands.

Pastor Astor put the bullhorn to his lips once more and delivered his closing line with all the power and drama he had in him that day:

"Beware the Ides of March!"

There was an uncertain pause as his audience weighed the proper response to that declaration. Pastor Astor sank back into his wheelchair and handed the bullhorn back to Herbert Dalton. Another strong gust of wind swirled around the protesters, ripping the sheaf of civic complaint petitions out of Herbert Dalton's hand, scattering them across the park.

Christabelle walked briskly toward the now chaotic group gathered at the base of the statue. She got to Pastor Astor just as Rose Posey attempted to hold onto her hat and put the lap blanket back across the pastor's knees.

"I'll take it from here Rose," Christabelle declared firmly as she tucked the blanket around Pastor Astor and started to wheel him toward the Buick. When the pastor saw Christabelle, he looked as docile and delighted to see her as ever. "I'm ready to go back home now, Christabelle. May I ride with you?"

"You most certainly may, dear," Christabelle said sweetly as Rose and Violet Posey glared daggers at her from behind the pastor's back. "I think you've caused enough excitement for one day."

Teenie, Marv, and Rhonelle watched from behind a stand of oak trees at the edge of the park as the windblown protesters scattered hurriedly toward their various forms of transportation.

Earlier that afternoon Teenie had noticed the Mansion Activity Bus pull into Herman Park while on his way home after his trip to the drugstore downtown. At first, he thought it was so nice for all those old people to have an outing in the park on such a pleasant day.

When he saw the Daltons arriving along with Violet Posey, he guessed there was more afoot than a simple walk in the park. By the time he got home and called Marv, loudspeaker sounds wafted faintly from the park. The two men found Rhonelle standing on the deck of the double-wide, hands on her hips, elbows flared and dark hair billowing about her in the wind. Without a word, she strode down the steps and all three walked in silence toward Herman Park, Teenie struggling to keep up with Marv and Rhonelle.

Arriving at the end of Herbert Dalton's speech, they heard the part about the petition. Marv sucked at his teeth and shook his head.

"That ain't good."

"Why?" Teenie asked looking worried. "He can't really do anything can he?"

"Actually he *can* if he gets enough signatures," Marv began to explain.

"Shhhh," Rhonelle held up her hand as she strained to hear.

Teenie pointed at Pastor Astor as he stood up from his wheelchair. "Oh my gawd, lookie who's a rising up like Lazarus from the grave!"

"Yep," Marv sighed. "Here comes the icing on the cake."

"Will you two shut up so I can listen," Rhonelle hissed at them before she turned back to watch. She could see Barry Zellhorn directing his linebacker cameraman as they circled the edges of the group. When clouds dramatically blocked the sun and the wind picked up, she couldn't stop a little snort of laughter. "I feel like I'm watching a scene from the 'Ten Commandments' movie."

Teenie's eyes were like saucers and he swallowed hard. "I think it's kind of spooky everything going all dark like this."

After Pastor Astor closed with his "Beware the Ides of March" line, Teenie tugged at Rhonelle's arm. "What does he mean by that? When are the Ides of March supposed to be here?"

The three friends stood there watching until most of the protesters had left and slips of paper were flying all over the park as the wind blew harder from the southwest and more clouds moved in. One of the errant petitions landed in the grass at their feet. Rhonelle leaned over and caught it. Holding hair out of her face, she looked it over quickly.

"Actually the Ides of March is the fifteenth – today as a matter of fact" – she said in a calm voice as she turned toward the highway. "Come on boys, this calls for pie and coffee." She handed the paper to Marv and looked ahead as she walked, head held high, the wind whipping her thick black hair in a wild dance around her face.

CHAPTER THIRTY-EIGHT

Winds of Change

Sergio had reluctantly left Rhonelle and returned to Memphis three days before the POO protest in Herman Park. He was planning to begin closing down his studio in Memphis. He and Rhonelle had decided he could rent or build a studio in Peavine a lot cheaper than his Memphis studio rent and still maintain a sales outlet near Graceland. He already had hired someone to run his small roadside gallery of yard ornaments.

This was a huge decision for Sergio. Rhonelle was amazed by how perfectly natural it had been for him to gradually move in with her. There was nothing pressured or dramatic about it; they just easily and mutually agreed that it was best for each of them. What anyone else thought about it really hadn't concerned Rhonelle one tiny bit . . . until she witnessed the protest.

The last thing Rhonelle wanted was for Sergio to be the target of some crazy bunch of self-righteous moral vigilantes. She pictured him living here as the beloved local artist who brought fame and prosperity to the little town she had grown to love and call home. Would he still want to live here if he had seen and heard such vitriol?

Silly as that protest had seemed at the time, the petition had the potential to spell trouble ahead. Marv had enough legal experience to know this could mean the eventual demolition and removal of Sergio's masterpiece if enough people signed on. Even Teenie had admitted to some aggravation about the Elvis fans taking over the town and possibly causing friction at the Annual Poodle Pageant. How many more citizens were harboring resentment of the Thirty-Foot Elvis? So on that blustery March night, Rhonelle sat in her moon and star chair feeling sad and lonely for the first time since . . . well . . . since she had moved to Peavine.

"*Hey, Cherie, you not alone. You got way too much love to feel dat way."* Granny Laurite was floating right in front of Rhonelle, smiling sympathetically.

Oh, Granny, I feel like I've just had my best friend turn on me. Rhonelle was so relieved to see the spirit of her granny she started to tear up.

"Your best friends are still your best friends. Jus cause all doze crazy peoples are makin' a big noise doan mean **nuthin***."'* Laurite snapped her fingers on the last word making a bright little spark that grew into a golden ball of light floating in between herself and Rhonelle. *"You and your soul mate, Sergio, done found each other. Dat's a really wonderful ting."*

The ball of golden light grew as Granny Laurite's face began to fade. Rhonelle felt the light surround her until the cold feeling of loneliness was replaced by warmth and well-being. She could still hear her grandmother's voice.

"Storms a comin' but doan you worry. It all gonna work out jus fine in de end. You see."

As Laurite's words faded to silence, the sound of the wind grew louder. Rhonelle reached for her chenille throw and wrapped it around her as she got up to look out the picture window. The pecan trees swayed and thrashed alarmingly as the wind blew harder from several directions at once. She turned on her small television to check for storm warnings.

Before she could find a local channel, her phone rang. It was Marv's wife, Pauline.

"Honey, I think we'd better gather everybody into the shelter," Pauline's voice was pitched even higher than usual with fear. "Tammy and Cecil came over a few minutes ago. Bo Astor's up at the radio station monitoring the weather radio and he says State Police spotted a funnel cloud west of El Dorado about thirty minutes ago."

This *was* alarming news, especially for folks living in a trailer park, the acknowledged "twister magnets" of the southeast. One of the smartest and most generous things Marv and Pauline ever did was to add a fully finished basement to their home when they built it several years ago.

This underground den was reinforced as a storm shelter, with all the comforts of a lavish recreation room and complete with an extra bathroom and shower. There was plenty of room in there for the residents of Homes-Sweet-Homes Park to be comfortable and even spend the night if necessary. It was a huge improvement over the cramped yet usable "fraidy hole" Doll Dumas had built when she took over.

Rhonelle, watching the TV warnings with the sound off, could see a Little Rock weatherman pointing to the counties surrounding Peavine. On his map, the Peavine area was covered with alarming red graphics. "Thanks, Pauline," Rhonelle attempted to keep her voice steady. "I'll call the Brices, Louise, and Lorna Mae. Don and Dorine had better join us, too. I've got a *bad* feeling about this one."

"Oh . . . okay honey," Pauline sounded even more frightened. "I'll call them right away. Y'all hurry up and get here. Don't take the time to bring anything with you. We're stocked up on flashlights, food, even blankets and pillows."

In ten minutes, Rhonelle was dressed and gathering her neighbors. They heard ominous rumblings of thunder and the first fat raindrops began to fall as they walked quickly along the 200-yard path from the lavender double-wide to Marv and Pauline's large modern home, built on property behind the trailer park just to the side of Tammy's small house. Mavis brought up the rear, holding onto a terrified poodle.

Don, Dorine, and *their* shivering poodle arrived by car at the same time. No sooner had they all ducked into the garage when a heavy downpour started, followed by a too-close-for-comfort bolt of lightning and a deafening clap of thunder that rolled across the field. Another growling of nonstop thunder was building in the distance.

"Come on folks," Marv called from the back door, which led to the basement through the garage. "Get on down there. The bar is open." He was grinning and attempting to sound jovial but Rhonelle could see the fear in his eyes as he looked past them out the open garage door.

Teenie screamed the highest and shrillest when the lights went out just as they walked in the door. Fortunately, Marv already had his flashlight on to lead the way downstairs. "Well, I beg your pardon," Teenie said quickly. "I had no idea I could still hit a C sharp in that octave!"

The others were grateful for the comic relief as they cautiously made their way down the stairs to the "den," as Pauline preferred to call it. Tammy jumped up to hug Teenie and Mavis. The room was well lit with several battery-powered lanterns. Marv quickly moved over to the fully stocked bar to mix himself a drink.

"I'm so glad y'all are safe," Tammy said with relief. "Momma is up at the radio station with Bo, makin' sure he doesn't wait too long to go into the storm shelter up there. He's obsessed with getting video of a tornado, even if it's too dark to see anything." The sounds of wind and thunder were getting louder. "Isn't that crazy to try and do something like that? It's like he and Coach Zellhorn are having some kind of a contest." Tammy had to almost shout to be heard.

Don turned up the volume of the radio on the bar next to Marv. All he could hear was static. "They went off the air a few seconds ago," Marv said into Don's ear.

Lorna Mae had been sitting quietly on one of the oversized leather sofas staring up at the ceiling. "Listen to *that!*" She shouted suddenly during a brief and sudden silence. Everybody froze. Don twiddled his hearing aids. Rhonelle felt a prickle of electricity as a low rumbling grew rapidly to sound much like a train engine. Sounds of trees breaking and alarming thumps shook the house above them.

Just as quickly as it had started, the sounds faded away to distant rumbles and the drumming of a heavy rain. Marv and Don went up the stairs and carefully opened the door. "House is still here," Marv happily shouted back down to the others. Pauline started to run up the stairs to have a look, but Don stopped her on the way.

"It'd be safer if we waited till morning when it gets light," Don explained. "Marv saw some broken glass on the kitchen floor. Might be a window blown out."

Marv came down behind Don and squeezed by to put his arm around Pauline. "He's right babe. Better safe than sorry. We have everything we need down here. Let's make a party of it. We can clean up tomorrow."

What he left unsaid was they could wait to see what was still left, if anything, of their homes and the rest of Peavine. "Drinks anyone?" Marv said, releasing Pauline, who stared worriedly toward the door at the top of the stairs. She turned back to her friends, sitting forlornly around the comfortable den.

Lorna Mae was staring up at the ceiling. "You know what this reminds me of," she asked no one in particular. "This is like that creepy old Twilight Zone episode when that guy went into a bomb shelter and everybody else got wiped out by an atom bomb." Her statement hung in the air like a verbal fart as she wrapped a blanket around her shoulders.

Pauline straightened up and plastered a very determined smile on her face. "Well Lorna, this was just a nasty old storm, *not* an A-Bomb! I've got snacks and board games down here too, y'all," she added cheerfully. "We might as well make the best of it."

So they did. Tammy managed to fall asleep within minutes on the sofa next to Cecil, who sat up stoically staring at the wall and listening intently for any sounds from above ground. Don, Marv, Louise, and Lorna Mae opened up a deck of cards and played a game of hearts. Mavis, Dorine, and Pauline sat over in a corner together discussing in hushed tones their plans to handle whatever emergencies they might discover when the sun came up.

Rhonelle picked a recliner away from the others, leaned back, and shut her eyes. She cast her awareness about the neighborhood, trying to glean any useful information. She did not sense anyone in pain or danger. She took that to mean everyone was safe. She was especially relieved that Don and Dorine had joined them.

Rhonelle's next chore was to attempt to reassure Sergio that she was safe. In the midst of the worst part of the storm, she had mentally called his name and seen a flash of his face wide-eyed with alarm. Over and over, she focused on Sergio repeating the same message over and over as she twiddled the ruby and diamond ring on her finger.

I'm fine. I'm safe and will let you know more tomorrow.

She was more curious than afraid of what the daylight would reveal. The reassuring words of Granny Laurite were still with her. She felt like everything would turn out to be fine. Perhaps the neighborhood would look even better once the mess was cleaned up. She had to smile at the irony of it all. Who would have guessed that old Pastor Astor would turn out to be such an accurate soothsayer?

Frantic knocking at the door up at the top of the stairs startled Rhonelle out of a light sleep. "Hey! Are y'all still alive down there?" Someone opened the door and shouted. "Tammy, you'd better be down there or I'll tan yore hide!" It was Lucille Lepanto shouting for her daughter. Despite the words, her voice quivered with tears. As soon as she got to the bottom of the stairs and saw Tammy sitting up rubbing the sleep from her eyes, Lucille ran over and hugged her daughter fiercely. Lucille's shoulders shook with sobs.

The next person to enter the room was Bo Astor, soaking wet and looking greatly relieved. "Boy, are we ever glad to see you guys." Marv stood up, filled with tension. "How bad is it out there, son?" He was not completely sure his house was all still there, in spite of his assurances to Pauline.

Cecil got up and left Tammy with her mother. "What is it?" he asked when he saw the look on Bo's face. "What have you seen?"

Bo looked at Cecil and put his hand on his shoulder. "Son, it looks like your house has been hit pretty bad. It's still too dark to tell much, but it done scared the shit out of Lucille – pardon my French."

Cecil swallowed hard. Bo peeled off his soaked windbreaker and Marv took it from him. "Here, Bo," Marv said, realizing that Bo was pretty shaken. Sit down here and I'll fix you a drink."

"Thanks Marv, I could sure use one." He gratefully took a towel and a blanket from Pauline. Everyone in the room moved in close to hear what Bo had to say. Lucille and Tammy sat close together on the sofa while Lucille cried silently into a wad of Kleenex, her arm around Tammy.

"There's definitely been a twister 'cause I saw it go by us out there on Radio Hill," Bo began.

Lucille interrupted at that moment. "I'd like to *never* got this idiot to come down to the storm shelter and away from the window."

"I *told* them you'd have to do that, Momma. Good thing you were there to save Bo from himself." Tammy patted her mother proudly.

"Sure was," Lucille agreed tearfully as she dabbed at her mascara smudges. "I'm sorry, Hon; you go ahead and tell it."

"Well as I was saying. We got knocked off the air because the power went out. It was too dangerous to hook up the generator, so I got on my ham radio set as soon as the storm passed and it was safe enough to set out the receiver. I heard all kinds of bad damage reports coming in.

"Somebody said it looked like there had been damage out at the Mansion Rest and Retirement Home and ambulances were on the way. I know they have a real safe place for all the people out there, but some of the weaker ones must have been in distress. I think my dad is probably okay. He's a pretty tough old fella.

"Then another guy reported damage over in the area of the trailer park and along the highway. That's when Lucille and I got scared. We had to come be sure you all got over here in time."

Lucille cut in now that she was able to stop crying. "We really dodged the bullet out there on the hill. There weren't but a few tree branches around, but by the time we got down the road nearer to town there were trees down all over the place . . . some of 'em blocked the road. We finally had to leave the car and come the rest of the way on foot."

"Momma," Tammy looked at Lucille in shock. "You shouldn't have done that in the dark. No telling what you might have stepped on out there."

"We had us some flashlights," Bo said. "There wasn't no stoppin' your mom until she knew you were safe. Then when we got over to your house and saw all those trees down around it and part of the roof off she had a fit."

"My roof came off?" Tammy put her hands to her face.
Lucille hugged her and began to get teary eyed again. "Yes, honey, it looked mighty scary and I'd hate to think what could have happened to you if … now you see why we had to be sure you were all right."

Tammy pulled back from her mother and started to smile. "Momma, I'm all right. As a matter of fact, Cecil and I are better than all right. I'm *pregnant*!"

She stood up and proudly stuck out her stomach. The beginning of a baby bump was evident. Tammy did a turn. "Ta da!"
Cecil blushed a deep red. "Tammy has a weird sense of timing … uh sometimes," he mumbled apologetically.

Rhonelle came forward and put her arms around Cecil and Tammy. "Why I think this is *perfect* timing. Nothing is wrong with hearing some really wonderful news to cancel out the bad. Congratulations!"

There was a brief initial silence to Tammy's unexpected announcement, but eventually the rest of the occupants in the room reacted joyfully to the news. Even Marv was delighted, despite the cold glare he shot toward poor Cecil.

"Now then," Tammy said sassily as she pointed at Lucille. "Since you are going to be a granny, you and Bo had better hurry up and get yourselves married."

"Well, listen to you Miss Priss," Lucille shot back. "What makes you think we haven't been working on that? Hey Unkie Marv," she shouted over toward the bar where he was pouring another drink. "How about you walking me down the aisle like you're my daddy?"

"I'd be honored to babe," Marv grinned at Lucille and raised his drink. "Let me know when you're ready."

A while later Rhonelle overheard Bo ask Lucille, "Now what exactly are we supposed to be doing about that wedding thing, sweet cheeks?"

"*I* don't know," Lucille muttered quietly. "But I'm sure between the two of us, we'll come up with something pretty dang cool." She looked over at Tammy and Cecil sitting across the room with Mavis and Teenie chatting excitedly about baby names.

Lucille elbowed Bo and added "We'd better do something sooner rather than later, 'cause that bun has been in the oven longer than you think."

The remainder of the long night passed quickly, but the early dawn came not a moment too soon. Marv was the first to get a good look at his house in the light of day. Sure enough, Bo had been correct when he'd told Marv that his house seemed to have weathered the storm intact even with tree limbs through a couple of windows.

Except for a corner of the roof, the basic structure of Tammy and Cecil's house was intact. They would need a new roof. While there was plenty of water damage in the bedroom, it was fixable. Most of their things were undamaged. Their wedding album was in pristine condition.

Cecil was enormously relieved to find that his new restoration garage was still standing amid debris from the trees and houses nearby. All five of the valuable classic cars he had been restoring were safe inside the building.

The lavender double-wide was miraculously unscathed despite two large tree limbs across the driveway and the metal carport blown over. The T-Bird was sitting there without a scratch on it. The six-foot replica of the Thirty-Foot Elvis had toppled over, but all that was damaged was his dignity. He was kind of muddy when Cecil and Bo set him back up.

Most of the damage at the trailer park was toward the back where old, unoccupied trailers were kept, and then off over behind Fred and Vaudine's unoccupied trailer where they kept the storage buildings. Two out of the three had been knocked over and the contents blown all over the place. The park looked a mess, but most of the damage was to the beautiful old pecan trees.

The Brices' Airstream had no damage but a toilet seat hung from one of the trees in their front yard. No idea where *that* came from.

The most frightening sight was an oak tree that fell right across the bedroom of Don and Dorine's house. If they had been in their bed, the tree would have crushed them. Dorine almost fainted when she first saw it. On the other hand, the Diner was untouched. At the Dew

Drop Inn, the only damage was a pink awning ripped off one cottage. The tornado seemed to have passed at tree-top level after touching down on Radio Hill, skipping over to the Dumas Plantation where it seriously damaged the roof and windows on the western wing of the Mansion Rest and Retirement Home.

After that, it came down near the trailer park and across the highway. It then went across one end of Herman Park before bouncing up and down on its way south of town. Out that way, the baseball field grandstand was damaged. The sign out at the Too-Tite Tavern blew over as a final touch before the twister exited Peavine.

Best news was it could have been worse. There were no serious injuries and very few homes with irreparable damage. There was one great big casualty, however.

When the twister blew across Herman Park, it left the Thirty-Foot Elvis tilted dangerously to one side. The park and the statue were declared a safety hazard by Sheriff Tilley and closed to the public until further notice.

CHAPTER THIRTY-NINE

What to Do With a
Leaning Tower of Rock and Roll

Peavine's cleanup effort began at the crack of dawn on the morning after the storm. Every able-bodied male over the age of eighteen possessed a chainsaw or knew how to use one. Even Teenie Brice had a stout set of pruning shears. The whine of chainsaws and aroma of cut wood filled the air. As soon as the roads were cleared, emergency rescue vehicles from Monticello arrived. Before the occupants of Marv and Pauline's basement shelter had a chance to climb the stairs, Arkansas State Troopers were on the scene searching for survivors and confirming that nobody was trapped in debris.

Don and Dorine's son, Donnie, was over at their house supervising cleanup when they arrived. He couldn't thank his parents enough for having the foresight to let him know ahead of time they would be over at Marv and Pauline's during the storm, and had the good sense to go over there.

"It was Rhonelle that saved us. She told Pauline to call us to come over," Dorine stated solemnly. "I'll never doubt that woman's intuition."

Rhonelle was delighted to discover that her phone was in working order by midmorning. She heard it ringing while she was outside sweeping leaves and branches off her deck. When she ran inside to answer, she knew it would be Sergio. He told her he was driving back to Peavine right away. Despite her reassurances, he *had* to see for himself that she was safe. He had heard dire stories on the morning news about all the destruction in south Arkansas caused by at least four tornadoes.

"There is something else I need to tell you first," Rhonelle said when she finally was given a chance to speak. "It's about the Big Boy (their nickname for the thirty-foot statue). He's got a seriously dangerous slant to him now. The tornado went right through the park. He hasn't fallen over but he looks like he could." There was a silence so long that Rhonelle wondered if she'd lost the connection. "Sergio? Are you still there?"

"I'm still here," he said. "There's another problem with the statue isn't there ... something else disturbing you."

Rhonelle reluctantly described the protest, petitions, the POO signs, culminating in Pastor Astor's "Moses Moment" and surprisingly accurate "Ides of March" warning. To her relief, they both got to laughing so hard over it all that she could barely finish her story.

"Ah, that is too rich," Sergio sighed. "You know what. I think Mother Nature may have solved more than one problem for us. I'll get my guys to bring the truck and their gear and come on down with me. Do you think we can find a place for them to stay for a while?"

"I'm sure we can work out something if they don't mind roughing it a little." Rhonelle was beginning to get a slight glimmer of a plan. "Darling, wait a couple more days before you try and come with the boys. It's such a mess down here I'm not sure the State Troopers will let you all come into town."

"I'll compromise with you," Sergio said after a pause. "I'll come on today and call my crew after we're sure it's okay."

"Sounds like a deal to me." Rhonelle smiled at the thought of Sergio arriving that night. "Tell anybody who tries to stop you that you're a resident and they should let you in."

"I *am* a resident," Sergio proclaimed. "And I love you!"

Mayor Buckshot Bradley proved an excellent organizer of cleanup efforts. He immediately contacted the governor's office to request National Guard troops to assist with recovery. Governor Clinton was happy to help in any way he could. He even came to Peavine personally the next day to officially declare the town a genuine disaster area – a big first on both counts. Clinton toured the destruction, giving out plenty of his famous "I feel your pain" hugs to the local residents with damaged homes.

All the television stations with their live trucks and cameras arrived the same day as Bill Clinton. Barry Zellhorn had two of his football player/assistants with him to be sure he didn't miss any photo opportunities. Bo Astor had KEPW back on the air by noon the day after the twister and provided constant updates and helpful information. He and his three other announcers were camping out at the radio station. They enjoyed copious amounts of nourishing food from the Brisket Basket. It was a huge sacrifice for Bo to stay on the radio and miss meeting Bill Clinton.

The governor did meet with Sergio and Mayor Buckshot when he was taken to Herman Park for a personal viewing of the ailing Thirty-Foot Elvis. Clinton stood in silence shaking his head and doing his familiar lower lip bite. "Aw man," he said as he put his hand on Sergio's shoulder, giving it a squeeze. "You *got* to fix this. This is just about the best likeness of the Elvis I've ever seen . . . a real regional treasure." He gazed up at the statue, an appreciative grin on his face. "He's great. Wish I could get away with having one of those in my backyard at the Governor's Mansion."

Mayor Buckshot reassured the governor that restoration of Peavine's newest landmark was one of the town's priorities because of its positive effect on the local economy. Sergio thanked Governor Clinton for his kind words and mentally began to picture how a sculpture of an Elvis with the face of Bill Clinton might look. He'd have to work on that some day.

With the roads cleared of debris, the energy repair trucks arrived and quickly restored electricity to a little over half of the residents by midweek. Don's Diner was one of the first to be up and running as a feeding center both for out-of-town workers and residents without power (or, in some cases, homes they could no longer stay in). Four families stayed at the Dew Drop Inn until they could find relatives or friends to house them.

Don and Dorine also slept in one of the pink and white cottages even before the power was restored. All had gas heaters and hot water so they were quite cozy. It sure beat spending the night at the Mortuary with Darla, Rupert, and Donnie's family. As usual, Astor's Eternal Rest Funeral Home had emergency power and provided a very comfortable temporary shelter. There was no way Don would get Dorine to even walk through the door, much less *sleep* there.

Because Doll Dumas had the funding and the foresight to install buried phone and electrical lines when she took over Madge's Mobile Home Park, all the residents were able to stay in their homes and their power was restored relatively quickly. While her neighbors were busy cleaning up tree limbs and Teenie was volunteering to answer the phones at Mayor Bradley's office, Mavis stayed busy finishing up Lucille's very *untraditional* wedding dress. No one but Lucille had laid eyes on it yet because Mavis quietly hid it under the bed whenever Teenie came home.

On March 22, Sergio's team of technical artisans arrived. This was the same group that had helped assemble and erect the Thirty-Foot Elvis on that fateful night back in December. Rhonelle and Sergio were able to clean up a couple of the vacant trailers that had escaped damage and make them comfortable for their stay. This time the crew would be around for several days to help Sergio put the Thirty-Foot Elvis to rights.

On the night of March twenty-third, there was a private meeting with Mayor Buckshot Bradley at the lavender double-wide. Attendance at this gathering – besides Sergio and Rhonelle – was limited to Lucille Lepanto and Bo Astor. After only twenty minutes, a plan was confirmed. Everybody shook hands and left happy.

Meanwhile, out at the Mansion Rest and Retirement Home, Christabelle Tingleberry had practically achieved sainthood. Her downright heroic efforts the night of the tornado had resulted in an orderly evacuation of all residents to the storm shelter in record time. Not taking any chances, she had convinced the staff early that evening of the possibility of severe weather and the need to begin moving the residents to safety. Well before the tornado approached, everybody was in place and having a loud sing-along. A majority of the residents hardly were aware of the storm, either because they were sleeping or singing.

One week after the storm, the residents who had been displaced when the storm damaged their wing had been relocated to other temporary rooms or, in a few cases, transported to nursing homes until the higher level care could be resumed at the Mansion. Pastor Astor had to be moved to another apartment since he had been staying in one of the damaged areas.

The pastor hadn't heard from Rose Posey since the POO protest in the park. She had left the morning after the tornado and was now staying with her sister Violet until repairs to her living quarters were completed.

One afternoon Christabelle decided to check in on the pastor and see how he was adjusting after such a trying week. He was now sharing a larger apartment with two other gentlemen until they could get him back into his own place. One of his roommates was extremely hard of hearing and the other had experienced a stroke that left him unable to communicate except by uttering, "Yer gawd damn right" in response to everything.

Pastor Astor spent most the daylight hours quietly sitting by the window, gazing out at the destruction left by the tornado and the cleanup work going on. A rather pitiful sight when Christabelle came to visit that day, he seemed to have shrunk a size or two since his powerful oration at Herman Park. She had to call his name several times before she could tear his attention away from the scene outside his window. When he realized who had come to see him his face broke out in a wide smile, then almost immediately he began to cry. Christabelle quickly came over to him. "Why Pastor, whatever is the matter? Are you in pain?" She gently took his hand and discreetly noted his pulse and skin temperature.

"No, Sister Christabelle," Pastor Astor replied in a weak voice. "My pain is not physical. It's my *soul* that is sick."

The two other gentlemen were seated at a card table across the room, working a jigsaw puzzle. The deaf one hadn't noticed Christabelle's presence, but the other roommate looked up and listened to every word with great interest.

Still holding onto the pastor's hand, Christabelle pulled up a chair and sat down facing him. "My my, that does sound serious," she said with great sympathy. "Maybe if you tell me what's bothering you it might ease your burden."

"You mean like a confession?" That idea seemed to bring a tiny light of hope to eyes.

"We could call it that if you want, but I prefer to call it telling a good friend what is troubling you." She patted his hand and patiently waited for him to speak.

Pastor Astor turned his gaze back to the window. "This is all *my* fault," he said in a voice so soft Christabelle could barely hear it. "I called upon the powers of the heavens and brought destruction to this town."

Christabelle's response was not at all what the pastor expected. "Lyle Bodine Astor, just who do you think you are . . . *God?*"

That got his attention. All he could do was stare open-mouthed in amazement at Christabelle. He finally answered "no" in a very small voice.

"Well, I think a preacher should know better than to think *he* would have the power to make himself his own personal tornado to come to town and do whatever he told it to." She was standing now with her hands on her hips. "Only God makes the weather and he doesn't use it to *punish* people, no matter how much you or some other holier-than-thou person may think they deserve it!"

Pastor Astor looked down at his hands. "What about Noah and the Ark?"

"Just my point." Christabelle didn't think much of the Old Testament-style God, but decided to go along with it. "Even *if* that was some kind of vengeance, God – not Noah – caused that flood."

Christabelle sat back down and took the pastor's hand again.

"So I'd say you're off the hook for causing a tornado, but you might want to ask Jesus for His forgiveness for your having such a great big ego to think you could tell God what to do. And ... maybe if you weren't so hard on yourself, you might be little kinder and more forgiving to others. I think that's what Jesus would want you to do." Now she was smiling. "I forgive you, Pastor, and I know you have love and kindness in your heart. Don't be afraid to show *that* to your family for a change."

"Yer gawd damn right!" shouted the roommate, nodding emphatically and waving at Christabelle Tingleberry.

CHAPTER FORTY

April Fool's Day

It was four-thirty on Monday morning, April first. Sergio quietly unlocked the door to the lavender double-wide and came inside. Rhonelle was asleep but stirred when he wearily slipped into the bed and kissed her lightly.

"Is it done?" she asked sleepily without opening her eyes.

"All done without a single glitch," Sergio whispered. He was so exhausted he immediately fell asleep and began to snore.

Rhonelle smiled and followed him off into dreamland.

In the apartment above the florist shop, Violet X-pressions, the alarm clock went off at five-thirty. Violet Posey quickly hit the **off** button before her sister Rose could hear it from the guest bedroom. Violet had to get up a little earlier each morning in order to walk Hero to the park and back before it got too light outside. She had to be especially cautious since the Ides of March tornado had come through. Now she carried her flashlight every morning.

Except for the week when she had that virus and the four days she spent at the regional Flower Club Conference, Violet had dutifully gotten up before daylight every morning since December first, when that giant Graven Image had appeared in Herman Park. She had made it her own private mission of revenge to train her poor dog Hero to hold "it" in every morning until they got to the statue, so he could leave his little brown gift at the base of the Thirty-Foot Elvis. It made for a very satisfying start to her day.

Since the Ides of March tornado, access to the park had been a challenge. The morning after the storm, she was almost was too frightened to try. However, her curiosity – and fervent hope that maybe Pastor Astor's prayer had worked and God had removed the cursed idol from their beloved park – drove her outside to see what had happened.

Seeing the downed trees that day got her hopes up. But when she saw the gleaming black pompadour above the wreckage, she was so angry she let loose such a stream of profanity … it made the dog whimper. On closer examination, she noticed the statue didn't look quite right after all. Its dangerous tilt filled her heart with gratitude for the probability it would soon fall down. She allowed Hero the right to do his business at the edge of the park for once, then used the rest of their morning constitutional to see what other havoc the Lord had unleashed upon Peavine.

Despite the warning signs and plastic fencing up to keep Herman Park and the Thirty-Foot Elvis closed to the public, Violet and Hero snuck past the barricades each morning and into the park. They paid their disrespect to the ailing statue as near to its' base as possible – without endangering themselves should it suddenly keel over.

On the first of April, Violet was busy admiring tulip shoots emerging from the Herman Park flower beds. Seeing them peek out of the soil rekindled an ecstatic joy that often followed Violet's observation of springtime. She was delighted that the storm had not destroyed the prize bulbs that she'd planted last fall. To their credit, the cleanup crews had been very conscientious about those flower gardens as they hauled off fallen trees and branches . . . and . . . *what's this?*

Violet stopped in her tracks and looked around. The sky was getting lighter so she didn't need her flashlight to see anymore. She suddenly felt disoriented and dizzy. She wasn't sure where she was. Hero stopped and whined as he looked at her, then ahead. The dog's leash fell from Violet's hand. Hero trotted ahead, right up to the edge of a large, bare concrete pad. Once Hero arrived, he squatted, dropped a load, and scratched at the dirt with his hind legs before returning proudly to his mistress.

She still couldn't believe what she was seeing . . . or more precisely, *not* seeing.

The Thirty-Foot Elvis had completely disappeared.

"Good morning, citizens of Peavine! And a fine good morning to all you good people out there who have come down here to help us get our little ole town set back to rights after the 'Ides of March Tornado' blew through. This is Bo Astor coming to you bright and early at six o'clock on KEPW radio."

Don had the Diner radio tuned to KEPW as usual while he fired up the griddle for Monday morning breakfast. Dorine shuffled over to unlock the front door. Lorna Mae set out pies and checked the coffee maker. One of the new waitresses, Suzanne Teeter, burst into the back door. "Oh my gawd y'all! You won't *believe* this," Suzanne noticed the radio chatter and pointed at it. "I'll bet you Bo Astor has something to say about it."

"Lordeee girl," Dorine still had the OPEN sign in her hand as she stared at Suzanne in alarm. "What's got into you?"
Lorna Mae turned up the volume on the radio just as Bo mentioned the Thirty-Foot Elvis.

"Yessir, as y'all know we brought in some specialists several days ago to see what they could do to get Peavine's newest major landmark back to rights. They've been hard at work – under the supervision of the artist Sergio Mandell – of course, attempting to straighten the big fella back into an upright position.

"Well, it has come to my attention this morning that there has been a *big* change in the position of our beloved Thirty-Foot Elvis all right . . .

"He's not there!"

Don twiddled at his hearing aids. "What the . . . did I hear that right?"

"Shush!" Dorine, Lorna, and Suzanne shouted together.

"You heard me right y'all . . . Elvis has *left* the building! Only in this case he's done left Herman Park. No April foolin' here, take a look for yourself if you don't believe me. For more on this breaking story stay tuned. We'll have an update after this message."

Everybody in the Diner started to talk at once.

"I *saw* it! That's what I've been trying to tell you!" shouted Suzanne the loudest. "I mean I saw it was gone when I was on my way over here. I noticed this old lady acting kind of crazy up by the highway and slowed down to see if she was okay. She was staggering around in her robe and curler bonnet while her dog yapped at her."

"That must have been Violet Posey," Dorine said. "She pretty much always acts a little crazy, if you ask me."

"Well, anyway," Suzanne continued. "When I asked her what was the matter she just kept laughing and pointing at Herman Park shouting 'Praise Jesus! It's gone away!' I couldn't figure what she was talking about. Then I looked where she was pointing . . . and that's when I seen it – a big gap where the Thirty-Foot Elvis *has been*."

"Lordeee," Dorine peered out the window. "You don't suppose somebody stole it do you?"

Don had started to snicker a little. "Nope, it ain't stolen. I think Bo Astor has been up to one great big April Fool's joke on us." He addressed Suzanne. "Are you sure it weren't just covered up or something?"

"No sir. It was gone because sunlight was coming up behind where it used to be."

"Hmmm, well I'll be dad gummed," Don stroked his chins and let out a guffaw. "If that son of a gun could get that statue set up in one night, I reckon he could take it down and move it overnight with no one the wiser. I'll be dad gummed . . . that Bo Astor is something else!"

Just then the ad jingle for Simpson's Piggly Wiggly faded out and Bo came back on the air.

"Good morning again Peavine, and a happy April Fool's Day to you. This is Bo Astor on KEPW with an update on the missing Thirty-

Foot Elvis.

(Sounds of a old time news ticker.) "This just in . . . Our largest favorite statue has not been stolen nor destroyed – as some of you might have hoped.

"The good news is our Elvis has *moved* to a new location and it's up to all you citizens of Peavine to find him. I'm giving away a free dinner for six at Seymour's Tex-Mex to the first caller who can tell me where the Thirty-Foot Elvis has gone. You have until the end of this next song, "Blue Suede Shoes" (in honor of our missing landmark).

"The number is 983-5555."

Immediately, Don grabbed the phone and started dialing.

"Don, what do you think you're doing?" Dorine couldn't believe he would be so eager to win a dinner at Seymour's. "Do you think you know where it is?"

"Heck no," Don grinned while holding his hand over the mouthpiece. "I just want to get in on this. . . . Hey, hello is this Bo? Hey you rascal, this is Don. That's some prank you done pulled off this time. . . . Yep, *surrrrrre* you didn't have anything to do with it." Don winked over at the women who were hanging on every word.

"Yeah . . . uh huh . . . really! . . . Well, I just wanted to sweeten the pot. How about you add four of my fresh-baked pies to that prize you're offering?

No . . . no charge . . . just my way of saying thanks for keeping life interesting around here. Alrighty, talk to you later, man."

The song was winding down on the radio and Bo started to talk again. Don listened with his ear right up to the radio and a huge grin on his face.

"Good news Peavine, you still have a chance to win! Nobody has found our Thirty-Foot Elvis yet and now Don's Diner has added to the reward prize for finding our wandering giant. Don is donating four of his famous, fresh homemade pies to the bounty!

"Now hold on everybody . . . before you run willy-nilly all over town, I have a very important *clue* for you.

"I'll be announcing that clue right after this message from Faulkner's Jewelry Store. I know that place all too well . . . that's

where Lucille and I picked out that pretty little engagement ring …
well it wasn't that little actually . . ."

During the Faulkner advertisement there was plenty of guessing
in the Diner on the whereabouts of the missing statue. They almost
didn't hear the drum roll on the radio. As it ended, Bo Astor came
back with reverb on the microphone.

"AND NOWwww . . . THE THIRTY-FOOT CLUE OF THE
DAYyyy!

"Listen up carefully everybody . . . here it is.

Elvis is gone but not forgotten
It's just a new location has been gotten
Turns out this place is going to be just right
Even if some say it's a little too tight.

". . . Okay folks, when the music starts, get your thinking caps on.
The first caller to guess the new location will win dinner at Seymour's
and Don's four wonderful pies! Here we go with 'Jail House Rock.'"

Don and Dorine looked at each other in astonishment that they
hadn't figured it out sooner. "The Too-Tite Tavern," they shouted in
unison.

"Why it's a perfect place for him," Dorine chuckled. "That's probably where they should have put him in the first place."

Like Don and Dorine, several KEPW listeners guessed that the
new home of the Thirty-Foot Elvis was the Too-Tite Tavern, which
also happened to be the property of Lucille Lepanto (fiancée to one
Bo Astor). The contest winners were announced – along with the correct location.

Lucille Lepanto came on the air with Bo and invited everybody
to come on out to the Too-Tite Tavern at six o'clock that evening for
a grand Elvis celebration. There would be live musical entertainment
along with plenty of free food and soda pop.

Throughout the day, Peavine was all abuzz over the latest shenanigans concerning the Thirty-Foot Elvis. Meanwhile, the Too-Tite
Tavern would be closed all day in order to make preparations for the
special event that evening. KEPW had updates and announcements
throughout the day and a large part of the population planned to at-

tend the celebration.

At five-thirty that evening, Rhonelle made a call to Pauline. She wanted to be sure that Pauline and Marv would be out at the Too-Tite Tavern celebration a little early that evening because Lucille wanted Marv to do her a big favor. He'd find out all about it when he got there.

Teenie Brice was asked to be sure that Mayor Buckshot Bradley would be prepared to deliver a short speech dedicating the new location of the Thirty-Foot Elvis. The mayor reassured Teenie he was more than ready to do some talking that night. Mavis was very quiet all day, with a small smile and a slightly smug expression on her face. When Teenie asked her why she was so happy about the celebration, her only answer was an emphatic, *"I ain't saying nothing."*

Finally, six o'clock arrived. A huge crowd had gathered out at the Too-Tite Tavern. It was "alcohol-free night," so anyone under-age was allowed to join in. It was a beautiful warm spring evening, not a cloud in the sky. Tables and a stage had been set up outside in front of the Tavern to accommodate the large crowd and allow the Thirty-Foot Elvis to be the centerpiece of the celebration.

The old Too-Tite Tavern sign had blown down during the tornado. A new sign had replaced it on the front of the building. For the time being a tarp covered it and would be removed later during the festivities to reveal the new one that Sergio Mandel had designed and painted.

The Party Girls had returned to Peavine and brought plenty of good food with them. Ozelle and Sally Washington also showed up with their entire family. The Brisket Basket crew with their portable smoker had been out at the Tavern all day filling the air the tantalizing odor of Ozelle's barbecue.

Weaving throughout the crowd was Coach Barry Zellhorn, earnestly directing two of his football player/assistants as they got plenty of excellent footage of the statue and the festivities. Barry stopped to interview several of the partygoers to get their reaction to the April Fool's surprise that had been pulled off by Bo Astor, Lucille Lepanto, and Sergio Mandell.

Live musical entertainment turned out to be none other than the Gay Caballeros. They were set up on a stage right beside the Thirty-Foot Elvis. The musicians stopped for a break at six-thirty and Mayor Buckshot Bradley strode up to the stage to wholehearted cheers and applause. He gave a spirited speech that turned into a pep rally for the town, promising they would rebuild a stronger and better Peavine.

"There's no wind strong enough to destroy the sense of *community* we have here in Peavine!" The mayor shook his fist at the sky. "When we all work together there's *nothing* that can get us down for long." The crowd loved it, especially since they all were comfortably filled with delicious food.

Nobody had noticed that Bo, Lucille, Marv, and Tammy were nowhere to be seen. They had discreetly gone inside the Tavern as soon as the mayor got up to speak.

The mayor wound his speech down and applause dwindled. Mayor Buckshot got a nod from Louise Dolesanger who had risen from her table and was coming toward the stage wearing her full "Louisa the entertainer" garb.

"Ladies and Gentlemen," the mayor announced as Louise climbed up onto the stage and took a seat at her grandson's electric jazz organ. "If you would please give us your attention, we have a very special musical presentation from Louise Dolesanger. Would the audience please stand?"

With a great rustling and scraping of chairs, the crowd seated at all the tables stood up. Some started to remove hats and place their hands over their hearts in anticipation of the national anthem.

Down at the end of the parking lot only the few people sitting or standing in that area noticed as a car door opened and a plump lady with the assistance of a tall slim man helped an elderly gentleman get out of the car and into a wheelchair. As the threesome drew closer to the area below the Thirty-Foot Elvis, a murmur went through the crowd. One by one, the citizens of Peavine recognized the old gent. It was Pastor Astor, accompanied by his eldest son, Rev. Joe Don Astor, and Nurse Christabelle Tingleberry.

Much to the onlookers' relief, the old pastor's face bore a peaceful and beneficent expression as he gazed up at the statue then over toward the entrance of the Too-Tite Tavern. Christabelle whispered in his ear and pointed toward the Tavern and the old man's face broke out in a smile.

At that moment Louise, began to play the opening chords of ... Mendelssohn's wedding march! The front doors of the Tavern opened with the assistance of Cecil and Pauline. There stood Lucille in her hot pink, rhinestone-studded wedding dress with matching cowgirl boots, grinning as she clung on to Marv. He had a somewhat befuddled yet happy look on his face as he walked forward to give the bride away. In her free hand Lucille gripped a large bouquet of vividly colored tropical flowers.

At the same time, the groom, Bo Astor, leapt out of the KEPW live broadcast truck where he had changed into the most dazzling outrageous Elvis jumpsuit and cape ever seen in these parts. He trotted up onto the stage and stood next to Mayor Bradley. He rocked back and forth on the heels of his white patent-leather boots grinning back at his equally resplendent bride.

Following Lucille was Tammy dressed in a bright pink-flowered Hawaiian muumuu made especially for this occasion (and her maternity wardrobe) – by Mavis, of course. Tammy was tossing pink rose petals into the air, laughing and crying at the same time.

When the bridal party had all arrived on the stage next to the mayor, Louise stopped the music and turned around to watch the ceremony. Mayor Bradley took the microphone again.

"Please be seated folks ... and I know what you might be thinking, but no ... this is the real thing!" This caused an excited undercurrent of murmurs as the audience took their seats.

"Dearly beloved friends, family and fellow citizens of Peavine," intoned Buckshot Bradley. "We are gathered here today to celebrate and witness the marriage of Lucille Anne Lepanto to Bodine Earl Astor

. . . and it's about time, right folks?" This brought laughter and cheers from the audience. "Okay," Buckshot nodded to Marv. "Who gives this woman's hand in marriage?

There was a pause while the mayor held the microphone toward Marv. A whirring sound could be heard as Coach Barry's video camera recorded the ceremony from the edge of the stage.

Marv leaned into the mike and said, "Uh . . . her daughter Tammy and I do." Then he smiled and playfully shoved Lucille toward Bo. Lucille whispered "Thanks!" and handed her large bouquet over to Tammy, who was starting to blubber as Marv put his arm around her.

"Now here goes the good part," Mayor Bradley said. "Do you Lucille take this man, Bo Astor, to be your lawfully wedded husband?"

"I doooooooo!" Lucille shouted out without the help of the mike.

"Do you Bo take this woman, Lucille Lepanto, to be your lawfully wedded wife?" The mayor held the mike up to Bo.

"Heck yeah I do!" Bo got a laugh on that, which prompted him to grab the mike and say, "Thank ya, thank ya vurrrrry much."

The mayor took possession of the microphone again. "Have y'all got some rings somewhere here?" He asked the bride and groom.

Bo and Lucille both held up their hands to show the gold bands. "Way ahead of you on that, Mayor," Lucille said. "Didn't want to take the chance we'd lose 'em."

"Then with the power invested in me as your mayor of Peavine ... I now pronounce you *legally* man and wife."

As Louise started up a jazzy tune, Bo laid a big one on Lucille. The crowd cheered as the newlyweds turned to take a bow.

That was when Bo spotted his father and brother standing there smiling up at him. After a nod from Lucille they both stepped down off the stage and warily approached Pastor Astor in his wheelchair. Bo offered his hand to his father, but the old man held out his arms for a hug instead. It was a tender moment as both Bo and his garish new bride were lovingly embraced by the family patriarch. Pastor Astor blinked and stared at the extravagantly bejeweled Elvis costume his son Bo was wearing. "Do you think you could find one of those outfits for me?" he asked in all seriousness.

"I don't know about that Daddy," Bo said. "Seeing you dressed like that might be more than those ladies out there at the Mansion could handle! Am I right Christabelle?"

"I think it would add a *whole new* dimension to your father's mission work," Christabelle said cheerfully.

Once the friends who had crowded near the bride and groom were reassured all was well, they swooped in for hugs, kisses, and congratulatory slaps on the back.

The band started to play a fanfare and the two bartenders pulled off the tarp that had covered the new sign.

Louise was back up on stage at the microphone. "Look over there everybody … it's the new sign," she shouted out excitedly. "Welcome to the new Blue Hawaiian Bar and Grill!"

The tarp fell away exposing a beautifully painted new sign for the Tavern outlined with a new turquoise neon light.

The old "Too-Tite Tavern" red neon light had been replaced by a large wooden sign with a painting of an ocean beach, a blue orchid and "Blue Hawaiian Bar and Grill" in tall fancy lettering.

Bo and Lucille sighed in admiration as they stood looking up at their original hand-painted wedding gift from Sergio and Rhonelle.

"Babe," said Bo as he put his arm around Lucille. "Looks like the beginning of a brand new era for Peavine."

Epilogue

Mother's Day that year was warm and lovely. Herman Municipal Park was resplendent with the flowers of early summer. The new gardenia bushes donated by David Posey and his Aunt Violet surrounded the concrete slab that had once been the foundation of the Thirty-Foot Elvis. Fragrance of the blooms filled the air with a perfume.

Newly situated in the center of the concrete platform was a tastefully done yet somewhat "modern" artistic fountain. It was a bronze sculpture of Doll Dumas and her beloved husband, Herman Junior, seated on a bench while they huddled together under a large umbrella. A fountain of water sprayed out of the top of the umbrella and rained down upon the sculpture. The faces of Doll and Herman Jr. expressed joy and deep affection for each other.

If you look closely at the base of the sculpture you can see the signature of the artist – Sergio Mandell.

A few simple words are engraved on the rim of the marble water basin surrounding the fountain.

They read as follows:

"Have no fear of loss, dear ones. Love does not end at the grave."

– Ernesto White Cloud Mandell

Essay for "Thirty Foot Elvis"

Okay . . . Here I go again! First of all I must remind you that Peavine is a make-believe town (somewhere between El Dorado and Monticello in south Arkansas) and all the people in it are my imaginary friends.

However in *this* book there are some new characters that were inspired by real people and places. Think of them as my characters being portrayed by local actors. Also placing the "present day" in my narrative as 1985 gave me a good deal more artistic license . . . I hope!

The "Cast List" is:

Buckshot Bradley . . . . .Gov. Mike Beebe
(It was Ginger's idea to name him "Buckshot." I came up with Bradley.)

Sugar Bradley . . . . First Lady Ginger Beebe

Coach Barry Zellhorn . . . . .Harry Z. Thomason
(When I heard him tell *his* story of how he got to be a producer, I knew a version of him belonged in my Peavine!)

Theodore Patterson, Editor of the Peavine Times Newspaper
. . . . Ted Parkhurst

Then Governor Bill Clinton . . . . As himself

I also took the liberty of borrowing the name of a really spectacular art museum and used it(remember this is in 1985) as the name of a very flamboyant new character, Krystal Bridges . . . played with hilarious gusto by her own self!
(I mean no disrespect!)

I must acknowledge that the inspiration for the idea of a thirty foot sculpture of Elvis came from passing through Portia Bay, Arkansas while I was finishing up "Madge's Mobile Home Park". I always wondered why on earth a tree trimming company would have decided to put a five foot sculpture of Elvis on top of their big ole ladder truck. Well . . . *why not?* It sure did catch my attention every time I passed it on my way from Jonesboro to Hardy!

Then it came to me that a huge statue of Elvis Presley could suddenly appear in Peavine's municipal park nearly one year after the demise of our beloved Doll Dumas. How did it get there? What would be the reactions of the citizens of Peavine and the residents of Doll's Home-Sweet-Homes on Wheels trailer park?

One thing was sure; the arrival of that thirty foot tall dark stranger caused a chain of events forever changing Peavine and the lives and loves of my dear imaginary friends!

"Q and A" Session with Author
Jane F. Hankins

This interview was conducted by budding movie documentarian and Peavine High School coach Barry Zellhorn. His technical assistant and camera man was star linebacker Oz Osbey.

Coach Barry: Hello there Mrs. Hankins. Since Bo Astor is off on his honeymoon with Lucille in the Hawaiian Islands, he asked me to do this interview. I hope you don't mind if we videotape it . . .

Jane: No, that's fine with me Coach, and you can call me Jane.

1. Coach: Okay . . . Well I understand it took you *eight years* to write your first novel, "Madge's Mobile Home Park". How did you manage to write this second book so quickly? It didn't take more than a year to do this one, right?

Jane: I had a steep learning curve! I got a lot better at writing directly onto my computer instead of having to handwrite it first. And I already had some material I saved for the second book that I cut from book 1. The main reason I wrote so fast was I had a movie going on in my head and I had to get it all written down. The ideas were coming at me fast and furious! I also had a publisher and readers that were ready for the sequel right away.

2. Coach: A movie in your head? That's cool. So when did you get the idea for the story line in Book 2?

Jane: Actually I wrote the opening chapters almost immediately after the editing process finished on "Madge." I got the idea for the plot while I was finishing up the editing on that first book, but put it on hold for a few months while I was promoting "Madge's Mobile Home Park." I got back to writing "Elvis" early in the summer of 2012.

3. Coach: Hmmm, sounds like you were pretty motivated.

Jane: Yes I was having too much fun in Peavine to stay away from it for long. Teenie, Doll Dumas and Rhonelle wouldn't leave me alone. Inspiration was everywhere I looked!

4. Coach: Speaking of inspiration, where on earth did you get the idea for a big statue of Elvis to turn up in Peavine?

Jane: I made several trips between Jonesboro and Hardy AR while I was seeing about my mother who was still living in Jonesboro at the time. I'd go to our cabin on Spring River to relax. On the way I'd pass through Portia Bay. There was a tree surgeon company truck always parked by the highway there that had a five foot statue of Elvis attached to the cab. Sure got my attention . . . then I could see all the possibilities for how the arrival of a huge statue of Elvis could shake up things in Peavine.

5. Coach: Why Elvis?

Jane: Because it was pretty well established in Book 1 that Doll Dumas was a huge fan of Elvis. Lucille thought that a "huge" Elvis statue would be the perfect memorial in honor of her mother.

6. Coach: In this book your main character is that Rhonelle DuBoise gal who kind of spooks us Peaviners because she's a psychic . . . very mysterious.

Jane: Yes, I guess she is the most mysterious person in Peavine, and that's why I found her so interesting. She was certainly full of surprises. A psychic who was a strip tease dancer in New Orleans before she came to Peavine is bound to have a very interesting private life.

7. Coach: Why did you have her get that makeover from Shirleen Naither? Not that I'm complaining about it. It was quite an improvement!

Jane: Southern women have a thing about hair color. Allowing oneself go gray is the equivalent of a lack of proper self care. Actually, for Rhonelle to allow Shirleen to dye her hair was the first example of Rhonelle paying some attention to taking care of her own needs instead of everybody else's . . . and it made her feel good about herself!

8. Coach: So . . . how did you come up with that boyfriend of hers- the sculptor of the Elvis, Sergio Mandell? Is he based on anyone in particular?

Jane: Sergio came to me just as he is, and not based on anyone I can think of in particular. I wasn't even expecting him to show up like he did in that clothing store in New Orleans when he referred to David Posey as Rhonelle's son! By the way, having him also a psychic made for more unusual possibilities! I'm certain they were together in a past life, too.

9. Coach: Alrighty . . . you're starting to creep me out now. So let's talk about Lucille and Bo. How did you come to put those two together?

Jane: I think they were meant to be a couple! Despite the age difference they have the same sense of humor and love having fun together. They started hitting it off at the Memorial Bash in "Madge". They also are perfect business partners. Lucille surprised the heck out of me when she announced she'd bought half interest in KPEW . . . but it worked so I kept it in the story. That's how the call letters got changed to KEPW (for Elvis Presley!)

10. Coach: One other thing, how'd you get the idea for that old stripper friend of Rhonelle's . . . Krystal Bridges? She was a real hoot. I like that gal!

Jane: Well . . . that's complicated. One day my husband said, "You know what . . . Krystal Bridges sounds like a stripper name." And I said, "Oh my goodness . . . it *is!*"(I . . . uh used a "K" to spell it in hopes I wouldn't offend anyone in future times.) Anyway Krystal bloomed in my imagination and I really enjoyed writing about her– especially her wedding!

Coach: Well Miss Jane I have no idea what you're talking about, but I guess that's all for today . . . What's that Oz? *You forgot to put the video cassette in the camera?!*

Uh . . . Mrs. Hankins, do you mind if we do this interview over again?

How Road Signs Became Sculptures that Begat a Novel by Jane F. Hankins

Fannie Flagg, you have no idea what you have started!" Those were the first words I blurted out when I met the talented actress and author at an event in Blytheville, Arkansas the fall of 2003. I wanted to tell her that reading her novel back in 1987; Fried Green Tomatoes at the Whistle Stop Café had inspired a whole series of sculptures of elderly southern ladies.

In 1992 I entered some of those pieces in a juried show for the National Museum of Women in the Arts and was one of ten artists chosen to represent Arkansas in an exhibit in Washington, DC. The juror, Grace Glueck, art critic for the New York Times, ended up purchasing one of the sculptures because it reminded her of her neighbor's mother. She wisely told me that, "it can be funny and it's still art!" Thus I became serious about making art with a sense of humor.

I proceeded to babble on to Ms Flagg about my latest creations; sculptures of characters inspired by road side signs, and making up little stories about them. Bless her heart, she was very kind – even had a photo taken with me, but I probably came across as a bit much. I relate this story because there is something about Fannie Flagg that seems to nudge my creativity into totally new territory. Foremost of all, I am a visual artist working with sculpture and paintings. I have also been at various times an actress, TV pitch person and singer, but never thought I'd be a writer. I can't tell you how many times people have looked at my fantasy paintings and said, "You ought to write a children's book." However, it turned out that my inner Muse had other plans: a full length novel about a group of people living in a south Arkansas trailer park!

In 2000 I did a one woman sculpture show of characters inspired by homemade road signs I saw on car trips between Little Rock and New Orleans.

The first characters that came to mind were Teenie and Mavis Brice when I saw "AKC Toy Poodles and Dog Outfits". (I offer my sincere apologies to the actual persons who put out that sign. No offense intended.). A Curl up and Dye sign begat Shirleen Naither the beautician, and so on. Once I invented the town where they all moved into a local trailer park, the possibilities were limitless. If there can be a Lake Woebegone, Wisconsin and a Tuna, Texas there can be my imaginary town, Peavine Arkansas.

Each of the sculptures came with a one page story about what they did, their connection to the town of Peavine, and a drawing of their trailer. The manager of the park, Loretta Doll Dumas, was the widow of the richest man in town who had moved from her mansion to a lavender doublewide and became friend and benefactor to her community of quirky residents. I gave her a tall dyed black beehive up-do, cat eye glasses, holding a cigarette in one hand and a cold PBR beer in the other.

The art show was a success, especially the refreshments served at the opening reception. I had a table full of junk food delights "catered" by two of the characters – Kristy and Misty, the Party Girls. There wasn't a single Vienna sausage left by the end of the evening! Over the next three years I kept adding characters to the collection of People of Peavine, and each had their own story. Doll Dumas had become my Muse, riding on my shoulder, whispering tales of her pals. By 2003 I had a collection of short stories, but no idea what to do with them.

Then I met Fannie Flagg.

Three days after Christmas following the Blytheville event, I figured out a way to connect all my character's stories through a single narrative. Doll Dumas was the connector and I now had developed a beginning, middle and end for a plot. I began to build upon that structure much as I would build a sculpture over an armature. My husband was out of town, so I sat in my writing chair for the next four days hand writing an outline, opening and ending to "The Mavens of

Madge's Mobile Home Park".

On New Year's Eve, my husband and I attended a party at the local Repertory Theatre. We were talking with the director, Bob Hupp when my husband announced, "Jane's writing a book."

Bob said, "Wonderful! Let's do a reading." He wanted to plan it for the following spring, but fortunately we could wait until later in summer after my daughter's wedding. As if I would have finished it by then . . . sure I could!

I guess my brave ignorance was a blessing, because I doubt I would ever have had the will or perseverance to write this novel had it not been for committing myself to getting a script ready for the reader's theater production. My gifted talented husband, daughter and son joined me in three sold out performances. Once again, Kristy and Misty's junk food buffet that preceded each show was served and gleefully devoured.

At the time of the reader's theater production I had completed writing the first seven chapters. Hearing the voices of my characters and seeing the positive reactions of the audience gave me the confidence to keep writing.

For the next year, I would take breaks from my studio and go on writer's dates several times a week at Barnes and Noble. I would order my latte and take a seat in the café, careful to position myself facing the New Releases book shelf. I would start writing by hand nonstop for the next hour. Later would come the painstaking chore of transferring what I'd written to typed text documents on my new laptop computer. I must add here that I never took typing in high school preferring drama and choir as electives.

My family joined me again in performing the reader's theater script a year later at my church as a fundraiser for Habitat for Humanity, again to a sellout crowd. By then I had written and typed most of the original novel. So why did it take me six more years to get it published?

For one thing this project was the proverbial red-headed-stepchild of my creative endeavors (and I'm not a real redhead by the way). My income is from my visual art, and that's where most of my time and energy was spent. Yet every time I talked about my novel, I'd get so excited I'd get goose bumps. I loved my characters and felt like I was writing down what they told me just as fast as I could.

Doll Dumas was patient as well as persistent. I kept coming back and finally after four versions the novel had grown from a "stranger comes to town" theme to that plus "hero's journey". I also have more than enough characters for a trilogy at the very least!

I decided I needed to find some way to share this story of Doll Dumas and Madge DuClaire and their redemption. After some kind and constructive reject letters from publishers, I decided to post the novel in serial form on my business Face Book page, one chapter at a time. The response was wonderful with close to 900 readers following the story at one point. I was getting close to the last third of the novel, when I got a call from Ted Parkhurst as I was driving my granddaughter home from nursery school. He said a little birdie had told him that I needed a publisher. I sure am glad I took that call, and didn't wreck the car!

So after a summer of more rewrites, I have the fifth and final version of the story of Madge's Mobile Home Park. It's a little different and better than the version I had on Face Book which I had promptly removed after getting my publisher. I also spent my summer working on illustrations and cover art.

One form of art feeds another in my creative world. I listen to music and see an image which tells a story, and it becomes a painting. I see a play or read a book and am compelled to create a sculpture of how I see a character. All my visual artwork is a form of storytelling, so it's not that much of a stretch for my sculpture to tell me so much of a story that I began to write it down. Eventually I ran out of room to write on the back of my sculptures.

That's how Jane the sculptor and painter wrote herself a novel.

As Dorine the waitress in Don's Diner located across from the mobile home park would say," Lordeee Hon, it's about time!"